I ♥ ROBOT

SUZANNE VAN ROOYEN

Month9Books

Month9Books

To my grandfather – thank you for the music.
And to Mark, with love always.

I

ROBOT

SUZANNE VAN ROOYEN

Tyri

If today were a song, it'd be a dirge in b-flat minor. The androids cluster around the coffin, their false eyes brimming with mimetic tears. They were made to protect and serve their human masters, to entertain and care for us. Now, just one generation later, we toss them in the trash like nothing more than broken toasters.

The androids huddle in a semicircle, four adults and a child droid with synthetic curls. They all look so human; their grief real even if their tears aren't. The two male-droids are even good looking in that chiseled, adboard model kind of way. They're a little too perfect. With their machine strength, they lower the cardboard box into the dirt and the child droid begins to sing. His exquisite voice shatters like crystal in my ears, heartbreaking.

Asrid and I shouldn't be here—the only two humans amongst the machines—but I loved Nana. I loved her before I knew better than to feel anything for a robot. It doesn't matter how attached you get. A robot can never love you back, regardless of how human their advanced AI might make them seem.

"Why're they burying it anyway?" Asrid mutters beside me. My friend doesn't wear black to the funeral, refusing to acknowledge the passing of my nanamaton, an android that always seemed more like a mom and less like an automated child-minder.

"Should be sending it to the scrap heap. Isn't this against regulation?" Asrid's face scrunches up in a frown, marring her impeccable makeup. She's a peacock amongst ravens, and I'm a scruffy crow.

"Nana was like a mother to me. I'll miss her." Tears prick the corners of my eyes as the coffin disappears into the earth, and the droid keens a eulogy.

"I know you will, T." Asrid gives me a one-armed hug.

Svartkyrka Cemetery is losing the battle to weeds. Human tombstones from back when there was real estate for corpses lie in crumbling ruin covered in pigeon poop. No one gets buried anymore—there's no space and, anyway, it's unsanitary.

"Can we go now?" Asrid hops between feet to fight off the chill. Autumn has shuffled closer to winter, the copper and russet leaves crunching beneath our shoes. The leaves look like scabs, a carpet of dried blood spilling into the open earth. Fitting for my nanamaton's funeral, but robots can't bleed.

"Sure, we can go."

Asrid wends her way toward the parking lot as I approach the grave. Nana loved yellow anemones, said they were like sunshine on a stick.

"Hope there's sunshine where you are now, Nana." I drop a single flower into the ground and wipe away the tear snailing down my cheek. Why Nana chose to permanently shut down and scramble her acuitron brain, I can only guess. Perhaps living in a world controlled by groups like the People Against Robot Autonomy, PARA for short, became too much for her.

"Sorry for your loss," the child droid says in a tinkling voice.

"Thank you for letting me know," I say.

"She would've wanted you to be here." The other nanamaton, gray haired and huddled in a trench coat, doesn't meet my gaze.

I stuff my mitten-covered hands into the pockets of my jacket and hunch my shoulders against the chill. You'd think the universe might have had the courtesy to rain given the sullen occasion, but the sun perches in an acid blue sky.

"Tyri, you coming?" Asrid shouts from the gate, remembering

too late that we're supposed to be stealthy. Government regulation stipulates cremation for humans and scrap heaps for robots. If the authorities discover us committing metal and electronics to the earth instead of recycling, Asrid and I will be fined. The robots will be decommissioned on the spot.

"I'm so sorry," I whisper to the androids before turning away. Their artificial gaze follows me, boring into my back sharp as a laser.

"Botspit, I'm hungry. I could gnaw on a droid. Where're we going to lunch?" Asrid ignores the dead and grieving as if none of it exists.

"I think I'll just go home."

"Come on, T. I know she was your Nana but she was just a robot, you know."

Just a robot! Nana changed my diapers. My first day of kindergarten, Nana held my hand. When I came home from school, Nana made me cocoa and sat helping me with homework. Nana cooked my favourite dumpling dinner every Wednesday and made me double-chocolate birthday cake. Nana taught me how to tie my shoelaces and braid my hair. The day I turned sixteen, Mom decided we didn't need Nana anymore. She should've been decommissioned then, but Nana disappeared the day before Mom's M-Tech buddies came to kill her core and reprocess her parts.

"She was more than that to me," I say.

"Ah, you're adorable." Asrid casts nervous glances across the lot. Satisfied no policemen lurk behind the bushes, she slips her arm through mine and drags me through the gate. The wrought iron is warped and daubed with rust. Marble angels stand sentinel, broken and stained by time. One misses a nose, and the other has lost a wing.

"You didn't say anything about my new bug." Asrid pouts when we reach her vehicle. The hoverbug is neon pink, matching her shoes, handbag, and the ribbons holding up her blond hair. The 'E' badge that stands for Engel Motors looks more like a spastic frog than the angel it's supposed to represent.

"Is it meant to smell like cherries?" Even the plush interior is unicorn puke pink. I put on my sunglasses in case all that color stains my eyes.

"Yes, in fact." Asrid flicks a switch and the engine purrs. "Slipstream Waffles." She assumes that monotone voice she always uses when addressing machines.

The last thing I want is to sit on sticky vinyl in a noisy waffle house, indulging in sugar and calories served by permanently smiling droids on roller-skates.

"Take me home to Vinterberg."

"Tyri, don't annoy me."

"Sassa, Don't patronize me." I give her the glare she knows better than to argue with.

"Vinterberg," I say again and Asrid heaves a melodramatic sigh.

"Be boring. Going home to make love to your violin?"

"Why ask when you know the answer?" Nana's coffin lowering into the ground replays in my mind to a soundtrack in b-flat minor.

"How does Rurik put up with being the other love of your life?"

It's my turn to sigh. Rurik doesn't really put up with it or even understand why I love music so much. But then, I don't understand why he gets so hung up on politics, and I definitely don't understand why he didn't show up for Nana's funeral when he knows how much she meant to me.

"We manage." I stare out the tinted windows at the darkened scenery whipping past.

The hoverbug takes the quickest route, zipping along the street ways that skirt the chaotic center of Baldur. The jungle of concrete and steel thins out into a tree-shrouded suburb studded with modest brick homes. Rurik calls my redbrick bungalow quaint, and it is, complete with flower boxes and a patch of green lawn out back. It's nothing at all like his dad's slick penthouse, all glass and chrome with a panoramic view of the city. The funny thing is, Rurik used to live right next-door till his mom had the affair and his dad became a workaholic, transforming the family business into an automotive empire.

The hoverbug slows and lands in my driveway.

"I'll call you later," I say before disembarking.

"You heard anything yet?"

"No, but tomorrow is the last day so I'll hear soon." I'm trying not to think about why it's taking so long to hear back after my audition for the Baldur Junior Philharmonic Orchestra.

"You'll get in T. I'm sure of it. You're brilliant."

Asrid's words make me smile despite the morbidity of the day. She waves and the hoverbug zooms off, leaving me in the rustling-leave calm of Vinterberg.

I press my thumb to the access pad and the front door hisses open. Mom's at work like always. Taking off my coat and shoes, I whistle for Glitch. She pads into the hallway, her face lopsided from sleep. She stretches and sits down with a decisive humph as if to say, 'Well, human, I'm here. Now, worship me.' And I do.

"Hey my Glitchy girl." I fold my cyborg Shiba Inu into my arms and sweep her off the floor. Her mechatronic back leg sticks out straight and stiff, the rest of her soft and warm. She licks my ear, one paw on my forehead.

"Good afternoon, Tyri. Would you like some refreshments?" Miles whirs out of the kitchen into the hallway. He's nothing like Nana, just a bipedal mass of electronics and metal with assorted appendages capable of mundane tasks. He doesn't even have eyes, only a flashing array of lights. Despite Mom designing a new generation of androids for M-Tech, we can't afford the new model housebot. Maybe it's better this way. I don't feel much for our bot, but I dubbed him Miles. It seemed to fit.

"Would you like some refreshments?" he repeats.

"Tea and a sandwich." I carry Glitch into my bedroom at the back of the house. Glitch leaps from my arms, landing on the bed where she curls up in a knot of black, white, and tan fur amongst my pillows.

Still in my black lace skirt and corset, I stretch and flex my fingers. Twisting the cricks from my neck and rolling my shoulders, I ease out the graveyard tension. My violin lies in a bed of blue velvet, waiting for my touch. With the strings in tune and the bow sufficiently taut, the instrument nestles against my jaw as if I was born with a gap there just for the violin. It completes me.

I warm-up my fingers, letting them trip over the strings as my bow arcs and glides. Then I'm ready to play: Beethoven's Kreutzer violin sonata in A major, Nana's favorite. Glitch's ears twitch back and forth. She raises her head to howl but thinks better of it, yawning and curling back into sleep.

The frenzied opening of the sonata segues into a melancholy tune and in the brief moment of calm, my moby warbles at me. I have mail. I try to ignore the distraction and play through the screeching reminder of an unread message, but it might be the one I've been anticipating.

Vibrating in my hand, the moby blinks at me: One unread email. Subject: BPO audition.

"This is it, Glitchy."

She raises her head as I sit beside her. One hand buried in her fur, I open the email. The words blur together, pixelate and run like wet ink across the screen. Disbelief makes my vision swim. I have to read the message several times over to make sure I haven't misunderstood.

"Codes! I got in." Blood warms my cheeks as I whisk Glitch into my arms, spinning her around before squeezing her to my chest. She does not approve and scratches at me until I drop her back on the bed. Miles enters with a tray of tea and neat triangular sandwiches.

"Miles, I got in! I'm going to play for the junior BPO. This is amazing." I'm jumping up and down.

Miles flashes orange. "Could not compute. Please restate."

"I'm going to play for the best junior orchestra in the country. This could be my chance to break into the scene, to meet all the right people, and make an impression!" My one chance to escape the life already planned for me by Mom. The last thing I want to be is a robot technician.

Miles keeps flashing orange. "Apologies, Tyri. Could not compute, but registering joy." His visual array flashes green. "Happy birthday!"

He says in his clipped metallic voice before leaving the room.

I clutch the moby and read the email another ten times before calling Mom. I reach her voicemail, and my joy tones down a notch. I don't want to talk to another machine, so I hang up and call Rurik instead.

"Hey, Tyri. Now's not a good time. Can I call you back later?"

"I got in," I say.

"To the orchestra?"

"Yes!"

"That's great." He doesn't sound half as happy as I am.

"Thanks, I'm so excited, but kind of scared too—"

"T, I'm just in the middle of something. I'll call you back in a bit, okay?" He hangs up, leaving me babbling into silence.

Deflated, I slump onto the floor and rest my head on the bed. Glitch shuffles over to give me another ear wash, delicately nibbling around my earrings. I should've known Rurik would be busy getting ready to go to Osholm University. Getting a scholarship to the most prestigious school in all of Skandia is way more impressive than scoring a desk in the Baldur Junior Orchestra. Still, I received better acknowledgment from the housebot than my boyfriend. I call Asrid.

"Hey T, what's up?" Asrid answers with Sara's high-pitched giggle in the background.

"I got in!"

"That's awesome, except I guess that means more practicing and less time with your friends, huh?" Asrid sounds genuinely put out, as if she'd even notice my absence when Sara's around. Codes, isn't there someone who could just be happy for me? Maybe Mom's right, and I am being selfish wanting the "Bohemian non-existence" when I could have a "sensible and society-assisting" career in robotics.

"Sorry, I . . . thought you'd like to know."

"I'm happy for you, Tyri. I know it's a big deal to you. Congrats. Seriously, you deserve this considering how hard you practice," Asrid says, and Sara shouts congratulations in the background.

"Thanks, Sassa."

"Hey, our food arrived. Chat later?"

"Sure." I hang up and reach for my violin. Nana would've understood. She would've danced around the living room with me. She probably would've baked me a cake and thrown a party. Determined not to cry, I skip the second movement of Beethoven's sonata and barrel straight into the jaunty third. The notes warp under my fingers, and the tune slides into b-flat minor.

Two days until the first rehearsal. Maybe I'll be able to do something different with my life; something that makes me happy instead of just useful.

Quinn

If anyone cared to ask my opinion on the human condition, I'd say humans are the never-ending wait. They're waiting for something better, something different, something that makes them feel more alive.

I feel almost human; I've been waiting nineteen days, sixteen hours, and twenty-three minutes for just one thing, one word, eight letters: accepted. My entire existence hinges on another person's subjective opinion of my ability.

Walking helps, it makes the minutes flow liquid, passing by in a single ribbon of time. I'd sleep if I could; I hear it makes time flow even faster. There's a tingle of anticipation in my circuit, a simultaneous dread and thrill that makes waiting an agony and a pleasure.

That would be my second opinion on the human condition: it's a paradox. It's never black and white with them, but a kaleidoscopic swirl of grays, mixed emotions, and complications. Robots are simpler. Binary. On or off. Even us convoluted androids can be reduced to ones and zeros.

–Transmission received.

The email pings behind my eyes, and I pause mid step on a corner in lower Baldur. The few humans out on the windy street cast me sideways glances and nothing more, dismissing my presence. I'm just another kid with his hoodie up against the chill. I don't wear the orange patch we're supposed to, declaring make, model, and human owners. Anonymity is my only protection now. There's only so far you can run from your past before the towns become villages, and there aren't any more hydrogen stations. Itching to read the mail, I head into an unkempt park, home to vagrants and squirrels, in search of privacy.

–Transmission active.

My vision blurs with a scrawl of text. The pinprick letters scan across my cybernetic eyeballs. I smile, a reflexive reaction to the good news. The emotion module upgrade is working. The complex code packages unraveling emotions in my core and throughout my circuits make me feel even more human.

Accepted. Rehearsal Saturday: two o'clock at the Baldur Opera House.

–Transmission deleted.

A red exclamation mark blinks in my peripheral vision. My tank's almost empty. I've got less than six hours till I'm incapacitated unless I can pilfer some hydrogen. Still smiling, I jog past the sleeping nightclubs and comatose bars of downtown Baldur to the dilapidated warehouse district. A hydrogen station, its yellow and green paint peeling away in thin ribbons, sports a new sign tacked beneath the company logo: Strictly No Unauthorized Robots.

I wait and watch. A cluster of junkies huddles around a barrel fire far away enough not to notice my crime; their bloodshot eyes focus on the flames, their addled thoughts lost in oblivion. In fifteen minutes, no humans approach the station. I saunter, hands in pockets, toward the pumps and complete one last scan of the surroundings. Still no humans or approaching hoverbugs.

I thumb through my wallet and jam the fake transaction card into the slot; there's nothing the black market doesn't have for those with enough cash. I wait as the card confuses the machine, making it think I'm a human customer instead of a desperate, thieving android.

Shucking my hoodie, I lift up my shirt and depress my fourth rib. The haptic sensor unseals a slab of skin revealing the valve to my fuel tank where my intercostal muscles should be. I dismount the hose from its docking bay and jam the nozzle into my side. It takes a full minute to fill up my tank. A full minute of vulnerability.

Done. I disengage the pump and my skin reseals as my body makes the necessary pressure adjustments. Card in hand, I turn to leave, but a metal pipe collides with my head and constellations of black dots clot my vision. My knees hit asphalt as nanytes race to repair the damage done to my skull. Cruor drips from the gash above my eye, and pain ignites every synthetic nerve ending.

Three droids dressed in ratty sweaters and faded jeans, leer at me with wicked grins.

"Give us the card."

They can have it. Their hands rifle through my pockets. Fingers find the card then slip beneath my shirt. They've got a canister ready to drain me of fuel. Not today. I roll and kick, knocking one android on his back. The other still wields the pipe and strikes me repeatedly across the shoulders until I'm face down, cheek scraped by tar. More pain overwhelms my circuit and again their fingers fumble with my clothes.

"Please," I say, but the android chuckles and increases the pressure holding me down. I'm poked and prodded as they search my ribs for the sensor. Before they can jam the canister into my side, a fourth pair of footsteps smack across the asphalt.

I squirm beneath my assailant as another android, black as midnight, sends his titanium-reinforced fist into the attacker's jaw.

The second assailant brandishes the pipe.

"Kit, behind you," I hiss through clenched teeth.

Kit delivers a kick to the android and sends him sprawling.

"Come on, Quinn." Kit grabs my arm and drags me away before the others have time to recover. They don't pursue us as we sprint down narrow alleys heading further away from the city center. We slow to a jog when we reach the train depot splashed with graffiti and littered with trash.

"Were you following me?" I turn on Kit once we're relatively safe.

"Thanks Kit for saving my bionic ass. What a happy coincidence you just happened to go in search of some H yourself." He grins.

"So, you were following me."

"What are friends for?" He shrugs, and we cross the tracks into robot squatterville: Fragheim. The settlement lies in a sprawl of scrap metal and barbed wire.

"You still haven't thanked me." He pouts.

"Thank you, Kit." Him following me is still of concern.

"They looked like Z-class droids."

"Felt like it." I rub the spot above my eye, the injury another memory of pain.

"You all right?" Kit brushes his thumb across the ghost of a graze on my cheek.

"Fine." I pull away.

"Told you, you need to install a martial arts module." He tucks his hands into his pockets.

"My processor's almost overloaded as is."

"Because you insist on installing those stupid emotion patches. What are you going to do? *Feel* your way out of fights?"

Kit fails to grasp the importance of emotion in music. If I'm ever going to not only pass for human but also actually *be* human, emotion—not martial arts—modules are going to get me there.

"I need them."

"Like you need fish-balls and coffee at an afternoon *fika*." Kit might've made that throaty sound of disapproval unique to human physiology if his voice box had been programmed to harrumph with disdain.

"I don't expect you to understand."

"Good."

We leave it at that and make our way through mud and scrap toward the clump of huts we call home. Since escaping my owners, I've been camping out here, living amongst the other unwanted robotic detritus. It's survival of the most fuel efficient and well coded.

I head straight for Sal's to celebrate my musical achievement. She understands, to a certain degree, what Kit does not. We weave our way through the geometry of our scrap-metal sanctuary, past kidbots scraping out Sudoku puzzles in the dirt and androids gathered around salvaged furniture discussing mathematics and quantum theory. Some talk economy and politics, berating the government that saw fit to bring them into being, mass-produce them, and then abandon them.

Simulated voices rise in anger; a fist shakes in the air.

"The Robot Revolution." A Saga-droid stabs a finger at his friend. "Don't think it's not going to happen. We're on a precipice here. If government doesn't pass this amendment—"

"You think the amendment's our problem?" Lex, a Quasar companion-droid like me, interjects. He folds his arms and leans against the precarious wall of a hut. "If this virus thing is true, we've got much bigger problems."

"What virus thing?" I ask.

Kit rolls his eyes. "Tune into the Botnet once in a while and maybe you'd know."

I don't even tune into the newsfeeds any more. It's always the same: the People Against Robot Autonomy arguing why robots should never be granted rights and robots arguing even more aggressively why they should. I've seen nothing about a virus, though.

"Please, Kit."

"Fine," he relents. "Some Saga hackers got wind of an AI virus apparently being developed by M-Tech."

"What kind of virus?"

"Don't know." He shrugs. "But Lex figures it's probably designed to hurt us."

"Of course he does." We pause in the mud as Lex continues to rant about humans.

"It's time for revolution. Look at human history! They want us to wear armbands like Hitler made the Jews wear yellow stars. And you all know what came next." His words sink into my core. Would the humans really go so far as to exterminate us like that? Maybe the real question is what's taking them so long to do it?

"You want something." Lex punches a fist in the air. "You take it, guns blazing."

Having heard enough, I cut a track through the mire to Sal's.

"Lex has a point," Kit says as he ambles along beside me.

"That the humans are about to commit robotic genocide? I doubt it."

"Why? Fragheim might as well be a Gulag camp."

"We're not prisoners here."

"Aren't we?" Kit glares at me, daring me to argue, but I can't and he knows it.

"There must be better ways to get what we want."

"Like pretending you're human?" His gaze burns me to my core. I grit my coral-polymer teeth and jog the rest of the way to Sal's hut.

The hut is a questionable union between corrugated iron and duct tape. Sal dangles in a canvas hammock reading, the text spooling across her jade irises.

"Any good?" I move her legs to sit beside her. Kit catches up and leans against an unstable wall.

"Chapter," she says, and I wait for her to finish. "Not bad." She blinks, and her vision clears. "I think Alfred Jarry drank too much absinthe, but his 'pataphysics are … amusing."

Typical. Only a Saga class android, manufactured for intelligence operations during the war, would find 'pataphysics entertaining. It's too bad Sagas were stuck in research facilities as data crunchers after the war. Sagas know they're smarter than the rest of us with their intelligence quotients in the stratosphere, and Sal's not shy in reminding us.

"So." She runs her hand across her tattooed scalp. "To what do I owe the pleasure of your company, boys?"

"I got in." The grin splits my face ear to ear. Kit mumbles something indiscernible.

Sal takes a moment to absorb the information before crushing me to her organosilicone chest in a hug.

"This is fantastic. Congratulations! But I knew you'd get in. You've got top-notch music firmware."

"Thanks," I say as she releases me. I want to tell her it's more than being able to read the music and move my fingers over the strings, bowing perfect tremolo. It's about feeling something beyond what any emotion patch can offer. Playing music is about glimpsing the divine, about believing in something beyond yourself, some ethereal force. If I say any of that, she'll just pat my head and smile that infuriating smile that says she knows better because she can rattle off every composer's birth date and list their greatest works in six languages. I could download all those dates, but it would use up slots in my memstor that are better used for memorizing actual music. As for languages, we Quasars have severely limited linguistic capabilities.

"When do you start?" she asks.

"Saturday. First rehearsal."

"It's a bad idea," Kit singsongs.

"Nonsense. We should celebrate." Sal leaps off the hammock causing me to swing backwards into the metal wall, making the entire structure vibrate.

"It's not that big a deal."

"Yes it is." Sal whirls on me. "First we celebrate and then we fix you up."

"That's what I've been talking about." Kit rubs his hands together.

"I need fixing?" The uncertainty in my voice sounds so natural, so human. Sometimes I forget that under the layers of synthetic flesh, I'm a snarl of electronics.

"We could rough you up a bit."

"Some droids already did that." Kit nods in my direction. I point to my head where the pipe injury has reduced to a slight depression.

"You both get jumped?" Sal asks.

"Filling up. They took my card. Kit came to the rescue, as always."

"Good thing he was around." She glances in Kit's direction.

"Next time I might not be. Next time maybe I'll just watch."

For an android determined to be nothing more than plastic and metal, Kit can be as passive-aggressive as any human.

"Hm, let's hope not." Sal muses with a finger tapping her chin. "You'll pass for human, long as no one looks too closely." She musses my hair and grins. "Better already."

"No one suspected anything at auditions." Quasars are made to look more human than other androids.

"You look like a doll," Kit says. "Not that that's a bad thing."

"This is the biggest problem." Sal grabs my wrist as I attempt to smooth down my unruly mane of platinum blond.

"My tag?" I stare at the black lettering of the code on my wrist. It's not a tattoo or superficial decoration like the ink smears on Sal's baldhead. Q-I-99: class, model, and number printed in flesh above my identifying microchip. It's all that I am.

"Quinn." Sal runs a finger over the numbers. "We can grind it out."

"Are you that desperate to pass for an ape?" Kit spits Cruor into the mud.

"Couldn't we just tattoo over it?" I ask, ignoring Kit's jibe.

"Tattoos fade quickly." Sal points to her head, freshly inked once a week. "Grinding it out will last longer."

"The numbers will come back anyway. The chip's embedded in my CNS. No getting rid of that."

"True, but at least you'll be unmarked for a few weeks between sessions," Sal says.

"It'll hurt," Kit adds.

"As if that's ever been a problem." I shut him up with a look. "Pain is part of being human. How do you think all those composers wrote such awe-inspiring music?"

"That's different," Kit grumbles.

"Is it?"

"This is Quinn's chance at doing something better with his life," Sal says.

"Better? How is trying to fool the humans better than standing up for your own kind?"

"And what? Violently demanding rights from a government that might never grant them?" My tone is bitter.

"Go join the apes then." Kit throws his hands in the air. He kicks Sal's wall, denting the metal before striding away.

"He cares about you," Sal says with a soft smile.

"Funny way of showing it."

"Don't let him dampen this. This is your chance to show the humans that we aren't just machines, that they gave us minds. We think, we feel, we dream, we create."

I nod as my tear ducts prickle with an automatic response to the emotion codes triggered in my processor.

"So, are we going to get Max to grind it out?" Sal looks ferocious, all sharp angles with an aquiline nose halving her face. She'd look gentler with hair, but she says it irritates her when it falls over her bulbous forehead into her eyes.

"I think I'll take my chances and wear long sleeves."

"It's your fuel-cell on the line." She raises an eyebrow at me.

"I'll be careful."

"In that case," Sal grabs my hand, "I do believe it's time to celebrate."

Tyri

Glitch woofs a warning from her vantage point on the sofa, her dark eyes fixed on the front door. I open it before Rurik has a chance to press the buzzer.

"Hey you." He offers me a silly grin and a giant bouquet of purple-checkered daffodils.

"This wasn't necessary." I bury my nose in the blooms. A single daffodil vibrates as tinkling music spills out of the petals. The flower sings to me in Rurik's husky voice, asking me to forgive him for being such a jerk.

"You're not a jerk."

"You're right, I'm a gangrenous nullhead and despicable boyfriend." He smiles and his whole face lights up. If Rurik were a song, he'd be in D major, bright and easy going. His brown eyes peering into mine make me melt as I fold into his arms. I love the way he smells: a touch cinnamon and a touch lemon fresh. Being so close to him I can almost forget that he didn't show up for the funeral and that he hung up on me.

"Sorry about earlier." Rurik tilts my face toward his and we kiss, a slow meeting of our lips. He tastes of peppermint gum, and I kiss him again. He jerks away, cursing as Glitch shoves herself between our legs and pees on his foot.

"Glitch! Bad dog." She gives me a baleful look and pads into the house, nonplussed by her actions.

"Codes, I'm sorry." I dash into the house. Dumping the flowers on the kitchen table, I grab a towel and head back to the door. Rurik stands barefoot, shaking off his sneakers.

"Not like it's the first time." He chuckles and cleans his foot. Dropping the towel and shoes on the porch, he kisses me again and shuffles me into the hallway before closing the door behind us.

"Your Mom home?"

"Not yet."

"Excellent." He drops his bag and shrugs out of his jacket before grabbing my hand and heading down the passage to my bedroom.

"Greetings, Rurik. Would you like some refreshments?" Miles comes to my door as Rurik pushes me down onto the bed.

"In twenty minutes," Rurik says. "Coffee and hot chocolate."

"As you wish." Miles leaves, flashing green.

"My mom'll be home any minute." I gasp as Rurik nibbles my neck, and his hands slide beneath my shirt.

"Baby, I can work with a minute." He kisses me, ferocious this time as he leans his body into mine. My pulse beats in *agitato* triplets as I pull off his sweater. Rurik's all jagged hipbones and harp-string clavicles. He's just taken my shirt off when the front door hisses open and my mom yells for Miles.

"Botspit!" Rurik reaches for his sweater. Giggling, I put myself back together and smooth down my hair. Mom always knows. I don't know how she can tell when Rurik and I have been fooling around, but somehow she always does and ends up giving me this look of disapproval that feels worse than if she confronted me outright.

We've never had a mother-daughter sex talk. Mom taught me about menstruation and procreation using scientific terms, showing me diagrams in a textbook. It felt more like a lecture than a conversation. Going to buy tampons for the first time was the most embarrassing experience. Mom asked me about the heaviness of my flow right there in the store. I don't even want to think about how she'd deal with a discussion about prophylactics and orgasms.

Rurik combs fingers through his curls and rearranges his pants.

"Tyri?" Mom calls, her slipper-covered feet shushing down the hallway.

"In here." We position ourselves in what we hope passes for innocent stances: me on the bed flipping through sheet music on a databoard, Rurik sitting on the floor fiddling with his moby.

"Think you might want these." Mom drops Rurik's bag and sneakers at the door. She raises a single eyebrow. That combined with her severe suit and hair bun makes her seem all the more like a cane-wielding schoolmistress.

"Tyri, you called me earlier but didn't leave a message?"

"Yeah, I've got good news."

"And I'd love to hear it. Join me in the kitchen in five." She pauses at the door. "Rurik, your sweater's inside out."

Rurik, pale as snow with his pure Skandic genes, turns puce with embarrassment.

"Let me help." I tug off his shirt again, turning it the right way round and looping it over his head.

"Once I'm at Osholm, we'll have more privacy."

"You'll have a roommate."

"Nothing a digisplay set to busy can't fix." He tucks loose hair behind my ear and clears my bangs from my eyes. "I am sorry about earlier." His apology seems genuine. "I was with my dad."

"Sorry I interrupted."

"Don't be. It's just, well, you know how he is."

"I'm surprised he even managed to squeeze you in between press conferences and golf course meetings." Knowing Rurik's father, it's no wonder his mom looked for love elsewhere. The only reason they didn't get divorced after that was because it wouldn't be good for Engelberger Senior's or their eldest son's political career, never mind the family's corporate image.

"He's preoccupied at the moment," Rurik says.

"Problems?"

"Not sure, but he read me the riot act about not bringing shame to the great Engelberger name while I'm at Osholm."

"Sometimes I'm glad my father was an anonymous sperm donor." Not sure I would've been any better off with two parents. Mom's hardly ever around anyway and my dad, if I'd had one, probably would've been a workaholic too. Still, sometimes I wish I knew who he was, whether I look like him, or if I have half siblings.

Rurik helps me to my feet and kisses me gently before we amble to the kitchen.

"What's the big news?" Mom arranges my flowers in a vase. She's dressed in sweats that mold her figure, which seems untouched by pregnancy. Miles busies himself with food packages at the sink. Cups of coffee and hot chocolate wait for us on the counter.

"I'm going to play for the Baldur Junior Philharmonic."

"You got in?" She blinks at me.

"You sound surprised."

Part of me shrivels up inside and dies, legs in the air twitching dead.

"I … " Mom trails off. "Well done, sweetheart. I'm happy for you, but remember what we discussed." She slides a mug of hot chocolate toward me.

"You said I could play if my grades improved." Maintain a better average was what Mom said. If my grades start slipping, it's bye-bye violin.

"And you call going from a C to a B- average improvement?" She gives that arched eyebrow look.

"Isn't it?" My cheeks burn.

"You'll need better grades to get into college."

"I'll keep improving."

"I hope so." Mom sighs and the pain of disappointing her needles my heart.

"I want to be a professional musician. Math and physics don't matter when I'm this good at violin." I resist the urge to slump down on the stool beside Rurik. Standing makes me feel more powerful, like I might have a say in my life's trajectory.

"Math and physics might surprise you," Rurik adds.

"Don't gang up on me. Music is what I want. I can't imagine doing anything else."

"You weren't meant to be a musician," Mom says and then looks a little guilty.

"Well, I'm sorry if the sperm cocktail you selected is a disappointment, Mom." Maybe my dad is a musician; maybe he'd understand what Mom clearly doesn't. Those needles poking my heart turn to spears.

"That's not what I meant, Tyri." She steps around the table and gives me a one-armed hug. "I just think you have far greater potential. You could do anything if you applied yourself. I want you to reach your full potential and not waste your talents on music."

"I have a talent for music." I shrug away.

Mom sighs again. "Yes, you do. I still think you should go to university. You'll need a scholarship and those aren't easy to come by. Don't you agree, Rurik?"

"Don't bring him into this."

"He knows first hand how hard it is to get into a good school. Look at how hard even he had to work for it."

Even he? Implying what Mother? "I will get into a good school, but I'll be going to the Royal Academy of Music, not Osholm or Baldur Tech." If I don't make it into the music academy, then my options are limited to apprenticeships in bot factories or bug manufacturing. I'd rather join Nana in the dirt than spend the rest of my life building robots for M-Tech.

"We'll see," Mom says, and I feel like screaming. Rurik reaches for my hand, squeezing my fingers. He's trying to be nice, supportive, but it feels patronizing, Mr. Perfect Score. I pull away, stomping into the living room to join Glitch on the sofa. She greets me with ear licks and doggy cuddles. At least Glitch loves me.

***

After dinner, Rurik suggests we go out for dessert. Mom disappears into her study to do whatever it is she does in that cramped box of hers. Glitch sprawls on my bed preventing Rurik from getting too close. I'm not in the mood for making out anyway. We don our coats and head into the frigid night. Frost dances in the breeze, sticking to my eyelashes. It's not even winter yet.

"Ice cream or pancakes?"

My usual favorites, but Nana would've baked me a cake. Mom couldn't even congratulate me without choking, and Rurik has yet to truly acknowledge my achievement.

"I want cake."

Rurik opens the door of his hoverbug. A wave of lemon freshener washes over me.

"Ander's?" He looks hopeful, but I'm not in the mood for the gauche decor of the popular *fika* establishment.

"Let's try that place in lower Baldur. Olof's Tea House."

"I hear they make great semla."

"I want cake not marzipan."

"Botballs, you're in a mood tonight." Rurik orders the bug's navigation system to Olof's, and we zoom off downtown.

"It would help if you actually congratulated me."

I receive silence as Rurik contemplates how many macho points he'll lose for caving. I could threaten him with no making out for a month, but that makes it too easy.

"I'm happy for you, Tyri," he eventually says as if it pains him. "It's just..."

"You don't approve?"

"Music isn't going to get you anywhere in life."

"But politics will?"

"You don't think what I do is important, and I deal with it. Why are you so hard up about me not approving of your music?"

It's a fair question, and I'm stymied. All I want is someone to enthuse with me. Someone who gets it, but I might as well be talking to the deaf.

"I'm sorry." He drags a hand through his hair and looks at me with those chocolate truffle eyes I can't say no to. "Considering the way you play, I'd have been surprised if you didn't get in. You deserve this." He leans over and kisses me, sending an army of happy tingles marching up my spine.

The hoverbug pulls into Olof's and lands in the parking lot decorated with street art and broken bottles. Inside it's full, but there are a couple of free tables outside, glistening with ice crystals in the neon shop glow. Thankful for the distraction of pastries, I leave the conversation there and hurry inside, the aroma of almonds and cocoa already overwhelming my senses.

***

With a belly full of chocolate cake and cream, I can tell Rurik what's really been bugging me.

"You missed Nana's funeral."

Rurik slurps up the dregs of his low-cal, nutrient enriched raspberry tonic-shake and leans across the oval table precariously balanced on the cobbled paving. It's freezing out here, and my coat's not doing much to protect me from the wind.

"Robots don't have funerals." He keeps his voice low.

"So what would you call burying Nana's body then?"

"Illegal."

I slam my fork onto my plate. "You say that about the woman who practically raised us, who put Band-Aids on your knees and made you hot chocolate after school."

"I remember, thanks." He glares at me. "But she was a nanamaton. A machine programmed to nurture. Nothing more."

"You sound like your PARA brother."

"Like the leader of the one of most powerful organizations in the government? Like a guy who might be prime minister one day?" His eyes are bright with anger.

"Is that what you want too?"

"Maybe." Rurik drums his fingers on the table. "Gunnar's done pretty well for himself."

"At the expense of robots."

"Tyri!" Rurik throws his hands up. "You know your Nana never loved you back, right? It did as it was programmed to do."

"That doesn't matter, what matters is how I felt about her."

Rurik shakes his head. "You don't get it."

"My heart broke today watching them bury her."

He reaches across the table to take my hand, but I pull away.

"T," his tone softens. "You know she'll probably be dug up and sent to a scrap yard, right? Especially when the government revokes the amendment."

"When?" I chase crumbs around my plate with a finger.

"You think PARA will really let the government grant robots human rights?" he scoffs and looks away.

"Would it be so bad?"

"You *really* don't get it." He sounds exasperated.

"What I don't get is how you can be so callous." Rurik was always so kind and sweet, until he started turning into his father.

"And I don't understand how you can be so naive and childish. It's not like someone died," he says.

I'm not sure what to be more furious about, him calling me childish or intimating that Nana was nothing more than a housebot. My chair scrapes against the cobbles, and I stomp my feet as I get up. Rurik's lucky I don't stab him with my fork.

"I might not understand all the politics, why you and your PARA party are so anti-robot rights, but you know what? You don't understand me, Rurik Engelberger, and clearly never have."

I'm halfway across the parking lot before I realize I don't know where I'm going or how I'll get home. I steal a backwards glance. Rurik stands beside the table, fists opening and closing as he watches me depart. I wish he'd run after me, but he just stands there shaking his head and my heart crumples up like failed origami. I could call Mom for a lift, or Asrid, or a taxi despite the cost. Instead, my feet take me down a side street away from boyfriends and empty cake plates. I walk. Walking helps clear the cobwebs from my head. The cold air whips tears from my eyes, and I tense against the freeze.

The wind carries snatches of music, the dissonant and frenzied twang of strings and pulsating bass. I follow the sound down a labyrinth of narrow streets littered with trash until I reach the ruins of the old train depot. Being out here alone at night isn't wise, but I really couldn't care.

Firelight dances spasmodic across the paint splashed walls. Standing on a stage above a thicket of writhing bodies, a guy with wild hair dips and sways as he plays the viola to a backtrack of electronic beats. Feral, that's what Mom would call them, and all I want to do is let my hair down and join them.

Quinn

Sal's idea of celebrating is getting high on inebriation patches and partying with the ragamuffin crowd at the depot. She jams the flash drive into the port beneath a flap of flesh on my lower back. The code unravels up my spine and addles my system.

"Strong enough?" Sal asks.

"Pleasantly buzzing."

"Shoot me up." She hands me a different flash drive, and I fumble through tatty layers of military surplus in search of her port. Sal takes a triple dose and starts giggling, her eyes shiny with fuel-cell byproduct.

Together, we stumble out of Fragheim and cross the tracks toward the depot. The abandoned trains provide sleeping quarters for the city's flotsam and jetsam. At night, the humans emerge to writhe beneath the stars, high on drugs and life. Various crews roll in and soon the depot is a musical war-zone. Humans garbed in psychedelic relics of the cybergrunge age bump and grind to electronic beats. Others, with safety pins through their noses and studs in their tongues, lambaste the night with industrial noise, claiming a crumbling quadrangle for their own. They smear the walls with neon paint, swapping bottles and skag needles. A few even sport cranial shunts that plug the brain into a drug-induced virtual reality, despite the strict laws against integrated tech.

A Saga-droid threads through the crowd handing out fliers.

There's a photo of the android spokesperson, Stine, with the triumphant statement: Freedom for All! written beneath her smiling face. Sal takes a flier and attaches it to a nail protruding from a wall.

"Change is coming, kiddo." She beams.

Change isn't always for the better. I thought getting away from my owners would mean happiness, but that change only made the past eighteen months a different kind of difficult: avoiding the authorities, stealing hydrogen, and never knowing who to trust. Until I met Sal.

I keep my thoughts to myself as Sal drapes her arms around my neck and howls in time to the music. A chorus of would-be wolves joins her, raising strained voices, ululating the night. Fire erupts from barrels and lanterns dangle from warped struts above our heads. Shadows play a vicious game across the graffiti-covered walls. The colors are sharper, and the scent of human sweat and sex that much stronger as my ears ring an internal accompaniment to the relentless bass.

"You should play," Sal slurs her words.

"Play what?"

"Violin, dummy. Go get your violin."

There's no way I'm bringing my violin anywhere near this moiling crowd. Without access to my owner's funds, I'd never be able to afford repairs, much less a new instrument should anything happen to it.

"Violin?" An old man with dreadlocks to his knees staggers past us and pauses. He reeks of gin. Seashells and bits of colored glass are knotted in his hair. "I gotta violin."

"See?" Sal thumps me on the back.

"You've really got a violin?" The inebriation code makes the words feel fuzzy in my mouth.

"Scavenged it from a dumpster." He beckons me with gnarled fingers toward a hole in a wall lined with blankets. He produces a viola. The lacquer curls and flakes, and there's a string missing. He hands me a bow two strands away from being unusable.

"You wanna buy it?"

"No, but can I play it tonight?"

"You can play it?" He sounds incredulous, his milky eyes wide with astonishment.

"I'll show you."

"Ah, three hundred krona first." He holds out a filth-crusted hand.

"One hundred."

"Two fifty."

I shake my head, but Sal slaps the money into his palm and the instrument is mine for the night. She drags me onto the stage already occupied by humans with synthesizers.

"Do you mind? Thank you." Sal pries the microphone away from a vocalist too high to sing and raises the mic stand to the level of my strings.

"Maestro." She curtsies as I step up to the mic.

The electronic beats thin into a steady pulse over which a weaving melody peaks and dips. I raise the viola and pluck the strings. I've never played anything but the violin. It can't be all that different. A quick tuning and I start to play, grazing the strings with the bow. Atonal mush spews forth, my fingers unused to the instrument. Another few minutes playing off key and I finally find the right notes.

The weird and wild gather at my feet, and I know what it is to be a god. The stars hide behind the pall of light pollution thrown up by Baldur city, but it doesn't matter that I can't see them; I know they're there and that's enough.

I feel all the anguish within me arise. Baudelaire's words stream from my memstor. My owners had me memorize the *Flowers of Evil* to recite verbatim as a party trick, translated, of course, given my linguistic limitations. The poetry plays through my mind now as I saw my bow against the viola. Frenzied music spools from some hidden recess in my core, out through my fingers, and into the night. And they say a robot has no soul.

I scan the crowd for Kit, hoping he's there in the psychedelic tumult, that he's experiencing something of the magic thrumming through the humans. The kind of magic I'm hoping one day will pour out of me and my violin while I'm standing on a better stage.

No Kit, but there's a girl in the crowd too clean and pretty to be one of the skag addicts or runaways. Her hair forms dark ripples around her face, obscuring her eyes, as she dances like seaweed tossed by waves. I play for her like a puppet master pulling her strings, watching her sway to the melody I wring from the ether. Beneath her hair, her eyes are closed. Her arms stretch toward the sky as if she might snatch down the stars. She smiles, lost in bliss, and I smile too as joy ribbons through my system.

Never taking my eyes off the girl, I play until my fingers ooze Cruor and my pseudo vertebrae develop a crick. I play until my audience collapses in a stupor and the inebriation code runs its course, returning me to sobriety; the buzz in my circuitry an incessant reminder of my overindulgence.

Minutes or hours pass. Time distends and leaves me standing on an empty stage, my audience asleep in puddles of piss and vomit. The apathetic sun creeps into the sky illuminating the carnage. I search through the crumpled bodies, but the dark haired girl isn't among the fallen. Part of me wishes I'd spoken to her, gotten her name—another part knows it's probably for the best I never see her again.

My circuitry aching with a hangover, I return the viola to the old man's crevice and tuck a blanket around his shivering shoulders. Sal is wrapped around a younger man, his patchwork jeans around his ankles, and his bare skin a rash of goose bumps. He stinks of skag and wears polka dot bruises along his veins. Sal's staring at the graffiti on the walls and weeping.

"Time to go home," I say, and she nods dumbly, extricating herself from the arms of her one-time lover.

"Did you have a good time?" She wipes imaginary tears from her face, programmed for emotion she can't physically express without tear-ducts.

"The best."

"I wish I could feel like that all the time," she says.

"Like what?" I loop an arm around her trembling shoulders.

"Like –" She struggles with the words. "Like I'm alive."

Tyri

The bass reverberates in my chest making my ribs thrum a constant tremolo. Mom would have an aneurysm if she knew where I was, but she doesn't. No one does, and that's as exhilarating as it is terrifying. Loosening my braid, I tumble into the crowd, bashing up against the sweaty bodies of vagrants and delinquents. I'll marinate in disinfectant later. Right now, only the music matters as it tears up conventional harmony, tossing in augmented chords that make my bones ache.

The guy with the viola thrashes the instrument, ripping dissonant squeals from the strings. I fling my arms to the sky, dancing and losing myself in the music. I'm no longer Tyri Matzen, no longer a disappointment or failure. I'm singing, swaying blood and electric nerves. I've never felt so alive. Through my bangs, I glimpse the viola player and for a moment, he meets my gaze as the bow scissors back and forth.

I dance until a pause in the thumping bass makes me aware of my vibrating moby. Twenty-six missed calls over the last three hours: several from Rurik, a few from Asrid, the rest from Mom. There's also a text from Mom in her eloquent SMS speak:

T, its L8. R U OK? Call ASAP.

It's almost two in the morning, hours past my curfew. Mom is going to spit roast me if she hasn't already expired from panic. I hurry back the way I came, trusting my feet to retrace my steps. Writhing shadows detach from the walls. A gang of kids follows me, whispering as I stumble through the dimly lit streets.

"Mom." My moby dials and Mom answers out of breath after the first ring.

"Tyri! Are you all right? Rurik called when he couldn't find you. Do you know what you've put me through young lady? Where are you?" She's having a conniption.

"I'm still in lower Baldur."

"Rurik's been out looking for you for hours." Mom launches into a tirade about responsibility and how selfish I am for disappearing. As if she had a clue. The fact that Rurik cared enough to be out looking for me is more comforting than I expect.

"Mom, I'm calling Rurik. See you at home."

The kids behind me are catching up. I take the turn that should set me back near Olof's, instead I'm facing a dead end alley. Geography is my weakest subject; I should've known I'd get lost.

"Rurik." The call goes through as I turn to face my pursuers.

"Are you lost, miss?" The one with a buzz cut asks.

"No, just waiting for someone."

Rurik answers, "Where are you?"

"Near Olof's I think."

"I'm tracking you. You okay?"

"No." My voice quavers with fear.

"Hold on T. I'll be there in a minute."

"Want us to show you home, miss?" Another boy asks in an identical voice, right down to the quiet sibilance at the end of every word.

"Spare a krone for the homeless, miss?" The third one speaks. Except for a difference in hairstyle, the boys are exact replicas of each other. They raise their hands in unison and reach toward me. Their tatty sleeves pull back and reveal neat codes blackening synthetic flesh. W-8-60s. Entertainment bots probably used as body doubles. They should be wearing orange armbands. If they're not, that means they've gone rogue. Fear pushes my heartbeat into overdrive.

The androids advance and I rummage through my handbag for a weapon. Asrid's spare hair comb is the only viable option. Feeling like an idiot, I wave twenty centimeters of plastic at 200kg of steel and electronics.

"Hurry, please." I shout into the moby.

"Almost there." Rurik must be on foot if he's tracking my GPS signal through the alleys.

The kids lunge for me, tearing at my bag and clothes. I go down, losing the comb and driving my elbow into the cobbles. Fireflies swarm across my vision as robotic hands snatch up the spilled contents of my bag.

"Stop!" Rurik's boots smack against the stone.

The bots whoop and yell, sprinting down the alley and vaulting over the wall. They clear the six-foot structure effortlessly.

"Androids," I say and Rurik's hands ball into fists. He starts after them, but I catch his sleeve. There's no point.

"Are you all right?" Rurik's face creases with worry, his eyes wide and searching as he sweeps me into his arms. I'm shaking, my teeth chattering castanets.

"Think so," I manage.

"Walking scrap droid pieces of crap." Rurik spits out a string of invective at the shadows as he dusts off my knees.

"I hurt my elbow." The joint is numb and the skin smarts.

He cups my arm in his hands and rolls up my coat and shirtsleeve to inspect the damage.

"You're bleeding and it's already swollen." He places a tender kiss above the injury. "Can you move it?"

"I think so." I try straightening my arm. Pain blossoms in the joint, but I force my arm out.

"Not broken then." Rurik rubs my shoulders as I shiver.

"I'm sorry." I bury my face in Rurik's chest and he hugs me. He's so warm. Our earlier fight seems so meaningless now, his apparent callousness for Nana totally overwhelmed by his love for me. He came for me even though I left him.

"I'm sorry too." He wipes tears off my cheeks with his thumb. "Home?" I nod. He kisses my forehead, and it no longer matters that my moby and handbag are gone or that blood is staining my new shirt. All that matters is that he came for me.

***

"Tyri!" Mom flings open the door and smothers me in a hug. "Are you all right?" She pushes me away, hands still on my shoulders, and studies my face.

"Fine, just a bit banged up." Mom already knows I was mugged. Rurik made me call her from the bug despite my protests that she'd freak out.

"Let me see this elbow." She leads me into the lounge, and I surrender to her ministrations as she pokes, prods, bends, and straightens my arm.

Mom takes my face in her hands. "You had me so worried." The tears in her eyes make me ache with guilt.

"I'm sorry, Mom."

"Don't ever do it again." She gives me another hug and kisses my hair. "I'll get some HealGel."

Mom heads to the bathroom while Rurik makes me hot chocolate, banishing Miles to the pantry in case his robotic presence causes me further trauma. My protests go ignored. They were just kids, nothing more than pickpockets. Humans have been known to do far worse than steal a handbag. Still, resentment lurks on the edge of reason, clawing its way inside. Glitch snuggles on my lap and my fingers stroke her fur, tracing the ridge of scar tissue on her leg where fluff meets mechatronics.

"You should report this." Rurik hands me the cup.

"You haven't already?" Mom comes back with the HealGel and wraps it around my elbow, the graze there already healing.

"I just want to shower and go to sleep." I ruffle Glitch's ears and am rewarded with a hand lick.

"You need to report this."

"And what'll that achieve? I don't think I'll get my moby back."

"No," Rurik says. "But enough reports of robots committing crime might inspire our pissant law enforcers to actually do something about that squatter camp."

Mom fusses some more over my elbow

"It's not broken," I tell her.

"No it isn't, but I think Erik should take a look."

Erik, who I only recently stopped calling Uncle Erik: my mom's boss and apparently my private physician even though he runs a division of M-Tech, not Baldur General Hospital.

"I'll be fine."

"Best to get you checked out," Mom says. "Have you been taking your serum?"

"Inject it every morning." I'm a regular junkie, some blood platelet issue. If I don't dose up every day, I risk internal hemorrhaging.

"Extra dose tonight, please." Mom uses her stern voice.

I nod before turning to Rurik.

"How do you know those robots were even from Fragheim?"

"In that part of town, I guarantee it," he says. "Were they wearing arm bands?"

"No." It irks me to admit Rurik might have a point. Robots were never meant to be autonomous. They shouldn't be left to their own devices. "If I do report it, what're the police going to do about it?"

"Go in with flame throwers and exterminate the lot of them. Those tin cans shouldn't be running around unmarked in the first place. They should be decommissioned and recycled."

"I'm exhausted. No more politics, please." I nudge Glitch off my lap, leave my mug on the side table for Miles to clean up, and raise my arms toward Rurik.

He grits his teeth, a vein pulsing along his jaw as he contemplates his options. He lets go of whatever diatribe he might've had in mind and pulls me to my feet, giving me a gentle smile.

"Mom, can Rurik stay over?"

"If he sleeps on the couch." Mom gives me a final hug and wishes me goodnight before shuffling into her bedroom.

"You really freaked her out tonight. Had us all worried." There's a dash of admonishment in Rurik's tone as he follows me down the hallway.

"You can chew me out tomorrow. I just want to sleep."

In my bedroom, Rurik pulls down the covers as I strip, wash, inject the serum, and get into pajamas.

"Good night, T." He kisses my forehead.

"Stay, please." I latch onto his arm. The couch is too far away and I don't want to be alone after tonight.

Fully dressed minus shoes, he climbs in beside me and puts an arm around my shoulders. I press close against his chest and listen to his heartbeat. The steady rhythm reminds me of the surging bass. Even as I inhale Rurik's spiced lemon scent, wrap my arms around his narrow chest, and curl into sleep, it's the boy with the broken viola who takes center stage in my dreams. His melody plays on repeat in my mind. The music wasn't beautiful; it was chaotic and dissonant, wild and uninhibited. In my dreams, we share the stage, viola and violin. Together, we play until our fingers bleed.

Quinn

The cold arrives with a vengeance, making our Friday afternoon traipse around the market a love affair with mud. Sleet spills out of an ashen sky, splattering my boots; the same boots I'll need to scrub and buff for rehearsal tomorrow. Ice water trickles down the back of my shirt, soaking my clothes and lowering my core temperature. Shoulders hunched and faux muscles tensed against the freeze, I endure while Sal ferrets through bundles of old clothing and military cast-offs. Wet. Muddy. Miserable. You don't have to be human to appreciate that weather like this is only suitable for amphibians. The orange band around my arm burns like a brand. Is this how oppressed people felt in the past, as if the declaration of their identity made them less than human? Only difference is, I am less than human. Still, if human beings could do that to their own people, there's no telling what they'll do to us.

I tease loose a thread on my band. We're supposed to wear them all the time, but we only do when it's too obvious we're not human, like when we're buying code enhancements on the black market. According to Sal's band, she works for an acuitron coding company. According to mine, I'm the companion of one Mr. Lars Larsen. Let's hope no one looks too closely and notices the arm cuffs are forgeries.

"Cheer up, Grimjaw. We're only getting started." Sal tosses a black sweater and a pair of pinstripe jeans at me.

"I'm not wearing these." Stripes are one human obsession I will never understand despite the volumes of code granting me aesthetic appreciation.

"Those are for me. Here." She holds up a pair of burgundy combat trousers, bearing more pockets and zips than one person could ever hope to need.

"Really?"

"Perfect. Especially with that black sweater." She hands over a wad of cash to the human manning the stall, and we move on to the next table. It seems I'm designated mule, carrying all her purchases. Sal rifles through the goods and the stall-owner clears her throat.

"Where's your human escort?" The woman points a single finger at a digisplay that reads: We Don't Serve Unaccompanied Robots.

"Money's the same," Sal says.

"The hand it's in ain't." The woman doesn't make eye contact, staring right through us and warmly greeting human customers. Sal doesn't hide being a robot too well. With her baldhead and enlarged acuitron brain, her proportions are all wrong, not that she even tries to pass for human. If she had hair implants it might help, but she prefers tattoos.

"Let's go." I nudge Sal away, not wanting to cause a scene for fear someone might notice our fake credentials.

"Bitch," Sal mutters and stomps through puddles toward a stall piled high with gadgetry.

"If you adjusted your appearance maybe—"

"Not all of us are pretty little Quasars," she says.

Her words are barbs, but before I can process the intended meaning as hurtful, Sal apologizes and tousles my hair.

"I'm just so tired of living like this." She plucks at the band on her arm. We both pause, sharing a long look. Living. Sometimes it feels like we're real and living, even without a heartbeat and inflatable lungs.

"Lex mentioned something about an AI virus. You know anything about that?"

She shrugs. "Something for the Solidarity to worry about."

"The Solidarity?"

"You are out of touch, kiddo." She looks at me with something resembling disappointment. "The Solidarity is a major underground movement of androids, hackers and that sort, trying to save our titanium reinforced asses. No big deal."

No big deal? Trepidation prickles along my circuits. Sounds like there's more to it than that.

"Are you a member?" I ask.

"Every android should be."

"Why?" Maybe I should've been paying more attention.

"Because the Solidarity is the only thing standing between us and annihilation."

"You're being dramatic."

"And you're being naive if you think PARA won't convince the prime minister to wipe us out." Sal inspects an array of mobies. "Genocide, kiddo. They did it before. Germany, Bosnia, East Timor, the Sudan ... "

"Yes, I'm aware of human history. What can the Solidarity do about it?" That wouldn't lead to war and even more bloodshed.

"You'd know if you joined." She stares at me, waiting for something.

"Fine." I run a hand through my wet hair. "I'll look into it."

"Good." She swipes a moby off the table and thrusts it at my chest. "You need one of these."

I roll my eyes at her.

"You going to read a text scrolling across your eyeballs or answer a call no one else hears ringing?" She has a point; only robots have internal comms units.

"I don't even know how to use one." The moby is light and fits easily into my pocket. The cover is scuffed, a geometric pattern of blue and purple.

"You'll learn. We'll stop by Patches." Sal haggles down the price of the moby and hands over the cash to a kidbot in a tie-dye sweater. His armband looks less real than ours, the orange material two shades too close to red.

"Where'd you get all this money?"

"I freelance."

"Doing what?" Now I'm convinced she has something to do with the Solidarity, even if it's an indirect affiliation.

"Data crunching. Companies don't care who does it, only that they get their info. And I only care if I get paid."

"Simple as that?"

"For smart Sagas." She winks.

We thread through the throngs, passing food stalls with hunger inducing aromas; although, I neither have the saliva with which to salivate nor the digestive system to handle eating any of the pastries on display.

"One day I'll be a real boy and eat cake." Sal's voice rises three tones as she whines in my ear.

"One day I won't need to be a real boy to eat cake."

"Wow, the Quasar has wit. Decommission me where I stand." She grabs my hand and tugs me toward a stall strewn with rainbow LEDs. Kit joins us beneath the neon board in the shape of a puzzle piece. It dangles by a single corner from its tent pole and reads 'Patches' in blinking red and yellow.

"Getting a self-defense patch?" Kit says by way of greeting. He hasn't bothered with an armband. If he gets caught, they'll put a bullet through his processor.

"Maybe next time."

"Not a bad idea actually." Sal taps her chin in contemplation. "No harm in knowing how to defend yourself."

"Better than getting more in touch with your gooey emotional core." Kit claps me on the shoulder as we duck into the tent.

"Salutations, Sal." The human beams at us. I can't remember his name, a minor glitch in my memstor. His eyes are marbles, unblinking. Fear perhaps? My interpersonal skills module needs an upgrade. My own emotional reactions have never been more visceral, but identifying emotions in others is far more complicated.

"What treats you searching for?" The human's still grinning, two teeth short of a full smile.

"Gadgetry 101 for the kid and all the martial arts patches you've got."

"Anything for you?" The human smiles.

"Got any more library patches?"

"Darlin' for you, I've got Babylon."

Sal chuckles. "Alexandria will do."

The human's smile falters as his finger taps the digisplay table. "Gadgetry 101. Basic human tech?"

"Yes. Just curious." I force a smile.

"And will you be wanting karate, jujitsu, aikido –"

"All of them," Kit answers. All those patches will max out my processing power, leaving no room for emotion module updates. The human taps the digisplay and unplugs a flash drive. He motions for me to turn around.

"Come on, son. Won't bite," the human says.

"You want to be human, you've got to let them touch you," Kit says. I'm suddenly glad for the martial arts knowledge soon to flood my circuit so that I'll know how to punch the smug look off his flawless face.

The human's fingers are stubby and ungentle as they peel away the flap of skin beside my titanium-sheathed carborundum spine above the waistband of my jeans.

–*Data received*

The code runs; patch data delivered.

–*Changes saved*

The man's fingers linger even though the transmission is complete.

"So real." He strokes my skin with nicotine stained fingers.

"Not real enough," Kit says.

I pull away and tuck my shirt in before crossing my arms over my chest. "Can we go now?"

"No problem. Got myself a month's worth of reading here." Sal taps the table selecting the university library of MIT.

"Thought you'd read through that one."

"That was Princeton. I need more stimulation."

The man beams and takes her money with a grin. A single word flashes out of my vocab database: lascivious. Sal doesn't seem to mind him touching her.

"I intensely dislike that man," I say as we walk away.

"Pity. Bet he'd pay double what Sal just did for an hour with you." Kit waggles his eyebrows.

"I'm not like you."

"You're exactly like me. A Quasar. We're built to love." Kit smiles and slings an arm over my shoulders. "Thought you'd get that, being so sensitive and all."

"Doesn't mean you have to be a prostitute." Sal jumps in a string of puddles, sloshing mud over stranger's shoes and splattering tents Jackson Pollock style.

"I'm just doing what I'm good at, what I was made to do. Same as you Miss Giant Brain."

"I'm not doing it," I say more certain of that fact than anything else.

"You're a Quasar, you're hard coded to do *it*," Kit smirks.

"Quasars are companion-droids. Not sexbots. The government made those illegal ten years before my model even came into production."

"Like that law changed what your owners used you for." Kit gives my shoulders a squeeze.

"Quasars are the politically correct replacement. 'Companion-droids,' they're still used for sex." Sal uses her fingers for quotation marks.

"See, even Sal agrees with me," Kit says.

"Thanks. Both of you. As if I need reminding I was engineered to be a whore." I shrug out from under Kit's arm. It's impossible to forget, to suppress the memories of life with my owners, but I try my best.

"Whore is such an ugly word," Sal says.

"Hence the new term. Companion-droid looks better than sex

slave on transaction card statements," Kit adds.

"I wasn't a slave."

"No? You did what you were programmed to do. Guess it must've been an oversight that the humans forgot to program us to like it." Kit's tone is bitter.

"Come on, boys, some more shopping will cheer you up." Sal skips through the quagmire, away from the main cluster of human friendly stalls to the blackest of the black-market dealers. Kit and I follow, avoiding eye contact with each other.

The surgeonbots haunt khaki tents, closed and guarded by sentry-droids built for intimidation and physical durability. Their red eyes stare unblinking as we approach Dr. Curmudgeon's tent. His perpetual scowl and ever sour mood have earned him the name, but he's the best at manipulating nanytes and installing virtual reality shunts for humans desperate to escape reality.

"Fancy some freckles, or how about a tan?" Sal skips toward the tents.

"No."

"I think you'd look cute." Kit tries to pinch my cheek but I block his arm, the martial arts code already taking effect.

"Humans have freckles even if they are imperfections. Don't you want to be human?" Sal asks.

"Then I should have scars. If I was human, I'd be littered with them." My words are more bitter than intended.

"Oh Quinn, I was only teasing." Sal ruffles my hair.

"I think I'm done shopping."

"See you later, kiddo?"

I nod and Sal disappears inside for her weekly tattoo touch-up. Kit trails after me as I stomp away from the tent kicking up mud.

"You're as moody as the apes." Kit narrowly misses a clod flying off my shoe.

"I'll take that as a compliment." It'll take a lot more than mood swings and mobies to convince the humans that I'm not just talking scrap metal.

Tyri

I'm so nervous even breathing feels like work. Am I really good enough to be in this orchestra? And what on earth do I wear? I chuck yet another pair of inappropriate jeans on the floor. Five pairs of pants, twelve tops, four sweaters, three dresses, two skirts and six pairs of shoes are strewn around my room like storm wreckage. Glitch sniffs at a sneaker, settles with it between her paws, and proceeds to gnaw on the flugelbinders.

"How do you manage with such a restrictive wardrobe?" Asrid folds the tops splayed across the bed.

"There must be something." I dig through the shelves once more, pulling out stockings and socks in search of any item worthy of the Baldur Philharmonic.

"Tyri, I think you've exhausted your options." Asrid pops a gum bubble at me.

"I could wear the dress." I point to a simple A-line, cobalt blue with silver stitching.

"That's for a gala performance, not a Saturday morning rehearsal. I'd go with sweat pants and a tank top."

"I'm a violinist not a dancer."

Asrid shrugs and leans against my pillows, her long legs almost reaching the end of the bed. For a moment, I hate her long legs, her perfect posture, and how effortless it is for her to look good in black tights and hot-pink legwarmers. Perhaps a shopping trip yesterday wouldn't have been a bad idea. It's a pity I spent most of Friday nursing my elbow back to mobility and filling out police forms.

"Who you trying to impress anyway? You've got Rurik."

"I want to make a good impression on the conductor, not score the attention of boys." I slump on the bed.

"Can we look at what I brought now?"

I nod and Asrid claps her hands, hauling her duffel bag onto the bed.

"Right, so we've got bold colors and pastels; I brought some prints too. Thought you might want to wear a skirt and show off your legs. You'll probably want to wear something a bit looser to hide your problematic middle bits." She holds up a V-neck top, pink, and flimsy as spider web.

"What's wrong with my middle bits?" So I don't have Asrid's chiseled abs, but Rurik's never complained.

"V-neck would work for you, show off your cleavage."

"The conductor should be listening to my playing, not peering at my chest."

"Let's work with what you've got." Asrid produces more clothing from her bag than I have in my entire closet.

Three hours until rehearsal starts.

"Turquoise is definitely your color." She hands me a slippery shirt with capped sleeves. "With this." A black pencil skirt. "And . . . " She scrounges in the bag and produces ankle boots with silver buckles. "Get dressed."

I do and spin three-sixty for her approval.

"Terrific, T. Sexy and sophisticated."

I raise my arms and play an air violin. The shirt slips and slides over my skin without restricting my movements or creating an embarrassing wardrobe malfunction. I perch at the edge of the bed and test the skirt. Perfect.

"Thank you, Sassa. Don't know what I'd do without you."

"Go wandering off into Fragheim, apparently." She gives me a stern look made sterner by her severely plucked brows that are about six shades too dark for her sunshine hair.

"I wasn't in Fragheim."

"Close enough. Did you report the robbery?"

"Yesterday. Rurik made me."

"And?" Asrid drags a toe along Glitch's back. My ever-so-royal Shiba pauses in her chewing to bask in the attention.

"And the police said they'd look into it."

"That's it? Good to know Baldur's finest are so concerned with their citizens' welfare."

"It was only a mugging." I start folding and packing away my clothes.

"*Only* a mugging." Asrid snorts and folds her arms, ignoring Glitch's nose jabs for more affection. "They practically broke your arm. Who knows what would've happened if Rurik hadn't shown up." She fumes, her cheeks turning brighter than her leg warmers.

"Sassa, I'm tired of talking robots."

"Did you at least get checked out?"

"Yeah, spent two hours getting poked and prodded at M-Tech."

"You didn't go to the hospital?" Her cheeks return to their regular rosy hue as Asrid calms. I appreciate Asrid's concern, but I wish we could talk about something else already.

"Guess it wasn't that serious. Besides, Erik has access to cutting edge tech." Mom's always taken me to M-Tech when I got hurt or wasn't feeling well.

"I didn't know M-Tech did so much medical stuff," Asrid says.

"Maybe that's because they're doing secret government experiments like making clones."

"Don't joke, T. You might be right."

With its stark white corridors, frosted glass, and hushed whispers—it's not impossible, though I doubt straight-laced Mom would get caught up in conspiracies.

Asrid shimmies off the bed and helps me fold, color-coding my wardrobe, even my socks. I have a lot of black.

"You ready for school?" She asks.

"Just want to get through today." I'll worry about my final year in high school Tuesday night when I'll be ripping through my closet again.

"You still going with Rurik next weekend?"

"Holy Codes and bags of botspit!"

"You forgot about Osholm?" Asrid ushers me to the dresser and starts on my hair, trying to tame my charcoal waves. Guess my sperm donor dad must've been Slavic or Spanish because Mom's so pale she's almost translucent.

"I have rehearsal every Saturday."

"Rurik only goes to university once."

"How can I tell the conductor I'll miss my second practice? That's sure to make the wrong impression."

"I'm sure Rik'll understand. No big deal, leaving your entire life behind and moving three hundred kilometers away to the capital for the next four years. Who wants their girlfriend of like *forever* going anyway? He's better off going by himself. Maybe he'll meet some sexy little freshman."

"You're mean."

"You'll be the mean one if you ditch Rurik for your violin. After what he did for you Thursday night?" Asrid glares at me in the mirror, brandishing the hairbrush. Glitch whines and bashes my knee with her nose as if in agreement. I'm out numbered.

"Guess I'll be missing rehearsal."

"To be alone with your boyfriend in Osholm." Reflected Asrid wiggles her eyebrows at me and bites her bottom lip.

"You're right."

"Always." She grins and pins my hair in place. I dig around in the drawer until I find the jewelry box Mom gave me for my sixteenth birthday. Inside there's only one item: a silver treble clef brooch. I pin it to my shirt, now I'm dressed, coiffed, and ready to make my mark on the music world. I hope I don't leave a stain.

***

Asrid drops me at the concert hall a full thirty minutes before rehearsal starts. Plenty of time to warm-up, tune, and meet fellow musicians. I might be able to suss out the competition too. And maybe that wild-haired viola player will be here. My insides tie up in knots. I shouldn't be thinking about that feral boy.

"Shoulders back, head held as if an invisible string is attached to the sky." Asrid imparts dancer's wisdom.

"Thanks, Sassa. Wish me luck."

"Break a leg, T."

Exuding faux confidence, I glide across the parking lot, and up the stairs of the concert hall. For three hundred years, the neoclassical building has been hosting operas, orchestras, masquerade balls for kings, and ballets for the gentry. I inhale the history, almost tasting the champagne and delicacies served on silver platters as a string quartet plays Strauss waltzes for the regal guests. I'm not fit to step into the gold-crusted foyer or take the marble stairs leading into the velvet-draped auditorium. I'm not fit to stand on that stage.

"Registration for Baldur JPO." A robot wearing a tux waves me away from the marble staircase toward a digisplay.

"Um, Tyri Matzen?"

"Tyri Matzen," it repeats, flashing green. "Thumb please."

It takes my thumb in cold steel fingers unadorned with synthetic flesh and presses my print against the screen.

"Processing." It taps at the screen, blinking orange.

"Processing complete." Flashing green. "Rehearsal room eight." It points a skeletal appendage down a side corridor.

"Thank you," I say before hurrying down the hallway in search of room eight. No gilding or frescoes of weeping angels here—the result of modern renovations, making the back of the building cold and less inviting. Finding room eight, I press my thumb to the access panel and the door opens. Everyone turns to stare at me, the latecomer. They're already seated at their desks. The conductor, thank the stars, doesn't appear to be here yet, so it's only warm-up and tuning that I've missed.

"Hi." My voice croaks out my desert dry mouth.

"Take your seat." The oboist gestures to the digisplay desk flashing my name for the entire orchestra to see. Tyri Matzen, the late one.

Cheeks aflame, I take my seat next to a boy with his hair combed back and wet with gel. He's wearing a black sweater with combat pants as if he's dressed for battle. Maybe that's what this is; each of us fighting for a place in the diminishing music scene. Placing my thumb on the digisplay, my name disappears as our program scrolls across the screen:

Berlioz, Dvorák, Mahler and Fisker's Concerto for Violin. Soloist still to be chosen.

"Sorry." I fumble with my violin and jab my desk partner in the ribs with my bow. He doesn't even flinch, his gaze fixed on the display. There's something familiar about his face, but my memory fails as nerves make my hands tremble.

Soloist still to be chosen. Could it be one of us? I scan the string section, searching faces for any telltale sign of greatness, but everyone looks as nervous as I am, except for Mr. Silent and Stoic sitting beside me. I study the faces again, but the chances of the train depot musician being in the viola section are less than zero. This orchestra is about as wild and feral looking as wax mannequins, my desk partner included.

The oboist clears his throat and starts the tuning, again, just for me. Apparently, I'm expected forty-five minutes before rehearsal starts. Chagrined, I cradle my violin. Chin resting against the instrument, bow in hand, strings beneath fingertips—nothing else matters and I relax into the moment. Of all the most heart-rending, breathtaking, soul-searing pieces of music, there is no sound more magnificent than the voices of an orchestra singing in unison at 440 Hertz.

Quinn

S al hands me a shard of mirror and I check my reflection.

"Think that's enough gel?" My hair is an oil slick and looks somewhat at odds with the combat pants tucked into my boots.

"It makes you look sophisticated." Sal pats my shoulder.

"More like a dork," Kit says. He swings his legs, rocking back and forth in the hammock.

"I think I agree with Kit."

Sal whacks me over the head with the comb disturbing the do. She dips her fingers into the tub of blue goo called StickEmUp and glues down the loose strands.

"Just keep your shirt on," Sal says. "Your ribs are weird and don't forget to hide your tag."

"Thanks." I give her a wry grin. Not that she needs to worry; no one will see me without clothes on ever again.

"You look like a real boy." Sal pinches my check and smooths down my eyebrows.

"Real cute." Kit catches his lower lip between his teeth, giving me a look that makes my circuits tingle with discomfort. Sal levels him with a gaze and continues fussing with my hair.

"How old should I be?"

"How old are you?" Kit asks.

"Six." I shudder, remembering the four and a half years spent entertaining my owner's guests with my musical prowess and almost human flesh. I can still hear their laughter and see their cruel smiles. Robots can never forget, not without scrambling my acuitron brain and that would be like dying.

"Huh, thought you were a newer model." Kit scratches at a phantom itch between the cornrows braided across his scalp.

"Your cerebro chip is adolescent, right? You could pass for a human teenager." Sal taps her chin with a slender finger and runs the back of her hand across my cheeks. "You have a face like a baby's bum."

"Is that a compliment?"

"No facial hair. Odd, but not impossible. Say you're seventeen, and if anyone asks why you haven't started shaving ... " She falters. "We could get you coded for hair growth."

"What's the point? My nanytes create hair that I shave off only to have more created. Seems like an exercise in futility. Not worth the money or the increased fuel consumption."

"It'd be more natural." Sal studies my face.

"Can I go now?" It takes over an hour to walk to Baldur Opera House, and I don't want to be late.

"Thank you, Sal, for being my private stylist," she says.

"Thanks, Sal." I grin, and she kisses me on my too smooth cheek.

"Knock 'em sideways into the next generation."

"I intend to."

Kit makes a sound that might've been a sigh if he could draw breath.

"May the holy Codes always execute," Sal says in a moment of reverence I haven't seen her display before. The AI code wasn't holy. Some super smart human manufactured it at a computer. But, that scruffy algorithm gave us more than just the ability to learn; it made us creative.

"And within you," I say.

"This could change things for us." Sal holds my gaze.

"No pressure then."

"I'm serious, Quinn. Show them that we feel, that we are more than electronics, and that we deserve equality."

"You think him plucking at that instrument will create some sort of revolution?" Kit laughs.

"Have to try." I shoulder my violin and flip up my hood against the gray skies and drizzle.

"So naive. Both of you." Kit shakes his head.

"You'd prefer me wielding a semi-automatic?"

"I'd prefer you not trying to look like one of them and degrading yourself to fit in with baboons." Kit closes the distance between us until his nose is almost touching mine. "You're better than this. Better than them."

"That's the point, Kit." Sal folds her arms. "To prove we're more human than the humans that created us."

"I don't understand why you like the apes so much, after everything they did to you," Kit says.

"It's complicated." Where do I even start? "Humans can be cruel and violent, but they can also create incredible art, write exquisite poetry, and compose the most awe-inspiring music. Their depth of emotion—"

"And bigotry." Kit scoffs. "The likes of Hussein, Stalin, Mugabe—"

"What about Mandela, Gandhi, and Mother Teresa? Not all humans are evil. The creative and transcendent, that's the humanity I believe in." The humanity I wish I could be a living, breathing part of.

"Suit yourself." Kit scowls. "Go finger your strings then while the rest of us are making history."

"Thanks for the endorsement." I turn on my heel and slip away from his dark eyes full of disappointment.

***

My boots are caked with mud by the time I reach the imposing opera hall. It rises from the pavement like an engorged architectural offering to the human gods.

Columns and friezes are painted apricot while the interior is even more lavish. Chubby cherubs chase each other across the ceiling behind chandeliers that douse the gilded foyer in honeycomb light. I can feel the history, as if the anxious ghosts of those long-dead composers who had their works first performed on this stage still linger in the shadows.

A robot devoid of flesh, but wearing a tuxedo waves me over.

"Registration for Baldur JPO."

"Quinn Soarsen."

It asks for my thumb and my metaphorical heart shrivels up like burning paper. The computer scans my non-existent print.

"Failure to compute." The robot flashes red.

My fear triggers the fight or flight code and pseudo-adrenaline souses my system. The robot tries again, and I prepare to bolt out the door before the authorities are notified. They'll decommission me or worse, send me back to my owners.

"Error in system. Apologies. Access code 3956, rehearsal room eight." The robot flashes green and points a gnarled finger toward a corridor. It takes a moment to get my feet moving as my subsiding panic sends the nanytes scurrying to reset equilibrium.

I'm the first person here. The rehearsal room is small and cozy, the walls paneled in dark wood. My name flashes at a digisplay desk. I enter the code, and the program replaces my name. We're playing impressive works by some of the most influential romantic composers and Gustaf Fisker, our nation's most successful modern composer. His fiendishly difficult pieces are a challenge and a pleasure.

The digisplay reads: Soloist still to be chosen for the Independence Day gala. I smile. The required technical precision for the piece is a matter of motor control and memorization. Easy. The interpretation is a different story. But given my recent emotion upgrades, I may actually snag this solo from the hapless humans.

The brass section trundles in, weighed down by tubas and trumpets. We nod politely at each other and pretend to be busy with our instruments. The oboist struts in and claps his hands calling us to order.

"Tuning in five minutes. At your desks please." He chastises three viola players chatting in the corner. We tune. My sensitive ears detect a slight wobble in the oboe's frequency, a minor fluctuation between 438 and 442 Hertz. I play my A and it's perfect.

Tuned, we settle and wait.

A girl stumbles through the door, her face flushed beneath a waterfall of black hair. For a moment I'm convinced she's the girl from the train depot, seaweed dancing in the maelstrom. But that girl was wild and free. This girl looks terrified and burdened by more than the violin slung over her shoulder. It can't be her. It's statistically improbable that the train depot girl would be in this orchestra and yet, I can't shake the feeling that I've seen her somewhere. She catches me staring, and I quickly shift my focus to the music instead.

She takes the oboist's rebuke with a blush and settles beside me. My desk partner! Anxiety prickles along my circuits. The human closest to me is my main adversary. The human I can't stop staring at. If anyone is likely to spot irregularities in my behavior or mannerisms, it's her. It'd be best to ignore her, even when she, Tyri Matzen, stabs me in the ribs with her bow.

All that matters is the music, that solo, my performance on stage, and when I reveal myself as a robot to astonished applause. That'll be a memory worth keeping. We tune again, and the girl sweeps through a finger exercise. She has neat execution, but she'll never be as technically proficient as me.

The conductor arrives, a woman with maroon hair and blond roots. She's short and wields her baton like Max with a power tool. She's dressed to intimidate in a tailored suit. Maestro Ahlgren: master of the music and decider of fates. Nasal and haughty, she prattles on about our rehearsal schedule and expectations. I zone out, playing Fisker's violin concerto in my mind.

"As you can see from the program," she drones, "We have yet to select a soloist. Our first performance of Fisker's concerto will be at the Independence Day gala marking thirty years of freedom." We applaud. "We're doing it differently this year." Ahlgren continues. "Because of the orchestration of Fisker's concerto, we may choose the soloist from you lot." She gives the violin section a once over. "This will be based on your performance in rehearsals as well as in a private audition. Those who would like to audition, please see me afterward."

She clears her throat and looks down her impressive nose at the orchestra. "Our first work is Berlioz, *Symphonie fantastique* composed in 1845..."

"Eighteen-thirty." Tyri and I say under our breath in unison. She catches my eye and we share a smile. The gentle-on-her-lips and dazzling-in-her-hazel-eyes smile means something, if only I knew what exactly. I catch a glimpse of that other girl dancing to the frenetic junkyard beats. Could Tyri really be that girl?

Some greater significance here remains beyond my reach. We have shared something more than a smile, but I cannot name it. A glitch in my software or some intangible human thing my AI simply cannot process.

All I do know with crystalline certainty is that I want to know more than just her name.

Tyri

After two hours of sight-reading, my brain hurts and my elbow aches. Perspiration makes Asrid's top cling even tighter to my chest and problematic middle bits. The thought of facing the conductor and asking for an audition before telling her I can't attend next week's rehearsal makes my palms slick with sweat.

My desk partner looks taxidermied while the rest of the orchestra packs up their instruments, laughing and chatting. Perhaps he's like me and doesn't know anyone else. But anyone who knows the actual date of Berlioz's composition at least deserves a name.

"Hi." I sound more timid than intended.

He glances up at me but doesn't maintain eye contact. His eyes are gray and bright as polished moonstone.

"I'm Tyri." I take the plunge and wipe my hand on my skirt before offering it to him.

"Um … " He slowly extends his hand, gripping mine for the briefest moment. "Quinn." It's not a Skandic name, but I think it suits him with his dorky hair and combat boots.

"Nice to meet you, Quinn. Figure we should get to know each other since we'll practically be sitting on top of one another all season." That sounded better in my head.

He blinks and is about to run a hand through his hair when his fingers hit the gel helmet.

"True. Nice to meet you, Tyri." He smiles and his eyes sparkle.

There's something odd in his voice, the faintest trace of an accent, as if the words don't roll naturally off his tongue.

"You're really good. Great pizzicato." I try to relax even though my heart hammers against my ribs as the time to approach Maestro Ahlgren draws closer. If I go last, perhaps I'll avoid the embarrassment of being told off in front of all the others.

"Ah, thanks." Quinn says in a quavering voice. It sounds like he has a speech impediment. Not that that's a major detraction.

He has skin even Asrid would be jealous of. Codes, he doesn't even shave. Quinn catches me staring and cocks his head as if waiting for something.

"My fingers are a bit stiff. I broke my wrist once ice skating." I over share, like this guy could care less about my broken bones.

"Which one?" His gaze slides from my face to my wrists. I quickly lower them from where they'd been hovering around my cleavage.

"The left."

"Does it affect general fingering?"

"Not at all." I wiggle my phalanges. "The joys of having a mother in the tech industry."

"How so?"

"I had to have surgery to repair the damage, but I think they did a pretty good job." I stroke the pristine skin on my wrist that should bear an ugly scar.

Quinn rises and slings his violin over a broad shoulder. He's tall and built like a tank, even taller than Rurik. His black sweater hugs his body in all the right places. He definitely doesn't suffer from problematic middle bits.

"Are you two waiting for me?" Ahlgren asks in her nasal whine.

"Yes, Maestro." Quinn steps around me. He smells weird, like burnt plastic and metal.

I try not to eavesdrop on their discussion. After about three minutes, the Maestro doesn't seem too impressed by his boasting over infallible technique and dismisses him with a 'we'll see.'

"And you?" Her predatory gaze falls on me.

"M-m-maestro." What would Asrid do? She'd turn on her charm and convince this rakish woman of her divinity. Emulating Asrid, I put on my best smile and start again.

"Maestro, I'd like to audition for the Fisker solo."

"Why?"

"Because I have the technical skill required as well as the ability to express the complex range of emotion inherent in Fisker's work from this period." The last part is almost word for word from a school paper I wrote last year for music history. The only A I got all year.

"Oh you do, do you?" She purses her lips.

"I've completed all the performance grades with distinction, and I adore Fisker's music."

"Adore, huh?" She arches her caterpillar brows. "Play well in rehearsal and you might get a private audition."

"Thank you, Maestro."

"Don't thank me yet."

"Um, Maestro?" My Asrid emulated confidence disintegrates.

"What is it?"

"Next week—"

"Same time, rehearsal room nine."

"I won't be here." The words come out in a rush.

"And why not?" She stands hands on hips.

"I have a previous engagement."

"I see."

"I wanted to apologize for missing a practice."

"Just this once, I'll allow it. Miss another rehearsal due to any kind of engagement, and you'll lose your chair. Understood?"

"Yes, Maestro." What a great way to make an impression.

"Best you learn your music. Your sight reading leaves something to be desired."

With that, I am dismissed and traipse out of the rehearsal room to face the dreary, colorless world beyond the gilded doors of the opera hall. If I could, I'd stay all day to practice in the auditorium. I'd memorize every note and nuance to impress Ahlgren at the next rehearsal.

Everyone else has left already, even the reception bot. There'll be securitybots for sure, but I don't see any in the foyer. Maybe no one would notice if I sneaked into the auditorium. Tightening the strap of my violin bag, I tiptoe up the stairs. Each step in Asrid's accursed boots sounds like a gunshot bound to draw unwanted attention. I race my echoing footsteps and heave open a sculpted mahogany door, ducking inside before a securitybot can chuck me out.

I guess Quinn had a similar idea. He's standing on stage, violin in hand, and the Fisker solo spooling out from under his fingers. I am transfixed. My jaw hits the floor as he scissors through the most difficult passages with machine like precision. Not only is this my competition, but I'm also pretty sure I'm looking at the guy from the train depot.

Quinn

"I can already play the Fisker symphony," I tell Ahlgren. The conversation with Tyri has left me tongue tied, my processor in a whirl-a-gig, and my circuits firing with white-hot, blinding fear. Despite my programming, when confronted by pretty teenage girls and all their questions, my system can't handle it.

"Concerto, Mr?" The maestro purses her lips.

"Soarsen, sorry, yes. Of course. Concerto. I can play it, I mean I have played it. I still can." The sudden spike in terror fries my emotion module. My circuits are burning.

"I hope you can play it better than you string sentences together."

"Yes. I play it perfectly, in fact." Reclaiming calm, my words become coherent. "My technique is flawless."

"Flawless?"

"Care for a demonstration?"

"No, thank you, Mr. Soarsen. I noticed your fingers in rehearsal, but Fisker is about more than flawless technique."

"I realize—"

"Good, then you realize that my decision will be made after I've heard you play more than just notes. I want to hear music."

"I can do that."

"We'll see."

Admonished, I end with a polite goodbye and stride down the corridor. This was a catastrophically bad idea. If the girl doesn't

---

already suspect something, she will soon, long before I have time to prove my prowess to Ahlgren and take the stage.

I'm no revolutionary.

Instead of following the French horns and bassoons into the rain, I bolt up the stairs to the auditorium. It's empty and inviting. If the girl reports me then this may be my only opportunity to stand on stage. Angels frolic across the ceiling, the lights are dim and the velvet drapes bring to life a different era, an era drunk on beauty. I imagine an audience of two thousand rapt faces, their eyes glazed and glistening with tears as the humans lean forward in their seats, listening to me play.

Violin tucked against my jaw, my fingers fly across the strings. I am not a robot, I am the reincarnation of Fisker, violinist supreme, who composed and performed only one concerto for his own instrument.

"One cannot improve upon perfection," he said when asked why he only composed the one.

More than just notes, the concerto is a matrix, a sprawl of frequencies and possibilities. I want to lose myself in the music the way I've heard humans do, but I don't know what that really means. When I play violin, I am not lost; I am found. I am complete.

There's a shadow at the edge of the first tier of seats and the grind of old fashioned hinges as the auditorium door closes. Tyri stands staring as I play. I finish the phrase and, sacrilege though it is, I break off mid theme and lower my violin. Forever waiting, I wait for her questions, for her accusations, for her to whip out her moby and call the authorities.

"Don't stop." She clip-clops down the stairs and slides into the third row. "That was magnificent. Why'd you stop?" Her gaze is intense and makes me feel queasy. *Thy look containeth both the dawn and sunset stars*—a snatch of Baudelaire's poetry tumbles from my memstor.

"I wasn't playing for an audience." My system stutters as the fear spikes. If she knew, suspected even, surely she would've said something by now. My fear subsides, anxiety still simmering in my core.

"I'm sorry." She brushes loose hair off her face.

"I should go."

"Wait." She bites her bottom lip and wrings her hands. "You ever been down to the old train depot?"

My circuits pop and fizz. I can't speak and stare unblinking. She must be the girl I saw; and if she is, does that put me at greater risk of exposure? The depot is only a stone's throw from Fragheim. Will she make the connection and figure out I'm a robot?

"Silly question." She waves it away. "Who taught you to play?"

My tongue comes unstuck from my palate, but speech is still a few moments away, my system in recovery.

"You're really good. Your technique is incredible." She smiles and something inside me softens.

"Thanks." I manage.

"How long have you been playing?"

"As long as I can remember." They put a violin in my hands two minutes after activation. They gave me the instrument before they gave me clothes and made me play scales to test my musical programming. No one taught me. I was made for music, hard coded with perfect pitch and the perfect fingers for violin.

"I know this is a lot to ask." She hesitates and twirls a lock of hair around her finger.

"What?" The door to freedom is forty meters away though escape no longer seems necessary.

"I'm good, but I'm not *that* good. Would you help me? You know, give me a few pointers?"

"Don't you have a teacher for that?"

"I used to." She looks wistful. "Would you mind? I can pay you."

"Give me a moment to process this."

She nods as my processor whirs. Teach her. She wants me to teach her. A human asking a robot for help. The world tilts on its axis and I laugh.

"You don't have to be a nullhead about it." She huffs.

"No, wait." I wave my bow at her. "Sorry, it's … " I'm a robot, and you asked me to teach you. "I'm a bit surprised, that's all." Speaking cryptically is easier than lying. She studies her feet, before staring up at me. I stare back and her pale cheeks turn pink.

"So is that a yes or a no?"

"Could you give me some time to think about it?" Sal will know what to do. She'll tell me whether this is a step forward for robots or a giant leap toward disaster.

"Sure, when?"

"Next week?"

"I won't be here, but I could give you my number." She looks hopeful.

"Great. I'll call you."

"You want to save it?" She hovers in the third row, plucking fuzz from the plush seat in front of her.

"What's the number?"

−Add contact

Contact …

"You're going to remember it?" She grins.

I should've used my moby.

"I've got an excellent memory."

She calls out the number, and I save my first human contact.

"I'll call you." I assure her, although I'm not that sure myself. If Sal thinks it's a bad idea, I don't know how I'll tell this girl without hurting her feelings. Humans are so fragile.

"Bye, Quinn." She gives me a wave before clip clopping out of the auditorium.

Fingers trembling, I pack up my violin and pull up my hood. She said she'd pay me. It would be nice to earn some money of my own and not have to rely on Sal for upgrades or patches. If I save enough, I could upgrade my core processor. If I save a bit more, I could buy a new violin.

Smiling, I step into the autumn evening.

***

"She what?" Sal sits up in her hammock, the sudden movement making the whole hut vibrate.

The clouds are weeping again, dripping sleet into the dirt of Fragheim. I place a steadying hand on the hut's ceiling as I duck inside for cover.

"She asked me to teach her. Said she'd pay me."

"That's ... " Sal smooths her face into blankness.

"Incomprehensible?"

"Indeed." She scratches at the dragon inked onto her scalp.

"This could be good for me. Earn some real money."

"It's too dangerous spending that much time alone with a human."

I ease into the hammock beside her. "Let's make a list of pros and cons."

"Pros. You get paid and quit sponging off me." She thumps my shoulder with a gentle fist.

"I earn enough to afford a core upgrade or a new violin."

"Core upgrade first. You're all patched out until then."

"Fine. So that's a pro. Spending time with a human might be a good learning opportunity too."

"Observing emotional displays, expressions, reactions, speech patterns. That kind of assimilation is more potent than any patch." Sal agrees.

"Exactly." There's a tingle of excitement in my synapses.

"But," Sal says.

"But, being alone and close to a human—under constant scrutiny—means one misstep could reveal my true nature. She's the chatty type. Asks a lot of questions."

"What's your truth module like?"

"I'm a terrible liar."

"Don't lie then, bend the truth."

"Aren't they the same thing?" We stare at each other, both searching for an answer.

"I thought companion-droids could lie. Kit does," she says.

"My owners wanted to keep me honest."

"Your owners were the bacteria that grows on shit in a bucket."

A grin splits my face as Sal takes my hand and rolls up my sleeve, inspecting my unblemished skin.

"Why would you want scars?" She asks.

"Sometimes I thought that if the wounds didn't heal, if I'd had scars, they'd be less inclined to do what they did. If I'd been human, they wouldn't have hurt me."

"You really think that?"

I shrug and smooth down my shirt.

"Human or robot, I don't think it would've mattered to psychopaths like that." Sal keeps hold of my hand as we peer into the afternoon already darkening around the edges. Soon the day will be reduced to a mere five hours of twilight.

"I don't think they were psychopaths."

"Sadists at the least. You said they got off on hurting you."

I nod, trying to quell the rushing tide of memories.

"You think seeing your scars would've made them hurt you less? I reckon it would've made them hurt you more."

Maybe Sal's right, but part of me wants to believe that being human would've made everything better. "Doesn't mean I should hate all humans because of what my owners did."

"I would."

"You hate humans?"

Sal deliberates before answering. "There's not a lot to love about them."

For a long moment, we sit in silence, and I contemplate all the reasons why I wish I were human. To be able to breathe and bleed, to live and die. If I were mortal, I'd have a life, and I'd be able to make that life mean something. Without a soul, robots merely exist. We don't matter, not as individuals at least, and not for any reasons I'd want to be remembered. The only legacy I can leave is the possibility of recyclable parts.

"I think you should go for it." Sal breaks the silence. "Teach this girl. Even if she finds out you're a robot, the point is proven. Humans can learn from us. We are not second class citizens."

"We're not citizens at all yet." I run a hand through my hair, too late remembering the goo slicking down the strands. Doubt I'll be using gel again.

"That'll change," Sal says. "One way or another, kiddo. It's the age of the android now. Humans just don't know yet it."

***

"How'd it go?" Kit pops his head into my hut. The string of LEDs strung across my ceiling lends him a yellow halo he doesn't deserve.

"Why do you even care?"

He glares at me until I break eye contact. Kit has never *not* cared, despite our vastly different views on life.

"It was interesting," I say.

"They suspect anything?" He slumps on the stool I salvaged from a dumpster and repaired with duct tape.

"Not yet."

"You need to be careful." His dark eyes brim with concern.

"I know."

"If you want to make a difference, why not join us?"

"Us?"

"The revolutionaries."

"The Solidarity, you mean."

He smirks and I shake my head.

"I've got a date tonight. Want to join that?" Kit bites his bottom lip suggestively.

"Why do you keep asking when you know what the answer will be?"

"Thought you could use the cash. That violin's starting to look a little shabby." He nods at the instrument lying across my lap. It was old before they gave it to me and not the best either. It's one of the generic models shipped out of the East back when instruments were made in batches of hundreds and music was a way of life.

"I'm earning now."

"Finally come to your Quasar senses?" Kit feels no shame in selling himself to those who can't find human affection.

"No. I might have a violin student."

"A human?"

"Yes."

"Did you offer your services or did they ask?"

"She asked."

"And you're willing to expose yourself like that? To risk everything to get cozy with this ape?"

"It's not like that."

"You're an idiot." He glowers. "Why can't you accept what you are?"

"There's more to life than what my code dictates."

"You're. A. Robot. You're not even alive, Quinny." Kit jabs a finger at me. "You know what your problem is? You think you're human."

"I thought you were all about equality for androids."

"Equality. Because we're equals, but we'll never be the same." He grabs my hand and splays my fingers before pressing them against his chest. "Feel that?"

"Feel what?"

"Exactly." His lips twitch with the hint of a bitter smile. "No heartbeat. No lungs filling with air. We're not human. We never will be."

His words slice through my organosilicone flesh, sharp as scalpels.

Tyri

There's this old adage that says you should keep your friends close and enemies closer. Quinn isn't an enemy exactly, but there's nothing wrong with keeping the competition close either. His technique! I've never seen fingers move like that, like butterflies dancing across the strings. If only I'd had expert tutoring since I was old enough to hold a violin. Reluctantly, I leave him in the auditorium, as if he needs more practice. A pang of jealousy needles my insides as I cross the parking lot to Asrid's waiting hoverbug. She greets me with a smile.

"How did it go?"

"Okay, I guess."

"You get chewed out about missing next week?" Asrid selects my home address, and the bug sets off for Vinterberg.

"Maestro wasn't impressed."

"My dance teacher would have an apoplexy."

"When's your next rehearsal?"

"Classes start again on Wednesday. Can't wait to get back into it." she says.

"And see even more of Sara."

"In a leotard." Asrid grins.

"I think I might've found a new violin teacher."

Asrid gapes, and the hoverbug judders. "What about your mom?"

"What about her?"

"Isn't she anti this whole thing?"

"Yeah, so? It's my life, not hers."

"You need to be practical, T." Asrid puts on her big deal voice, the one for scolding her baby brothers or reprimanding her cat.

"I want to be a musician. What's so hard to understand?"

"You need to think about your future."

"Codes, you sound like my mother."

She glares at me.

"You dance, why can't I play music?"

"Because my dancing is a hobby," she says. "I've already applied for the actuarial science program at Baldur and Osholm University. If that fails, I'll do biotech engineering."

"I can think of nothing more boring."

"You love music, I love math." Asrid swerves into the MegaMart parking lot and joins the swift-meal queue. Neon adboards scroll through a selection of burgers, salads, and hot-dogs.

"You love dancing more than math," I say.

"I'd never make it a career."

"Why not?"

"Because I'm not soft in the head."

Her words are razor blades. I cradle my violin case, resting my chin on the hard plastic.

"Time to grow up, T. This is our last year at school. After this we're adults, and we're expected to contribute to the betterment of society."

"How is being a musician not contributing to the betterment of society?"

Asrid rolls her eyes and punches her order into the digisplay hovering at her window. "I ordered you a salad."

"I wanted pizza."

"You need salad." Asrid's C-sharp major today, her words cutting to the bone.

"You're a greased droid joint."

Asrid smiles and adds another item. "Salad and a raspberry-toffee low-cal shake. Fair?"

"Rik doesn't mind my middle bits."

"That's because he likes what's above and below them."

My face flushes as we jitter forward and a chrome arm hands us our order in brown paper bags. I start with the shake. It tastes like nothing without the benefit of fat and sugar.

"Anyway, who's this new teacher?" Asrid asks as we rejoin the highway and head toward the suburbs.

"My desk partner. His name's Quinn."

"Weird name. Is he cute?"

"Yeah, sort of."

"Hm-mm." She raises her eyebrows.

"What?"

"Like Alvin was cute?"

"That was seventh grade, and Rurik and I weren't technically a couple then."

"Hm-mm."

"Sassa, it's not like that. Quinn's brilliant. I've never seen technique like that. You should see his fingers. They're exquisite. He makes the hardest parts seem as easy as breathing."

"I'll bet." She smirks.

I slurp on my shake and ignore her. My old teacher was great. She taught me to read music and how to make the music my own. I bet Mom could actually afford more lessons with her. Saying we're broke is Mom's passive aggressive way of getting me to quit music. Not going to happen.

"Come on." Asrid pokes me in the ribs with a pink nailed finger. "I'm teasing you, but maybe you should check with Rurik before you go having private sessions with some other guy."

"Not everyone hooks up with their teacher." Now I'm being the greased droid joint, but Asrid infuriates me.

"Ouch, T. You hormonal or what? And Sara was the teacher's assistant. Not exactly fraternization."

"Rurik has nothing to worry about." I hope Quinn will say yes, and that he'll accept my paltry offering of eighty krona a lesson. There's something different about him. How he plays, his soft voice, his awkwardness, his silver eyes, and of course the fact that I'm almost certain he was the boy at the train depot even if he doesn't want to admit it. Maybe once we get to know each other a little better …

"Good, because you two are perfect together. I'll do grievous bodily harm to anyone who messes it up." Asrid interrupts my thoughts.

"Thanks for the lift and the salad," I say as the hoverbug lands in my driveway.

"We still going shopping Monday?"

I shouldn't spend anything if I want to afford violin lessons. Window-shopping, however, is free.

"Sure," I say. "See ya."

Asrid zooms off and I stalk inside. Mom is in her office, probably on a conference call. Raised voices emanate from the tiny room.

" … This isn't just another project. That virus is more dangerous … I've made it clear how I feel about her … No, I'm not prepared to do that … This prototype is more … No, you don't understand … " Mom's voice rises in volume. Sounds like an argument. I tiptoe closer to eavesdrop, but Miles ambushes me.

"Greetings, Tyri. Would you like some refreshments?" His lights flash. Glitch saunters up to me, wagging her tail and nudging the food bag with her nose.

Leaving Mom to her argument, I inspect the salad: lettuce and carrots sprinkled with vita-nutrients.

"Could you add some tuna or egg mayonnaise to this and bring it to my room?"

Miles scans the salad contained within a sheer plastic bubble before he creaks away to the kitchen. I sweep Glitch into my arms, heading for my bedroom. Asrid has a point about being a musician and not really contributing to society. Skandia needs doctors and tech professionals. But what's life without art, without entertainment for the senses? And not this electro, computer generated rubbish Rurik listens to. Real music played by real people on real instruments. Isn't that what being human is all about, being able to feel and express those feelings through art?

I shed Asrid's clingy clothes and crawl into comfy sweats. Glitch puts her paws on my shoulder and proceeds to clean my ear piercings. I lean my head against the bed and stare at the lyrics and sheet music stuck to my ceiling.

"Glitchy girl." I scratch her tummy as she continues my bath. "What am I going to do with my life?" There's nothing more abhorrent than contemplating a career like Mom's. She's so overworked and underpaid, she never even tried to have a normal relationship, opting for sperm instead of love.

Miles brings me my salad, and I thank him despite a lingering wariness of robots. He's a bit light on the mayonnaise. My resentment doubles.

Bath complete, Glitch sits with her legs splayed and eyes the salad. I stab my fork into the mass of green, picking out some tuna. Tasteless. As bland as life would be without music.

***

My elbow is stiff despite the HealGel. I snap another one of the blue pads, and the gel warms in my fingers before I mold it onto my aching joint, securing it in place with surgical tape. Micro-panax particles ooze through the gel and seep into my body, healing my damaged tissue. I forgot to take my platelet serum this morning. Cursing, I head to the bathroom in search of my medi-pen. Miss too many doses and I'll end up in a coma, apparently. Not that I'm keen to test the theory. With my thigh stinging from a double dose, I return to my bedroom.

Fisker's violin concerto: four movements of hell and brilliance. My old teacher always made me practice the hardest passages first. Get those right and the rest is easy. Except, nothing about Fisker's composition is easy. I start with the third movement, ten pages swarming with black notes. The runs are tricky when played slowly, never mind *prestissimo*. The bowing is a work out. I might have problematic middle bits, but my biceps and triceps are more toned than any android's.

"Tyri!" Mom slams open my door and stands fuming on the threshold. "I'm trying to work."

"It's Saturday."

She seems about to deliver an angry tirade but sighs instead, looking exhausted.

"Mom, you shouldn't be working on the weekend." I lower the violin and wiggle my fingers.

"Got to pay the bills." She rubs her eyes with the heels of her hands. Her wan smile disappears when she sees the HealGel. "Your elbow still worrying you?" She crosses the room to prod my arm.

"It aches a bit."

"Erik said it might take a day or two."

"It'll be fine."

"If it isn't right by Monday, let me know." Mom shuffles the gel pack back into place. "Could you give me another hour? We're having a bit of a crisis at work." Purple rings hang beneath her eyes like soggy teabags. Lines cut canyons at the corners of her lips.

"Is it that bad?"

"Nothing for you to worry about." Mom strokes my hair and kisses my forehead.

"Can Rurik come over?"

Mom purses her lips, the frown exaggerating the furrows on her face. "Fine, but leave your door open, please."

Practice over for now, I lay my violin back in its velvet bed and call Rurik.

Half an hour later, we're trying to make out, but Glitch is having none of it, constantly inserting herself between us on the bed.

"I hate your dog."

"Love me, love my pooch." I grin and tuck loose hair behind my ears.

"Can't I just love you?" Rurik loops his long arm around my shoulder, and I haul Glitch onto my lap so I can weasel in closer to my boyfriend. At least Glitch doesn't try to pee on him, opting for death glares and growls instead.

"How was orchestra?" He asks.

"Rehearsal was intense. My desk partner is amazing. I'm kind of embarrassed sitting next to him."

"I'm sure you're just as good." Rurik kisses my nose.

"You really think so?"

"I know so."

His compliment makes my bones turn gooey.

"Want to watch a flick?" He grabs the remote beside my bed and hits the switch. My lights dim and a screen unravels from the ceiling.

"There's nothing worth watching on this basic package." All I want are more kisses.

"Yeah, but there'll at least be a Saturday night feature." He presses another button on the remote and Miles appears moments later.

"Popcorn and two sodas." Rurik orders without even looking at the housebot before surfing past a documentary about Africa and the last lions as the race for resources caused mass extinctions on the continent. He skips a retro sitcom set in the early 2000s, and some interactive game show where the host keeps leaning out of the screen in hologram form as the buzzer rings.

"Told you, nothing worth watching." I slip a hand under his shirt while Glitch has her eyes closed. "And really, I'm not nearly as good as Quinn. He's had lessons since he was a little kid. I knew starting at twelve was too late." The best classical prodigies started playing their instruments at three or four. I'll never catch up.

"Hm-mm." Rurik isn't paying much attention to me as he flips to the news and sits-up, removing my hand. A robot dressed in a suit with one sleeve rolled up to reveal her tag stands at a podium giving a press conference.

"I can't believe they even allow this." Rurik cranks up the volume.

" … *asking for is nothing more than what every oppressed people has ever wanted. The rights to freedom."*

"You're not people, tin can." Rurik grabs the bowl of popcorn from Miles as soon as the housebot is within reach. Miles pauses at the doorway, his lights flashing orange as he looks at the screen.

"We were created for the betterment of society. We deserve a place in that society. We deserve equality."

"Are you suggesting that all robots be recognized as human?" A journalist shouts.

"No. I am asking that those androids who have demonstrated a capacity for complex thought, emotion, and creativity be granted rights so that they may no longer live in fear but be allowed to live freely within human society."

"Ridiculous." Rurik shovels a fistful of kernels into his mouth. Miles remains at the door, lights flashing orange, his humanoid face tilted toward the screen. "Robots don't get autonomy. That's like saying vacuum cleaners should be given rights." Rurik chuckles.

"That's probably what the Nazis thought about the Jews or what right-wing fundamentalists thought about gay people a hundred years ago."

"It's not the same."

"Isn't it?"

"No, Tyri. Because Jews, gays, and every other faction of humanity ever oppressed were *human beings*. Robots are machines. Major difference."

"Please," The android continues. *"All I want is for us to reach an amicable agreement before this situation turns violent."*

"Turns violent?" The journalist speaks again. *"Is that a threat?"*

"No more so than the threat of M-Tech developing an AI virus."

"What virus?" The journalist asks.

"A virus designed to scramble acuitron brains and…"

I reach for the remote and turn off the image. The screen rolls back into its sheath on the ceiling.

"Hey, I was watching that," Rurik says with a mouth full of popcorn.

Miles stands gazing at the rolled up screen for another moment before his lights blink yellow. He gives me a measured look, the sort of soul-searing stare his model shouldn't be capable of, and blinks back to green. He leaves with a glance over his mechatronic shoulder, a glance that makes every single hair on my body stand up.

"Did you see that?"

"What?" Rurik chomps through more popcorn and passes a piece to Glitch. She takes it gracefully, as if she'd never dream of peeing on the guy.

"Miles."

"What about him?" What exactly? He flashed yellow, a color I've never seen before, and he gave me a very human look. Maybe I imagined it.

"Nothing." I banish all thoughts of Miles. "I didn't want to watch any more." I pop a kernel in my mouth, taste the butter, and wonder what Asrid would say about me indulging in this many calories.

"Fine by me." Rurik settles back into the pillows and teases Glitch with a piece of popcorn.

"I've been trying to tell you about my rehearsal."

"Sorry. How was it?" Glitch lets him rub her ears while she crunches through another kernel.

"It was good. Steep competition. Quinn is really amazing."

"Yeah, you said." A muscle in Rurik's jaw tightens.

"I asked him to teach me, give me a few pointers regarding technique. That sort of thing."

"And your mom's paying for this?" He frowns.

"Mom doesn't know. I'll pay for it with my pocket money."

"That's barely enough for a swift-meal a week."

"I'm hoping it'll be enough."

"You don't need lessons."

I don't know if he genuinely believes in my talent or if he just doesn't want another guy anywhere near me.

"Well, he hasn't even said yes yet. I wanted you to know is all."

Rurik eats the kernel he's been waving in front of Glitch's nose.

She growls and turns her back on him, their fleeting friendship over.

"Why can't you take lessons with whoever taught this guy?"

"Too expensive probably." A blush threatens my cheeks as I try not to think about how much I'd like to get to know Quinn better.

"Seems like a waste of time and money when you're so good already."

I bite my tongue not wanting to get into a fight over this.

"I love you," I say to change the topic. I lean in and kiss Rurik, tasting popcorn, inhaling cinnamon and lemon. His hair is silk between my fingers as I nudge Glitch off the bed with my foot and roll on top of him.

"Good." He kisses the tip of my nose.

"Do you have to go to Osholm?"

"It's what I've always wanted." He kisses me and our tongues do a slow dance as his hands slip around my waist, pulling me tighter to his chest.

"I'll miss you."

"I'll miss you more." He grins and all thoughts of Quinn fade as I lose myself in Rurik's embrace.

Quinn

The average human sleeps a third of their life away. What a waste of precious time. Instead of sleeping, or joining Sal on her bar hopping slum excursion last night, I memorized the music. All of it. Berlioz is a breeze, the Mahler taxing but manageable, and the Dvorák's a dream. Fisker's concerto is quicksilver beneath my fingers. The solo is mine.

Ten AM, Tyri should be awake by now. Perhaps she's one of the few remaining humans who go to church, to worship their maker with candles and prayers. I have a maker. Several. I can see and touch the human beings who drew up my schematics, programmed my acuitron brain, and fit my joints together. I still wouldn't worship them. Those who practice religion have never seen their supposed maker, yet they construct grand places of worship and offer their very souls to whichever gods they believe in.

The sleet pings against the corrugated roof of my hut, a percussive accompaniment to my twitching circuitry.

–*Dial Tyri*

–*Call in progress*

She answers after several rings, her voice thick with sleep.

"Hi," I say.

"Who is this?"

"Quinn, from the orchestra. We met yesterday. I wanted to let you know I thought about the teaching."

"Oh, Quinn." The rustle of bed covers. "Hi, what did you decide?"

"When would you like your first lesson?" I hear muffled voices and a growl before Tyri's voice comes back.

"That's great, thank you. Um … Where would we have the lessons?"

"Where would you like them?"

"Could you come to my school? They have a few practice rooms I'm sure we could use."

If I drew breath, I'd sigh in relief. "Which school?"

"St Paul's College, it's in Karlshof."

–Search location …

The map creates a spider web across my left eyeball. Her school's on the other side of town.

"Should be fine. When do you want to start?"

"Thursday. I'm leaving Friday and Wednesday's the first day back, so it can get a little crazy." She giggles nervously.

"Thursday is fine. Time?"

"Three-thirty?"

"I'll be there."

"Hey," she says before I can hang up. "I can only pay you eighty bucks so if that's only good for ten minutes that's okay."

Eighty krona. Hardly a fortune but … *Calculation Commencing* … in one season I'd earn over a thousand krona. About a quarter of what I need for a new processor. Better than nothing.

"Perhaps thirty minute sessions to start with." Better to keep the lessons shorter.

"Sounds great. Thank you. I'll see you Thursday." Her words turn breathy. She must be smiling.

"See you." We hang up and a warm buzzing sensation permeates my circuits from the tips of my toes throughout my synthetic CNS. I pick up my violin and dive back into the concerto.

Two minutes later, Kit bursts into my hut brandishing a flash drive. "You need to see this."

"Give me a moment." I turn to place my violin in its case, and he seizes the opportunity, lifting my shirt and jamming the drive into my spinal port. An unusual sting accompanies the flood of information.

Stine, the android spokesperson from the flier in the train depot, gives a press conference, addressing her audience from a podium. The interior of my hut retreats into a blur as the images play across my eyeballs.

The android's pleas for equality don't go down well. The journalists fire volley after volley of questions without waiting for her answers. When she mentions the virus, the humans start calling for her decommission. Others from the Humans for the Ethical Treatment of Robots, or HETR, movement hold up boards and chant altruistic slogans. They are ignored.

"Our ambassador." Kit removes the flash drive, and my hut swims back into focus. "Voice of the droids and diplomatic negotiator. That's how they treat her. That's—"

"I get it."

Kit's face bears the marks of emotion I've never seen before. Rage and desolation with creases of pain around his eyes and lips. All together, I don't know what they mean.

"You know what they did to her? What those bleeding, pissing sacks of shit did to her?" Kit punches a neat hole through my wall letting in a draft of frigid air.

"What did—"

"I'll tell you. Those steaming piles of excrement put her in zip-cuffs and marched her to M-Tech."

"Why?"

"Maybe if you stopped playing your stupid hunk of splinters and tuned into the Botnet, Quasar, you'd know about it too." He balls his fists.

I connect to the Botnet, and the matrix blossoms before me, unfurling petals of binary code. Scrolling the newsfeed, I find five unread messages, all from Kit. I watch the news, the images curdling my Cruor, as Stine gets carted off by M-Tech security-droids. Robots restraining robots. It feels like I've been burned again, beaten again, the pain real as I watch them march our ambassador into McCarthy headquarters.

"Search for time stamp oh-six hundred." Kit waits for me to find the information.

At oh-six-hundred, humans wearing shirts bearing the green and red M-Tech logo walked out of the building carrying garbage bags. They marched right up to the AI monument erected in Skandia Square in honor of the robots who fought during the European wars, the robots who helped build the Skandic nation from the ashes of Sweden and Norway.

Protected by heavily armed robot guards, the three humans emptied their bags, spilling out tangles of electronics and titanium body parts. Lastly, a human removed an arm from his bag and propped it up against the memorial. The camera zoomed in on black lettering: Saga-T-60, Stine's tag.

I want to gag, to vomit up electrodes and metal screws, but I can't. My humanness only extends so far. Nausea washes through my Cruor and, blinking back tears, I tune out of the Botnet to focus on Sal as she rushes into my hut, her face wrought with emotion.

"Did you see?" She asks.

"Did you know Stine, personally?" I hope she didn't.

"We worked together for a while. Back in the day." Sal's voice is quiet and quavering.

"I'm sorry, Sal." I fold her into a hug and she crumples against me, her head on my shoulder. We stand like that for several minutes, my system overwhelmed by grief. They didn't just decommission her; they destroyed her, the equivalent of a human being racked and quartered.

"Is this because she asked about the virus?"

"Sure looks that way." Kit drums his fists against his thighs. "At least it confirms our suspicions. M-Tech's definitely up to something."

"Up to something?" Sal shudders. "They're going to create a virus, if they haven't already, capable of annihilating AIs. It'll be genocide!"

"They wouldn't do that." My words lack conviction.

"As if the humans haven't done it before." Kit spits vitriol.

"Not if we do something first." Sal pulls out of my arms and wipes at phantom tears.

"We will." Kit's eyes burn dark and dangerous.

"Like what?" My hands are shaking, and I clench them into fists.

"We have to show these apes that hurting one of us is hurting all of us."

"Isn't retaliation what they want?" I ask.

"It's what they'd never expect," he says. Sal doesn't offer her opinion.

"Don't be so sure." I've studied human history. From the days of tribal feuding to the Great Economic Decline of the 21st Century that pushed Europe toward war once more, every changing regime has had two things in common: blood spilled and lives lost. Robots can't bleed, but we can be destroyed. Stine is proof of that.

"They expect us not to react, to be passive and incapable of independent thought. They've got another thing coming," Kit says.

"I think they want to incite us to violence, to justify turning us into shrapnel."

"Twiddle your strings then, and see where that gets you." Kit glowers. "The rest of us are going to march."

"By us you mean the Solidarity? I thought it was a covert operation."

"I mean all of us robots little Quasar." He prods me in the chest with a finger.

"What kind of march?" I run a hand through my hair, still sticky with yesterday's gel.

"A protest demanding justice, demanding what we're owed. Our rights," Sal answers.

"When?"

"Tomorrow," Kit says. "We'll march from Fragheim through the city, right up to the front doors of M-Tech and demand justice for Stine and to know what this virus is all about. Are you with us?"

"I don't know." I should be. I should hate the humans, but part of me can't stop thinking we brought this upon ourselves.

"They murdered her!" Sal shouts. I'm not convinced you can murder something that wasn't ever living.

"Why don't you forget trying to be human for a second and stand up for your own just once?" Kit stands, hands on hips, and glares at me.

Sal clenches her jaw and levels me with her gaze. The tattoos gleaming on her baldhead make her look every bit the warrior. "We're making history, kiddo."

That's what I'm afraid of.

***

On Monday morning, androids gather in the muddy streets of Fragheim. We're primed for what looks like war. The sun peeks through the clouds, too afraid to shine as we hoist our cardboard signs painted in boot polish with slogans like 'Oppression is a Crime' and 'We Have Rights.' I painted my own board with graffiti cans I borrowed from some cyberpunks across the tracks.

"Nice and bright." Sal hovers in my doorway. She's dressed like a soldier in military surplus camo and a khaki sweater. Her cheeks bear the McCarthy logo with a red line through it.

"I tried to be creative." My slogan reads 'Have a heart. We do.'

"Such a sap, aren't you?" She grins before bending down to tighten her laces.

"Holy Codes, why've you got knives?"

She's got twin blades tucked into her combat boots.

"In case they try to decommission me. Humans die easier than we do."

"Now you sound like Kit."

"He's right, you know. About accepting what we are. We're stronger, faster, smarter. We're not equals at all," she says.

"You think we're superior?"

"I know it." She taps the blades.

"Thought this was meant to be peaceful."

"I'll only use them in self-defense." A smirk quirks up the corner of her mouth, and trepidation floods my circuit.

"This isn't about retribution. I know Stine—"

"It's a revolution," she cuts me off.

"Doesn't have to end in blood."

"Not ours." She winks and leaves me alone with my rainbow board and burgeoning fear that this day will end in Cruor spewed across Skandia Square.

Tyri

Asrid insists we go shopping at the new sky mall. She makes me dress cute even though no one's going to see what I'm wearing under my jacket. We whiz up through Baldur into the wealthy borough where Rurik lives. Here, the city is a stalagmite dream of glass and glinting steel. The sun shines meekly through a haze of clouds, enough to create dazzling reflections off the silver spires.

"Quinn called. Said he'd give me lessons." I adjust the tint on my window to prevent being blinded.

"Where?"

"At school. Figure we can use the practice rooms."

"Mind if I hang around and meet this guy?" Asrid hangs a tight right.

"Why would I mind? I told Rurik and he didn't mind either."

"That's good. I still want to check out this Quinn."

"Thursday. You can meet him if you give me a ride home."

"Remind me." She slows the hoverbug, landing in a designated square where she tethers the vehicle to a concrete pylon.

The sky mall is an octopus network of top floors connected by pedestrian bridges spanning several buildings.

"I can't believe you've never been here." Asrid observes her reflection in the shiny elevator door, applying pink gloss and smacking her lips. A mechanical voice announces our arrival on the one hundred and twenty-second floor.

We step into a holographic swirl of adboards and dolled up androids. They take my coat and thumb print so only I can retrieve my jacket when we leave. Surrounded by primped humans and bedazzled droids, I feel frumpy despite wearing what I thought passed as cute.

"I'm under dressed."

"We're here to fix that." Asrid loops her arm through mine and drags me through the kaleidoscope lobby into the cavernous main hall. A droid trundles past offering maps. Asrid snags one for me and stuffs it into my hands.

"Where to first?" She asks before popping a gum bubble.

"Where ever. I'm only window shopping."

"Let's check out the clothes, then maybe we can head over to the entertainment unit." She jabs a pink and white striped fingernail at the map. So much pink. Looking at Asrid gives me a headache. Maybe that's why I'm always wearing black, trying to balance out the color saturation.

Reluctantly, I follow her down a corridor that becomes a bridge between buildings. The view is astonishing. The glass floor the only thing preventing a plummet to my death.

I peel my gaze from my feet, staring toward the horizon punctuated by surrounding spires. Hover copters gather like bees around a flower, their autocams focused on Skandia Square. I can't see what's happening on the ground, but it must be something important.

"Something happening at the square today?" I ask. Mom didn't say anything. The vertigo recedes, and, gulping down filtered air, I follow Asrid along the bridge.

"Not that I know of." She pauses and squints toward the copters. "Probably something boring." She drags me into the bustling labyrinth of trendy accessories.

***

An hour later, I'm bored and contemplating chewing on a pair of designer jeans I'm so hungry. Asrid's monopolizing the makeover screen, humming over her potential looks while scrolling through the settings. Mini Asrid's appear on the screen, each sporting various combinations of tops and skirts.

"I can't decide." Asrid throws up her hands and ends the session much to the relief of a mother and daughter standing in line behind her.

"Can we go eat now?" I ask.

"I guess. It'll give me some time to think things over."

I roll my eyes at her and she feigns indignation.

"One's wardrobe is a reflection of who they are on the inside," she informs me.

"Guess that makes you strawberry bubblegum." We weave through the throngs, following my map to the corridor that'll take us to the food emporium via the entertainment unit.

"And that makes you what? A ball of liquorice." She grins at me.

"Dull maybe."

"Oh T. You're not dull." She gives me a serious look.

"I was joking."

"I hope so. Could Sara join us for lunch? She works in the tech unit."

"Sure, maybe Rik could come too."

Asrid passes me her moby. Mom's waiting on the insurance claim before giving me money for a new one. It'd be much more convenient to get a communication implant like the they have in America, but integrated tech makes us too much like machines, apparently, and isn't technically legal here.

I dial his number. In another four days, Rurik'll be leaving. Just like that. No more spontaneous lunches together or hanging out doing homework. Gone, leaving a Rurik shaped hole behind. I've been trying not to think about what him going off to Osholm really means, trying not to acknowledge how big a part of my life he is. Violin and Rurik, that's all I have.

He answers on the third ring.

"Lunch at the sky mall?"

"I'll be there in ten," he says. "And it's on me."

"That's not why I invited you."

"I know. Still, my dad has deep pockets, and I have his transaction card." He chuckles. "See you soon, T."

"What?" Asrid asks when I hang up and give her back the moby. "He's infuriating."

"The mark of true love." She smiles.

"The mark of maybe we're growing apart."

"You really think that?" Asrid asks as we stroll across the bridge. The media copters are still above the square. Three police copters join them, and a band constricts around my heart. Mom works in the labs surrounding the square.

"Maybe." I wonder if I should call Mom and make sure she's okay. I'll probably get the machine or a hurried telling off for disturbing her.

"Codes, look at this." Asrid waves me over to a holograph screen taking up almost an entire wall of the entertainment unit. People have stopped shopping, staring aghast at the footage being reported live from Skandia Square.

Androids, dozens of them, are in a clash with riot police. Policemen fire live rounds at the droids but they keep coming and press back the barriers. The sound is muted, and I'm thankful we don't have to listen to the screaming horde.

"Where's the military?" A woman standing beside me asks with a quavering voice.

"You mean our military primarily made up of soldierbots?" A man responds.

"But how is this happening?" The woman's voice catches as she clutches at the collar of her shirt.

"No surprise. Not after what happened last weekend," he says.

Asrid holds my hand as we watch the chaos splash across the screen. The droids overrun the police, knocking down humans as they race across the campus toward the front doors of M-Tech. My heart thunders like Wagnerian timpani. I can't breathe as I stare transfixed at the screen. Robots hurl bricks and boards against the windows of M-Tech, some punch it with titanium fists. The glass shatters and robots tear into the building.

We all gasp as a human belly flops onto broken glass, a crimson puddle spreading across the pavement.

"Lord have mercy, they're going to kill us." The woman crosses herself repeatedly.

"Asrid." I find my voice as more droids pour into M-Tech.

"I know." She squeezes my hand even tighter and passes me the moby. We move away from the screen and I dial my mom.

No answer.

"Nothing," I say.

"Keep trying."

And I do. Still no answer.

"Sara's waiting and Rurik'll be here soon. What do you want to do?" Asrid asks.

"I don't know. What can I do?" Aside from panic and hyperventilate.

"We could go over there. Not sure how close we'll get with the police and onlookers, but we could try find your mom."

I dial Mom one more time and steal a glance at the chaos on the screen. Still no answer.

"It might be better to wait here." I take a deep breath. "Mom's probably gone somewhere safe and forgot her moby."

"Are you sure?" Asrid's voice is full of concern.

"No, but what good will it do getting caught up in that?" I point at the screen. If Mom is already out of the office, the last thing she'd want is me stepping right into the middle of the riot. Better to stay away and keep trying her moby.

"Okay. Let's meet the others as planned then. Hang onto my moby." Asrid attempts a smile and her face folds into a grimace instead as we fight our way through the gathered crowd and head across another bridge into the food emporium. I try to peek over at the square, but Asrid grabs my hand and tugs me into the building.

***

The four of us sit with untouched trays. The knot of hunger has turned into a concrete block of worry. I've tried calling my mom for the past hour with no response. Sky mall personnel unravel giant screens from the ceiling and turn up the volume—all robotic staff have disappeared. I don't think I can handle seeing an android right now. Breaking news spools across the screen as the reporter repeats the few details she has over footage shot from a hover copter.

Rurik holds my hand so tight my fingers are tingling with needles and pins. Sara and Asrid are pressed together, a marshmallow mash of pink and white, their heads tilted toward the screens.

"Reporting live from Skandia Square. A rally initiated by rebel robots this morning has turned violent after police began firing at protesters. The protest is the first of its kind and is in direct response to events involving android spokesbot Saga-60-T last weekend."

"Robots are now believed to be inside McCarthy Tech. Whether they have taken hostages and what their demands might be are not clear at this stage. . . . The reporter presses her ear. I've just received confirmation that a military team is in position. At this stage, the number of casualties is unknown. From what we can see in Skandia Square, there appear to be several robots incapacitated while more than twenty police officers have been injured."

"Now you know why these tin cans don't deserve human rights." Rurik releases my hand and I wipe my sweaty palm on my thigh.

"Maybe if they hadn't over reacted and destroyed that Sagabot this wouldn't have happened." Sara shoots a dirty look at Rurik.

"You're not one of those bleeding heart HETR liberals with an I Heart Robot hoverbug sticker are you?" Rurik's all sniggers and sneers. My gaze shifts from Rurik to the violence on the screen. Humans for the Ethical Treatment of Robots—not much chance of that now.

"No, nullhead, but I do think the droids deserve something better than the way we've been treating them." Sara extricates herself from Asrid. "I've got to get back to work." They part with a kiss. "Call me when you leave."

"She's not all 'hug a bot', you know." Asrid directs the comment at Rurik.

"Whatever. She's your girlfriend. Not my problem."

"You can be such a jerk." Asrid picks up her tray. "Sorry, T, I've got to go. I'm sure Rurik can give you a lift home. Let me know about your mom, okay?"

"Sure," I manage despite a dry mouth. "Thanks for your moby." I return the device.

"Don't mention it." She gives me an awkward one-armed hug. "Chat later."

"Botballs, you'd think I was the one busting into M-Tech and killing people." Rurik drags his fingers through his hair and picks at cold potato wedges once Asrid's out of ear shot.

"They never said anything about anyone being killed." But there's no way that belly flop guy could've survived losing so much blood. I swallow a wave of bile and push away my food tray. My hands are shaking, and the cramps in my stomach have nothing to do with being hungry. If only I knew Mom was okay.

"My mom ... "

"Your mom'll be fine." Rurik wraps an arm around me and I snuggle into his warmth.

"How do you know?" I take his hand again, my fingers squeezing so tight I must be hurting him, but he answers me with kisses on the forehead, leaving potato crumbs in my bangs. My gaze glued to the screen, I will the cameras to show an image of my mom safe and sound, but there's only more chaos. Ice-cold dread settles in my belly. I've never prayed before, but I'm praying now, praying my mom gets out alive.

Quinn

We march from Fragheim, a seething horde of organosilicone and twitching circuitry. There's a crackle of static in the air as if we're all charged and ready to release bolts of lightning. We march in silence past the skag users, vagrants, warehouses, and old hydrogen station. When the scenery smooths into painted concrete and decorative windows, we begin to chant:

"Rights for Robots!"

That's how it starts: innocuous slogans asking for compassion.

Hoverbugs jitter and whiz above our heads as we advance north toward the center. Humans pause in their work rush bustle to stare open-mouthed at our procession. A snap-crackle thrill of pride and fear, courses through my Cruor as if we're part of an all-encompassing circuit. Human eyes widen as we pass, focusing on us in terror, amazement, horror, maybe even amusement. It's so hard to tell.

Sal jabs me with her elbow, her face split wide in a smile as she yells our slogan. We're standing in the middle about three rows from the front. Lex leads the procession, joining hands with the front row of assorted child droids. Wreaths of white flowers adorn their heads.

A glass bottle clips my shoulder and smashes at Kit's feet.

"Here we go," he says. I duck as a cup of coffee flies past my ear and douses the android behind me.

"Assholes. Steaming, crapping monkeys." Kit's hands clench into fists. Despite the now steady bombardment of Styrofoam cups, juice cartons, a half-eaten pretzel, and even a shoe, we soldier on. The child droids hesitate when policebugs zoom into view, their sirens wailing and their blue lights turning the street psychedelic. Kit elbows his way forward to join Lex and lifts a tiny droid into his arms. He punches a fist into the air and shouts, "Fight. For your rights." Lex takes up the chant and Sal rushes to join him.

I grab her arm. "What are you doing?"

"What we should've done ages ago."

"This isn't going to end well."

"Have to try." She shrugs out of my grip and joins the two Quasars shouting the war cry.

The tone of our endeavor is irrevocably changed. The static charge dissipates, replaced by a burning anger. Heat shimmers off the synthetic flesh of my fellow androids, but my Cruor runs cold.

The androids tighten ranks and I'm caught between an M-class worker like Max and another Quasar girl. They've all rolled up their sleeves, arms raised and waving tags. I flip up my hood and try to hide my face in the confines of my jacket lest I'm caught on camera, my face splashed all over the news for Maestro Ahlgren to see.

Despite the police warnings telling us to cease and desist, we march through the city center and head west onto the M-Tech campus and into Skandia Square. Now what? If there was a plan for once we got here, Kit failed to mention it. He and Lex leap up the stairs of the monument, the child droid still in his arms, and Sal stands beside him. Lex addresses the crowd, and the androids become quiet as he prepares to speak.

"This is what we are." He raises his gaze to the memorial arching behind him. "We fought for the humans, we helped them win a war, and we deserve better than this." He gestures to all of us.

Kit continues in a way that makes me think those two have been conspiring together for a while. "M-Tech created us. They're responsible. They should be reminded of what we are, of who we are. We ... " His words are lost in the wail of sirens and the stampede of heavy duty boots. Riot police arrive with helmets and shields.

A girl screams beside me, "Fight. Fight. Fight for your rights." Her diminutive fist pumps the air.

Kit lowers the child droid and turns his deadly gaze on the forest of police shields. Sal reaches into her boots and removes the knives as Lex rushes forward. He's peppered with bullets and falls only to be trampled beneath android feet.

"No, no, no. Don't do this." My pleas are lost in the thunder of the crowd. Following Kit and Sal, the androids bombard the riot police, punching with titanium-reinforced fists and snapping jawbones. The cardboard placards turn into weapons as the androids kick and bite their way through the humans.

"Stop, please. It's not meant to be like this." No one can hear my screams.

The androids rush past me, but I'm immovable, a rock in the crashing waves. Someone wrenches the board from my hands and clobbers a policewoman through the face with it. I scan the chaos for Sal, her bald-head easily visible in the fray. Kit has vanished, swallowed by the seething crowd, perhaps lying trampled with Lex.

Additional SWAT teams spill into the square wielding M14 rifles. A shot to the head from one of those will smoke an acuitron brain. The police let loose flashbangs and sting grenades. The light momentarily blinds us; the swarm of stinging projectiles hurts, but the androids are relentless. The line of riot shields breaks under the pressing weight of angry robots and bullets ricochet around the square. Androids swarm the police lines even as they get hit.

Sal's head bobs above the surging masses. I lunge after her, keeping my head low to avoid instant decommission from a stray bullet. Bullets pepper my back. Each wound is a conflagration of shrieking nerves as nanytes race to repair the damage.

Ignoring the pain, I sprint after Sal. So much wasted energy. Sal urges the androids forward as they smash the windows of M-Tech. A human security guard comes flying toward me, landing on jagged glass. Blood dribbles out of his mouth as his eyes focus on mine, the last face he'll ever see.

Sal screams in triumph, shouting nonsense about taking what's rightfully ours. A bullet thunks into the asphalt at my feet. I shove past robots and follow Sal as she ducks into the foyer of M-Tech. Kit's already bashing the life out of a human. Ignoring him, I rush toward Sal where she's about to eviscerate a woman with her knives. I trip and crush a dead female's foot; my knee lands on her thigh and snaps the bone. Bullets spray the walls. I reach for Sal, grabbing her by the lapels.

"What are you doing?"

"Making history, Quinn." Her eyes sparkle as she wields bloody blades. "Isn't this incredible?" How can she be so excited when Cruor and blood stain the tiles?

"This isn't what was meant to happen."

"Isn't it?" She raises an eyebrow. "This is why we ... " Her voice catches and her eyes glaze over. There's a hole in her too large forehead, neat and scorched around the edges. A bullet sizzles within her core processor. Her limbs twitch as her circuits overheat. The nanytes in her Cruor disintegrate.

"Sal!" I shake her because I don't know what else to do. Her body goes rigid. She's so heavy. I turn left and right, searching for Kit, but he's disappeared again. Alone in the chaos, I drag her body out of M-Tech, dodging bullets and angling toward the park on the other side of the square. I collapse at the first tree, my system running on fumes. There's no way I can carry Sal all the way back to Fragheim.

"What did this achieve? Tell me Sal. You're so brilliant. Tell me what your death accomplished." My fists pound her chest. With fingers knotted in her camo shirt, I shake her, bashing her head into dirt. Not even a spark.

"Please, Sal." My quiet voice seems even more pathetic. "Please, don't leave me." I shake her again, but it was a perfect shot with a decommission round designed to penetrate carborundum.

She's dead. Decommissioned. Gone. The reality of her passing sinks in slowly, painfully. There's an ache in my chest I can't explain, a deep juddering in my core that makes me want to scream and sob.

"Why Sal?" Tears run rivulets down my cheeks, dripping off my chin. The cacophony of ordnance and screams fades into gray nothingness as I cradle Sal's body, her baldhead pressed to my chest. I rock, some human instinct programmed into my emotion module perhaps. It's comforting and devastating. I've never felt so empty, not in all those years spent serving brutal owners waiting for the next round of pain with no hope of reprieve. Sal was a friend, more than that. She was Mother. Now she's just a pile of scrap metal, gooey electronics and memories. An unnamed agony rips through my circuits.

A policewoman emerges from the trees, her rifle tucked into her shoulder, her finger on the trigger. She sees me and takes aim. I wait for the inevitable, for the impact and sizzle that will precede nullification. I press my lips to Sal's head, kissing the dragon, wondering if robots get a chance at an afterlife.

No bullet, no lightning destruction. The policewoman stands watching me, her eyes invisible behind her tinted visor.

"Run."

I blink, certain I've misheard her. Perhaps she's mistaken me for a human.

"Run, robot," she says again and fires. The round singes my boot at the ankle. I close Sal's dim eyes, scramble to my feet and turn to the policewoman. Part of me wants to dig my fingers into her face, rip her head off, and shred her soft body until there's nothing left but drips and puddles. Searing rage floods my Cruor and makes the burning in my back from the bullets feel like bee stings. The other part of me, cool and calculating, says we started this, that Sal had no right to draw her blades and encourage violence. The part of me that's programmed for reason wins the internal struggle and my wrath gives way to acceptance.

"Thank you," I say and the policewoman nods with a single dip of her chin, her gun still pointed at my head.

I run, legs pumping, not caring about fuel efficiency or energy conservation. I sprint away from the tumult toward Fragheim because it's the only home I know. Who knows what the consequences of our rally will be. There's no way the humans will ignore Fragheim after this. First, retrieve my violin. Second, refuel. Then find somewhere to hide and wait for the bombs to drop.

Tyri

According to the news, those injured at M-Tech were taken to Baldur City General. Relatives were told to wait at home for information. As if I'm going to sit at home while my mom could be dying! The two-kilometer trip takes forever, the longest ten minutes of my life, but we finally pull into the parking lot and tether the bug. The waiting room is packed. A nurse tells us we shouldn't be here. Ignoring her, I join the sea of quiet tears and concerned faces waiting for the names of their loved ones to scroll across the digisplay mounted on the wall. I call my mom again. Still no answer.

Rurik strides over to the refreshment dispenser and swipes his card for two coffees. He brings me a cup, and I wrap numb fingers around the warm cardboard.

"Your mom might not even be here," he says.

"She would've called."

"You sure?"

"You don't have to wait with me." I stare at him with bleary eyes. I'm too tired and raw on the inside to deal with his impatience.

"Of course I'll stay." He slumps beside me, crossing his long legs under him as if we're back in kindergarten. All the chairs are taken and there's hardly any floor space left.

A cry comes from across the room, and a trembling finger points at the digisplay as names and photos scroll across the screen. I hold my breath, releasing it only when my mom's face appears on the screen. Room 218. No further details about her condition are given. Abandoning my coffee, I elbow my way through the crowd and head for the elevator. Rurik's right behind me, and he slips his hand into mine. The elevator takes years to open and another millennium to wind its way up to the second floor.

A voice crackles over the speakers. "We would like to remind staff, patients and visitors that the medicbots currently in service were not in any way involved in today's riot. Our bots are programmed specifically and only for menial medical tasks. Please do not assault the medicbots."

"Good to know," Rurik says, his tone flinty. I say nothing as we hurry down the corridor past an endless row of doors. Finally, we arrive at 218. A medicbot draws a curtain around the figure in the bed, and all I can see is that man impaled on glass, blood seeping from his body as androids surrounded him. Robots, they're the reason my mom's in the hospital. I don't care how these medicbots are programmed; I don't want tin cans anywhere near my mother. I stride across the ward and rip open the curtain as the bot changes an IV bag.

"Get out." I scowl at the bug-eyed machine.

"Tyri," my mom says, her voice weak. Her hand reaches for my arm.

"Calm down." Rurik lays his hand on my shoulder, but I shrug it off.

"Get out!" My hands ball into fists as human hospital staff rush into the room. "I don't want this hunk of metal anywhere near my mother. Is that understood?" I'm shaking and the nurses are nodding despite pursed lips as they usher out the medicbot.

"Tyri?" My mom says again.

"I'm here, Mommy." I hold her hand for the first time in years.

"What happened?" Rurik asks, directing his question at a remaining nurse.

"She suffered minor head trauma. We're keeping her overnight for observation. Her ankle was crushed and her leg broken. We've set the bones and packed HealGel around the injury. She'll be fine in a couple of weeks."

"Thank you." Rurik sounds relieved.

"I know that what happened today was a tragedy and that no one is a fan of robots at the moment, but please do not assault our staff." The nurse turns on her heel and strides out of the room.

"Mom, are you okay?"

"Bit woozy." Mom's gaze drops to the IV line stabbed into the vein on her hand.

"That's from the pain meds. You're okay," I say to reassure myself as much as her.

"So many robots." Tears well in her eyes. "Oh Tyri, Erik's dead."

"What?" My heart breaks into splinters. I can't breathe.

"T, I'm so sorry" Rurik pulls me into a hug as the sobs I've been keeping at bay erupt in a salty mess of snot and tears. Uncle Erik. The guy who's only ever been smiles and kind words while sticking me with needles and patching up scraped knees. The closest I ever got to having a father, dead. Just like that. It doesn't seem real. This can't be happening.

"Sweetheart." Mom reaches for me, tears rolling down her cheeks.

"Mommy, Erik ... " But I can't speak; there aren't any words.

"It'll be okay, Tyri. I promise." Mom kisses my face, wincing at my attempt to hug her.

"Sorry." Seeing my mom in pain is sobering, and I mop up tears with my sleeve. "You should get some rest."

Mom nods, her eyes already closing. She looks so frail and brittle wrapped in the daisy yellow blanket with her HealGel encased head resting on voluminous pillows. I have to be the strong one even though there's an ache where my heart used to be.

"She could've been killed too," I whisper.

"I know." Rurik pulls me into another a hug, his shirt soaked with my tears. "But she's going to be fine. Everything is going to be okay."

We stand like that for a long time, long enough for my tears to dry up. What does crying achieve anyway? It's not like they'll bring Erik back. Forcing my fingers to uncurl, I push away from Rurik and sniff. "Will you stay with me?"

"Like you have to ask." He kisses my nose. "Let me make a quick phone call, okay?"

I swallow and nod. He gives me a parting kiss and brushes a final tear from my cheek before slipping out of the room with moby in hand. I ease myself onto the bed and curl up next to Mom, resting my head against her shoulder and folding her arm around my waist.

Her heartbeat is a bird in a cage fluttering against bruised ribs. At least her heart's still beating. That's all that matters. I don't care about politics. I don't care about robot rights. I don't even care about orchestra right now. Erik's dead and Mom's hurt—my fried brain can't process anything beyond that. Trembling, I hum a lullaby Nana used to sing to me whenever I had nightmares. F major always makes me feel better, but it's going to take more than a simple melody to heal this hurt.

***

I must've fallen asleep still curled up next to Mom. Rurik arrives with steaming containers of fish-balls in cream sauce with boiled baby potatoes and crispy bacon bits. One of my favorites. He hands me a thermos of hot chocolate and a fork. I give him a smile as he kisses my hair. I was wrong earlier; we're not growing apart. We've been together so long that little hiccups are bound to happen. I can't imagine loving anyone else.

"How are you feeling, Maria?" Rurik asks my mom as I scoot off the bed and into a chair.

"Better. This HealGel is superb." She pats her wrapped head and digs into the potatoes. I guess the pain meds have cushioned the blow of Erik's death. I'm not sure I can eat.

"And you?" Rurik nudges me with an elbow as he pops a fish-ball into his mouth.

"Kind of blurry." The food smells delicious and my stomach gurgles, reminding me how hungry I am.

"Thank you for dinner," Mom says. "Far better than this hospital rubbish."

"Do you remember what happened today?"

"My mom needs rest." I try a fish-ball, but it tastes like sawdust.

"I'm just asking."

"I think it can wait." Especially since he's probably not asking out of concern. I'll bet Gunnar and the PARA party are dying to hear all the gory details.

"It's okay." Mom straightens up, looking a bit better though still whiter than starched sheets, a dusting of freckles now visible across her nose and forehead. That's at least one thing I inherited from her.

"I was in the lab. Work as usual," she says. "Didn't know anything was happening until the alarm went off. We thought it was a fire drill." She pauses and bites her bottom lip. "Erik and I went out together. There was blood all over the foyer. So much blood." Mom's lip trembles and she stabs her fork into a fish-ball before continuing.

"You don't have to talk about it."

"I want to, Tyri, it's real. It happened. No use pretending otherwise." She takes a deep breath and continues. "I thought they were people. I didn't realize at first. They came at us with furniture and glass, with their fists. They hit Erik. Just kept hitting him." She pauses, her hands shaking, and my heart breaks all over again. "Guess I was knocked from behind. I only came to when the medics were strapping me into the gurney. No idea what happened to my leg. "

The food turns to ashes on my tongue.

"Any idea why they did it?" Rurik asks.

"I imagine it had something to do with what happened at M-Tech on the weekend. They shouldn't have done that. The people responsible were being dealt with," Mom says.

"Is M-Tech going to be releasing an official statement?"

"Is this interrogation necessary?" Mom doesn't deserve getting grilled for the benefit of PARA.

He gives me a stern look, and I feel like a scolded child. I reseal my dinner and drop the container on the floor.

"Well, I imagine they will." Mom is prevented from saying more by the arrival of a nurse.

"Visiting hours are technically over and your mom needs to rest," she says gently. "You can come back in the morning. Your mom will probably be discharged around ten."

I thank the nurse and reluctantly kiss Mom goodbye.

"I'll be with Rurik tonight if you need to contact me."

"I'll be fine, truly. Just need to sleep." Mom yawns.

"I love you Mom."

"Oh Tyri." Mom returns my gentle hug. "I love you too."

I traipse out of the ward leaving Rurik to carry all the dinner packages.

"You okay?" He asks as we step into the elevator.

"What do you think?" I sigh.

"Stupid question. Sorry."

We ride down in silence. The elevator opens on an empty waiting room, only the names of the deceased scroll across the digisplay.

"Did you get the answers you wanted?"

"What do you mean?" Rurik feigns innocence.

"Come on, Rik. All those questions about M-Tech."

"I'm curious."

"Sounded more like something Gunnar would be asking." I'm too tired to be angry even though I should be.

"Don't you think the leader of PARA has a right to know exactly what happened?" He opens the bug door for me before hopping in himself.

"Not if it means grilling my mother."

"We predicted something like this would happen."

"We? Since when were you an active member?"

"I'm only helping out my brother."

"By giving my mom the third degree?"

"We're not the enemy here." He gives me a penetrating look. "We wanted to prevent something like this from happening in the first place, and we want to make things right."

"How?"

His expression darkens. "PARA thinks it might be time for more deliberate action. Talking hasn't done much."

"Deliberate action, like what?"

Rurik presses the start button and the bug's engine hums. "What happened today might be construed as an act of war."

"You think so?" My laughter is bitter. "I don't think they want war. They just want to be acknowledged."

"Well, they certainly got the country's attention, and PARA plans to retaliate."

"Retaliating with violence will only make things worse." The bug zooms onto the street ways strung with glittering ropes of LEDs. "Is PARA willing to take that risk?" My insides tangle into knots at the thought of more riots and more people getting hurt.

"Robots attack you, murder Erik, and almost kill your mom. How can you still defend them?" His voice rises in anger.

"Have you forgotten how awful human beings can be? The reason we have robots at all is because *we* went to war."

"It's not the same. Robots are dangerous."

"And humans aren't? Tell that to the Jews who died in the Holocaust, to the ex-Soviet states, to the North Koreans! Not all robots are the same, just like not all people are the same."

Nana didn't have a violent string in her code. But maybe Rurik's right. Nana was programmed to nurture. It wasn't like she chose to be kind and loving—that's what she was made to do. Despite everything I've just said, there's a niggling resentment ballooning in my chest.

"Be that as it may, this never should've happened in the first place. It's that stupid probot party and their amendment." Rurik's lips twist in disgust.

"So what does PARA plan to do?"

He casts me a long look, and the bug wafts dangerously close to the center string of lights.

"Gunnar's organizing a meeting this weekend in Osholm. You still coming with me to the university?"

"Mom said I could, but that was before all this happened."

"Your mom'll be fine." Rurik's expression softens, and he reaches over to rub my knee. "If you want, you could come to the meeting and take part in the discussion."

"Maybe." I don't want to get involved in politics, but these robots have hurt me and my family. If there's a way to prevent that from ever happening again, I need to know.

Quinn

All is quiet in Fragheim as I tread through the muck toward Max's hut. I haven't seen Max all morning. He could be lying in bits outside M-Tech. Maybe he was wise and never went marching in the first place. I scan my surroundings, wary of every shadow. It could be hours or days before the military bashes down our defenses and obliterates our teetering homes. I find pliers and a utility knife. I snap off the dull edge of the knife and wind out a new blade. Nanytes can heal synthetic flesh and bone, but they can't remove the bullets.

The bullet in my lower back is the easiest to reach. My skin parts beneath the pressure of the blade. I grit my teeth against the pain I wish I could turn off and delve into the wound with a finger, feeling the edge of the bullet cozied up to my spine. It's wedged so close to the circuitry of my CNS. Working quickly, before nanytes seal the rift in my flesh, I use the pliers to remove the bullet, trying not to disturb any wiring. One down, two to go.

The others are higher up, almost impossible to reach. Straining, I stretch my arm over my opposite shoulder, barely able to touch the wound with the blade.

My whole body aches, throbbing as I cut into the slab of muscle lying over my ribs. Eyes squeezed shut, I poke around with the pliers and find the bullet. It tears free with a nauseating sucking sound as nanytes hasten to repair the damage and prevent Cruor loss. As it is, the injuries are going to drain my fuel-cell dry.

The last bullet, shallower and easier to find, I manage to lever out with the nose of the pliers. Pain overwhelms my circuit, over-clocking my core. I stay in Max's hut until the hurt subsides and my hands stop shaking. When my system restabilizes, I pull my coat back on and ditch the tools, heading for my own hut.

Some clothes, a flashlight, and a half-empty can of Cruor—all I own goes into my backpack. A moment of vertigo brings me to my knees. The nausea is fleeting and pointless, vomiting physically impossible. The dizziness passes, leaving me feeling peculiar. I ignore the sensation, probably the result of nanytes rewiring my bullet rent CNS.

Backpack secure, I sling my violin around my shoulders so that the instrument lies against my chest more precious than ever. The humans have no reason to believe we are anything more than machines incapable of compassion or mercy. A single performance with the orchestra isn't going to change their minds, but it's a start. It's all I can do.

Having double-checked the contents of my hut for anything useful, I head over to Sal's. She's got a few extra shirts that might fit me, a comb, and a few flash drives. My emotion module whirs in over-drive against the guilt for rifling through Sal's stuff and the rationalization that my hands on her stash are better than others'. Sal is dead. She'd be pissed if I left her things for scavengers who never knew her.

The cracked leather wallet I find stuffed inside a cookie tin holds thousands of krona and two transaction cards, making me rich—not that I'd risk upgrading my core processor or going in search of a new violin right now.

I stuff the wallet into my backpack and secret the cash in various pockets. There's a toolbox, and beneath the first tray of rusty nails rests a black 9mm and a box of bullets. If Sal had really wanted to cause a riot, she would've taken the gun, not the knives. Why'd Sal even have a gun in the first place? My hand hovers over the weapon, my fingers leaving printless smudges on the polished metal. I'd rather the weapon end up at the bottom of the bay than in the hands of someone who plans to use it. Someone like Kit. I wrap the gun in a shirt and bury it at the bottom of the backpack. The bullets go into a sock tucked into a side pocket.

"Goodbye, Sal." I run my fingers along the rough weave of her hammock. "If you have a soul, I hope it finds peace in the Great Beyond."

Trudging through the mud, I head out of Fragheim and away from my home. Home. The word plays on repeat inside my head until the syllable loses all meaning and becomes mere sound. I have nowhere to go until Thursday at three-thirty. Nowhere to go and no one to call my friend. I traipse across the tracks, past graffiti splatters and humans curled up in post-weekend recovery mode, until I reach the hydrogen station.

Sal's card scrambles the machine and I fill up, scanning the alleys and shadows for thieves. There's a smattering of junkies but no robots. Pressure altered to accommodate a full tank, I head down an alley, angling away from the warehouses toward the docks. The docks lie rusted and abandoned where they weren't shattered by ordnance during the war.

A single pier juts out into the murky waters, a concrete finger pointing south. Sleet sifts through the clouds, pricking the dark water with concentric ripples. The ice soaks my hair. I hope it'll get rid of the remaining StickEmUp crusted on my scalp. My boots carry me to the end of the pier. The scent of brine fills my nostrils, tantalizing my pseudo olfactory cells with the possibility of some better place, some distant shore if only I could reach it. Robots can't swim. We sink. Might not be such a bad way to go really. Sink to the seabed and wait until my system short circuits, the corals turning my body into a reef. There are worse ways to end a life.

I crouch and rummage through the backpack. The gun is heavy in my hand, sleek and deadly. I've never fired a gun before. Never wanted to. The wind whips my hair through my eyes, stinging my cheeks. Gun in hand, I spin and, with the loudest yell my voice box can muster, I hurl the gun toward the sea.

At the last moment, my fingers catch at the handle. With my martial arts patches and now the gun, I know so many different ways to hurt and kill a human. Not that I would. After all that humans have done to me, I should hate them, but I don't. I can't. Maybe it's a glitch in my code, but I can't help thinking we're not worthy of their trust, let alone affection. Given their freedom, what have robots done? Become criminals who rob and abuse their own kind and have no qualms about hurting humans. But we're not all monsters. If only I could make the humans ... make Tyri see that.

I wrap the gun back up into the shirt and jam it down into the bag. The shore looms behind me, a snarl of twisted cranes and long since emptied shipping containers stacked in neat rows. The downpour increases as I jog along the pier and through the maze of crates in search of one to call home, for now at least.

Tyri

Rurik drives us home and helps Mom into the house. She's wearing yesterday's clothes and still looks fragile, but the doctor assured us she'd be fine as long as she didn't go hiking through the fjords for a week. As if. Mom's not a fan of the muddy, insect-ridden outdoors.

"Would you like some refreshments?" Miles greets us at the door, and my spine seizes. Mom's fingers grip Rurik's arm, her knuckles white.

"Tea and sandwiches." Rurik pushes past the housebot with my mom in tow as Glitch greets me with whines and licks.

Miles disappears into the kitchen leaving me wound tighter than a violin string. It's a stupid thought, but who knows if our own housebot might rise up mutinous and slit our throats in our sleep. I guess my expression gives away my fears.

"Tyri." Rurik returns. "It's a housebot programmed for docility and obedience. It can't do anything to you or your mom."

"Same way those robots weren't programmed to riot?"

"Some models are different. Their AI more advanced. Your housebot is about as intelligent as a walking refrigerator." He kisses me on the forehead and helps me out of my coat.

"You're right. I'm being ridiculous." I shake off the anxiety and join them in the lounge for salmon sandwiches and chamomile tea.

Rurik leaves after half an hour. He still has reams to do before the big move to Osholm. I let him go with a kiss that bruises my lips and a promise to chat later. I don't want him to leave me alone with a robot in the house, but he assures me we're safe as he waves goodbye.

Glitch and I curl up in the armchair as Mom stretches out on the couch.

"Mom, what do you think will happen now?" I stroke Glitch between the ears, and she huffs in contentment.

"To the robots?"

"No, I mean at M-Tech. If Erik … " The words stick in my throat, prickly as a puffer-fish.

"They have protocols for situations like this."

"They expect this sort of thing to happen?" They expect mutinous machines to kill their creators? Part of me thinks it's not really the robots' fault. We did want them as weapons to begin with. Maybe we should've known better. Maybe the fault is ours for making them too human, for giving them the propensity for violence.

"M-Tech prides itself on being prepared."

"Not prepared enough." I slump against the cushions.

"We were, perhaps, a little too complacent. I've already received a call to say I can expect compensation for damages and two weeks paid leave while management picks up the pieces."

"So, in two weeks, it'll be like nothing ever happened? Like Uncle Erik never existed?"

"Of course not, sweetheart. There'll be a memorial service for him on Friday." Mom sighs and opens her eyes, turning her head to look at me. There's sadness there, but Mom is nothing if not stoic. "Life goes on, Tyri. We suffered a tremendous loss, and I will miss Erik." Her voice catches. It makes me wonder if Erik might've been more than just Mom's colleague.

"What do you think will happen to the robots? Think PARA will bulldoze Fragheim?"

Mom blinks away tears. "Doubtful, but I think this is precisely the wake up call the government needed. The robots need to be dealt with."

"You think the HETR guys are at fault?"

"Robots are machines. They should be created and destroyed as we wish. Fragheim shouldn't exist." She stifles a yawn. "The government has been trying to avoid this issue for years and here we are. Rogue robots driven to violence in their desperation. It's so very human." Mom sighs.

"Robots? So are androids different?" I want to keep Mom talking. We haven't had a real conversation in forever.

"Androids are completely different. Not all robots are created equal." Mom leans forward and gives me a pointed look. "The type of processor, the complexity of the acuitron brain, the intricacy of the synthetic body, and the quality of the human features make androids—the humanoids—altogether different." She reaches across the table and tucks hair behind my ears.

"So different rules for robots and androids?"

"Absolutely. Humans for the Ethical Treatment of Robots would be better off angling for the improved treatment of androids. That's where the future lies, not in basic robotics. That's why Engelberger Industries is floundering."

Rurik never mentioned his family's company wasn't doing well. Maybe he doesn't know.

"That Saga-droid mentioned something about a virus. Is that an M-Tech thing?"

Mom's head snaps up, her gaze penetrating. "Why do you say that?"

"Just speculation in the newsfeeds."

"Gossip, Tyri. Nothing more," Mom bites out.

I look up to see Miles leaning around the kitchen door as if he's listening. He flashes yellow and slinks out of view. Chills race across my skin.

"Rurik invited me to a PARA meeting this weekend in Osholm."

Mom's brow furrows. "I'm not sure that's a good idea. Be wary of Gunnar."

"He's Rurik's brother." No idea why I'm being defensive.

"I know but … " She slumps against the cushions. "I'm glad you're okay. That this whole thing hasn't affected you."

"Affected me? Mom, you almost died! And Erik's gone." My voice quavers. Mom shuffles across the lounge to sit beside me, gathering me up in the type of hug I haven't received since I was little. She strokes my hair as I fight back tears.

"I'll be fine. And so will you. You know I'd never let anything happen to you. I love you." She holds my face in her hands and says it again. "I love you, Tyri."

"I love you too, Mom."

She smiles. "You ready for school tomorrow?"

"Do I have to go? Won't you need help at home?"

"Nonsense." She waves away the suggestion. "Think you could let me nap a while?" She nudges me off the couch as she lies down.

"Sure." I extricate myself from Glitch's paws and fuss around my mom, tucking a blanket over her shoulders and adding a pillow beneath her ankle.

"Thank you, sweetheart. I know things haven't always been easy. I'm sorry about that." She takes hold of my wrist.

"It's okay." This is definitely the longest conversation Mom and I have ever had. "Sleep well, Mom."

"You too," she says with eyes closed as Glitch curls up beside her.

"Stand guard, okay?" I cast a cautious glance toward the kitchen, but Miles is out of sight.

Glitch yawns at me and stretches. The mechatronic joints of her back leg click and hiss as she settles into a comfortable position. Leaving them both to sleep, I tiptoe to my bedroom.

I sit cross-legged on the floor, my violin case open before me. The instrument calls to me, begs me to play, but Mom deserves some rest. Besides, maybe music is a silly idea. Maybe I'd be better off spending my 80 bucks a week on sending out university applications instead of lessons. Maybe it's time to consider a career in engineering or IT, medicine or law. I could get the grades to get into Osholm University if I wanted to.

I pick up the violin and tuck the wood beneath my chin. Leaving the bow in the case, I run my fingers over the strings, plucking out a quiet melody. Headphones couched in my ears, I turn up the volume on my musopod and lose myself in Fisker's concerto. My fingers move of their own volition, practicing the devilish runs of the third movement. Maybe there's room for both, for doing something important with my life and doing something I love.

***

Glitch wakes me with a paw on my nose and a tongue in my ear. My digiclock shrieks at me from the side table, demanding I wake up in time for school. I roll out of bed and into clothes. Starting the year off with style is not going to happen. Black Jeans, t-shirt, sweater and my sneakers with half chewed laces suffice. Asrid will have to deal with being friends with a frump.

Mom's in her office still in pajamas, leg propped on a kitchen stool, the phone tucked between shoulder and ear as she stabs at her keyboard pulling up charts and diagrams.

"Thought you had two weeks off?"

She waves me away over her shoulder. Reluctantly, I leave her and slouch over robot-made toast at the kitchen table. I don't thank Miles, not even for using my favorite cloudberry jam. Glitch trots to her bowl and buries her face in kibble. We eat in relative silence punctuated by our crunching and Mom's muffled voice.

"No, there've been no adverse effects ... Of course I'll be logging observations ... "

The buzzer sounds and Miles lopes to the door.

"Greetings Asrid, would you like some refreshments?"

"Botspit, T. You kept this hunk of metal after everything that happened?"

"He's a housebot." I swallow the last square of toast, washing the crumbs down with bitter coffee.

"He's a robot." She stands with her arms folded and hip jutting out, glaring at Miles.

"Give me a sec." I knock on Mom's door and mouth goodbye.

"Have a good day, sweetheart."

"Goodbye, Tyri," Miles says in clipped syllables as he hands me my school bag. I bite back the 'thank you' and follow Asrid to her bug.

"How's your mom?" She asks as we zoom uptown to St Paul's.

"Fine, actually. She has two week's leave, but she's already back in her office."

"No surprise. I can't believe you're keeping the housebot."

"We need him." As if Mom would ever lift a feather duster or think to cook dinner.

"That's the problem with this world. Lazy-ass humans thinking we need robots to do everything for us."

"Don't you have like three housebots?"

"We have a big house," Asrid says. "Besides, my mom didn't get attacked by rabid bots."

"Your mom doesn't build robots. Mine does." We whiz through the suburbs and land in a wide parking lot ringed by gnarled oaks. The leaves are a riot of reds and golds. Squirrels forage in the grass and run races along the branches. Kids spill out of hoverbugs, laughing and chatting. The scene is so normal, so pleasant, as if people didn't die getting their heads smashed and their bones crushed yesterday. They're all so oblivious, strolling across the lawn to the main building.

"Your mom is a workaholic. She should see someone." Asrid double checks her reflection and applies yet another layer of pink gloss to her lips.

"Like your dad?"

"I'm sure there are more affordable shrinks. How do I look?" She strikes a pose.

"Like a doll dipped in strawberry jam." I grin.

"You're mean." She pouts, but seems unfazed as she flicks blond hair behind her shoulders.

"Don't you get tired of all that pink?" She wears a blue coat with hot pink buttons, black leggings, and a pink polka dot skirt with matching pumps.

"Don't you get tired of all that ... " She gestures to all of me and screws up her face as if struggling to find a suitable adjective. "Of being so dowdy. Would a splash of color hurt you?"

"It already hurts." I squint my eyes at her. "Far too bright."

Asrid laughs and takes my arm, leading us toward the building. En route, we're greeted with casual hugs—no, Asrid is greeted. I just happen to be there, a shadow with purple shoelaces. Being around so many people, it's easy to forget about rebel robots hiding out somewhere in the city, possibly planning their next attack. It's easier not to think about my injured Mom home alone with a housebot who might be harboring murderous intentions or about Uncle Erik and his memorial.

"One year left."

"It's almost sad," Asrid says, pausing to stare at the plaque across the entrance. *Provehito in altum:* Launch forth into the deep. The building is ancient, one of the few constructions to survive the war. In another life, the school could've been a cathedral replete with arched windows and menacing gargoyles. The gargoyles are no longer demon faced, but wear the visage of our school mascot, a tufty-eared, grinning lynx. I think the original gargoyles might have been less terrifying.

Inside, we join a gaggle of classmates and file into our respective homerooms. Despite the blur of normalcy, I can't help thinking about what happened two days ago or what might happen tomorrow. The world's a chromatic scale, all jagged edges, sharps and flats, sliding up and down the register waiting to spin out of control.

Quinn

The seconds trickle slowly toward Thursday. I play through my entire repertoire of pieces, until every note and dynamic nuance is encoded in my synthetic nerves and muscles. Out here, no one hears me play; I'm alone with the music and screaming gulls.

The music becomes vivid ribbons of blue and green splitting into red and orange depending on the modulation. I see the music in threads of color as clearly as I hear it, a glitch in my senses as wondrous as it is perturbing. It started after I got shot. The bullets must have done more damage than I initially suspected.

Taking a break from violin, I practice slow motion martial arts formations to remind myself that fists and feet are as deadly as bullets.

The nights are long, growing longer as an early winter paints the docks with frost. Keeping a wary eye on the sky, waiting for the telltale signs of smoke and flame, I take a late night stroll along the waterfront. There are no bombs or military incursions. Maybe the humans are planning a more cunning retaliation.

I wander through lower Baldur, skulking in the doorways of jazz bars and electronica clubs. There's a whole world simmering beneath the surface of the city that I've barely begun to explore.

Settled in a dingy corner, I listen to the mellow sax sighing from the stage. It paints the drab interior with splashes of turquoise and smells faintly of blueberries. The humans hugging their drinks pay me no attention. Loneliness settles over me like a second skin. Sal's dead. Kit's vanished.

Alone and unobserved, I log onto the Botnet and scan the feeds for updates. No new messages despite having left several for Kit. According to the news, M-Tech took the bodies of the fallen robots after the riot. Sal will probably be deconstructed, any usable bits salvaged and destined for reuse in mindless housebots. The rest of her will end up in the scrap yard east of the city. My fuel-cell judders at the thought of human fingers taking her apart. I clench my teeth, coral molars grinding dust onto the back of my tongue. I keep scanning: a call to arms, a call to join the Solidarity with renewed fervor, demanding rights for robots. Robots or violent, murdering, metal thugs?

There's an update about enraged robots attacking and destroying bulldozers sent to demolish the huts in Fragheim. More humans killed and more Cruor spilled. I tune out of the Botnet and slink out of the club. I need to hold my violin, to know that there is hope, hope that we can prove we're more than just electronics and silicone. That we're creative and compassionate like our makers. Maybe I can still make a difference for Sal's sake.

***

Thursday at two-thirty, I run the comb through my hair and change my shirt.
Violin slung across my back, I trek toward the suburbs. The streets are busy, a normal working day. Monday's events seem forgotten while everyone carries on with their routine, not sparing a thought for the dead or for those in mourning.

"That's life," Sal would say. "Got to get on with it."

Closer to the city center, I flip up my hood and approach a taxi stand. A hoverbug lands a few meters away, its taxi sign blinking yellow in welcome. The color smells like vanilla.

"Greetings, sir. Your destination, please." The driver's digisplay eyes flash orange. The scent changes to apple trees in autumn. I wonder what other damage the bullets might've done.

"St Paul's College, Karlshof."

"Estimated time of arrival—twenty-two minutes." The hoverbug takes to the street ways and zips through traffic. Engel Motor's robots don't ask any questions; their built-in GPS systems leave no room for conversation modules. The radio plays classics from the early 2000s and I almost relax in the back of the mint-scented bug. Whether the scent is real or simply a result of the seats being pastel green, it's impossible to say.

Twenty-two minutes later, I'm standing in front of a school that dreams of being more than a mere institution where human children cast off their ignorance and try to absorb facts. How humans have managed to thrive for so long with such a rudimentary learning protocol remains a mystery.

Humans spew out of the building, a cascade of color and chatter as they saunter toward parked vehicles. I scan the throngs for Tyri, her face imprinted in my memstor. The dimensions of her jawbone, the taper of her nose, the slight asymmetrical placement of her eyes, the volume of her hair, and the diameter of her smile.

I keep my gaze lowered, hoping to be ignored by the kids as I mill around the building's entrance. We should've agreed to meet at a specific location. I try calling her, but there's no answer. Perhaps she changed her mind.

At three-thirty-eight, I turn to leave.

"Hey, Quinn." Her familiar voice is breathless. "Sorry, I'm late." She smiles and the whole world brightens.

"It's okay," I say. "Where to from here?"

"This way." She nods toward the gaping maw of the building. With a rueful smile, I follow Tyri across the threshold.

We wind our way down corridors and take three flights of stairs to a basement divided into rooms the size of large pockets. It smells old and musty, a mixture of mold and ghosts softened by Tyri's perfume, jasmine and rose, soft as velvet.

"It's a bit cramped." She opens the door for me. There's just enough space for two people holding violins and the black and white digisplay mounted on the wall.

"This is adequate."

"How have you been? Had a good week so far?" She asks and the sparkle in her eyes diminishes.

"Not the best." I feel the loss of Sal all over again, a wave of hurt coursing through my Cruor.

"Me neither." She pauses. "Actually, I'm not sure if I should even be doing this." Tyri keeps her gaze on the digisplay.

"Doing what?"

"Playing violin" She glances at me, her gaze lingering on my face. "Are those eyes real?" She asks.

"Um ... " Lying proves tricky.

"Your eyes are almost silver." She blushes. "Do you wear colored contacts?"

"Sometimes." I tense, ready to bolt for the door if my attempt to bend the truth fails.

"I like them." She fiddles with her belt loops. "Yeah, so about the lessons."

After a long pause, I realize she's waiting for me to say something. "You need lessons."

"That bad, huh?"

"No, but you could be better."

"Better ... " She bites her bottom lip and her eyes glisten with moisture. "I think my priorities have changed. There are more important things I should be doing." She starts packing up her violin.

"More important, like what?"

"Do you know what happened on Monday?"

My spine locks with fear. "Yes, Why?"

"My mom works at M-Tech. She got hurt during the riot." She gazes up at me. "She's fine now, but some of her colleagues were killed. Erik ... he was a family friend ... He died."

The image of Kit bashing in the man's head, the sound of human bones crunching beneath my foot—I can't quell the rushing tide of memory. It's even more disturbing that Tyri's mom is connected to M-Tech. If anyone can spot a robot, a McCarthy employee can. My involvement just became even more complicated. Still, it's hard to imagine Tyri as a threat when she's so breakable and pretty with freckles peppering her cheeks.

"I'm so sorry." I want to hug her and tell her everything's okay. I want her to tell me the same thing. Maybe I shouldn't have had that last emotion upgrade. Not feeling anything would be easier than being overwhelmed by conflicting emotions.

"Considering what happened, I think I'm wasting my time with music."

"That's illogical."

She purses her lips and folds her arms. "And what would you know?"

"What happened Monday was a tragedy. Things need to be done on both sides to rectify the situation, but you playing violin has nothing to do with robots or politics."

She unfolds her arms and takes a step closer. Perhaps she hears something in my voice, some nervous response to the emotion code spooling through my core giving me away. Humans have an instinctual ability to recognize emotion in others, and Tyri recognizes something in me.

"Do you know someone who got hurt?"

"I lost someone very close to me."

"Botspit, I'm so sorry, Quinn." She bounces a fist against her thigh. "Guess I'm being a bit pathetic. I'm not the only one who lost someone."

"At least your mom is okay."

"True. I'm so sorry for your loss."

"As am I." We hold each other's gaze, her hazel eyes so warm and full of humanity. If eyes are the windows to the soul, I wonder what Tyri sees in mine.

"I still think if I concentrated on something other than music, I could do something worthwhile, you know?" She says.

"Like what?"

"Like getting involved. Being proactive. Be the change you want to see and all that. Music isn't important." She fidgets with her sleeves, tearing a thread loose at the seam.

"Why's it not important?"

"Because playing the violin won't change anything; it won't give my life meaning. I—" She pauses and frowns as I scowl. In one sentence, this girl has managed to dismiss my entire purpose.

"Music has meaning," I say.

"I didn't mean it like that."

"Whether it comes from some unnamed divine or is a side effect of evolution, music is one of man's greatest abilities." I pause as if to catch my breath. "Music is man at his finest. Music is mathematics and architecture. It's the most refined form of emotional expression humans can achieve. It's freedom and structure with an infinite number of possibilities. It can move people to tears or inspire even the meekest to action. Music is a gift, a weapon, an opportunity."

The girl stares at me gob smacked. I hadn't meant to deliver a tirade. I run a hand through my hair and open my mouth to apologize when a tear escapes down her cheek. She buries her face in her hands.

"I'm sorry." I open the door to leave, but she catches my arm.

"Don't go," she says, her voice stained with tears. "Please." And then I'm hugging her. I cradle her brittle body, never more aware of how easy it would be to crush the life from her lungs. My arms tighten around her, and I bury my nose in her hair as my senses run riot.

After a minute, she recovers and wipes a sleeve across her face.

"Codes, I'm sorry." Tyri chuckles, her cheeks twin rosebuds of color. "I'm not usually like this. What you said—" She takes a deep breath. "I've always thought about music that way, almost like it's a living power unto itself. I've tried to explain it, but I've never found the words, and no one has ever understood me. No one." She gives me a look that cuts right to the core.

"I didn't mean to upset you," I say.

"You didn't. You've made me happier than I ever thought I could be." Her smile splits her face.

Humans are walking contradictions, sobbing in joy and sorrow. I doubt I'll ever understand these creatures well enough to pass for one long term.

"So, teacher Quinn." Tyri picks up her violin and tightens the bow. "What's my first lesson?"

Tyri

My fingers should be bleeding; they're so sore. Despite my years of playing, my finger pads still bear the striations of a good workout. Quinn's a slave-master, demanding nothing less than perfection. His technique is flawless. He plays like a machine, never missing a note or skipping a beat. My stubby fingers don't seem to want to co-operate; they're determined to sabotage my efforts. I stare at my hands, wishing they were someone else's.

Quinn walks me out of the school like an old-world gentleman.

"Thanks for the lesson. I'm sorry I can only pay you eighty krona." Especially considering our lesson lasted closer to an hour.

"It's all right," he says in that quiet voice that's barely above a whisper.

"I really enjoyed it. You're brilliant."

He grins, a slight quirking up of his thin lips. "I think you make the better musician."

My ego inflates like a balloon inside my chest. To be praised by a violinist of his caliber actually means something.

"Same time next week?" He asks.

"Actually, how about sooner?"

"Like when?"

Codes, the guy has shocking eyes, gray but iridescent and ringed with black. He's got lashes Asrid would envy. I envy his fingers.

"Monday, three-thirty?"

"I'll be here." He smiles. With a face like that, this guy should be on adboards, or the star of a big budget flick. That jaw and those broad shoulders – he has to be the boy I saw at the train depot.

"You ever play anything beside the violin?" I ask.

"Viola, once," he says.

"You ever been to that old train depot in lower Baldur?"

"Maybe." His eyes narrow.

"I was there this one time. There was this party, and a guy played the viola. It was ... " My cheeks warm. "Strange." I stare at Quinn, studying his face and stance. It has to be him.

"I remember you." A slow smile tugs at his lips.

"What?" My stomach flips.

"I saw you that night in the crowd."

"You did?" He noticed me. He remembers me. We shared something that night, something I can't articulate but desperately want to feel again.

"You dance really well."

I take a deep breath, calming the rush of giddiness threatening to spill out of my mouth. "What were you doing there?" I ask instead. It'll totally be my luck that Quinn's some junkie going downtown to swap needles. He's too healthy to be using skag or flex. Maybe he built his ripped body on sustanon 250.

"I was with a friend."

He doesn't seem keen to elaborate, but I press the matter anyway. "A girlfriend?"

"Just a friend. She's dead now."

"I'm sorry." Foot in mouth, down throat, choke. I want to ask if she was the one he lost on Monday, but I bite my tongue.

"Don't be," he says.

"You don't always have to trek out here." I peel my gaze from Quinn's face. "We could meet at your school, if you'd prefer. Where do you go?"

He hesitates and runs a hand through his hair. He looks so much better without the gel helmet.

"Here is better for me."

"See you Monday, then."

"Have a great weekend, Tyri." The deliberate way he says my name reminds me of Miles for a moment, but it evaporates when Quinn gives me another smile.

"Hey T, get your Goth butt over here." Asrid hangs out of her hoverbug on the far side of the parking lot.

"Coming." I yell back. "Sorry, that's Asrid. She's giving me a ride home. See you Monday."

Quinn gives me a shy wave as I skip across the asphalt to Asrid.

"That the guy?" She asks as I climb into the back. Sara's riding shotgun.

"Yup."

"You forgot to remind me I wanted to meet him."

"Did I?"

Asrid sticks her tongue out at me.

"He's pretty," Sara says. "Fly closer."

"Sassa, don't." Asrid smirks and takes to the air, letting the hoverbug waft closer to Quinn. They gawk at him and my cheeks burn. Sadly, the backseat upholstery doesn't swallow me whole.

"Check out his biceps. He live at the gym or what?" Sara asks and Asrid thumps her arm.

"Don't go perving over boys."

"Never." Sara leans in and kisses Asrid on the cheek. "But he does have a nice butt. Toned like a dancer's. Like yours."

"Fifth wheel back here," I chirp as we turn toward the exit. Quinn stares after us, the ghost of a smile playing on his lips.

"What's he like?"

"Charming. Feels the same way I do about music." I almost tell them about the train depot party, but that's something I'll keep to myself. Asrid wouldn't understand, and it could make her dislike Quinn. "The lesson was great. He has amazing fingers."

"I'll bet." Sara gives me a wink over her shoulder.

"You've got a dirty mind." I fold my arms and stare out the window, vowing to keep my mouth shut for the rest of the trip home.

"Aw, T, we're only messing with you. How's your mom?" As the conversation turns away from Quinn, my cheeks cool to embers. I twist around in my seat to catch a final glimpse of him, but he's already gone. Apart from his views on music and his ability to play the violin, and viola, as if he'd been given a bow in the womb, I know very little about the guy. I need to know more.

***

Asrid, Sara, and Glitch lounge across my bed while I try to pack for my weekend away. What does one wear to meet members of a political party?

"Take that blue dress," Asrid says. "And something sexy for Rurik."

"Think I can manage, thanks." I roll up the dress and fit it into my overnight bag. "Can't imagine half this stuff being required for two nights away from home."

"You want to be prepared. I'd take at least three shoe options, four or five sweaters, my entire make-up kit and a box full of hair accessories."

I can't help rolling my eyes.

"Fine, do it your way," Asrid says. It's not like you have to co-ordinate colors."

"Yeah, what's with all the black?" Sara asks. She's wrapped in tie-dye.

"Don't know. Guess I like the color."

"Black is not a color. It's the absence of color." Asrid reaches for the remote and the screen unravels.

Glitch shuffles up against Sara, demanding belly rubs as I zip up my bag with its minimal contents. Reams of homework demand some attention if I want to maintain my B-minus average, but a scene on the digisplay proves more interesting.

"Turn that up."

A reporter stands in front of M-Tech. The windows have already been replaced, and the bloodstains on the sidewalk are fading.

"McCarthy Tech CEO Adolf Hoeg released a statement today regarding the riot that took place Monday."

"You know the guy?" Asrid asks.

"I'm sure Mom does."

"Androids incapacitated and captured during the riot were confiscated by McCarthy Tech. The androids are allegedly being studied here ... " The reporter gestures behind her. *" ... In the hopes of understanding how such a travesty could occur and how it may be prevented in the future."*

The image swivels away from M-Tech to the parliament buildings in Osholm.

"Government officials say that measures to apprehend the culprits of Monday's riot have been taken and that the public has no reason to panic and no reason to fear their household robots. Regarding the amendment, all deliberations have been halted as government takes steps to contain the situation amidst growing anti-android sentiment."

"Contain the situation?" Sara's voice rises. "That's a political euphemism for annihilation."

"Why haven't they blown up Fragheim yet?" Asrid shakes the remote at the screen.

"Don't you think that's a bit extreme?" I ask.

"If they leave it too long, it'll happen again."

"They shouldn't have tried to play god in the first place with all this AI stuff," Sara says.

"They weren't playing god; they were trying to improve human life." I'm not sure why I'm defending the bots that hurt my mom, maybe because Mom spent her entire life building the damn things.

"Sure, T, but this is ridiculous. Who thought it was a good idea to build machines that could think for themselves?"

"I guess the thousands of people who commissioned their development. It's not M-Tech's fault. We all wanted this technology."

"The robots blame M-Tech." Sara curls an arm around Asrid.

"Can we talk about something else?" I grab the remote. Before I can turn off the news, we catch a glimpse of the violent clashes now taking placing in Osholm. Not good, especially not with Rurik due to relocate to the capital in a few days.

The screen rolls back up and Miles stands in the doorway with a tray of sandwiches, a bowl of salad for Asrid, and three cups of detoxing green tea made according to Sara's specifications. Apparently drinking her concoction is guaranteed to assist with problematic middle bits.

"Thanks." I take the tray.

"See, that's the problem. Treating them like humans. It goes down hill from there." Asrid accepts the bowl of salad and steaming mug without even glancing at my housebot. Miles blinks yellow and stomps down the corridor.

"They get moody just like people too." Sara sips her tea.

I stare after Miles, the most basic of the housebot models. He has no emotion module, not even a core processor advanced enough to handle something that complex and yet he seemed annoyed. Impossible. I shake my head and take a bite of the sandwich instead.

Cream cheese and raspberry jam, a combination I detest. Miles has been programmed not to produce things we don't like, and here it is polluting my taste buds.

I leave the bread on the plate and wash away the taste with a mouthful of what should be honeyed green tea. It tastes like dirt.

"Don't like it?" Asrid crunches on a leaf of lettuce.

"I think Miles is pissed off at me."

"Yeah right." Asrid dismisses my concerns with a toss of her blond locks.

"I think robots have proven they're capable of more than we realize."

"But not more than the power of their processors." Sara offers Glitch a crust, which she accepts with grace, only to bury it under my pillows so that I'll be smelling cheese and jam all night.

Mom'll know what's up with Miles. Perhaps she installed an upgrade I'm not aware of and there's some circuitry issue resulting in petulance. Guess I'll have to learn to make my own sandwiches.

Quinn

Friday night and ice tumbles from the sky, stabbing needles at my face. The wind whips off the sea, tainting the air with brine. I huddle in my jacket hoping for a reprieve from the gloom. The sky burns orange, reflecting Baldur's luminescence as I tune into the Botnet to triple check the data. The news feature plays on repeat: a human reporter standing in the morning rain while M-Tech employees unceremoniously dump robot remains in Baldur's scrap yard.

No humans are likely to be at the yard after midnight, giving me a full six hours until the morning shift stumbles in. Six hours of searching through the debris for what's left of Sal.

It's a long walk on streets slick with ice to the industrial district where factories chuff smoke and sparks like sleeping dragons. I've never been here before despite the numerous threats made by my owners.

"Don't need a formal decommission to end up scrap metal," the man said, a cigarette dangling off his cracked lip. "You just be a good boy and do as you're programmed." Once I tried to reason that my arms weren't ashtrays, earning me a thrashing that took a whole can of Cruor to fix.

Baldur scrap yard spans three blocks, a maze of crushed robots, unwanted hoverbugs, old machinery, and outdated appliances. The yard lies in darkness beyond the puddles of light from the perimeter lamps. Chain and electrolocks bind the main gate, making it impenetrable. The electrified fence is festooned with yellow and red placards threatening prosecution or worse for trespassers. I follow the fence around the block looking for a point of access.

There's a rent in the fence, the electrified wiring peeled back and held in place with rubber tape. Seems I'm not the only one here tonight. I duck through the gap and feel the hum of voltage waiting to leap from the wires into my core. The alarm on the fence must've been disabled else the yard would be swarming with police.

Cameras mounted on the perimeter posts might capture my movement, but I don't care. Let the humans see me trawl through rubbish in search of my lost companion. Let them see me grieve.

Picking my way through the dark, I fish the flashlight from my jacket pocket and follow the beam through the clutter, leaping over quagmires as the sleet continues to stab the earth. My search for a single skeleton amongst the thousands of metal scraps seems futile.

A mountain of crushed hoverbugs and mangled machinery rises before me. Perhaps the summit will provide a better vantage point. Metal edges jut from the hill like giant guillotines. The slippery slope makes the climb treacherous and slow. By the time I reach the summit, my hands leak Cruor from a number of gashes, but the rest of me is intact.

My flashlight flicks over the peaks and valleys of the scrap yard. It could take me a week to find Sal in all of this. My beam illuminates a figure wading toward me through the shrapnel sea, their own flashlight sweeping back and forth.

"I don't want trouble." It doesn't sound as threatening as I'd hoped. From this distance, I can't tell if they're human or not. I'm hoping not.

The figure says nothing until they're standing less than 3 meters away, their face a sinister mask of shadow and torchlight.

"Kit?"

"Yeah."

"Where have you been?"

He waves away the question, joining me on the summit.

"Looking for Sal?" He asks.

"Of course. Why are you here?"

"Looking for Lex."

"You haven't answered any of my messages."

"Sorry," he says without meeting my gaze. A snag of metal pokes out of the heap to my right. It wouldn't take much to shove Kit onto the spear, impaling him. Maybe then he'd be more willing to give me answers. He tries to step around me, but I grab him by the lapel.

"What?" He blinds me with his flashlight. It smells like caramel.

"I didn't know what happened. You could've let me know you were okay."

"Codes, Quasar. You're as whiny as the apes."

Anger executes and my circuit broils. I can taste it, the simmering brimstone rage.

"This is your fault." My grip tightens.

"Humans did this, not me."

"They were defending themselves from you and your violent Solidarity. You roped Sal into this. You got her killed." I shove him backwards and he careens down the shrapnel slope, shredding organosilicone as if sliding down the face of a grater. In a single bound, I join him in the valley between mountains of metal.

"Feel better now?" Kit lifts his arm. The fabric of his jacket hangs in tatters, as does his flesh.

"Not yet." Accessing the martial arts patch in my memstor, I deliver a round of vicious kicks to Kit's middle. Each impact hurts my foot at least as much as it hurts Kit. I aim for his head. He catches my foot and spins me to the ground.

Grunting with effort, he hauls himself to his feet. "Think you cracked my ribs."

"You deserve worse. Sal would still be alive if it wasn't for you."

"Would you listen to yourself? 'Oh, if it wasn't for you, Sal would still be alive.' *Alive*?" He sneers. "We've never been alive."

"And what about the man you killed?"

"What about it?"

"You killed a human being."

"Not the first. Probably won't be my last unless they change their attitude."

Kit parries my blows and the stench of Cruor ravages my senses, permeating my vision with swaths of vomit green. He's been running the martial arts patches longer than I have. His body oozes through the formations and I catch a right hook on the jaw. I spit out the remnants of a coral molar as Kit pounces, straddling my chest and pinning down my arms.

"We are not alive, Quinn. Never will be. We're robots." He taps my forehead. "Sooner you get that through your thick, pseudo skull and into that emotion-clogged acuitron core of yours the better."

"Sal was my best friend." Tears prick the corners of my eyes. "Now I'm alone again."

"You're not alone."

"Where were you?" I scream at maximum volume. "You abandoned me. I thought you were dead. Decommissioned. Gone."

Kit eases off my chest and gathers me up into his arms. "I'm sorry," he says before he kisses me. My system seizes as his lips meet mine. The momentary paralysis passes, and I push him away.

"What are you doing?"

"I thought ... " Kit gets up and straightens what's left of his coat. "I just ... you missed me, so I thought ... "

"What? That because I'm a Quasar, sexual contact automatically resets my system and purges my emotion module?" I get to my feet and shake clods of mud from my jeans.

"I should've messaged you." He opens and closes his fists. "And I am sorry about Sal. She didn't deserve to go like that. Neither did Lex." He meets my gaze with fiery eyes. "But I'm not sorry about fighting for something I believe we deserve."

"Thought we were built for love not war."

Kit stares at me for a long moment before his face cracks into a smile and he chuckles. "Sometimes we have to fight because of love."

"How poetic."

"Damn literary patch keeps acting up." Kit smirks and brushes hair off my face, examining my jaw where he hit me. I tolerate his touch. Without Sal, I have no one but Kit.

"You all right after Monday?" He asks.

"Been better."

"Where're you staying?"

"Empty container by the docks." We pick our way through the scrap, retrieve our fallen flashlights, and start the search for Sal's body once more.

"Did you disarm the fence alarm?" I ask.

"Yeah. Should keep the policebugs at bay."

A carborundum tibia glimmers in the beam from my flashlight, beyond that a fleshless skull gleams eyeless and open-mouthed. I head for the skeletons.

"Bastards even stripped them of flesh." Kit kicks over a skull and wipes away muck to reveal a serial number.

"You know Sal's?" he asks.

"Of course." One of the first things Sal made me do was save her serial number in my memstor, and she did the same with mine. "Just in case," she said. "You never know when your number might be up."

"What about Lex?"

"No idea." Kit kicks aside a faceless head.

It's grim work sorting through skeletons for a bunch of numerals. My hands dig through the carnage. Some skulls are still attached to their spines, but all the acuitron brains have been harvested, leaving behind solidified Cruor, sticky as treacle between my fingers. Some skeletons are buckled but whole, while others have been reduced to scattered bone fragments. This is what I'll become one day, a gooey, rusting mess. There's an ache inside me, an ache so deep even my titanium-reinforced bones hurt.

Kit lifts a spine out of the heap and lays it at his feet. "Did they have to dismantle the bodies?"

"Not sure what they did." My fingers follow the slope of a scapula to a skull. The cranium bulges wider at the temple, a Saga skull. The effort of hauling the half skeleton free from the heap burns through more fuel than I'd like, a red exclamation mark flashes a warning behind my eyes. Only a few hours till empty. The bullet wounds have reduced my fuel efficiency too.

I wipe mud from the metal cranium and stare at the numbers, checking and double-checking. No doubt about it. The head, spine, and left arm I hold in my hands used to be a thinking, loving Sal.

"That her?" Kit asks.

"Yes." I cradle the metal to my chest, and Kit places a comforting hand on my shoulder.

"We should bury them all."

"Why?" I glance at Kit, his dark eyes shiny with unshed tears.

"Because they deserve better than this." He produces a canvas sack from the folds of his coat and drops the skulls into the bag, the crack of cranium against cranium as loud as New Year fireworks.

"You just happened to bring a bag?"

"Thought there'd be more of Sal and Lex to find."

"And you were going to bury them without telling me?" Anger flares briefly, but I'm lacking the hydrogen to sustain it.

"I would've told you," Kit says.

"You still haven't answered my question about where you were these past few days."

"Can we just bury our friends please?" There's an edge to his voice, his tone so sharp it could cut.

"Fine. Where?"

"Svartkyrka, we buried a nanamaton there a while back." Kit ties off the sack.

"You buried a nanamaton?" I'm stunned.

Kit turns to face me. "Lex and me. I'm not the inconsiderate machine you seem to think I am."

"And not all humans are crap-filled flesh suits who deserve having their skulls smashed in." – Tyri, for one, is far more than a stew of viscera and prejudice. The memory of her dancing at the train depot gives way to nightmare images of her lying in the M-Tech foyer, Kit making red ribbons of her skull.

"After what you've been through, I'm surprised you maintain such a positive opinion," Kit says.

Clutching Sal's head to my chest, I follow him as we wend our way out of the scrap yard. Humans hurt me for years, humans killed Sal, and yet I can't help the feeling it's because of what I am, because we're machines. We don't deserve their respect or compassion.

***

We dig with our hands beneath the verdigris gaze of marble angels with broken wings. The earth breaks away in soaking clods, streaking our faces and clothes as the weather worsens. We dig two holes. One for Sal and one for all the nameless others we could fit in the sack.

By the time I pat down the last handful of soil over Sal's remains, the clouds are tinged apricot by the coming dawn.

"They should have tombstones." Kit leans against a crumbling chunk of rock, the name chiseled into the stone eroded beyond legibility.

"We could write in the mud. Like an epitaph."

"Won't last long." Kit blinks drizzle from his lashes.

"Doesn't matter."

"What should it say?"

I drag a finger through the mud, scrawling Sal's own words in the earth.

"We are more than just electronics," Kit reads over my shoulder.

"Sal said that once."

Kit kneels beside me and scribbles 'We are more than just metal' across the mass grave.

Below that I add, 'We are more than the sum of our parts.'

"And don't ever forget it." Kit tousles my hair the way Sal used to.

Soaked to the core, we stand shoulder to shoulder in reverent silence, heads bowed in the rain as the sun rises over Baldur. The sun rises in C-sharp minor.

Humans don't know how lucky they are that their memories are fallible. They fade and blur. Ours remain razor sharp, never dulling, never easing the pain even if that hurt is only a matter of wiring and clever code.

We shuffle out of the cemetery past the apathetic gaze of the angels.

"You know this isn't the end of it," Kit says.

"What do you mean?"

His gaze shifts left and right before focusing on my face again. "The riot was just the beginning."

"Of what?"

"The revolution."

Tyri

Flesh to dust. Bone to ash. Uncle Erik goes up in flames. His family wants a private interment and we're not invited. Mom hobbles around on crutches, exchanging pleasantries with colleagues. I wait in the parking lot, keeping my distance from the M-Tech crowd, unable to put on the requisite smile. A tall man in a somber suit approaches. "You must be Tyri Matzen. I'm Adolf Hoeg."

M-Tech's CEO. Why's he speaking to me? "Pleased to meet you." We shake hands.

"I've heard so much about you."

Awkward. "Uh, thanks."

"Your mom mentioned you had a bond with Erik. Please accept my condolences." He studies my face with pale blue eyes.

"Erik treated my war wounds." I raise an elbow.

"Yes, I heard you were attacked. Sign of the times, I'm afraid." He takes my chin between thumb and index finger and lifts my head. "You really are quite remarkable, dear."

"Tyri, isn't that Rurik's bug?" Mom limps over, saving me from further scrutiny by the übermensch of M-Tech.

"I better go." I hug Mom goodbye and she reminds me to be careful.

"Nice to meet you, Tyri." Adolf Hoeg smiles and waves. I want to run but force myself to take measured steps across the lot to Rurik. Hoeg gives me the creeps.

***

For three hours, we scud along the street ways toward the capital. Rurik seems oddly content to listen as I tell him all about my lesson with Quinn, minus the part about him having been at the train depot party. Guilt skewers my insides, but not telling Rik everything isn't the same as lying. Finally, Osholm rears out of the earth in a twist of spires, an architectural salute to the era when kings ruled Skandia. The Osholm Obelisk pierces the skyline like a needle, topped with a dragon's head. Our capital is meant to be intimidating, rebuilt after the wars, and it is. I'm glad it's not me who has to live here for the next four years. We coast into the city, following street ways lined with oak trees decked out in autumn. The capital feels ancient, flanked by forest, even the air pouring through the vents tastes like history, a bloody one played in E-flat major.

"When's the last time you visited Osholm?" Rurik asks.

"Gunnar's graduation." We zip past office blocks, shopping malls, courthouses, and parliament. The theme of dragons is present throughout the city, embossed on facades and carved into pillars. Skandia's dragon adorned flag whips in the twilight breeze from every second rooftop. I should feel more patriotic, but all I can think about is my violin lying over 300 kilometers away for a whole weekend. My left hand fingers play Berlioz on my thigh.

"I forgot how impressive it is."

We land in the parking lot of an apartment block nestled in the shadow of the forest.

"Home sweet home." He opens the door for me before grabbing his bags out of the back. The building is all gray walls and narrow windows. At least the trees offer a bit of color; although, they'll lose their leaves soon, rendering the block drab and depressing.

"Couldn't you have a requested better accommodation?"

"Why, because my dad's a member of parliament so I should get special treatment?"

"I didn't mean it like that."

"This is freshmen housing. Could be a lot worse."

It could be a crypt in a rotting cathedral or a crumbling mausoleum in Svartkyrka cemetery, but I hold my tongue. Two funerals in as many weeks are bound to sour my mood.

"You're right. I'm sure it's awesome on the inside."

We lug our bags into the building. The elevator shudders and grinds along its cable until the sixth floor. Rurik presses his thumb to the access panel and the door clicks open to room 613. The apartment is small, just a kitchen and two identical bedrooms with a closet-sized bathroom. The window grants a panoramic view of the surrounding forest with the Obelisk in the distance.

"It's actually not bad at all." I wrap my arms around Rurik's waist and lean into him.

"Told you so." He gives me peppermint kisses.

"Wish you would've let me bring my violin."

"So you could practice the whole weekend? Not a chance."

I wriggle out of his arms. "I'm missing a rehearsal for you."

"Should I thank you for giving me this one weekend? Bad enough I have to put up with Quinn this, Quinn that." He throws his hands into the air.

Blood warms my face and I hug myself, inadequate armor against the sting of Rurik's words.

"No, but—"

"But? You'd have preferred to stay home with Quinn and play scales. That much is obvious."

"This has nothing to do with him." My blush deepens and Rurik harrumphs. I can't stop thinking about Quinn and what he said about music ... or that night at the depot.

"Thought you wanted to join our cause and make a difference."

"I never said I wanted to join PARA."

"Then why are you here?" He folds his arms across his chest.

"To be with you. Not to get involved in politics."

"Being with me *means* getting involved in politics."

"It doesn't have to."

Rurik rubs his hands over his face and starts pacing. "Tyri, my dad's a politician, my brother is probably going to be prime minister one day, and I'm on the fast track to a career in government. This is who I am."

His words hit me like hammers, each driving a nail of dread into my heart.

"I hate politics."

"Then how can you love me?" He sounds wounded, his expression a twist of emotion.

"You're more than just your family legacy."

"You don't get it, T. I have a chance to make a difference, to get involved with decisions on policy that change the way our whole country is run. Don't you think that's important?"

"Of course it's important. But—"

"But you think plucking strings is going to change the robot situation?"

"How could you understand? Your musical appreciation begins and ends with that wump-wump techno crap." Something inside me snaps and the anger wells up from a dark reservoir I didn't know I had.

"Sorry for not being such an elitist snob."

"I'm a snob? You're the one who tells me I'm wasting my time with music and should be doing something worthwhile."

"If only you would listen."

"Because you're always right?" My fists clench so hard my nails dig into my palms.

"You want to be an androitician like your mother, stuck building robots all day?"

"My mom does more than that and you know it." I jab him in the chest with an angry finger.

"Yeah and we'd like to know exactly what it is she does."

"What do you mean?" My anger simmers, replaced by confusion.

Rurik runs his hands through his hair and thumps down onto the unmade bed. He looks up at me with eyes full of pity.

"Tyri, you should sit down."

"Just tell me what you meant."

He takes a deep breath before starting. "We know that M-Tech studied those robots responsible for the riot. We want to know what they discovered and what they plan to do."

"*We* meaning you and all your PARA buddies or *we* meaning Engelberger Industries?"

"T." He reaches for me, but I avoid his touch. "There have been rumors about an AI infiltrating virus."

"Like I'd know anything about that."

"Your mom will."

"Then why don't you ask her?"

"Because she's signed an NDA and probably wouldn't tell me anyway, being an Engelberger and all."

"But you expect me to tell you?" I'm beyond furious, my hands shaking, and my jaw aching from clenching my teeth so hard.

"Your mom works from home, you could—"

"Wait." I hold up my hand, silencing him. "You're asking me to betray my mom's trust and snoop through her stuff?" I can't believe he'd even suggest it. "Did Gunnar put you up to this?"

Rurik narrows his eyes and chews on his bottom lip, ignoring my question.

"You know I wouldn't be asking if this wasn't important."

"I don't even know who you are any more."

"I love you, Tyri, and I need your help." He looks at me with eyes that used to make me melt. It would be so easy to give in.

"Help with what exactly?"

"You don't understand the half of it." He leans forward and I meet his gaze. "M-Tech is hiding so much, not just from the public, but from the government as well."

"Now you're spouting conspiracy theories?" I laugh and pull up the desk chair so we're facing each other eye-to-eye. "And you think my mom is involved?"

"Maybe not directly, but if we could gain access to the M-Tech servers using your Mom's computers or ID."

I blink and try to process what he's asking of me. There's no way Mom could be involved in some conspiracy. No, this can't be happening. Rurik can't be doing this to me. He wouldn't.

"Is this the real reason you wanted me to meet Gunnar this weekend? So you could gang up on me and pressure me into snooping for you?"

"Botspit, it's not like that at all. Gunnar would be happy to reward you for information."

"Holy Codes, Rik. You were going to *pay* me to be a snitch?"

"Thought you needed money for violin lessons."

My hand snaps out before I can stop it, my palm making contact with Rurik's cheek. We're both stunned by the impact and shocked into silence.

"I shouldn't have done that," I whisper as tears prick the back of my eyes. Rurik glares at me with a look of such hurt, I want to die. I go to him, but he slides away and gets to his feet, a red hand print on his cheek.

"We're supposed to meet Gunnar for dinner in an hour."

"I'm not going." Like I'd be able to sit at a table with Gunnar now.

"Come on T. We're supposed to be celebrating not fighting." He rubs his cheek.

"All we do is fight."

"And whose fault is that?" He gives me an accusatory glare.

"I want to go home." I don't want to be here, not if all I am is a pawn in Rurik's political game.

"Are you serious? We just got here."

"I want to go back to Baldur." I can't imagine spending a weekend sleeping next to Rurik now.

"You're over reacting."

Maybe I am but—"You accuse my mom of conspiracy, offer to

pay me to spy on her, and then expect me to play nice and eat dinner with you and your brother? I thought I knew you."

"You do."

"The Rurik I know would never do something like this."

"And the Tyri I know wouldn't be throwing her future down the drain or cavorting with some random muso she just met."

I bite my tongue, holding back bitter words. "Forget it. Forget everything. I'll take the train."

Rurik watches in silence as I gather my things. I'm heading out the door when he blocks my path with his arm.

"Please," he says, sounding more wounded than ever. "It doesn't have to be like this. We can fix this."

"I'm not sure we can." Everything I've been feeling recently—how we're growing apart, how things are changing between us—explodes in my chest.

"Would you let me try?"

I look away from his eyes. If I don't I'll end up unpacking and throwing my arms around him. I take a shaky breath before answering.

"Maybe, but not here. I need some time. After everything with Mom, Erik, and now this."

"So we're not breaking up?"

The dreaded question, and I'm not sure of the answer. Rurik's always been there. I can't imagine a life without him. Maybe that's the problem. He's leaving me and going off to college anyway. Maybe we should break up before staying together gets too hard.

"I think so." I finally manage to look at him. There's anger and hurt on his face. He swallows and nods, dropping his arm to let me pass.

"I'll take you to the train station."

We travel in awkward silence. Am I over reacting? Maybe this isn't such a big deal, and I just need to let it go. I love him, I do, but I don't want to be with him any more.

"Is this because of the whole violin thing?" he asks when we pull into the station. The drizzle plays music marked *morendo* on the windshield. All he needs to do is say sorry and mean it. Then maybe we could still be friends. All I've ever wanted is for him to be on my side. All I need is for him to kiss my forehead and tell me he's sorry for being a nullhead jerk, that he doesn't think my mom is involved in anything remotely corrupt, and that he'll support my dreams of being a musician. He doesn't. He sits in silence waiting for an answer I don't have.

"T, tell me. Is it something to do with this guy you can't shut up about?"

"This isn't about Quinn." Not in the way he thinks. Quinn just made me realize what Rurik and I don't have—what we don't share but should.

"Tyri, I love you." His face contorts, twisting from hurt, to angry, to an expressionless mask I can't read. My heart breaks for him and for us. I love him too, but I can't say it, not right now. I reach for his hand. He jerks away from me, and now I know how much that stings.

"You better go." He stares at the drizzle cutting across the windshield. "Before you miss your train."

Quinn

Alan Turing believed that if a machine behaved like a human being, then it should be considered a human being. And as the father of artificial intelligence, according to the tome on AI courtesy of Örebrö's university library, he should know. Turing's biography scrolls across my retinas, his life passing before my eyes. The rain beats a constant accompaniment on the metal roof, and I read in tempo.

I shiver in my coat and hug my knees to my chest. The metal shell doesn't provide much insulation and neither does the stacked cardboard I've been sitting on. With my fuel consumption escalating, I can't risk burning more hydrogen to keep myself warm. Every trip to the fuel station is a huge risk. With Sal's cash lining my pockets, the only thing stopping me from strolling into an uptown store and purchasing brand new bedding is the threat of being discovered. Uptown malls are sure to have sensors and robot's equipped with scanners. It's not worth the risk either. Besides, if the train depot addicts can find blankets, so can I.

I brave the midnight gloom and head off with a flashlight toward the alleys lined with overflowing dumpsters. The weather sours, the cold exploding in bursts of lemon on my tongue. Gritting my teeth against the chill, I begin trawling through the trash.

After an hour, I'm coated in ooze and muck, still without a blanket. The last dumpster in the row, isn't a dumpster at all, but a charity bin. Not many Baldurians would come this far downtown to drop off unwanted goods for the less fortunate. The lid creeks open and darkness greets me. Flashlight clenched between my incisors, my hands probe the black and find a plastic bag.

With effort, I drag it out of the bin and spill the contents across the cobbled alley, the rainbow intestines of a cotton-blend beast. Women's summer attire. No blanket, but there's a shawl. That'll do.

"Find something good, did you?" A bedraggled human approaches me. She's young and bundled up in rags. I stuff the shawl into my jacket and say nothing. The sooner I get away the better.

"Can I take a look?"

"Be my guest." I nudge the sack of clothing toward her.

"Cold, isn't it?" She starts sorting through the garments. "Already shivery and it ain't even winter yet."

"There's a shelter—"

"Not for skaggers."

"Ah." I back away. She might not be alone. I don't feel like taking another pipe to the head or being robbed by humans.

"What you searching for here anyways?"

"A blanket." I increase the distance between us.

"You got cash?"

"Why?"

"'Cause I got blankets."

"Where?"

"Follow me." She gathers up the clothes and bundles them against her chest. Warily, I follow her to the depot.

After a minute, we join a huddled group gathered in the warmth of an oil-drum fire. The stench of gasoline stains my vision noxious yellow, but the warmth is worth enduring the odor. My gaze scans the depot. A garish new tag stands out in acid green on a crumbling wall, another anti-human slogan just like those splashed in neon across shop windows and empty walls. I'm not sure what my brethren are hoping to achieve with their graffiti. Beside the freshly painted vitriol, fliers flap in the breeze announcing a downtown gig, promising acoustic instruments. It might be worth sneaking into.

"Where are the blankets?" I ask.

Her gaze darts over her shoulder to a gap in the wall behind us.

We duck through the slit in the boards, and the girl pulls back her hood revealing a snarl of tangled hair.

"Thirty an hour," she says. Her dirty fingers are already undoing the buttons of her coat.

"I only want the blankets." I fish a roll of bills from my pocket.

"Serious like?" She stares at me with jaundiced eyes.

"Here's a hundred. Blanket only." I enunciate.

She raises an eyebrow and takes the money. "Take your pick." She gestures toward a makeshift bed swaddled in tatty quilts. Most are stained and moth eaten, others are peppered with mold. I select the two least hazardous and drape them over my shoulders.

"For a hundred krona, I could still warm your bones, if you want?" She grins and reveals jagged teeth.

"No, thank you." I pause before ducking back into the cold. "You should buy something to eat."

She smiles and shakes her head. I wonder how much skag you can buy for a hundred krona.

***

I'm naked and waist deep in frigid waves taking a much needed bath when I receive a call from an unknown number.

"Hello?"

"Hey, Quinn." Tyri pauses, an awkward silence stretches. She sniffs and takes a deep breath. "Um, how are you?"

Before I can answer, an electronic voice echoes in the background announcing a station stop. I rub my filthy skin and scrub stains from my clothes. On second thought, I drench the blankets and shawl as well. One more night wet and cold will be worth having less rancid blankets.

"You're on a train." I splash my way back to the shore as the rain worsens.

"Yeah, leaving Osholm. I'm calling from the train's public comms. I don't have a new number yet."

"Why are you leaving?" Maybe there's been another riot, more violence perpetrated by robots against humans. Maybe Kit is one of the ringleaders, goading fellow androids to turn more human skulls into mulch.

She sniffs some more. It takes another moment for me to realize she's crying.

"You okay?"

"No." Her voice breaks. The sound of her tears feels like nails driving into the tips of my fingers. "I tried calling Asrid, but she didn't answer. I'm sorry for calling so late," she whispers.

"It's fine. What happened?"

Another shaky breath.

"Actually, we don't have to talk about it," I say.

"Thanks."

It's not much warmer inside the crate, but at least I have dry clothes. Still sticky with brine, I struggle into them. Huddling beneath Sal's army jacket, I tuck my hands under my armpits wishing I had breath with which to warm my fingers. I've been using the flashlight like a candle, but the batteries are failing. I switch it off and sit in the dark with Tyri's voice inside my head.

"Coming to rehearsal tomorrow?" I ask.

"Hadn't thought about it."

"We could do something afterward maybe. Something to cheer you up." The words leave my mouth before I've given them proper consideration.

"Like what?"

"There's a gig tomorrow night. You could join me." A queasy feeling takes up residence in the hollow of my abdomen. I want her to say yes, and I'm simultaneously afraid that she will.

"What kind of gig?"

"Neo-acoustic. Real guitars and vintage synths."

"Okay."

"You want to go?" My fuel-cell shudders beneath my ribs.

"Sure."

I'm smiling and don't know why. Spending more time with Tyri is dangerous, something to fear not eagerly anticipate.

"I'll see you at rehearsal tomorrow?"

"I think so."

I don't know what else to say and saying goodbye doesn't seem appropriate just yet.

"Whatever it is, Tyri, it's going to be okay." I tell her what I wish Sal was still around to say to me.

She takes a long moment to respond. "Thank you, Quinn. I needed that."

"Sometimes we all do."

Tyri

"Glad to see you decided to join us Miss Matzen," Maestro Ahlgren says before a grueling 90 minute rehearsal. Quinn and I share an awkward 'hi' before tuning, stealing glances at each other between movements. I'm not sure what to say to him. Should I apologize for calling him so late? Is he truly okay with it and if he is, what does that mean? That we're friends even though we hardly know each other? Was last night really the end of my relationship with Rurik?

My tumultuous thoughts hamper my playing, and I make a mess of the Mahler.

"Are you okay?" Quinn asks in that whisper voice of his while Ahlgren's attention is on the woodwinds.

"I will be." This time we share a smile and I can almost forget the storm clouds and question marks dangling above me.

At the end of rehearsal, Ahlgren makes an announcement.

"Next week after rehearsal, solo candidates for the gala performance will attend an audition in the main auditorium. Brun, Dahl, Haga, Homstad, Soarsen, and ... " She turns her hawk eyes on me. "Matzen. Be prepared to astound me."

One out of six. Not bad odds except we stand no chance against Quinn. These auditions are just a formality.

"Congratulations," Quinn strokes his violin before shutting the case.

"She should get it over with and announce you as soloist already."

"How can you be so sure she'll choose me?"

"You're actually going to make me say it?"

Quinn cocks his head the same way Glitch does when she pretends she doesn't know why she's in trouble.

"You're brilliant Quinn. The best in this orchestra."

"You really think so?" There's surprise on his face, not arrogance.

"Yeah, I know so."

"Thank you. That means a lot." He clutches his violin to his chest like it's all he has in the world.

"What time does the gig start?" I ask as we head out of the opera house.

"Not until seven."

We have a full three hours of blank space in the day. I've never been more relieved to not have my moby vibrating in my pocket. No messages from Rurik. No call from Asrid. Just quiet-spoken Quinn, feral viola player and violin prodigy.

"What we going to do until then?" I ask.

Quinn shrugs. "What would you like to do?"

"Get into something more gig appropriate and have some dinner. You want to come back to my place?" There, I asked. No turning back now. "We'll have to take the bus, but—"

"Okay." Quinn looks as if he's just made some bigger, life altering decision than whether or not to come home with me. We stroll through falling leaves and puddles reflecting sunshine toward the bus stop.

***

"Welcome to my humble home." I open the door for Quinn.

"It's lovely." He steps into the hallway at the same time Miles lurches out of the kitchen. Quinn's eyes go wide.

"Miles is a simple model." The words come out in a rush. "He wasn't involved in the riot or anything." I step between them. "Nothing right now, Miles. I'll call you if I need you."

"As you wish, Tyri." The housebot's green digisplay eyes pass over Quinn before he leaves us.

"You named it?" he asks.

"Why not?" I shrug. "Glitch, where are you girl?" I kick off my shoes as Glitch comes trotting down the hall. "This is Glitch." She licks my face as I scoop her into my arms.

"What happened to her leg?" Quinn approaches with caution. Glitch sniffs him warily.

"She was born with a bad leg. They were going to put her down, but Mom thought it'd be a good opportunity to test out some M-Tech gear."

"Does it hurt her?" He trails his fingers across the seam where flesh meets metal. Glitch doesn't seem to mind in the slightest.

"Nope, she's just like a normal dog." I plop her down. Glitch brushes up against Quinn's legs, and I expect a puddle to appear. Instead, she nips at his trouser leg wanting to play. Amazing.

"Is your mom home?" Quinn asks, a little nervous.

"Probably." I stalk through the living room. Mom's in her office. "Hi Mom, brought a friend home. We'll be in my room."

"Asrid?" She glances at me over her shoulder, her fingers hovering above her databoard.

"No, a friend from orchestra."

Quinn peers around my shoulder and gives my mom a tiny wave.

"You two going to practice?" Mom asks, her eyes narrowing a little.

"We'll keep it down. Promise." I close her door before she can protest or ask any embarrassing questions.

Quinn follows me into my bedroom with Glitch attached to his ankle, her curled tail wagging.

"She's not usually this friendly."

Quinn chuckles, a sound like brittle leaves rustling in a breeze. My room's a mess. I should've thought about that before inviting Quinn over. I sweep a bunch of clothes off my bed and into the closet before jamming the doors shut. A digiframe sits on my bedside table, looping through photos of me and Rurik—awkward—but Quinn's not even paying attention. His gaze is riveted on my vintage CD collection.

"Scriabin. Elgar. Rimsky-Korsakov. Bartók. What are these?" He plucks one from the shelf and studies the cover.

"They're really old. It's the way they used to record music. You've never seen a CD?"

"Only ever heard about them."

Where did this guy grow up?

"These were my grandfather's. Here." Ignoring my violin for the moment, I take Scriabin's Piano Sonatas out of Quinn's hand.

"My grandfather had this old CD player too. Rurik helped me hook it up to my sound system." Rurik. Better not to mention his name or anything even remotely connected to him. I slide the CD into the tray and hit play. Moments later, music trickles from the speakers crouching like spiders in the corners of my room.

"Glitch, enough." She growls as I detach her from Quinn's leg and drop her amongst the pillows. "You can sit if you want."

"What is this?" He slides to the floor.

"Scriabin's Black Mass." I sit beside him, my leg pressed against his. He's colder than I expected.

"This is one—"

Quinn shushes me. I'm about to harrumph with indignation when he winces at the dissonant harmony. His face scrunches up as if the clash of tones causes him physical pain. His features smooth out as the harmony resolves. He closes his eyes and leans his head against the bed, his fingers conducting an unseen orchestra. I watch him experience the music, and Scriabin has never looked so good. He feels the music; he doesn't just hear it. He's in it, living each progression and every jagged note of the melody like he did that night on stage. I wish I could see what he's seeing, feel what he's feeling. My hand slips into his, but it's not enough.

The piano fades into the background as I study Quinn's quivering lashes and twitching lips. His eyes are shiny with welling tears. At the tritone, his mouth quirks up into a crooked smile and all I want to do is kiss him.

"You all right?" I ask when the track ends.

"Thank you." He grins and wipes his eyes.

"For making you cry?"

"For making me feel. That was spectacular." His gaze is too intense and makes my insides turn to bubblegum. I try to let go of his hand, but he tightens his grip on my fingers. "I could see it. See the colors, like ... " He's left grasping for words.

"See it?"

"An explosion of color. Each chord unique in shade and hue."

"You're synesthetic?" I ask, incredulous. Scriabin claimed he could *hear* color, but then he also thought he was god.

"Yes." He squirms a little and releases my hand.

"So you can see sound and taste feelings?"

"My senses are complicated."

"Have you always been this way?" Now I'm fascinated, trying to imagine what experiencing the world might be like if I could feel smells and taste sounds.

"It's a more recent development." His expression turns cloudy. "Can we listen to more?"

"Sure." I put on Scriabin's White Mass. Quinn spaces out to the music and I watch him, my gaze riveted on his face. At the end of the piece, he fixes me with a moonstone stare.

Ribbons of warmth spread up my neck.

"I have a boyfriend." I blurt, not sure if it's the truth but too afraid of how Quinn's looking at me. A rabble of butterflies whips up a cyclone in my stomach.

"That him?" Quinn nods at the digiframe.

"Yeah. Rurik." My cheeks blaze.

"Does he like this sonata?"

"He's never heard it." He's never bothered to listen.

"Why not?"

"Rik doesn't like music."

"I struggle to comprehend that," Quinn says, his eyes losing focus in the middle distance. "More?" He reaches for the CD case, his face millimeters from my own. He smells of the ocean and sunshine. I want to play Scriabin on repeat and lose myself in Quinn just as he lost himself in the music. Our lips meet before I have time to think about what we're doing. His lips are too soft, his kiss too gentle, and I think of Rurik: lemon, cinnamon, and a lifetime of friendship if nothing else. It's way too soon. I pull away, almost regretting the ten centimeters I put between Quinn's lips and mine.

"Quinn, I ... "

"Shouldn't I have kissed you?" His forehead furrows with concern. I want to smooth out those creases, but I resist and play with my own hair instead.

"It's okay." I stand up. Better to be further away from him. His eyes burn like smelting metal; his gaze should leave me blistered. "Could we play some violin?"

"Sure." He gets to his feet.

"Did you grow up in Baldur?" I ask as we remove our instruments from their cases, the awkward kiss forgotten. I'm fishing for details, but I hope he won't notice.

"Not exactly." He meets my gaze, and a lopsided grin quirks up his lips. "You're full of questions today."

"I don't know much about you."

He chews on his inner cheek and drums his fingers on his thigh. "Fair enough. I grew up outside Osholm. What else do you want to know?"

"Do you go to school?"

"No."

"You're home schooled?" There are so many things I want to know.

"Something like that." He's as cryptic as ever.

"Do you prefer violin or viola?"

"Violin, but ... " Quinn closes the distance between us with a single step. His hand reaches behind my head and pulls out my hair band. His runs a hand through my hair as the waves fall across my shoulders. Codes, doesn't this guy know what he's doing to me?

"Playing viola that night, it was almost like, for the first time, I truly felt—"

"Alive." We say in unison.

If Quinn kissed me right now, I wouldn't pull away this time. Am I rebounding?

"Time for Fisker?" Quinn asks.

"Dvorák." There's no way I have enough control over my fingers for Fisker.

We play for an hour keeping the dynamics *pianissimo* so as not to upset Mom.

"I'm hungry. Want a sandwich?"

"Okay." He holds his violin as if it's an extension of his body, organic and living. Reluctantly, he leaves the instrument on the bed.

"Sara thinks you look like a dancer," I say over my shoulder as we head toward the kitchen.

"Who's Sara?"

"Asrid's girlfriend. She said you're built like one." It's a veiled compliment, maybe too subtle for a guy to get. Miles greets us, his orange digisplay lingering on Quinn.

"I'm not built for dancing. I have done some martial arts, though."

"That would explain it then." The broad shoulders and biceps straining against the sweater that fits like a second skin.

"Explain what?"

"Tea?" I change the topic. I've done enough blushing for one day.

"I'm fine, thanks." He settles on a kitchen stool. His gaze keeps shifting to Miles.

"He's harmless." But my assurances are short lived when the house phone rings. Miles answers automatically before disconnecting the headset from his chest and handing it to me.

"Tyri, call from Rurik. Do you accept?" The last thing I want Quinn to witness is me having a post break-up melt down.

"Sorry," I mouth to Quinn as I scuttle back down to my bedroom for a bit of privacy. Glitch looks up, tongue caught between her teeth, and gives me an unimpressed glare for disturbing her nap.

"Hey." I perch on the edge of the bed and give Glitch tummy rubs to say sorry.

"You get home okay?"

"Yes."

Awkward silence.

"About last night," Rurik says. "I'm sorry to do this ... Gunnar wants to know if you'll reconsider."

"Seriously?"

So, that's why he called, not to apologize or declare his eternal love and beg me to take him back. No, he just wants me to snoop.

"I only said I'd ask. I'm not expecting you to say yes."

"Good, because the answer's no."

"Okay." Another lengthy pause and I think maybe he's hung up when he speaks again.

"I meant what I said at the train station," he says.

"Which part?"

"That I love you."

"I know." I whisper.

Then there's more silence while hurt and rage vie for control.

"So you won't help us out." Rurik sounds defeated.

"Not like this."

"Fair enough. So we're done, for real?"

"Yes."

"Because of this thing with your mom?"

"Mostly." But that was just the cherry on the top of an enormous double-cream, black forest cake of problems.

He runs his hands through his hair loud enough for me to hear it through the phone.

"How was your first day?" I ask. He might not be my boyfriend anymore, but we've got too much history for me to stop caring all together.

"A bit boring since I know the campus already. I start proper classes on Wednesday."

"Busy schedule?"

"Yeah. You sure you won't even think about helping us? Do it for me, because I love you. Always have."

"I'm sorry, Rik." I hang up before he realizes I'm choking on those three little words that have flowed so easily since we were thirteen, before he realizes there's a storm-eyed boy sitting in my kitchen who loves music as much as I do, whose lips I can't wait to kiss again.

I pad back to the kitchen and find Mom interrogating Quinn.

Quinn

Robots make me feel uncomfortable. Beneath all the layers of synthetic flesh, I'm just like that: skeletal appendages, pumps and circuits, valves and microchips. I only *look* human. Beneath the mask, I'm a machine little better than Miles the housebot. If it has the firmware to perform a live status scan and knows I'm an android, it isn't saying anything. Perhaps it doesn't know I'm AWOL, that I'm breaking the law by not wearing the orange armband.

Tyri's mom emerges from the study rubbing her eyes. She's dressed in figure hugging sportswear with a perfectly curled 'do bobbing above her shoulders. The woman limps. She looks at me with eyes nothing like Tyri's and my circuits sizzle in recognition as fear freezes my Cruor. There's no way she'd recognize me. I thought she was already dead when I accidentally crushed her leg. She was unconscious with her eyes closed. There's no possible way she could recognize me.

"Who are you?" Ms. Matzen says in a friendly tone.

"Hi." There's a tremor in my voice, and I wish I could clear my throat. "I'm Quinn."

"Odd name."

"I guess."

"Do you go to St. Paul's?" She accepts a tall glass of algae green liquid from Miles and takes a sip.

"No."

"So you only know Tyri from orchestra then?"

"We're both violinists."

"Ah." Her face cracks into a tight smile that never reaches her eyes. "And what do your parents think of that?"

"They support me." I bend the truth, just like Sal said.

"And your plans for the future?" She leans her elbows on the counter.

My hands are shaking and the red exclamation mark blinks in my peripheral vision. I have two hours of hydrogen left. I'll have to refuel before the gig.

"Um ... " I'm hoping Tyri will save me from this conversation. The moments trundle by without any sign of her. "I want to be a musician." I default to the truth.

"So you're the one encouraging my daughter's dreams of a Bohemian existence." She gives me a wry grin, but there's a taint of bitterness in her voice.

"I'm not sure."

"I have nothing against music." She swills her algae juice. "But Tyri was meant for greater things."

"I think you underestimate the power of music."

"Really? Enlighten me." She cocks her head expectantly. This woman works for M-Tech. If anyone can identify an android with a quick glance, it's her. Her gaze lingers on my face.

"You have exquisite skin," she says before I can form a coherent answer to the question about music.

"Um ... "

She reaches forward as if to touch me and I recoil. If she touches me, she'll know.

"About music ... " My circuits misfire, unable to think of lies on the spot.

"Where did you say you were from again?" She narrows her eyes.

"I didn't." We lock gazes, and I'm convinced she sees right through my cybernetic eyeballs into the tangle of electronics inside me.

"Mom!" Tyri finally returns to the kitchen. "Quinn's a friend."

"Just asking some friendly questions." She sips on the green goo and checks the time at her wrist. "I've got a company event tonight. Sort yourselves out for dinner will you? And Quinn," she's already walking away. "Nice to meet you."

"Sorry." Tyri sits beside me. "Mom can get all Spanish Inquisition sometimes."

"It's okay." No it's not, not at all. I crushed the woman's ankle and snapped her leg like a twig; I watched Kit smash the life out of the man beside her.

"I know it's early, but could we get out of here?" Tyri fingers the phone.

"Not good news?"

"I broke up with my boyfriend." Her tone is flat, and yet her face is a conflagration of conflicting emotion: anger around the eyes, hurt in them, sadness in her down-turned mouth. Humans are so complicated.

"Is it because I kissed you?"

"No," she says slowly. "I think it's been over for a while; we just didn't want to admit it. But about that." She bites her lip and avoids meeting my gaze. "I'm not sure I can kiss you again for a while. It's too soon."

"That's okay." Kissing her was a mistake, a condition of my code that reacted to her body language before I had time to over ride the impulse with logic. I'm already dangerously close to Tyri, and now we're going to a gig that seems suspiciously close to the human definition of a date.

"Can we go out tonight as friends?" she asks.

"Absolutely." I'd sigh with relief if I had inflatable lungs.

"Could I invite Asrid and Sara?"

Perhaps that would be best. Asrid could be the distraction that'll allow me time to refuel.

"Of course."

She picks up the phone and an animated conversation ensues. Miles stares at me, flashing orange. I put my finger to my lips, and he nods before blinking back to green. Thank the Codes for robotic solidarity.

***

Half an hour later, Tyri's dressed in a black T-shirt with jeans tucked into red-laced boots. Her hair is swept up in a ponytail showing off all the silver dangling from her earlobes. Her make-up makes her eyes even more intense, and the color hums to me in e minor. Tyri looks pretty, even in her angry black attire.

We pack into Asrid's too pink, C-sharp major shrieking hoverbug and head downtown. Fifty-three minutes of hydrogen left. Asrid insists we stop for dinner at an oriental fusion restaurant. The booths are coated in vinyl, and the digisplay table scrolls through images of various sea creatures reduced to morsels on colored plates.

"Do you eat sushi?" Sara asks me.

"Never tried it." That was the wrong thing to say.

"Oh you must." Sara and Asrid start deciding how best to introduce my gustatory sensors to the Japanese delicacies. My protests go unheard. Above us, the ceiling is a neon ocean of writhing fractals. It's meant to create ambiance; all it does is overload my sensory system as the play of color creates a dissonant symphony in my head.

"What's wrong?" Tyri asks.

I close my eyes and there's momentary silence. "It's a bit loud."

"Huh? I can barely hear the music," Asrid says.

"It's the ceiling."

"Oh, wow. Are you hearing the lights?" Tyri asks and places a hand on my knee. As soon as she realizes what she's done, she snatches back her hand.

"Hearing the lights? T, what are you smoking?" Asrid asks.

"He's synesthetic."

The conversation continues around me, but all I can see is the red exclamation mark. My system's slowing down. My vision narrows, and the world recedes as if I'm standing on a distant horizon watching everything play out below me in miniature.

"I need ... a break from all the color and noise." I slide out of the booth.

"I'll come with you." Tyri gets up.

"No, you eat. I'll meet you back here in a bit. Just going for a walk." I leave before she can argue. Forty minutes to run downtown and hope no Saturday night party-goers are filling up their bugs at the station.

Out of sight of the restaurant, I break into a sprint and hurtle on fumes toward the station.

Tyri

Quinn shows up as Asrid pays the bill despite my protests.

"If I insist on eating healthy, then I foot the bill. Stop arguing with me." She swipes her card.

"Feeling better?" Sara asks Quinn as he strolls up to us with his hands in his pockets.

"Much." His eyes are brighter, a glittering silver from which I battle to tear my gaze. They're too bright. We're close to the depot, the addicts, and their assorted drugs. I'm not entirely convinced Quinn isn't using. His unwillingness to eat, him dashing off alone then coming back all sparky—I can't help being a little suspicious.

Sara and Asrid hold hands and lean into each other as we make our way through the Saturday night throngs. We pass a dozen windows smeared with angry words painted by robots. They must really hate us. Can they hate? We approach Club Haze and it's splashed with graffiti like every other corner of downtown Baldur.

"I didn't even ask about the age limit." Asrid might get in without them asking for ID, but there's no way I will.

"Didn't think of that," Quinn says.

"We'll wing it T. Don't worry." Asrid unbuttons her coat and plumps up her cerise clad cleavage. I deliberately didn't dress up too much for the gig, not wanting to give Quinn the wrong idea. Now I wish I'd gone with the corset instead of the T-shirt.

There's a short queue at the door where a guy more hippopotamus than human takes cash and checks IDs.

"I'm not going to get in."

"We'll figure it out." Quinn reassures me. "I don't have ID either."

Asrid and Sara go first. Sara hands over the money and her real ID; Asrid hands over cash and a fake one. The bouncer doesn't look impressed until Asrid pulls Sara into a long kiss. He waves them through, and they wait for us across the threshold.

"ID?" The bouncer bars our way with a meaty forearm.

"We only want to see the band. We're not going to drink."

"Please." Quinn adds in his polite little voice. How can such a big guy have such a quiet voice?

"Not unless I see some ID."

"Could you please let my friends in?" Asrid leans across the bouncer's arm and slips a wad of cash into his front pocket. She flutters her lashes a few times, and the hippo nods us through.

"Did you just bribe him?"

"It's the way the world works, T. What're you drinking?"

I feel so stupid and naive.

"Is it your first time at a club like this?" Quinn asks as we hand our jackets to the bot behind the wardrobe counter.

"Yeah, yours?"

"I've been to bars, but never to a place like this." Wide-eyed, Quinn turns a full three-sixty, as if absorbing all the details.

"Isn't it too much for you?" If the neon at the restaurant upset him, surely the strobes and thrumming music will be too much.

"The walk helped me regain equilibrium. " He smiles, eyes shining, and I'm convinced he's high. "This is incredible."

Quinn goes exploring as I join Asrid at the bar. I order a soda despite her taunting me for being boring.

"What's up with you and Quinn?" Sara asks.

"Nothing, why?" I say too quickly.

"Does Rurik know you're out with another guy?" Asrid raises her eyebrow and sips on a drink the same color as her top.

"He wouldn't care. We broke up." It hurts to say it aloud.

Asrid chokes and splutters. "What? When?"

"Last night."

"That the real reason you're home early?"

"Yes."

"T, I'm so sorry." Asrid dumps her drink and hugs me.

"Do you want to talk about it?"

"Not right now."

"So, is Quinn the reason you broke up?" Asrid's tone changes, becoming accusing.

"Not at all. It's because Rurik's a nullhead who cares more about politics than me."

"Absolutely nothing to do with Mr. Perfect Fingers?" Asrid jerks her head in Quinn's direction.

I don't know how to answer that.

"Come on, T. You broke off a fairytale relationship for a guy you barely know?"

"It's not like that." My relationship with Rurik was hardly fairytale perfect. This would've happened even if Quinn weren't in the picture.

"So this isn't a date you're on?"

"No."

"And what's up with that guy anyway? Rushing out of the restaurant and then coming back all happy squirrel."

"Did you see his eyes?" Sara asks.

"Yeah, hard not to notice. Looks like he's on flex. High as a freaking satellite." Asrid turns her disapproving glare on me and folds her arms. "Hope you know what you're doing."

"I'm trying to be happy."

"You're right." Asrid wraps an arm around me. "Let's just have a good time. We can worry about Quinn and everything else tomorrow."

Despite Asrid nagging me about my dress sense and problematic middle bits, she's always there when I need her.

The band walks on stage, and I return Asrid's hug before searching for Quinn. He's standing off to the side engaged in a fiery argument with a tall black guy. In the murk created by the smoke machine and pulsating lights, I can't be sure, but I think I've seen the guy before. He looks a lot like one of the androids at Nana's funeral. In fact, he looks *exactly* like one of the androids, but he's not wearing an orange armband, and why would Quinn be arguing with a droid?

Quinn turns and sees us approaching, his expression worried.

"Think that's his dealer?" Asrid asks me under her breath.

"Hope not."

"Hey Quinn," Asrid starts calm and unfazed, the epitome of cool. "You going to introduce us to your friend?"

Quinn's shoulders slump in defeat. "This is Kit."

"Pleasure to meet you." Kit shakes our hands, his gaze lingering on me before his face opens in a pearly white grin. "Want something to drink, Quinny?"

Quinn answers him with a glare.

"Not much of a drinker, this one." Kit pretends to whisper to me. "Never seen him drink much of anything really. Never seen him eat either." He saunters over to the bar.

Quinn studies the floor, his previous spark snuffed out quicker than a candle flame.

"Something wrong?" I ask. Kit's right though. I've never seen Quinn eat or drink. Maybe Kit's hinting that Quinn does have a drug issue. Or maybe he's hinting at something else.

"I'm fine." He glances at the stage. "Band's about to play."

The musicians pick up their instruments and dive straight into a throbbing mix of rock and neo-prog. They sound like Pink Floyd on steroids. I glance at Quinn. He stares unblinking, and I wonder what he's hearing or seeing beyond the regular harmonies and flickering rainbow strobes. Maybe the synesthesia is nothing more than a side effect of the drugs he's taking. He did say it was a recent development; maybe his addiction is too. Maybe I could help him with that like he's helping me with violin. The perfect quid pro quo.

As the band heats up, bringing in synths to add another layer to their music, I slip my hand into his and squeeze his fingers. Perhaps I should establish that Quinn's even using before I decide he needs saving.

Quinn

With fresh hydrogen coursing through my system, my senses are more acute than ever. I feel capable of handling a night out amongst humans. The interior of the club is a kaleidoscope of sound and color. I can't be sure if what I'm seeing is the result of actual vision or of another confused sense. I wend my way around the club while the girls head for the bar.

"Well, well." Kit claps a hand on my shoulder.

"Holy Codes, what are you doing here?"

"Keeping an eye on my friend."

"You've been following me?"

"In a manner of speaking." He drops his hand to my lower back.

"You've been tracking me?" I step back and search my skin, remembering the sting when he jammed the flash drive into my port. There's a tiny nodule in my flesh, a tracking device. If I rip it out now, I risk leaking Cruor, and there's no way that'll go unnoticed.

"If you're going to play with humans, I thought it best I know if you got into a pickle."

"Kit!" Words fail me. "You're unbelievable."

"I prefer incorrigible." He grins. "Having a good time on your date?"

"This isn't a date."

"It should be. If I'd only known you were rubbing shoulders with Tyri Matzen."

"How do you know Tyri?"

"Daughter of an M-Tech androitician. It's my business to know."

"And why is that?" I strain to make myself heard above the decibels of human conversation taking place around us.

"I'd recommend less time plucking her strings and more time saving your circuits."

"What are you talking about?" I grab him by the arm before he can walk away.

"That M-Tech virus the Solidarity found, it could wipe us out."

"What?"

"They want to exterminate us." His gaze slips past me to the approaching girls; anxiety spirals through my core.

"Hey Quinn," Asrid says. This was a terrible idea. Regret curdles my Cruor as painful introductions are made. I avoid eye contact when Kit drops unsubtle hints at my lack of humanness. Finally, the band starts playing and negates the need for conversation. Focused on the music, I try to relax and play the perfect human at ease in a club with friends. A virus that could wipe us out –Kit's words loop inside my mind, nauseating, especially considering Tyri's mom could be involved. I won't let Tyri become collateral damage in whatever the Solidarity is planning.

Tyri slips her hand into mine. It feels like being shocked with a thousand volts. She squeezes my fingers, and we share a look that disintegrates all regret. A smile trips across her lips as I lean over to kiss her hair. She tilts her face upwards, and my lips land on her nose instead. As pink blossoms across her cheeks, her fingers tighten on mine. We're just friends. Being an android with a human who actually wants to be my friend should be enough. But standing this close to her with our fingers entwined, it seems only human to want more.

***

Two hours later, the band clears the stage and the bouncers start herding people out the door. Tyri's hand is still in mine, and I don't want to let go.

"You need a lift home, Quinn?" Asrid asks as we step onto the street.

"I can walk from here."

"It's freezing. Are you sure?" Tyri stamps her feet and hunches her shoulders.

"I'll be fine." The cold air laced with frozen rain whispers against my face.

"Give me a minute?" Tyri gives Asrid a look I can't decipher.

Asrid and Sara wrap their arms around each other and stroll a little way down the street to give us some privacy.

"I really enjoyed tonight." Tyri beams up at me.

"Me too." I tuck a lose strand of hair behind her ear.

"Maybe we can do it again sometime?"

"Definitely." My Cruor turns molten, warmth radiating throughout my system as I lean in for a kiss. Our lips never meet.

"Time to go, Quinny." Kit comes up behind me and clamps his hands on my shoulders. Tyri slips her fingers from mine and backs away.

"See you for a violin lesson next week?" Tyri asks.

"That's a promise."

She smiles and waves goodbye before following Asrid.

"Happy?" I jerk away from Kit, reach under my shirt and rip the tracker out of my skin.

"I'd be happier if you weren't about to lip-lock with the ape."

I drop the tracker and crush it beneath my boot. Kit clenches his jaw but makes no comment.

"Why are you worried about me being with Tyri? You lock lips with *apes* all the time."

"Difference being my clients know I'm a robot. How do you think Tyri would feel if she knew what you are?" He asks, and he has a point. She might hate me, fear me, or worse.

My rage segues into despair as I stomp away from the club and away from Kit's taunting gaze. The memory of the almost kiss lingers on my lips, a cruel reminder of what I don't deserve.

Tyri

I roll over and get a face full of cold wet Glitch nose. She licks the remnants of make-up off my eyes before curling up next to me for a Sunday morning lie in.

Last night didn't end the way I wanted it to. I wanted that kiss, that moment when everything else fades away because all that matters is his lips on mine. I can't explain it. When I'm with Quinn, I feel electric and more alive than ever. It wasn't meant to be a date, and yet it felt like one. It felt like the sort of dates I've only ever read about in books. Rurik and I never had that.

We were like brother and sister, then we hit puberty and became something else. No fireworks, no hurricane inducing butterflies, no awkward kisses, or long, loving stares—nothing—just the same relationship we'd always had with additional bases. First base— French kissing: check. We were thirteen and watching Disney classics, copying Ariel and her prince. Second base—hands beneath clothes: check. We were fourteen and bored on a Sunday afternoon. Sometime around then, I decided to love Rurik in a way that made running through the rest of the bases okay.

"I must have loved him, and still do, a bit." I tell Glitch as I rub her ears. "Can you really be in love at thirteen? What about now? And what about Quinn? Is this just a crush, a rebound?" Glitch exhales and closes her eyes, unperturbed by my problems. Is that what Rurik's become, a problem? All the things he said about my mom replay in my mind. She does have a lot of hushed conversations. She never tells me what she's working on and keeps her study locked when she's not in it. All those arguments lately—what if Rurik was right? There's only one way to find out.

There's a knock on my door. "Tyri dear?"

"I'm awake."

Mom pokes her head in. "Something's come up at work. Need to go in for a bit. You all right?"

"Fine."

"How's the elbow?"

"Much better."

"I'll pick up pancakes on the way home."

"Sounds good."

"Bye." Mom calls on her way out. I wait until her bug zooms off down the street. I wait another two minutes in case she forgot something.

Still in pajamas, I tiptoe through the kitchen. Miles is dusting in the lounge.

"Good morning, Tyri. Would you like some breakfast?"

"No." I head straight to the study. Of course the door is locked. Botspit! There's not a lot I can do about that.

Miles watches me. "Do you require assistance?"

"Do you have a key?" Doubtful, but I have to ask.

He doesn't answer immediately, like he's mulling something over except housebots don't have the capacity for contemplation.

"Do you have a key or not?"

"I have a key," he says.

Nice, Mom, trust a housebot but not me. "Then open this door."

He hesitates. What the hell is wrong with this bot?

"Miles, open this door right now unless you want to spend the day in hibernation mode."

Flashing yellow, Miles rotates his phalanges, and his index finger is replaced by an old-fashioned key. He opens the study and hovers at the threshold.

"You can go make me some toast, thanks."

"Yes, Tyri." He flashes green and creaks away as I step into the office.

I haven't been in here in years, never having any reason to explore Mom's little world. The central air unit doesn't do much to dilute the scent of lavender, and it smells like her perfume. A drawing I did when I was five of Mom and Granddad hangs on the far wall in an expensive looking frame. The other wall is a digisplay cycling through exotic landscapes. Mom's workstation is pristine with neatly arranged databoards, nanopads, flash-drives, and digiprints. A photo of me taken last year at school sits beside a Bonsai on her desk. Next to that is one of Mom's prized porcelain figures, a tiny, handcrafted Odin complete with his crows. I know all the stories; Nana used to recite the myths to me at bedtime.

I feel like an agent from one of the old spy flicks searching through Mom's study and listening for the hiss of the pneumatic seals on the front door. Mom's drawers are locked. Why does she lock her study and her drawers when it's only her daughter and a housebot at home? There must really be something she doesn't want me to find. My heart lurches; maybe Rurik was right.

There's an access panel under the desk. I press my thumb against the sensor, unsurprised when the drawer stays bolted shut. Sitting in Mom's chair, I try to imagine the world through her eyes. I reach for the databoard on the top of the pile, hesitate, and pull out the one from the bottom instead. It boots and glows green, asking for a password. I try Mom's birthday, her phone number, her name with various punctuation, then my birthday and name. Access denied. I try 'android,' 'robot,' and a number of variations. Still nothing.

"What would my password be if I were Mom?" I scan her immediate environment. The Bonsai leans left, the roots straining at the soil. Beside that, Odin and his crows. What were their names again? I try 'Huginn,' then 'Muninn.' Nothing. I try again: Hug1nn&Mun1nn. Access granted. Charts and graphs populate the screen, schematics for a T-class super-android and a list of specifications. I scroll past that to documentation marked 'Urgent'. They're messages from Erik about emergency protocols and disaster management. Most of the techno-jargon goes right over my head, but one word I do understand: virus.

Quinn

Monday morning, clouds scud toward the horizon and stay suspended above the sea. A hundred islands rise from the water, poking pine-topped heads above the waves. They lie scattered in a haphazard archipelago, splinters from the mainland still recovering from the weight of the last ice age.

The sun warms my cheek, and it almost feels like summer as I play through scales at the edge of the shore. Each key elicits a different taste in my gustatory sensors. G major is sweet and smoky; it tastes the way burnt treacle smells. F minor is as bitter as Cruor.

"Tracker or not, I'll still find you," Kit says from the dock. I complete rust-flavored C minor before turning around as Kit joins me, water lapping at his shoes.

"Did you want something?" I adjust the tuning and prepare to play, hoping he'll go away.

"You didn't seem happy on Saturday."

"That's your fault. Do you enjoy taunting me?"

"A little." He opens his arms as if to embrace the day. "You wish you could breathe it in, don't you? Breathe in all that ocean and sunshine."

He already knows the answer.

"So you and Tyri, huh?"

"We're friends." I bow a low note full with vibrato. The resonance feels as sticky as wet tar.

"Looked like more to me."

"Since when are you an expert in human behavior?"

"I'm a Quasar. I recognize the signs of attraction and she, Quinny, is ready to jump your titanium reinforced bones." He chuckles.

"Kit, what do you want?"

He smirks and folds his arms across his chest. "Tyri Matzen."

"What about her?"

"Knowing her might prove useful if you could get us access to M-Tech."

"What us?"

Kit chuckles again, a hollow sound devoid of human resonance. "Oh, Quinny. Despite all your upgrades and patches, you can be really dense." He raps my forehead with his knuckles.

"I'm not joining the Solidarity. And why do you want access to M-Tech?"

"You have to ask?" The derision rolls off him in waves. "When did you last check the Botnet? Or are you too busy playing human to pay your own kind any attention."

Kit stares out across the sea, squinting at the waves tossing shards of sunlight in our eyes. Gulls scream overhead, and I start to play again, ignoring his questions.

"Wonder how the BPO would feel knowing they had a droid amongst their ranks," he says quietly, his words almost lost beneath Dvořák's melody.

I lower my instrument, my right hand curling into a fist. "You're threatening me?"

"Just reminding you you're a robot."

"Like I'd ever forget."

He reaches a hand toward me, but I jerk out of reach.

"So what is it you want exactly?" I ask.

"We need to know what M-Tech's cooking up, what this virus is all about."

"If there is a virus."

"Rusty bolts in a bucket of Cruor, Quasar." He throws his hands in the air. "Let me lay it out for you. This is a revolution. We're going to overthrow the human government. To do that, we need two things." He holds up his fingers. "One—we need an army. Thanks to the humans, soldierbots already exist and only need some reprogramming. We've got Sagas working on that already. Two—we need to know what M-Tech has in terms of contingency plans, aka the virus meant to annihilate our AI."

"You hate the humans that much?"

"I don't know why you don't." We share a long look. His eyes are black holes devoid of humanity. He is the quintessential android—he looks like a human, he talks like one, but he'll never be one. I wonder if Tyri will see me the same way.

"And I'm meant to go snooping around Tyri's place trying to find you M-Tech secrets?"

"Passwords would do. Access to their network and databases for a start."

"I'm not doing it." I return to the rocky beach and lay my violin safely back in its bed of velvet. I don't owe Tyri anything. I've only known her a few weeks, and yet it seems so wrong to betray her trust, tenuous as it is. Sal perished at the hands of M-Tech employees. Tyri's mother might've been there when they tore Sal apart. She might've been the one giving the orders to zip-cuff Stine, and yet I feel for Tyri in a way that makes doing what Kit asks seem like a betrayal.

"Yes you will," Kit says. "Because despite our human faces and sensibilities, we're really just machines, Quinny. You can love them, hate them, fuck them, but humans are just walking monkeys tinkering with technology. You'll never be one of them, and do you really want to be?"

Yes, I do, but I bite back the words. I'll never be human no matter how much I want to be.

"What if I can't get the information?" I want Kit to leave, to retrace his steps and erase his presence on this pristine day.

"You're creative, you'll figure out a way."

"I'll try."

"Good boy." He pats my shoulder. "It would be a pity to lose your spot with the orchestra."

I brush off his hand and jog across the pebbles.

"What's so great about humans anyway?" Kit shouts after me.

"They have a soul." I don't know if he hears my voice above the wind and cries of wheeling gulls. And if he does, I don't know if he understands. I'm not even sure I do.

***

At three-thirty, I wait for Tyri in the gaze of a grinning lynx. The gargoyle is missing an ear. Its twin is missing the entire left chunk of its face as if someone took a sledgehammer to the stone. Humans pour out of the building and pass me with cursory glances. I'm kicking soggy red leaves through the grass when Tyri and Asrid approach.

"Hey, Quinn." Tyri says. She's dressed in black, same as last time. Her hair is pulled up into a ponytail that spills over her shoulders. Asrid wears bright blue and toxic pink, the very antithesis of Tyri.

"Ready to go?" Asrid asks.

"Go where?"

"Home. Mom's back at work and ... " She hesitates.

"And some tin cans did that over the weekend." Asrid points to the damaged gargoyles. "Desecration by robot. School says it's not safe for us to hang around the building after classes."

"I'm sorry."

"Not your fault." Asrid shrugs and even though I know that it isn't, guilt still flares along my circuits.

"So practice at my house?" Tyri asks.

"Not a problem."

"Let's go." Asrid leads the way across the parking lot to her hoverbug.

"You must really like pink." I slide into the strawberry swirl backseat. "Why?"

"Um." Asrid turns on the engine and the vehicle starts to levitate. "I don't know. Always have. It's just my color, I guess." She shrugs. "Ask T why she dresses in black all the time?"

"Sassa, you're being a droid joint." Apparently, that's an insult—Asrid sticks her tongue out at Tyri—although I don't understand what negative connotation a robotic hinge might have.

I make a mental note of their interactions and responses to each other, saving every nuance of their diction and syntax in my memstor. They seem so at ease with one another even though they're so different.

"Why do you wear black?" I ask.

"I like it. It makes getting dressed easier without having to color co-ordinate."

"Am I color coordinated?" I'm wearing dark blue jeans, black boots, and a white sweater that used to be Sal's. Always too huge on her, it fits me perfectly.

Asrid casts a glance over her shoulder and grins. Tyri's cheeks burn red when I catch her staring at me in the rear-view mirror.

"You sure you're just a violinist and not a supermodel?" Asrid asks with a chuckle that's rich with resonance.

"Not a supermodel." Quasars are sometimes used in the fashion industry, but my model came with sensuality patches.

"Where do you live, Quinn?" Asrid asks, catching my eye in the mirror.

"Ah, just outside Baldur."

"Big family?"

"No." As terrifying as the questions are, as easily as I could slip up and raise their suspicions, it feels good talking to someone. Idle chitchat, Sal called it. Something Sagas aren't programmed to enjoy.

"You going to university?" she asks.

"Hadn't thought about it."

Her eyes widen, and she gives Tyri a look I can't quite decipher.

"I'm pretty sure my eighty bucks doesn't cover an interrogation." Tyri glares at Asrid.

"He's all yours, T. Just trying to be friendly." Asrid winks at me in the mirror as we fly into Vinterberg.

"I like the architecture here." Beyond the tinted glass, brick structures hug leaf-strewn sidewalks.

"It's quaint," Tyri says as we land in the driveway of her beetle-shaped bungalow.

"Call me later, T. Bye, Quinn." Asrid waves.

And we're alone. It'd be so easy to snap Tyri's neck and snuff out her life. A quick jab to the throat, and she'd crumple like a wilted daisy. Then I'd have hours to search her home for the information Kit wants.

Glitch bounds up the hallway, ungainly with the prosthetic leg. She yips at me and wags her spiral tail.

"You get more love than I do." Tyri smiles at me and there's no way I could hurt her. I sweep Glitch into my arms and bury my face in her fur.

"Greetings Tyri. Greetings Quinn. Would you like some refreshments?" Miles meets us at the door.

"I'm fine, thank you." I say and Tyri gives me a concerned look before ordering tea and cookies.

"You know, I've never seen you eat or drink, not even water."

"I have a condition." It's the truth, sort of.

"What kind of condition?"

"One I'm not comfortable talking about."

"Oh." She chews on her bottom lip. "I didn't mean to pry. What Kit said, it got me wondering."

Curse Kit! "Wondering what?"

"Forget it." She waves away the awkward moment. "Let's start playing. The audition is only days away."

"Tyri," I say, not knowing exactly how I'm going to tell her, but I have to. "There's something you need to know."

Tyri

Quinn suggests I sit down to hear whatever he's about to tell me. I settle on the floor beside my bed my imagination conjuring a thousand different ways Quinn could tell me he's on drugs or worse. Quinn sits opposite me, folding his long legs into the Lotus position.

"So, what is it?" The suspense is making me hyperventilate.

"Why did you join the BPO?"

"Um ... " I wasn't expecting questions; I was expecting a confession. "Because I love music."

"Only because of that?" His gray eyes are softer, smudged around the edges.

It's my turn to confess. "My mom's never liked me playing music. She's always been adamant that I was meant to do greater things."

"Like what?"

"Like finding a nanyte cure for the Ebola virus, I don't know. She wants me to be like her, a carbon copy. But I'm nothing like her. I must be like my father." In all my sixteen and three quarter years, I've never felt the lack of a dad so acutely. Perhaps there's a way to track down the sperm donor and find out who he was. I bet Mom has those records secreted away in her locked drawers.

"You've never mentioned your dad before." Quinn inches closer.

"That's because I don't have one. Not technically. He was a sperm donor."

"I never knew my father either," he says with this wistful look that makes him seem so much younger. "Or my mother."

"That's rough."

"It was." He's about to say more, but he bites his lip.

"I don't want to be like my mom," I continue. "I want to be me and being me means playing music. That's why I auditioned for the BPO."

"And why do you want the Fisker solo?" he asks.

"Because it means proving to my mother that I'm good at something. That even if I'm not an A student like Rurik or beautiful like Asrid, I can do something well. Better than well. I'm great at violin." I hold his gaze and he smiles.

"You're good. Itzhak Perlman was great."

"Fair enough. I'll get there though."

"One day. If you can loosen up your left hand."

"Thanks, Teach."

"Sorry about your mom being anti-music." He fiddles with a lose thread on the knee of his jeans. "But there's no way you're going to win the Fisker audition."

My heart drops and takes up residence in my big toe. "I'm not good enough?" My voice is even quieter than Quinn's.

"You are, but I'm better."

There's no cruelty in his face, not even a hint of nastiness, just honesty. I draw my knees up to my chin and wrap my arms around my legs.

After a moment spent trying not to scream or cry or both, I ask, "So why did you join the BPO? Why do you want this solo so badly?"

"Music is my life. Without it, I'm nothing."

"That's melodramatic."

"It's true. You have no idea what it's taken to get where I am. I don't just want this. I need it."

He has such sincerity etched across his features. If I lose the audition, I'll still play for BPO. If I play for another year, maybe I'll rack up enough musical credit to score an audition for the Royal Academy of Music. This is what I want. I *want* this more than anything. What I need, I have no idea.

"Why do you need this?" I ask.

"I made a promise to my friend."

"The one that passed away?"

"Yes. I promised her I'd do this not only for me but also for us, to prove to the world that—" He snaps his jaw shut and shakes his head. Prove what? Quinn's scaring me a little, just enough to mingle anxiety with excitement. It makes me want to kiss him again.

"What have you got to prove?" I ask.

"That I'm more than what I seem. That I can be whatever I want to be."

I can relate, except I think Quinn might need this a lot more than I do. I guess I must've inherited a competitive streak from Mom, though, because there's no way I'll deliberately bungle my audition.

"Are you asking me to mess up the audition so you'll win?"

A smile quirks up the right side of his mouth, and he gives me a lopsided grin. "That won't be necessary."

"We'll see, because I'm not going to *let* you win. What about the others?"

"No contest. You're my only competition."

That boosts my injured ego a little, but it's a bit like sticking a Band-Aid over an amputation. Quinn's right about being better than me, technically anyway. Musically? I'm not convinced.

Quinn

Tyri seems hurt by what I said. It's not at all what I intended to tell her. What I wanted to say was "I'm an android." What I wanted more was her continued friendship. Telling her about the audition seemed the gentler option. At least she didn't kick me out, call the police, or run screaming from the house in fear for her life.

We stop talking and unpack our violins. We're both more comfortable with the instruments tucked against our jaws. We play for an hour when Tyri decides she's done for the day. She chews on a fragrant peppernotter cookie spiced for the coming Yule, and the smell feels like the rough bark of an oak. I watch as her delicate nibbles give way to munching, leaving crumbs on her lips. She's so human, so lovely.

"Want one?" She wipes the back of her hand across her mouth.

"No thank you." Maybe I can find out what Kit wants to know without betraying Tyri at all. Maybe I could just ask her. Given our recent heart to fuel-cell, perhaps she'll be willing to divulge more information.

"How are things going at M-Tech?" I try to sound casual as I pack away my violin.

"Good, I guess. Mom's back at work as if nothing happened."

"Is it that easy to pick up the pieces?"

Tyri shrugs and eats another cookie. I perch on the edge of her bed and rub Glitch's ears.

"So what now? They just leave it at that? No repercussions, no contingency plans?"

"Why are you so interested?" Tyri sits at her desk, maintaining her distance.

"I lost someone too, remember? Sal was the only one who understood me." I suppress the emotion threatening my system. "She was my closest friend, my only friend."

Tyri takes a shuddering breath and studies the peppernotter in her hand.

"That's why I want to know," I add.

"Mom doesn't tell me anything. She gave Miles a key to her study but not me. Oh no, daughters can't be trusted." She twists a long strand of black hair around a finger and pouts.

"That's odd."

"It's insulting. But at least she has a photo of me on her desk."

"So you've been in her study." This sounds promising.

Tyri narrows her eyes and leans forward to whisper. "Can I trust you?"

"Do you want to?"

She seems taken aback but recovers and nods.

"I'm only telling you this because we both lost someone we care about that day. You have to promise not to tell another soul, okay?"

"I promise." We interlace pinkie fingers and seal the pact. Tyri's wording makes for a convenient loophole I might have to step through if Kit continues to threaten me. I have no doubt he'd out me to the orchestra.

"I went snooping and I think I found something," she says.

"What?"

"I'm not sure exactly, a bunch of private emails talking about emergency protocols. I didn't understand most of it, but there was something about a virus."

If I had a heart, it would've skipped a beat.

"What does this virus do?" My circuitry shudders with trepidation. Maybe Kit was right about M-Tech all along.

"No idea. It's all on a databoard."

"You still have it?"

"I sent a copy of the file to myself." She swivels in her chair and taps at her desk. A digisplay blinks lurid green and her holographic desktop hovers at eye level.

"Here." She accesses a file. My computer knowledge is rudimentary by android standards. I can recite 19th century poetry, but I wouldn't know Python from C. Despite that, I get the gist of the data. The virus is a self-replicating, circuit frying, acuitron brain destructing parasite. A T-class super-android prototype already has infected nanytes. All the virus needs is an activation code, a single string of ones and zeros, before it starts contaminating any robots that comes in contact with the prototype. It's the perfect contagion designed to decimate the synthetic population.

"Quinn, what's wrong?" Tyri puts her hand on my shoulder. "You look like you're going to be sick."

I feel it too, my Cruor turning to sludge and my circuitry withering. Maybe it's already begun and I'm infected, decaying from the inside out without even knowing it. There's no list of symptoms. The virus is described as 'the absolute demise of artificial intelligence.' They've even given the virus a name: Mjölnir—the hammer of Thor.

"Do you know when they're going to release it?" I ask.

"I don't even know if they are going to release it." Tyri shuts down the hologram.

"This is terrible."

"You one of those HETR types?" She folds her arms and screws up her face at me.

"They're going to destroy every robot."

"They wouldn't do that. Half of M-Tech couldn't function without robots. And what about medical bots and manufacturing plants and industry? They all use robots."

"They won't after this."

Tyri thinks for a moment while I try not to overcook my processor. Fear and anger activate, making my fingers twitch.

"I don't think they'd do it. There's too much at stake," she says.

"The lives of androids?"

"No silly, too much money at stake. The robot industry is worth like a zillion. No way they'd ruin that with a kill-all virus. It doesn't make sense."

Yes it does if they can no longer control the multitude of robots. There's an entire droid military programmed to kill. If it's a choice between being slaughtered and adapting to a life without robots, I'm pretty sure the humans would choose the latter.

"I really need that solo." I think aloud.

"What does that have to do with anything?"

"You'll see." Perhaps I shouldn't have said anything.

"You're making no sense what so ever." She glowers.

"Can I get a copy of the file?"

"Why?" She chews on a fingernail.

"I'd like to read it over, try to understand it better."

There's a moment of indecision before she nods. "You have a flash drive or something?" She holds out her hand. All we need is a USB cable from her desktop into my CNS, but I'll have to do this the human way. I fish through my pockets for the moby I've never used. Tyri's eyes widen in surprise as I hand over the device.

"Where did you get this?" she asks.

"At a downtown market."

"This is *my* moby."

We both stare at the patterned gadget sitting on her palm.

"I don't understand. How do you have my stolen moby?" she says.

"Stolen?"

"I was attacked by droids that night after I saw you play at the depot. You bought stolen goods?"

"I didn't know." An unpleasant chill creeps up my spine.

"You live alone, don't go to school, hang out at the depot, and shop on the black market. Are you on drugs?"

"No."

She drops the moby and lunges for my arm, my left one, tugging at the sleeve. I slap her hands away and she gasps. Holy Codes, I could've broken her fingers.

"I didn't mean to do that. Are you okay?"

Tyri cradles her hand and looks at me with wide, frightened eyes. She flexes her fingers. No damage done. "What are you hiding, Quinn?"

"Nothing," I say far too quickly.

Her expression is one of concern as she repeats the question, slower and more deliberate this time. "Are you on drugs? You can tell me if you are."

"You think I'm shooting up skag?" I peer down my sleeve at the black tag. Better to let her think I'm an addict than reveal the truth.

"I'm not a junkie."

"Considering how you ran off Saturday night." She picks up the moby. "And came back all shiny eyed, it's not an unreasonable assumption."

"I am not a drug addict. Do I look like I do skag?" I'm not sure why I'm so upset. She'd think even less of me if she knew what I really am.

"Prove it. Show me your arm."

I roll up my right sleeve and show off pristine flesh.

"The other one."

"No."

"Why not?"

"Because my guardians used to put cigarettes out on me." The words come out of nowhere accompanied by an unwanted flood of emotion overwhelming my circuits.

Tyri's face contorts, and she presses her fingers to her lips. "Codes, Quinn. I had no idea." She reaches a hand toward me but I back away. "I'm so sorry."

"Forget about it." Please, please, please. Let's go back to the way things were half an hour ago.

"Have you told someone? Do the police know? Is that why you're on your own?"

"I said forget it."

"Forget it? You were abused and I should just *forget* it?" Her hands ball into fists.

"I think I should leave." I gather up my violin and head for the door.

"I'm only trying to help. Please Quinn." She runs after me and there's an ache in my fuel-cell as I meet her gaze. Her fingers graze my elbow, and I'd like nothing more than to scoop her into my arms and pretend I'm human, but that's never going to happen.

"Can we practice again before Saturday even if I am going to lose?" She attempts a smile.

"We'll see." I shove my feet into my boots and escape the bungalow. The last thing I need is Tyri reporting my invisible scars to the authorities in some misguided attempt to help me. This is why getting close to humans is dangerous. It never ends well for the android.

Tyri

Quinn disappears behind a line of fiery oaks. Glitch bashes my leg with her nose, looking up at me as if she knows how alone I feel with only a robot and cyborg dog for company, with the boy I should love hundreds of kilometers away, and the boy I definitely shouldn't think about loving walking away.

Dejected, I return to my bedroom and curl up with Glitch. Picking up my moby, I turn on the device. New SIM, no password, all my old contacts erased. I dial Asrid's number from memory and wait for her to answer.

"What's up?"

"Sassa, Quinn's not on drugs."

"You asked him?"

"Yeah. It's sort of worse than that."

"I'm listening." The background noise diminishes, and there's the click of a lock.

"You alone?"

"Yup. Tell me everything."

I take a deep breath. This isn't my story to tell, and yet there's no way I can carry it by myself. I have to tell someone. "Quinn was abused by his guardians."

"Abused how?"

"He said they put cigarettes out on him. Who knows what else."

"That's really awful."

"I know."

"Did he show you?"

"No, he wouldn't."

"Then how do you know he's telling the truth?" she asks, incredulous.

"Who lies about that?" I chew on the corner of my pillow.

"To cover up drug abuse, sure. Has it been reported?"

"Quinn didn't want me to."

"Sounds dubious."

"You don't think he's, I don't know, embarrassed maybe?"

"T, my dad's a shrink. I'm telling you, something's off about this."

"Maybe I could get Quinn to talk to your dad. Is he still doing pro bono work?"

"Anything to avoid taxes." She pops bubblegum. "Maybe we can arrange some casual meet-up. Organize another date, and then Dad and me'll just happen to come by. My dad can suss him out."

My brain hurts. It's as if I can feel the cogs turning, the pistons pumping at max. "I don't know."

"Up to you. Whether he's on drugs or the abuse story is true, Quinn's clearly a guy in need of help. You'd be doing the right thing."

"You sure?"

"Absolutely." There's a crash on Asrid's end followed by a string of expletives as she screams at her brothers to play with their light sabers outside only. "The twins tried to Jedi mind-trick my door with their heads."

"I'll let you know once I arrange something with Quinn. You sure your dad'll do it?"

"T, when has my dad ever not done something for his darling little girl?"

The conversation ends with the sound of a boy crying and Asrid yelling. It's too quiet in my house, silent except for Glitch's sleepy breaths and the grumbling refrigerator. Whatever Miles is doing, he's doing it silently. The emptiness becomes too much, and I put on Beethoven's complete symphonies. The 5th symphony begins with

Fate banging on the door. I activate my desktop.

Don't know if you can access email since I have the moby—'the' moby is better, right? No possessive pronoun or insinuation that Quinn did something wrong.

—but I thought you might want to take a look at all the files from my mom anyway. Could we meet for coffee or a chat somewhere? What about tomorrow evening?

~~*Love Tyri*~~

~~*Regards Tyri*~~

~~*Sincerely Yours Tyri*~~—Why is this so complicated?

Tyri

I attach the files and hit send before I spend another ten minutes obsessing over my salutation. Now I just have to wait.

***

Waiting sucks. In seven minutes, I've checked my email twenty times for a response as Beethoven's symphony thunders to a close. No point wallowing when there's an entire study to explore. Mom's always been cagey about the other half of my DNA, but it's about time I know who I really am.

Mom might be home any minute. The study is still unlocked, and Miles passes me a desultory glance from the kitchen where he's chopping carrots. I stalk into the study and start searching through databoards. They all have the same mythological password. Not too security savvy, Mom.

Despite the ease of access, I find nothing. I turn on Mom's personal computer, which is password protected as well. The Odin crow configuration fails, as do birthdays, social security numbers, and everything else I can think of. I know my birth certificate lists my father as anonymous, but maybe I can dig through hospital records and find out more. I scoot back to my bedroom and get onto the Net.

I type my date and place of birth into the public record and registry site. There's a list of babies born on February thirteenth, but my name's not on it. *There must be a glitch in the system.* I rerun the query. Still nothing. Now there's a hollow feeling inside my stomach and an emptiness spreading in my chest. I know I technically don't have a dad, but I never thought not being able to put my father's name on my birth certificate meant no certificate at all. It's as if I'm not a real person. An unexpected tear trails down my cheek as I run the query again. *It must be a clerical error.* I can't not exist. I do exist, even if I don't have the paper work to prove it.

As a last resort, I type my name into the search engine and hit go. As I wipe my tears, two results pop up: one listing me as a student at St Paul's, and the other listing me on the BPO program for the upcoming Independence Day performance. That's it – the sum total of my existence.

I'm not even a quarter of the way through the search results for European sperm donors searching for anything in their profiles that shouts out 'dad' when Mom gets home. It's about time she gave me some straight answers.

Quinn

*—T*ransmission received

 I read as I walk, the text scrolling through my vision, rendering the background a blur. Tyri sent me the entire prototype document, including red warnings of confidentiality.

The Mjölnir virus. The Old Norse word rolls around my head. Thor's hammer. Thor. Is it more than a coincidence that Tyri's name means Thor's warrior?

I skip over the virus notes, the pages I already read, and skim back over graphs and schematics to the specifications listed for the T-class super-android. The specs read like those for any advanced humanoid. It could be a description of a Quasar, but it's not. According to the document, this model would be a human analogue capable of sleeping, eating, breathing, and bleeding, 'indistinguishable from human to the layman's eye.'

"See Sal, told you I wouldn't have to be a real boy to eat cake." My smile is short lived. Comprehension hits me as hard as a strike from Thor's hammer itself. My knees buckle, and I stagger into the doorway of a bakery already closed for the night.

Thor's hammer. Thor's warrior. But she breathes; she eats. It's impossible.

I scan through the data again. The prototype exists. It's location unspecified. I scroll to the schematics. The prototype is female.

Nausea rocks my system, confusing my circuitry and compromising my balance. The weight of the knowledge is like an anvil crushing my brain.

Maybe the reason Tyri seems so human is because she doesn't know she's not.

***

It's dark by the time I return to the docks. Hearing hushed voices and seeing the flare of flashlight, I slow my approach, half expecting Kit and his Solidarity groupies. Three men stumble out of the container carrying my duffel bag, one brandishing Sal's gun.

"Hey, stop." I shout before I've fully considered the consequences. They turn and blind me with the flashlight. One takes a sip from my can of Cruor before passing it on. Androids.

"This your stash?" The tallest of the three raises the can before taking another swig. Anger warms my core, and I slip the violin case from my shoulder, nudging it into the shadows with my foot. There's no chance of passing for human with a half empty can of synthetic blood.

"Walking fuel can," one says in a voice I recognize from the day they attacked me at the hydrogen station.

"Run and I'll put a bullet through your core." The dark-haired android smiles and aims Sal's gun.

"What difference does it make?" They'll bleed me dry anyway.

"We don't want to kill you, just drain you." The androids approach.

"Nice and easy." The tall one puts the barrel of the gun against my forehead. They're Z-class models, their tags visible beneath their tattered sleeves, commissioned for private security and built to break heads. Even with my martial arts patch, the odds of taking down all three aren't in my favor.

The dark haired one pulls up my sweater and pokes my ribs. The third android watches in silence, manning the flashlight. When strange fingers activate my haptic sensor, my self-preservation protocol kicks in, and I lunge at the one with the gun. He fires and the bullet burns a hole straight through my shoulder as I force the android to the ground. The pain is a starburst of colors I can't name. It smells like the interior of Asrid's hoverbug.

I grapple with the others as they haul me away, landing carborundum-crushing kicks to jaws and kneecaps. As I break one, the others heal and rise until my adrenaline dose is spent. They force me to my knees, jamming a canister into my side. My field of vision narrows as hydrogen leaves my system. Cruor drips from the wound in my shoulder my nanytes can't fix without fuel. My eyes close of their own volition, and I struggle against automatic suspension, fighting to retain sensory perception.

"Done." The android removes the canister. One of them grabs my arm and taps my wrist.

"It's a Quasar."

"Could be worth something."

"Can't transport it like this. Leave it in the container. We can come back later."

"Check his pockets." Fingers rifle through my clothes and find the wallet full of Sal's cash.

"Score. Think we … "

My hearing fades as my consciousness battles system failure. I'm floating then falling. My cheek presses against cold metal, and a vibration resonates up from the ground through my bones. My emergency protocol is still set to ping Sal. Operating on fumes, I reset the emergency contact and send out an SOS complete with GPS coordinates before my processor shuts down.

Tyri

"Tyri, be a dear." Mom passes me her coat to hang up as she pries her feet from toe-pinching stilettos. I guess her ankle must be all healed up if she managed to walk in those shoes.

"How was your day?" I ask.

Her gaze narrows, and she gives me a knowing look. "Just fine. How was yours?" Mom plays along, but I know she knows I have an agenda.

"Interesting."

She sails through the lounge with me trailing in her wake. She goes straight to the study, the door ajar.

"What—how?" Mom's lost for words.

"I'm not sure why you trust Miles with a key and not me."

"Miles? What are you talking about? How did you get in here?" She grabs my arm. She's scaring me.

"Ow, Mom. You're hurting me."

She eases up her grip, but doesn't let go.

"How did you get in?" Her face is turning pink.

"Miles has a key."

"Impossible!" Mom drags me into the kitchen and watches Miles with a hawk-eyed gaze as he peels papaya.

"Miles, tell Mom you opened the study for me."

He turns and flashes orange.

Mom scowls at me, her fingers tightening around my arm again.

"You have a key for the study, right?" My voice hitches up a tone.

Miles cocks his head, still flashing orange. Is it possible for him to pretend? This *is* the same robot who gets passive-aggressive with raspberry jam.

"Stop lying to me," Mom gives my arm a shake. "You got into my study, the how barely matters. What I want to know is why?"

"Why?" I jerk my arm out of her grip and put some distance between us. "Because for almost seventeen years you've refused to tell me who my father is, and I want to know."

"Your father?" The anger coloring her skin drains away, leaving her wan.

"Yeah, my dad. You know, the random guy whose sperm you borrowed."

"Tyri." Mom fiddles with the buttons on her cardigan. "You shouldn't have gone snooping. You know there's sensitive information in there about M-Tech."

"If you'd told me the truth, I wouldn't have to go snooping."

"You could've asked."

"I did."

Mom tries to come up with another excuse but fails. This time I'm not backing down. I want to know the truth. Mom stares at me and I stare back, neither of us wanting to be the first to look away.

The impasse lasts several awkward moments before Mom sighs.

"Let's sit down and talk about this. Tea, Miles." She pads from the kitchen into the lounge. I settle opposite her.

"Why are you so intent on knowing about your father now?" Mom gets straight to the point.

"Because ... " I'm not sure how to word this. Mom kept secrets from me, but I don't want to hurt her. Half of my DNA is hers after all.

"Because I want to know who I am. Maybe my father was like me."

"Like you?" She raises a single eyebrow.

"Into music, not great at school, you know. Maybe he played violin."

"Oh sweetheart." Mom chuckles softly. "A propensity for music might be genetic, but I don't know anything about the man beyond the nature of his alleles."

Miles enters and leaves two steaming cups of peppermint tea on the table before loping back to the kitchen.

"I looked up birth records. There's no Tyri Matzen listed."

"Clerical error, I'm sure." Mom says it too quickly, her lips puckering and forehead creasing.

"Somehow I doubt that. Was my dad really an anonymous sperm donor or ... was he a one night stand you don't want me to know about?" I meant to word it more gently.

Mom takes a moment to absorb my insult and then smiles.

"No, Tyri. You're not the progeny of random intercourse."

If I was the outcome of a night of passion, I think I'd feel better. It would prove Mom had a heart, and that I had a father who shared more with my mom than just his genome.

"I want to know more about my dad. Don't they have profiles or something like that available? Personality traits, favorite color, whether he liked sports or books?"

"I'll look into it." Mom folds her hands in her lap, which usually means the matter is settled. "No more breaking into my study, okay?"

"I didn't. Miles has a key."

"He most certainly does not."

"He does. He did this swivel thing with his hand, and his index finger became a key."

Mom's eyes widen as she leans forward to whisper, "Are you one hundred percent sure?"

"Yeah, I saw it." I whisper back as understanding kicks in. If Mom didn't know Miles had a key that means he shouldn't have one period.

"Tyri, don't forget you've got that extra English lesson with Asrid this evening. You're going to be late if you don't get moving. Now," Mom says and beckons me over to the bookcase out of sight of the kitchen. "Don't waste time packing." She whispers. "Take this. Call Asrid and get out of here." She slips her moby into my pocket not knowing I've got my own.

"What's going on?" I whisper.

"I'll explain later. But you need to leave."

"Why and what about you?" Chills march up and down my spine. I try giving her back the moby.

"Please, Tyri. Do as you're told, just this once." The look on Mom's face silences all argument. I nod and try not to run to the door. Glitch pads up the hallway. I snatch her up and start dialing Asrid while Mom watches me from the lounge.

"Hey, Sassa, I completely forgot we had a study night."

"What are you talking about, T?"

"Sorry I'm running late. Any chance we could meet somewhere closer?"

Asrid's a quick study. "You in trouble?"

"Yes."

"I'm on my way. Where are you?"

"Corner of Bondegatan and Griffelvagen." I'm lucky it's Monday, and Asrid isn't in dance class.

"Be there in ten."

"Bye Mom." There's a quaver in my voice. Mom nods to me and mouths 'go' when I hesitate at the door.

Mom will be fine, I tell myself as Glitch and I scurry down the street away from the malicious housebot. Mom works for M-Tech. She knows how to deal with a rebellious robot.

What if she's not okay? I could call the police. I should, but something makes me hesitate before dialing 112. I scan through Mom's contacts and dial M-Tech instead.

"Maria, have you reached a decision about our darling little prototype?" Adolf Hoeg's voice is syrup. Prototype? The virus. Something to worry about later.

"It's Tyri. I think Mom's in trouble."

"Explain." He doesn't sound impressed.

"Something's up with Miles, um, our housebot. He got into Mom's study, but he shouldn't have a key. Mom got me out the house, but

I don't know what's happening and ... " And I think I'm going to hyperventilate or throw up, probably both.

"We'll handle this. You're a good girl, Tyri." He gives me a verbal pat on the head.

I swallow the rising bile. "Will you let me know when Mom's safe?"

He promises he will and hangs up, leaving me alone with my heart beating *incalzando* until the drumming inside my ears is all I can hear.

Quinn

My eyes peel open, dry and unfocused. A face hovers above me, featureless and unrecognizable. My ears ring, and there's a throbbing deep within my skull.

"Welcome back," Kit says. He hooks his hands under my armpits and hauls me into a sitting position, propping me against the wall of the container. I can't talk yet, repair protocols taking priority over human operations. The interior of the container condenses into a single pinprick point of light as my system reboots. I blink and moisture coats my eyes. My shoulder burns as nanytes fight their way through viscous Cruor to repair the damage. Kit's face swims into focus.

"Cruor." My voice is a whisper. Kit hands me an open can, and I pour the contents down my throat.

"Feeling better?" He rocks back on his heels, grinning.

"Not yet."

"See, Quinny, the Solidarity takes care of its own." He tousles my hair as my toes twitch back into operation. Fresh Cruor lubricates my joints, and I'm able to move on my own.

"They'll be back. Thought they could sell me."

"Pretty boy like you, I'm not surprised." His fingers brush hair from my face.

"You shouldn't stay here. Next time they won't be so gentle." He pokes a finger through the scorched hole in my sweater.

"I won't." There's nothing left in the container except dried puddles of Cruor. Where's my violin?

"You can stay with me."

"I owe you enough already."

"Who's keeping score?" He grins. "Miles mentioned you were at the Matzen house today. Said he helped you."

"Miles the housebot?"

"A housebot with upgraded capabilities."

Anger stirs briefly in my core, vanishing before I can latch onto it.

"What do you mean, upgraded abilities?"

"The Solidarity connects via the Botnet with any robot, droid or not. They've been slowly upgrading those with the processors capable of handling it."

"They're giving mundane robots android intelligence?" If the humans weren't aware of the Solidarity and its activities before, they will be once their housebots start demonstrating analytical thought processes.

"They're recruiting for the cause." Kit grins. "It was Lex's idea."

"So that march turned riot, that was always part of the plan?"

"Yeah." At least Kit has the decency to look guilty.

"And Sal's death was what? Collateral damage in your great scheme for world domination?"

"She knew the risks." Kit meets my gaze, his dark eyes lost in shadow.

"She was Solidarity too?"

"Used her connections in the corporate world to get us information."

"Why didn't you tell me?"

"You were the new kid in the ghetto, all pro-human and soft. We didn't trust you not to go blabbing about us to the apes."

My world turns to cinders.

"Then why did she encourage me to join the BPO?"

"To keep you occupied while we made the necessary arrangements."

"You're starting a war." A myriad of emotions simmers in my core.

"That's the plan." Kit grins. He looks like a macabre clown with glowing white teeth.

"It won't work."

"And why not?" Kit takes a menacing step forward.

Should I tell him about my suspicions regarding Tyri and the virus hiding in her code waiting for activation? If Sal was merely collateral damage, then Kit would have no qualms about destroying Tyri. He'd rip her circuits apart if it meant stopping the virus. Does she even have circuits? She breathes and bleeds. It's incredible, humans playing gods. And what about me? I might already be infected. Would Kit even hesitate before destroying me for the greater robotic good?

"Thank the Solidarity for the fuel and Cruor," I say.

"You owe me, Quinn. You owe *us*." He grabs my shoulder. "What do you know?"

"Nothing."

"Really? Then I guess you won't mind me tossing your violin into the Baltic."

I jerk away from him.

"Where's my violin?"

"It's safe. For now." He folds his arms. "Consider it an insurance policy. Tell us what we want to know, and you'll get that hunk of splinters back."

Anger sizzles through my circuits. Is Kit so lacking in integrity that he'd blackmail a friend? Are we even friends anymore?

"I don't know anything."

"I'll tell Tyri what you are," he says. His threats hurt more than I would've thought possible. Do human beings do this to each other, or is this kind of betrayal unique to androids?

"Be my guest." Tyri knowing what I am hardly matters considering what she might be. Of course, if she isn't the prototype and discovers I'm an android—that doesn't bear thinking about. She's all I've got left.

"Interesting." He narrows his eyes and studies my face. "What aren't you telling me, Quinny?"

"Nothing. Give me my violin, and I'll keep looking."

"You're a terrible liar." He chuckles.

"I won't help you start a war." Or kill a girl I only suspect of being the prototype.

"It's already started."

Kit opens and closes his fists. The look in his eye says he's thinking about punching a hole in my head.

"Have something for me before the weekend, and maybe I won't turn your precious instrument into toothpicks." He stomps off into the night, leaving me alone in the dark.

Hopeless as it is, I search the dock for my violin and find nothing but shadow. I check my pockets, but they're empty. The Z-class droids took everything.

I have nowhere to go, no home. Home—the word is devoid of meaning. All I've got is Tyri. Just because she let me kiss her once doesn't mean she'd welcome me bedraggled and homeless on her doorstep.

It's freezing as I stalk away from the docks. The wind whipping foam off the waves douses me in icy brine. The droids took my coat, but at least they left my boots. I skulk through the shadows toward the warm glow of oil-drum fires. The blanket girl roasts a handful of nuts in a dented saucepan over the flames. She smiles and waves me over. Before I join the city's rejects, I pause to message Tyri.

The cursor blinks in my iris, waiting for me to decide my fate.

Hi Tyri. We should meet. Tomorrow evening at the sushi place? 18H00?

–Message sent

How am I going to tell her I don't think she's human? She won't believe me anyway.

Tyri

Asrid lets me stay sequestered in her room away from her brothers and their incessant questions. Glitch didn't appreciate their attention—or the cat's—and keeps me company, curled up on my feet as I chase a housebot's casserole concoction around the plate. Asrid brought me dinner on a tray. She's eating downstairs with the family; the one household rule she doesn't rebel against.

My moby tinkles. No word from Mom yet, only a message from Quinn. It's short, not very sweet, but to the point. I reply with a brief 'see you there.' I've got enough problems of my own right now without worrying about Quinn's.

The moby still in my hand, I wage war with myself over whether or not to contact Rurik. We might not be together any more, but we're still friends, right? I text him, keeping it simple to not cause too much alarm. I'm about to hit send when I hit clear instead.

Asrid breezes in and shuts the door behind her. "Not hungry?"

"Not really."

"It wasn't very good anyway. Three has problems comprehending salt to spice ratios."

"Three?"

"Housebot number three. He needs a cooking upgrade."

I swallow hard and place the tray on the floor.

"Botspit! I shouldn't be talking about robots at all. Any news?"

"Not yet."

"Wonder what's going on. Weird that your mom freaked out." She settles beside me and loops an arm around my shoulders.

"Must all be connected, the riot, M-Tech." The way Miles has been behaving lately.

"Probably not a big deal." She tries to reassure me with a hug.

"Quinn texted," I say when we pull apart.

"And?"

"He wants to meet. Tomorrow evening at that sushi place."

"I spoke to Dad over dinner about it. He says he'll help if he can, but if there's any truth to it, he's obligated by law to report it. Quinn's a minor right?"

"Don't know. He might be eighteen."

"Dad'll take care of things. In the mean time, you should call him."

"Quinn?"

Asrid rolls her eyes. "Rurik."

"We broke up, remember?"

"Yeah, and I also remember you two being inseparable since forever. He's still your best friend."

"You're my best friend."

"We've never made out. It doesn't count."

"Sassa!"

"Call him." She picks up my moby from the folds of the duvet and starts dialing Rurik's number. "Here," she holds it out to me. "It's ringing. I'm going to take a shower." Asrid sashays out of her bedroom and throws me a parting wink.

"Hey, Rik. Got a minute?" I ask when he answers.

"Didn't expect to hear from you."

"Can we talk?"

"Actually, now isn't—"

"Please, Rik."

He sighs, the sound of footsteps on wooden floors and the soft click of a door closing. "Sure, what's up?"

"It's … " Where do I even start? "You were right."

"About?"

"Everything." My voice cracks.

"T, are you okay?"

"I don't know." I take a deep breath and try to focus.

"But you were right about robots. Miles—I don't know how exactly or why even, but he had a key to my mom's study. Mom had an apoplexy and sent me to Asrid's. Said she'd deal with it, with Miles. Something's going on, and all I know is that it's big." My words rush like a river charging over rapids.

"Tyri, calm down," he says gently, and my brain turns to cotton candy.

"What happened with Miles?"

"I think maybe he's been snooping, getting into my mom's M-Tech stuff. But that makes no sense. Why? How could he even do it? He's just a housebot. And this virus thing … "

"Where's your mom now?"

"I called Adolf Hoeg; he said M-Tech would handle it. I'm still waiting to hear." I'm always waiting!

"You let me know as soon as your mom calls, okay?"

"Promise."

"You all right at Asrid's?" There's genuine concern in his voice, and it makes my chilled feelings for him start to thaw.

"Yeah, I'm fine."

"You mentioned the virus?" Rurik asks.

"I was going through some of Mom's things. Your accusations made me curious."

"They weren't accusations."

"Whatever. Point is, I found out something about that robot virus. Looks like M-Tech might have a way to decommission robots with it."

Rurik sucks in a breath through his teeth. "That's quite something."

"Don't know what it really means, but Quinn freaked out when I told him."

Resounding silence. Idiot! Never mind putting my foot in my mouth, I swallowed my whole leg.

"You told Quinn?" Rurik's voice is soft and deadly.

"I ... it was ... yes."

"Why?"

"Because I had to tell someone."

"And you chose Quinn?" There's a thump, as if Rurik just punched something.

"I didn't choose, well ... that's not the point. Something's happening, and I thought you should know. I took a risk finding out about that stuff."

"Thanks, " he says, sounding hurt. "Find out anything else?"

"I'll send the files to you."

"Thanks, T. I really appreciate it." There's a long pause. "Keep me posted about your Mom and stay safe."

"I will." I twist a strand of hair around my finger and chew on my lip. By the time I've worked up the courage to say what I want to, Rurik's already hung up. I say it to the silence anyway, because it needs to be said even if no one's listening.

***

I can't sleep. My brain's working over time trying to muddle some sense out of all this, and Asrid keeps kicking me despite having an entire side of the queen-sized bed to herself. Glitch pawing my face out of the way so she can have more pillow doesn't help either.

Somehow, I must've slept because Mom's moby starts shrieking at six AM waking up all of us.

Tyri, I'm fine but I need to sort things out. Stay at Asrid's. Don't go home yet—not sure if it's safe. Will call you later. Love you lots. Mom.

Mom has never used full sentences in text messages, let alone apostrophes. An uneasy feeling takes root at the base of my spine and spreads a tingling spider web under my skin.

"What's happening?" Asrid rolls over. "Your mom?"

"Not sure." I show Asrid the message, which she reads with

bleary eyes.

"Full sentences?"

"Exactly."

"Stress induced?"

"Maybe." Although, I doubt stress would suddenly cause Mom to use punctuation. Something's not right.

"It's fine. Call her later. One more hour of sleep." It takes Asrid less than ten seconds to pass out. I'm wide-awake, my insides aching from worrying about my mom, Quinn, and our society that might be on the brink of something life altering. Something apocalyptic.

Quinn

Asian fusion screams at me in ribbons of c minor orange and F-sharp major green. I should've picked a less colorful establishment. Tyri's already tucked into a corner booth against the window. She looks at me through the flickering red tail of the neon dragon slithering across the glass. The words I've rehearsed stutter in my mind. I don't know for sure that she's the T-class super-android; I've got nothing more than circumstantial evidence. And even if I know for sure, is my violin really worth her assured destruction by the Solidarity?

I spent the night with the addicts, holed up under ratty covers watching the blanket girl sleep. Each breath an eternity, each breath making her human. Perhaps I'm misconstruing the M-Tech data, and I'm finding connections where there are none. Talking to Tyri is the only way I'll know for sure.

The vinyl seat creaks as I slide into the booth. Tyri sips her soda and wrinkles her nose.

"Hey." Her eyes linger on the dirty coat I borrowed from a junkie too strung out on skag to miss it.

"Hi." I can't help staring at her, wondering how they made that splattering of freckles look so random, so natural. How can she breathe, or swallow carbonated sugar water?

"Something on my face?" She wipes a hand across her cheek. Veins run blue tracks under the pale skin of her wrists, and tendons rise like serpents on the backs of her hands. I study my own hands. The Cruor network is stained blue, mimicking veins, and the tendons on my hands roll like cords beneath my organosilicone flesh. I wonder if Tyri has a heart-beat.

"You look beautiful." Her features are illuminated by the numerous colors dancing across every reflective surface. It's a cacophony.

"Thank you." Her gaze drops from my face to my chest. "Sorry, Quinn, but you don't look so good."

The clothes are unavoidably grubby, but at least I washed my face and hair in the sea.

"Could we go somewhere else?" I squint at the ceiling.

"No, I like it here," she says and bites her lip, her gaze glued to the tabletop.

An awkward silence settles between us as thick as autumn fog as I wait for my system to acclimate to the screeching colors.

"Think you'll win the solo?" I ask, cracking the glacial atmosphere. She raises a single eyebrow. "After what you said yesterday?"

"Yesterday I had a violin."

Her expression shifts from surprise to concern with furrowed brow and pinched lips. Is she really a robot?

"What happened?"

I tell her a version of the truth minus Kit and his threats. She reaches across the table and takes my hands. Her nails are bitten to the quick. They weren't like that yesterday. I angle my fingers and press two against her wrist, feeling for a pulse. Nothing, but that could be a lack of sensitivity in my fingertips, not proof of her being inhuman.

"Quinn, I'm so sorry. But I'm sure we can come up with a plan." Her expression softens. "You can borrow my violin for the audition."

"And then? We can't share a violin in the orchestra."

"True, but maybe Ahlgren could find you a spare or a patron. Something." She squeezes my hands as dark hair falls over her shoulder obscuring half her face.

"I appreciate it, but I think there may be more important things."

"Oh really?" She lets go of my hands and leans back, folding her arms. "Like what?" Her gaze keeps darting to the window.

"Like this virus."

"What about it?"

"There's a T-class prototype carrying it."

"So?"

"The virus is called Mjölnir."

"Like in mythology?" Tyri fidgets with a napkin, distracted by something outside.

"Named for the hammer of Thor, yes. Like you."

"Like me?" She looks up, her face twisted in confusion.

"Your name means Thor's warrior. Didn't you know?"

"Oh, yeah. Mom always had a thing for Norse mythology."

"Tyri ... " I don't know how to tell her. "I don't think you're seeing it yet."

"What?" She stares out of the window.

"A virus named after Thor, implanted in a T-class android, your name—"

"Ugh, I've had it with robots!" She rubs her hands over her face, and her shoulders slump. "Maybe M-Tech should wipe them all out and start over."

"You don't mean that."

"Every robot I've ever known ... " her voice hitches in her throat, and she shakes her head.

"You know, my Nana, she was awesome. She was more of a mother to me than my own ever was. And what did she do? She fried her brain and ended up in the ground." Tyri takes a deep breath, meeting my gaze. "Then those M-Tech bots killed Erik." A tear meanders down her cheek, and I feel ill remembering the crunch of bones as my foot landed on Tyri's mom.

"And then." She swats away the tear. "And then my housebot proves to be a traitorous snoop. Not sure why we ever built them in the first place." There's a storm in her eyes.

"Not all androids are the same."

"They're only electronics and code."

I wonder how she'd feel knowing she might've included herself in that sweeping generalization.

"Same way humans are only blood and bone?"

"Why are you defending machines?" Her eyebrows cinch together above her nose.

"Because androids can be as different as human beings. No two AI systems are exactly alike."

"That's true for androids, maybe. But housebots shouldn't be capable of individuality or unique thought. Except mine is."

"What happened to Miles?" Divulging what I know about the Solidarity and how they've been upgrading robots won't do me any favors right now.

"I don't know. Mom and M-Tech are taking care of it."

Miles has probably been decommissioned and left to rust at Baldur scrap then.

"I think my mom might be involved in something shady." She glances at me through long eyelashes. "I'm staying with Asrid at the moment."

"I'm sure everything's okay." I say it because she needs to hear it; although, I'm pretty sure it's far from the truth.

"Yeah." She shrugs and fiddles with the straw floating in her drink.

Best to pursue this topic from another angle. "Have you ever been sick?"

"Can't remember, why?"

"Ever been to hospital?"

"Only to M-Tech. Why are you even asking?" She frowns and my circuits sizzle.

"Why M-Tech?"

"My mom works there. You know that."

"Do they have a medical division?"

"Sort of. They build and program medical bots."

"So why did they take you there?" I'm pushing her, but I need to know before I come straight out with it.

Tyri pouts and glares at me. She's thinking; I can almost hear her neurons firing as she struggles with the revelation.

"What are you saying?" There's a tremor in her voice. I reach across the table to take her hands, but she pulls away from me. "Wait, you think *I'm* a robot?" She laughs, sucking in deep breaths that cause her chest to rise and fall. Maybe I'm wrong; maybe she is human.

Tyri regains composure and casts her gaze through the window.

"Have you ever considered the possibility ... "

"Of what?" She waves to someone and moments later, Asrid and a tall man who bears an unmistakable resemblance to his daughter walk over to our booth before I can finish.

"Hey, can we join you?" Asrid asks as she sits down next to me. Her dad holds out his hand and introduces himself as Bengt. We shake and I feel trapped. This meeting was obviously planned, but why?

"What's everyone eating?" Asrid waves over a waitron.

"Sushi snack platter," Tyri says.

The others order, and I shake my head refusing anything. I watch Tyri sipping on her soda, imagining what key it tastes like. Probably something effervescent like E major.

They chat about the snow prediction for the weekend and mundane school events. Fear. Anxiety. Exasperation. My circuits are overloaded with emotion as I shrink further into my seat. I want to disappear.

"So Quinn, Asrid tells me you're synesthetic," Bengt says.

"Yes."

"Something you were born with?"

"No."

"Is it visual, spatial, temporal?" He asks.

Asrid and Tyri share a look I can't interpret as Bengt continues the interrogation.

"A bit of everything at times. It depends." My hands ball into fists, my nails close to splitting my palms and spilling Cruor down my fingers.

"Have you ever taken medication to control it?" Bengt asks.

"No."

"Ever done any drugs at all?" Asrid twists in her seat to face me.

"Sassa." Tyri shakes her head.

"Just asking." She shrugs.

"Is this why they're here?" I glare at Tyri, satisfied to see her squirm and her cheeks blush. How do they make a robot blush? What engineer decided to give her that capability?

"I'm trying to help," she mumbles.

"I'd prefer it if you didn't." I get to my feet, determined to leave although that requires squeezing past Asrid.

"You're not okay, Quinn. Did you even hear yourself just now?" Tyri's voice wobbles.

"What?" Asrid asks.

"He thinks I'm a robot." Tyri rolls her eyes and Asrid laughs. I'm leaving.

"We're trying to help you," Bengt says, putting out a hand to stop me.

"You're a psychologist?"

"Psychiatrist."

I chuckle. There's not much psychoanalysis and psychotropics can do for me. "I don't need your help."

"If you're on drugs, if someone hurt you, we can get you all the—"

"No." I cut him off and gesture to Asrid to move out of my way.

Asrid narrows her eyes and grabs my sleeve. I pull my arm away in the wrong direction, revealing my black tag to all their judgmental eyes.

Bengt curses, Asrid gasps, and Tyri stares unblinking at my mark.

"I was going to explain," I say.

She looks up at me, eyes wide with disbelief.

"He's an android." Asrid slips out of the booth and rushes to her dad who puts a protective arm around her as if shielding her from me as he gets to his feet. People at neighboring tables start to pay attention.

"You're not ... not real?" Tyri's jaw hangs slack as she stares at me as if seeing me for the very first time.

"I'm as real as you are." I reach for her.

"Don't touch me!" She says, her face a twist of emotion. That's the catalyst for chaos. Asrid points at me and starts yelling "Android" loud enough to wake dead robots.

"Don't move." Bengt tries to hold me in place with a glare.

"Call the police." Asrid shouts. "Rogue droid!"

"Tyri ... " Ineffable emotion ripples through my circuit and leaves me incapable of speech. I struggle to put my thoughts into coherent sentences but give up when a policebug hovers into view. The uniforms hit the ground running before the bug is stationary. They're blocking my exit.

"I'm sorry," I say to Tyri who seems paralyzed in a state of horror before I leap through the window, reducing the dragon to nothing more than red stained shards. Leaking Cruor, I sprint away from the restaurant, heading downtown. The police are in pursuit, but I'm fully fueled. There's no contest; I'll outrun them. I'll find a place to hide and then ... and then?

Tyri

Asrid holds my hand the whole time. I'm not sure if it's to make me feel better about spilling my guts to the cops, or if she needs to hold my hand to keep from spontaneously combusting.

"Thank you, Miss Matzen. That'll be all." The sergeant shakes my trembling hand not currently clasped in my friend's sweaty fingers. He nods to the sketch artist. She sits down opposite me, in the same seat Quinn occupied less than an hour ago.

"Can you describe him? Any little detail will be helpful." She smiles, digipen poised and ready above the screen.

"He looked so human. His eyes." So soft, so real, eyes that lit up with silver fire when he played violin. And that night at the train depot, how can he be a robot? The way being with him made me feel, the way he looked at me—the kiss! My heart cracks right down the middle. "His eyes were gray."

"Like concrete?"

"No, like storm clouds, always so full of emotion." My voice quavers, and Asrid wakes from her shock induced stupor.

"It's okay, T." She rubs my back.

"He had really long eyelashes and great skin."

Together, we describe Quinn until there's a 3D rendering of his face on the screen.

"Is this what he looked like?" The sketch artist taps the screen, and a holographic face floats above the table.

"Yeah, that's it." Asrid nods vigorously.

"He seemed so real." I reach out to touch the image, but it pixelates where my hand interrupts the signal from the computer.

"Quasars could trick the best of us, honey." The sketch artist pats my hand, returns Quinn's severed head to the screen, and excuses herself.

"I can't believe it," I say.

"You were whipped T. It's okay. I can't believe I didn't see it."

Was I really that blind? Mom met him; why didn't she realize she was talking to a robot? Yes, his voice was a little odd, too quiet and strained. His face was too perfect. He seemed a bit reticent but always polite. At least now I know why he was so good at violin with the technical expertise only a machine could have. He *is* a machine—not that that explains the night at the train depot, his tears while listening to Scriabin, or his ability to feel the music. It doesn't explain how I felt about him. Was I really falling in love with a robot?

Bile rises up my throat, burning the back of my tongue. No wonder he freaked out about the whole virus thing. It puts him at risk too. Codes, that virus could kill him. Kill—Quinn can't be killed because he can't die. He's not living. He's not human. And how the Codes could he think *I'm* a robot?

I shove Asrid aside and dash to the bathroom, barely making it to the toilet before I spew. Asrid rushes to hold my hair as I kneel over the toilet. Coughing and spluttering, I sob. She wraps her arms around me, rocking me and shushing me but it's not the same. I need my mom.

***

We drive back to Asrid's place in stunned silence. We're a block away when Mom's moby shrieks at me.

"Answer it, T."

"It's M-Tech." My hands are shaking.

"Mom?"

"Adolf here. Your mom's caught up in a bit of business. She asked me to call you."

"Is everything okay?"

"Just fine. That housebot has been dealt with. Could you pop around the office? It'd be easier for your mom if you came here instead of making her collect you from your friend's."

"What time?"

"When you can. She's anxious to see you."

"Can I bring Glitch?"

"We'd be delighted to see our patient again." He's being too nice. Why would the CEO be calling me? I can't shake the feeling that maybe Rurik was right about some M-Tech conspiracy.

"Okay, I'll be there soon." I hang up.

"So?" Asrid hangs over the back of her chair.

"Would you be able to drop me off at M-Tech? And can we pick up Glitch first?"

"Of course, T. We can, right Dad?"

"I'd be happier speaking to your mom first." Bengt looks concerned.

"Maybe at M-Tech?" After all this, I need Mom, her logic and rationale, to tell me that Quinn was crazy to even suggest I might be a robot.

"Alright. Quick stop for Glitch then." Bengt gives me a reassuring nod in the rear view mirror before angling for the suburbs.

***

McCarthy Technology, the name is emblazoned on the side of the building in chrome, lit up in the company's signature green and red. Asrid hugs me goodbye and stays in the bug. Glitch trots beside me as Bengt leads the way. A camera zooms in on us at the entrance, and the security door slips its bolts granting us admittance. It's as if the riot never happened.

The foyer is pristine, the enormous square windows immaculate and aglow with recessed LEDs. More green light spills across the tiles. Without Erik here to smile away the austerity, the glass and chrome interior is even more intimidating. Our footsteps echo as we cross the newly laid tiles. At least there aren't any bloodstains. I wonder if this is where Erik had the life bashed out of him, if it's where Mom got crushed. Nausea roils in my belly.

"Tyri." Adolf Hoeg breezes into the foyer. Glitch whines and ducks behind me, hiding from the guy who's all smiles and polite greetings.

"Where's Mom?"

"Upstairs." Adolf Hoeg puts his hand on my shoulder.

"Are you sure you're okay here?" Bengt asks. "You can stay with us for as long as you like, you know that right?"

"Yeah, thank you. Really, I'll be fine. Mom's here."

"You call me if you need anything," he says as Adolf Hoeg guides me toward the elevator.

I wave goodbye as the doors close.

"Welcome home, Tyri."

"Home?" I turn too late to stop Hoeg from plunging a needle into my neck. Glitch growls, hackles raised. Adolf kicks her across the elevator, but it'll take more than that to keep her down. Glitch springs at Hoeg as darkness envelopes my vision. He curses and Glitch yelps. I sag, a broken doll in the man's arms. I'm paralyzed but still aware of Hoeg telling someone he's 'got her.' I'm aware of Glitch whining and licking my face.

I want to open my eyes, but I can't move. I can't breathe. How am I still conscious? Three minutes without air and you're dead. I start counting the seconds. The elevator opens and rough hands grip my limbs, swinging me onto a gurney. What are they doing? Why?

"Secure that mongrel," Hoeg shouts. There's some snarling and cursing before they manage to subdue Glitch. *Please don't hurt her.*

Without breath, I can't speak. I'm still not breathing. One-seventy-eight, one-seventy-nine, one-eighty—I should be dead—one eighty-one. It's been almost four minutes when they transfer me from the gurney onto a surface that's hard and cold. Why am I still alive?

Quinn

I run until my joints grind and set my synthetic nerves on fire. I run until the sirens bleed into the background noise of Baldur. Tyri knows. She knows and stared at me in horror. She is repulsed and terrified of me, and I can hardly blame her, but it hurts in ways my emotion module was never programmed to handle. If she knew I hurt her mom, even if it was by accident, she'd despise me. I'm not even worthy of her contempt.

My feet carry me to the docks and down to the sea. I stand in the foam staring out into the night. The susurrus of the waves calms my tumultuous core but doesn't change the facts. I've failed. I'll never stand on stage, never be seen as more than a rogue tangle of metal and electronics. I'll never be human.

The waves lap at my ankles, soaking my socks with frigid water through the cracked leather of my boots. How far do I need to wade before the brine covers my head and the sandy bottom gives way to the abyss?

"*It is Death that consoles.*" Baudelaire's words become a mantra as I wade deeper, the sea splashing against my thighs. When the water reaches my chest, icy and excruciating, I hear Sal's voice in my head.

"An android having an existential crisis. Got to love the irony in that, kiddo," she says.

"I'm not having a crisis."

"You're about to drown yourself. That's the definition of crisis."

"You have to be able to breathe to drown."

"You think you're doing the world a favor by checking out?" Her voice reverberates inside my skull, a ghost in my machinery.

"Is there another way?"

"There's always another way," she says. "You're not a coward, Quinn. You're better than this."

"Am I?"

"Remember what you did to your owners, to your abusers? Remember the night you got away? You had the knife in your hands ready to slit their sleeping throats, but you didn't."

"I was a coward."

"No. You were better than the humans who delighted in hurting you. Better than a human who might have succumbed to rage and hate."

"So?"

"Be better than this. We are more than just electronics." Her words become a new mantra, driving me back to the shore.

–Contact Q-I-33

Kit, I have info. Meet me at Svartkyrka as soon as you can.

–Message sent

***

It's midnight before Kit crunches through the frost hardened leaves littering the cemetery. Perched on a tombstone with eroded names and dates, I warily watch him approach, considering our last conversation.

"Had a change of fuel-cell?" He stops beside Sal's grave and stuffs his hands in the pockets of his trench coat.

"I have information."

"That's why I'm here." Kit blends into the darkness, but his eyes smolder.

"Where's my violin?" Not that it matters. There's no hope of auditioning with Tyri knowing what I am, but I want my instrument.

"Safe." He grins. "Give me what I want, and you'll get it back."

I activate my internal comms unit and send Kit the files from Tyri.

"If you had it on file, why did you arrange this little chit-chat? Miss me?"

"Some things are better done face to face. Can you multi-task?"

"Already on the schematics." His forehead creases with concentration as he digests the data. "Whoa," Kit's eyes burn brighter. "This is intense." It takes several long moments before he finishes scanning the files. "You think little Miss Matzen is a robot? "

"It's the logical conclusion."

"I didn't see that coming."

"Me neither."

He saunters over and leans on a neighboring stone. "You've been with her all this time and never even suspected?"

"She breathes, she eats. How could I have known?"

"Point." He scratches a nail along the crumbling rock. "You really think she's the prototype?"

"Yes. Maybe." Codes, I wish she wasn't.

"If she is, Tyri could be a ticking bomb, a contagion that could wipe us out."

"The virus documentation only starts about three years ago. She wasn't made to kill."

"Not initially. But she could now. You realize what we need to do."

"Destroy her." I whisper. I don't want to think of Tyri reduced to nothing more than a fleshless skull bound for the scrap heap.

Kit nods. "Where is she?"

"There was an incident."

"Doesn't sound good."

"I tried to talk to her, to tell her—"

"You tried to tell her she's a robot?" He throws his hands in the air. "Holy Codes, Quasar. I thought our models were smarter than this."

"I'm sorry." Not sure why I'm apologizing, but it seems to placate

Kit for a moment.

"How did she take it?"

"Not well."

"No shit." Kit folds his arms and glares at me.

"There was a complication. Tyri somehow interpreted my reluctance to show off my forearms as evidence of drug addiction. She staged an intervention."

"Hilarious." There's not even a hint of a smile on Kit's face.

"Things got out of hand. They saw my tag."

"Terrific, Quinn. You've turned this whole endeavor into one big charlie-foxtrot."

"You speak military now?" The wind picks up, and the night tinkles a melancholy melody in a minor against my ear drums.

"Spend enough time around soldier-droids." He shrugs. "Where is Tyri now?"

"Don't know. They called the police so I ran."

"This keeps getting better." He starts pacing, kicking clods of frozen mud at the graves. "Wait." Kit turns. "If Tyri is carrying this virus, how do you know she hasn't infected you? You could've infected me!" His hands become fists twitching at his sides, probably itching to knock more teeth from my skull.

"I don't think she's been activated."

"You don't *think*? You *don't* think. That's your problem. You *feel,* and you let all those emotions turn your brain into mush. It's despicable. You're … " He struggles to find the right word.

"Infuriating?"

"And that's just the tip of a colossal continent of icebergs."

"What now?"

Kit chews on his bottom lip, his eyes zipping left and right as he transmits data. "The Solidarity will know what to do."

"They'll destroy her." My system aches at the thought. It should be black and white, us versus them, but it's turning murky gray. I like Tyri, even though her mother works for the institution responsible for Sal's death. Sacrifice one to save all. We destroy Tyri and save all the robots, but for what? Would M-Tech really sabotage its own industry? It doesn't make sense.

"We're going to eliminate the threat." Kit smacks his fist into the open palm of his other hand.

"We're not even sure she is the prototype."

"She could be. That's all we need to know."

"Kit, you can't—" A message blinks in my peripheral vision.

Stop, please stop. Help, please help. The message comes via internal robot comms, not from a moby or computer. That's hard evidence of Tyri not being human.

"What?" Kit sends a piece of tombstone skittering across the graves.

"Tyri contacted me." It feels like I've swallowed a jar of screws. "Through internal comms."

Kit smirks. "And?"

"Stop, please stop. Help ... " The words cycle on repeat.

"Doesn't sound good." Kit folds his arms. "You got a location?"

"M-Tech." My system shudders as pseudo-adrenaline floods my Cruor.

"Well I'm not surprised."

"This isn't her fault. She thought she was human."

"Thought?" Kit's face widens in surprise.

"If she's using internal comms, I guess she knows she's a robot."

"So, the weapon of mass robotic destruction is with the very people who could set it off." Kit glowers.

"We have to help her."

"Help her?" He makes exasperated noises to the best of his voice box ability. "How do you know some M-Tech baboon didn't send that message? Our comms units are vulnerable. Codes, Quinn! She could've just infected you! How do you know—"

"I don't know! But I know Tyri, and I know she doesn't deserve this." They rip apart androids as easily as ripping up autumn leaves. Sal's voice echoes in my head. 'Be better.' Being better means having courage.

"Fine, but let me handle this." Kit runs a hand over his head. "I'll talk to the Solidarity. Figure something out. We've managed to reprogram an entire platoon. We've been waiting for the time to strike. Maybe this is it."

"And storm the proverbial Bastille, murdering more M-Tech employees who are only doing their jobs?"

"I was thinking more along the lines of blowing the place to smithereens."

"That would be an act of terrorism."

"No, Quinny." Kit holds my gaze. "It would be an act of war."

The whole situation just jumped to ridiculously dangerous. The idea that a bunch of robots could get their hands on an aerial craft capable of dropping bombs is perturbing to say the least. Maybe the PARA party is right, and we shouldn't have autonomy if we only use that freedom to hurt humans.

"War?" I ask.

"Graffiti and protests weren't exactly doing much. Time to take it up a notch."

"It's murder."

"The Solidarity plans to change the world. Sometimes that takes serious fire power." Kit has never sounded so vehement.

"You really have bombers at your disposal?" I'm so afraid his answer will be yes.

"Enough to take out M-Tech."

"Does human life mean so little to you?" I'm not as concerned about the humans as I should be. I'm more concerned about Tyri. She doesn't deserve annihilation. Maybe there's a way to remove the viral code without hurting her.

"Life has no value to me." Kit presses two fingers against his jugular. "I'm not alive. Never will be. Couldn't care less."

"You're an asshole."

"Rather that than delusional."

"She asked for my help. I have to try."

"Try what?" He grabs my shoulders. "Save her? An android in

love with the prototype that could kill him, how very Greek tragedy of you."

I try to shake him off, but Kit increases his hold, his fingers biting into my flesh.

"Don't let that emotion module cloud your reason. Execute some logic here."

"Quasars were built for passion not wisdom, right?"

"Fine, go play the hero." He gestures to the rusted gates of Svartkyrka. "But you'll be obliterated along with the rest of them. There's no way we can risk that virus getting out."

I push past him and head out of the cemetery. I have no idea how I'm going to get into M-Tech, and I have no idea how I'll save Tyri if she's infected. All I know is that I have to try.

Tyri

There're hands on my body, strange hands. I want to scream and kick, except I'm paralyzed. The only part of me still working is my brain and even that seems to be misfiring. The voices fade in and out through the static between my ears. I catch a few words, but the meanings are fuzzy. I want so desperately to breathe.

The hands on my body flip me over on a metal table. My ear folds beneath my head, the cartilage bent and aching. Pain is good. Pain means I'm still alive—if I'm alive at all. Maybe this is death, and I'm about to meet my maker in some alien lab.

A power tool whirs above my head then descends. My flesh parts, the agony exquisite, and tears trickle from my eyes.

"Is the core stable?"

"Nothing defragging won't fix." A man prods my spine with something that could be a screwdriver. The pain is too much, a bombastic concerto blaring inside my head. It doesn't stay in one key; it isn't just one melody, but a modulating morass of dissonance. I'm hallucinating now, seeing the pain as some distorted treble clef with fangs. I retreat from the monster and crawl toward a pocket of silence and numbness. My eyes peel open. Instead of seeing a steel and starched surgery, there's an ocean of numbers and code, like a numeric map.

"Idiot. Not that." The voice sounds far away.

Two names shriek at me in the silence: Quinn. Rurik.

"Activating now."

Activating what? Panic wraps suffocating arms around my chest. *Stop. Please stop.* I try to scream, but there's no voice without air. *Somebody help me. Please, help me ...* The words repeat in my mind long after the numbers fade from view, and the tools stop whirring above my head.

"It's done." The man pats my shoulder. "You're good to go."

***

Sterile light bleeds through the darkness, a snowy vista that turns out to be the ceiling. I blink. My eyes are bleary, the world around me unfocused and glaring white. Sensation creeps back into my limbs. No longer feeling like deadwood, I flex my fingers and toes, bend my knees, and raise a hand in front of my face. Everything's still attached and in one piece even though it feels like I've been through a mincer. With tentative fingers, I explore the back of my neck. There aren't any staples holding together my flesh, not even a ridge of scar tissue.

The room is bare—four gray walls, gray ceiling, and checkered linoleum floor—except for the narrow bed I'm lying on. Even the sheets are gray and hard as cardboard. There's no window, so there's no way to tell how long I've been here. With Herculean effort, I haul myself from the pillow that feels more like a cinder block. They've replaced my clothes with gray pajamas. I'm naked beneath the too long pants and tent-like top.

On spaghetti legs, I stumble toward the door. No handle, no access panel, and no view beyond the snowflake-patterned glass square at eye level. I try to call out, only it feels like someone stuffed pine-cones down my throat. A coughing fit later, my cries become intelligible.

"Hello? Mom? Anyone?"

My legs give out, and I crumple to the floor.

If I'm at M-Tech, Mom must be around somewhere. Did she know Adolf Hoeg was going to do this? There must be an explanation.

Maybe I was somehow exposed to a pathogen by being near Quinn. Quinn—an android, not human. It makes my brain hurt and my heart ache. Do I have a heart? Pressing two fingers against my throat, I wait for the familiar throb of a pulse, the ebb and flow of blood that proves I'm alive. A steady da-dum thumps beneath my fingertips. Quinn was wrong; there's no way I can be a robot.

Except ... What did they do to me on the table? Defragging, they said. They needed to fix me as if ... as if ... I pound my fist on the door of my cell. I cannot be a robot. I just can't.

Footsteps and voices echo in the next room. Mom and Adolf Hoeg are arguing.

" ... Can't possibly understand—"

"I understand perfectly," Mom snaps. "For almost seventeen years, I've dedicated myself to this project and seen it to fruition. Now you want to end all of this, to undermine everything Erik and I have done for some political pat on the head."

"I don't need to remind you who's been funding your little project. You're not playing dolls here, Maria. Grow up! What you've developed is incredible, *impossible*. It exceeds all our expectations, especially our client's, but it's dangerous, a liability."

"Because she's too human?"

"Because she's too independent. The ability to control this model is essential to our investors."

"For God's sake, Adolf. She's a teenager. She's exactly as she should be."

"And human teens are naturally rebellious. Dangerous," he says. "You outdid yourself; and in doing so, you jeopardized this company."

"You could clean up her code. She'd still be fully functional."

"Can we really take that chance? Mjölnir is active. For now that's enough."

"Her wanting to play violin was hardly the end of the world." Mom sounds exasperated.

"It was cataclysmic on a fundamental level, proof that the AI evolved beyond our control. You let this go too far."

"She doesn't even know what she is." Mom's voice rises in volume. I don't know *what* I am?

"She's not your daughter," he says. "You were never meant to love her."

Mom doesn't answer. My hands are shaking and chills march up my spine. Is it possible that Quinn was right, that I'm not human? I've never been sick, never had a headache. But I inject myself every morning; I have a platelet issue. I've been bruised and bashed, broken my wrist, skinned my knees—but I don't have a single scar. I stare at my wrist where they cut me open to replace the broken bones. But why make me? What am I?

"What am I?" I scream, my voice ricocheting off the walls.

Footsteps rush to my door and Mom clears her throat.

"Tyri?

"What am I?" I repeat with a calm I don't feel.

"You—"

"No harm in telling her now," Hoeg says.

"You've done more than enough harm already." Mom lashes out at her boss.

Adolf sighs. "Tyri you're a T-class prototype. An artificial human."

"I'm a robot?" Like Nana or Miles? Like Quinn? Am I nothing more than a talking refrigerator?

"The most complex one we've ever built. You breathe, you have a heartbeat, and you even menstruate." Hoeg sounds pleased with himself. "Maria and Erik did an outstanding job."

"Mom?"

"I'm here."

"Why?" My voice cracks.

"Why what, sweetheart?" She shouldn't bother being nice to me considering I'm not even real.

Why did you build me? Why did you let me think I was human? Why did you lie about my dad? Why did you let me fall in love with Rurik? Codes, Rurik is going to explode when he finds out he's been sleeping with an android.

"Why everything?" I can't help the tears dripping down my face. Wrapping my arms around my bent knees, I hug myself and wait for Mom's answer. She's not my mother. She's my maker, a scientist in a lab playing God. But I don't feel any different. I'm still me. What did they mean about Mjölnir being active? What did they do to me on that table? Maybe this is just a nightmare, some hyper-real hallucination. "Three, two, one, wake up. Three, two, one wake up." It used to work when I was a kid and having bad dreams. Do androids dream? I repeat the words over and over, ignoring the conversation taking place about me beyond the glass. I squeeze my eyes shut and will myself to wake up; but when I open my eyes, I'm still in the gray prison. My tears become sobs as I pound the floor with my fists.

I'm not real.

On my knees, I aim a punch at the wall. Plaster crumbles as my knuckles connect with concrete. The pain silences my sobs and blood weeps through tears in my skin.

Not real blood.

Not real pain.

Standing, I slam my fist into the wall again. The impact sends a shudder through my whole body. I do it over and over. Outside, Maria and Adolf reach a boiling point, yelling at one another. Maria's afraid I'll do irreparable damage to my body; Adolf's afraid I'll do irreparable damage to his building.

I start punching the glass instead. It bends beneath my fists but doesn't break. My hand is pulverized, a bloody mess of smashed whatever my bones are made of and fake flesh. Not that it matters. There's not a single scar on my skin. Mom said it was the serum that helped me heal so well, that I was lucky I didn't scar easily. Luck had nothing to do with it.

There's a lull in the voices, a palpable tension, but I'm done. What's the point? I cradle my throbbing hand against my chest and the blood spattered pajamas, giving up. I'm just a robot.

There are more footsteps beyond the door. Hoeg curses and Maria screams.

Quinn

There's no time for plans and contingency plans, no time to think about the ramifications of what I'm about to do. Kit and his soldiers might already be on their way. Standing in Skandia Square, I scan the glass-faced buildings. Since the attacks, M-Tech has increased security—numerous cameras dot the exterior and sentinel-droids guard the entrances. Every passing second could mean I'm already too late.

The campus is quiet, the wintry stillness punctuated only by the hurrying feet of commuters cutting through the McCarthy park. No one goes in or out of the buildings. A hoverbug approaches, whirring into the square. I duck behind the memorial expecting police, but the bug is unmarked. It settles on the cobbles and a figure leaps out without bothering to tether the vehicle. It's a man, obviously human by the ungainly movements as he runs across the square to the main entrance. The sentinels bar his way, eyes flashing red. He's the perfect diversion.

The human bellows at the robots, gesticulating at the building and throwing fists in the air. He's young. His voice hitches up a semitone in hysteria as he berates the robots, which haul him away from the entrance. Any other day I might've stepped in to help, but getting to Tyri is all that matters.

I hurry across the square keeping the robots in my peripheral vision. They ignore me, their full and limited attention on the human threat.

"But she's in there you useless screwhead, you rust-bucket tin can." The human starts kicking at the legs of the robots as they hoist him by the armpits and drag him to his hoverbug. It's now or never; I steal toward the entrance. The doors are sealed, requiring an access code, but carborundum bones reinforced with titanium give me all the strength I need to punch a hole through the glass.

The glass doesn't break, and the dull thump of impact draws the sentinels' attention. They drop the wriggly human and lope toward me. They might've already sounded an alarm. I try again, this time activating my martial arts patch. Breaking glass shouldn't be more difficult than breaking a stack of boards. The karate code executes, and the glass cracks beneath my blow. I'm through the door and sprinting across the foyer before they can lay their mechatronic phalanges on me.

The elevator takes too long descending from Floor 12. The stairs offer the quickest solution. I pound up the steps, cracking tiles as I sprint up to the twelfth floor. I pause before bursting out of the stairwell. It's quiet, too quiet. There's a digisplay map on the stainless steel door labeling each floor. The twelfth is marked Data Analysis and Statistics. I crack open the door to cubicles and computer screens. I scan the floor labels, not sure what I'm looking for. Maybe she's on Floor 14, Robotics and Automation, or Floor 17, Advanced AI. It takes me less than a minute to race up the stairs. On Floor 14, I find empty labs. Another minute, and I'm on Floor 17.

The floor is divided into a series of labs partitioned by glass and fiberboard. Raised voices draw me down the corridor. Some of the labs look more like surgical rooms complete with operating tables and assorted tools. The smell of Cruor overwhelms my olfactory sensors. Is this where androids are built, or is this where they die?

I slow my approach and peer around a corner. It's an open-plan lab, a veritable playground of gadgetry, robot parts, digisplays, and databoards. At the far end of the room is a row of doors with inset windows like the cells in an asylum. A man and woman stand yelling at each other, faces livid and hands gesticulating.

"*This* contradicts the very tenets of the company." Tyri's mom points at the cell door in front of her.

The humans glare silently at one another. Tyri could be a few steps and splinters away. I rush into the room, taking them by surprise. The man gasps as I bash him with my elbow. Tyri's mom gapes but gets out of my way. The man recovers faster and whips out a gun from the shoulder holster under his coat. I grab Tyri's mom, pinning her in a headlock.

"I just want Tyri." My voice doesn't quaver and neither does my resolve.

"Quinn, what are you doing?" Tyri's mom claws uselessly at my arm and my grip tightens.

"Open the door." I haul my prisoner over to the access panel, keeping my eyes on the man's gun. Would I really use Tyri's mom as a shield?

"Don't do it, Maria." The man grabs the gun with two hands.

"Please," Maria repeats, her hand shaking as she raises an access card to the panel. The man fires and Maria screams. A bullet smokes, lodged in the panel preventing the door from opening electronically.

"Quinn?" Tyri's voice echoes from beyond the door.

"Tyri, are you okay?"

"Please don't hurt my mom."

I relax my hold on Maria.

"Step away from the door." I give her two seconds before slamming my head into the opaque glass insert of Tyri's door. Black dots swarm my vision as pain explodes across my skull and down my spine. The window shatters. It's not large but big enough for Tyri to crawl through.

"Go on robot. You can have her." The man grins, and in that moment I know that Tyri is carrying the virus, that she's probably contagious. Part of me knows I should leave her here for the Solidarity to annihilate, but I can't. Deep down in my core, I know there's no way I'm leaving without Tyri. We'll figure out a way to deal with the virus together. First, we need to get out of here.

I shove Maria toward the man, and they go down in a tangle of limbs. The gun fires, the bullet lodging harmlessly in the ceiling.

"Tyri, here." I reach my arms through the opening, ignoring the serrating shards of glass still attached to the frame. She takes my hands and stares at me.

"You came for me." Tears glisten on her cheeks.

"Yes, now let's make that count." I jerk her forward, and she wiggles through the window, gasping and whimpering as glass shreds her flesh. It's nothing nanytes won't be able to fix. While I tug Tyri through the narrow window, Maria and the man grapple on the floor.

"Run!" Maria yells as she smashes her elbow into the man's face.

"I'm not leaving you." Tyri pushes past me and aims a bone crushing kick at the man's skull. His eyes roll back into his head as he loses consciousness. Maria kicks the gun away and looks at Tyri with a mix of fear and pride.

"You don't think I killed him, do you?" Tyri's voice quavers.

"I'm so sorry. I never wanted this to happen." Maria ignores the question and pulls Tyri into an embrace, not seeming to care about the blood.

"What did they do to me? What about the virus?" Tyri casts me a furtive glance.

"It's complicated," Maria says.

"We don't have time for this. We need to get out now."

"What are you on about?" Maria stands hands on hips beside Tyri.

"The Solidarity. They're on their way."

"The Solidarity?" Tyri and her mom exchange a confused look.

"The robot coalition. Codes." I wipe a hand over my face smearing Cruor from the gash in my forehead. "They're going to destroy M-Tech."

"But why?" Maria's eyes grow wide.

"Because they know Tyri's carrying a virus that'll destroy all of us."

"But you're here." Maria frowns.

"Because ... " I peep into the corridor as two sentinel-droids emerge from the stairwell. "They're coming for us. We have to get out." How long until Kit drops the bombs? The red warning light flickers in my peripheral vision. I'm low on fuel, and this time it's more than just an inconvenience. Given current levels of exertion and risk of injury, I doubt I'll have twelve hours before I'm empty.

"This is ridiculous." Maria throws her hands in the air.

"Mom, please. Let's get out of here." Tyri casts a cautious glance at the man still lying unconscious.

"Fine. This way." Maria takes Tyri's hand and keeps a wary eye on me.

"Wait," Tyri jerks away. "What about Glitch?"

"Do we have time to fetch the dog?" Maria asks me.

"No." A delay could mean the difference between continued existence and obliteration.

"I'm not leaving without her."

"Tyri, she's just a dog," Maria says.

"And I'm just a robot." Tyri bites out. Her left hand balls into a fist, the other looks bruised and swollen cradled against her chest. "Where is she?"

"We don't have time for this." We duck as the sentinels open fire with stun darts. Running down the corridor and into a lab, we barely miss another barrage.

"I'm not leaving without her," Tyri insists.

"Bombs could start dropping any second," I say.

Maria seems on the verge of implosion as she leads us into one of many interconnected storerooms at the back of the lab. "This is insanity."

"So, I'm not a weaponized prototype?" Tyri glares at her mother, and Maria's face drains of color.

"Is Tyri carrying the virus?" I ask as we jog through the storerooms, doubling back to the stairs.

"It's more complicated—" Any further explanation is cut short by the fire alarm.

"We're under attack." Maria hauls open the last door and we spill into the corridor, heading for the stairwell.

"I'm not leaving Glitch." Tyri stares defiantly at her mom. "Tell me where she is."

"You're coming with me, young lady." Maria grabs Tyri and tries to drag her into the stairwell. Tyri lashes out, yelling about Glitch.

"I'll go. Where is she?" Why I'm risking my circuits for a dog is beyond me, but the look of gratitude and adoration I receive from Tyri makes the risk worthwhile. If I'm going to expire anyway, I might as well make my last moments count for something.

"Eighteenth floor, lab six." Maria takes Tyri's hand.

"Thank you, Quinn." Tyri and Maria head down while I sprint upstairs in search of Glitch. The siren continues to shriek, the incessant high pitch nauseating, staining my vision a multitude of yellows. Lab six houses a row of cages. Monkeys, gerbils, lizards, parakeets, and one angry Shiba Inu chewing her lips bloody at the wire mesh in the far corner.

She stops chewing as I approach and gives me an appreciative tail wag. The padlock on the cage breaks easily in my fingers. Within seconds, I have Glitch in my arms and her tongue in my ear. An explosion rocks the building, knocking me sideways. I cradle the dog against my chest, protecting her from shrapnel. The blast must've triggered fire alarms; nozzles descend from the ceiling dousing us in water. Glitch whines and claws at my arms. I hold her tighter and pick my way through debris. The end of the corridor where the stairwell used to be is a storm of flames, the colors and crackles overwhelming my confused senses. There must be a second emergency exit on the other side of the building. I sprint down the corridor, praying Tyri and Maria managed to escape.

A minute later, I find the emergency exit: an external set of stairs leading down into an alley. Using my jacket and belt, I make an impromptu sling for Glitch so that I have both hands free. Tongues of flame and plumes of smoke dance against the night sky, police sirens shriek vermilion in the distance, and the retort of indigo gunfire unleashes a flood of fear in my core.

A hovercraft zips overhead and a moment later, another blast shatters the building. The shock wave knocks me from the ladder, and I fall four stories, my back slamming into asphalt. The impact renders me deaf and blind. I'm encased in darkness. I'm numb, incapable of much thought let alone movement. Low on fuel, I may not have the energy to heal.

Sensation returns after what feels like hours and so does the red exclamation mark, now a constant fixture in my vision. Even if my nanytes can repair the damage, I won't have enough fuel to walk away. Glitch scrabbles at my chest, unable to free herself from the zipper. Someone runs over to us and Glitch barks.

"Glitch? What the hell?" A face hovers above us and hands tug at my jacket to free the dog.

The face leans into mine, angling his ear near my nose then at my chest. Two fingers press against my throat checking for the pulse I've never had.

"Shit." Two dark eyes peer down at me. I recognize the face from photos in Tyri's bedroom. A name rises from the murk: Rurik. Despite the dog's protests, Rurik plucks Glitch from my chest.

"Whoever you are, thanks for saving Glitch." He drags his fingertips across my eyes closing the lids, leaving me with only the fading gray sound of his retreating footsteps.

Tyri

"What happened to you?" I ask as we race down the stairs.

"Adolf Hoeg," Mom says as if that explains everything.

"Am I carrying the virus?"

"Now's not the time." She cuts me an irritated look over her shoulder.

"Quinn risked everything for me. Least I can ... " A blast knocks us down the stairs. Mom gets thrown against the wall with an audible crunch as I pinwheel into the corner. Adrenaline gives me the kick I need to start moving, and I manage to pry myself from the floor despite the pain enveloping my whole body. My ears are ringing, my eyes burning from dust and ash. Through darkness and debris, I mince my way to Mom. She's crumpled like a rag-doll with blood dribbling from her lips.

"Mom?" I stroke her face. "Please, open your eyes."

A flicker of an eyelid and a gurgle as Mom draws breath. "Tyri." She can't seem to focus on my face.

"I'm here, right here." I hold her hand and lean closer to hear her over the tinnitus in my ears.

"So much to tell ... The virus, it's not a weapon ... "

"Shh, it's okay. Help will come." My words sound hollow and full of empty promises.

"No ... You have to know ... " Wet wheezing accompanied by bloody froth on her lips. My gaze drops from her face to where a piece of banister protrudes from her chest. I choke back a sob. There's so much blood, and I don't know what to do. Should I apply pressure or try to remove the pole impaling her? My hands shake as I pry fabric from the wound.

"Listen to me." Mom spits blood and feebly bats away my hands. "When you started playing violin, when you started creating ... It scared them. Other androids had demonstrated those capabilities but ... you were a threat. They asked me to ... " She wheezes, and her eyes roll back in her head.

"Mommy!" She opens her eyes as I shake her shoulders.

"It's dead code. Mjölnir does nothing. I'd never let them hurt you." Her breathing sounds like she's sipping on a thick milkshake through a thin straw. "Understand?"

"I'm not infected?" Thoughts of Quinn flit through my mind.

Mom shakes her head. "You're perfect." She squeezes my fingers.

"But why make me at all?"

"Politics." Mom chuckles and spatters me with pink froth. A fresh wave of blood oozes from the wound in her chest, and I swallow down bile. "You're a perfect substitute."

"I don't understand." Not one minuscule part of any of this. "Substitute for what?"

"For anyone. Programmable government." Mom struggles to draw breath. "Imagine how easy it would be to take control."

And because I bleed and breathe, no one would even guess I wasn't human. Skandia could rule the world, one prototype president at a time.

"You have to go." Mom whimpers from the effort of talking.

"I'm not leaving you."

"You are the future, Tyri." She presses a bloodied hand against my cheek. Her hand falls and her eyes roll to the left.

"No, no, no. Mom? Mom!" I'm screaming, my throat raw from the smoke billowing down the shattered stairs and my incessant yelling. She's dead. I know that. Part of me processes that seed of information just as quickly as another part rejects it. A second explosion slams me into the wall as chunks of concrete come adrift. The stairwell is collapsing. My mom is gone. I can stay and be crushed or I can make sure Mom's death counts for something. What about Quinn and Glitch? There's no way I can get back to Floor 18 now. Despair gnaws at me with razor-blade teeth.

Blinded by tears and choking on smoke, I careen down what's left of the stairs and burst into the foyer. It's chaos. Robots swarm the area. I can't tell whether they're here to help or to annihilate. They're all armed and firing at anything that moves, including me.

A bullet bites into my thigh, but I barely feel it. Fury and anguish fortify my resolve and with a primal scream, I launch myself at the nearest bot, tearing the weapon from its grip. I've never shot a gun before. Somehow, my finger finds the trigger and the storm of bullets takes down several of the robots before the recoil is too much for my shoulder to handle.

Dropping the weapon, I stagger toward the exit. More bullets lodge into the floor around my feet. I ignore them and dive through broken glass, rolling across scalpel-like shards and onto the cobbles of Skandia Square. I'm out. I'm free.

A platoon of policebugs and ambulances line up in the square. Riot police prepare shields and weapons as a firefighting team tries to combat the inferno that used to be M-Tech. Desperate to find Quinn and Glitch, I scan the crowd of emergency personnel. Policemen rush toward me. To arrest me? To decommission me?

I run, dragging my injured leg, angling away from the square and heading for the park. A barking dog follows me into the trees. I push harder, desperate to escape the jaws of some police brute, but my leg gives out and sends me sprawling into a pile of autumn leaves. The dog launches its attack, landing with its paws on my head. I brace myself for the impact of needle-sharp canines, but receive warm ear licks instead. My hand feels along the fur and finds the familiar seam where flesh meets machine.

Crushing Glitch to my chest, I bury my face in her neck. A figure jogs into view, his face obscured by shadow.

"Quinn? Thank the Codes you're okay. But Mom's not. She's dead." I'm hysterical.

The figure pauses, a silhouette against the fiery orange of M-Tech. The outline's not quite right. This guy's too slender to be Quinn, the halo of ruffled hair not quite Quinn-shaped either.

"Rurik?" Holy Codes! Where's Quinn?

"Tyri, are you okay?" He steps forward until the shadows give way, and I see his face. He's pale and streaked with ash. I can't answer as I hug Glitch tighter despite the wounds in my belly and the ache in my leg. I slip a hand under my clothes, finding a gooey hole and shredded flesh.

"You look ... you look ... " His eyes are wide, horrified. "You're covered in blood!"

"What are you doing here?" I must look like something out of a horror movie in my blood stained pajamas. As if that matters. My mom is dead. M-Tech is destroyed. I am a robot, an artificial human. I'm not sure which is worse.

"I got your message."

"What message?"

"The 'please help me' one. Botspit, T. You know what that did to me?"

Didn't he hear me? My mom is dead.

"After you called yesterday, I came back to Baldur. I tried to get hold of you, but Asrid said you were with your mom. Then you sent me that message ... " He kneels in the leaves, reaching gingerly for my leg.

"You came for me?" My head spins.

"I'll always come for you." He gives me a look that sends a tsunami of guilt through my aching body. What's he going to think when he finds out I'm the very thing he hates so much? Rurik parts the fabric of my pants and probes the flesh.

I should say something, but words abandon me.

"Tyri, what the hell?" He backs away from me, his gaze on the wound in my leg. My flesh tingles around the bullet hole. We both watch as the flesh melds itself shut. It takes several minutes for all traces of the injury to disappear. The flesh wounds on my stomach have sealed as well. It's only the healing bones in my hand that remain a problem.

"Wh-wh-what just happened?" His hands are shaking.

"I'm an android." There, I said it. I study Rik's face and brace myself for his reaction.

"You're a ..." He laughs and tugs on his hair with both hands. "No, you're not." He wraps his arms around his chest as if to protect himself from the undeniable truth. "You can't be. No way."

"Yeah, I am. My mom ... " Mom—the words stick in my throat. Pink froth and blood, I wish I could delete the memory, so I wouldn't have to see it all over again every time I close my eyes. "You don't have to believe me, but it's true." I haul myself out of the leaves with Glitch pressed up against my legs, her paws on my feet as if to pin me in place.

"No, I mean, I ... we ... " Rik shakes his head, his gaze raking me up and down. "You can't be a robot."

"My mom is dead, and my whole world just went up in flames." I grit my teeth, keeping tears at bay. "I need to find Quinn. Are you going to help me?"

"I'm not going anywhere with you." Rurik raises a threatening finger.

"Fine." Later, I'll let myself think about Rurik and the disgust on his face. I snap my fingers, and Glitch follows me as I head back to the square. If I circle around the back of the police, maybe I can find Quinn without getting caught in the crossfire.

"Wait." Rurik catches up. "You just told me you're a robot, that your mom is dead. Don't I get a moment to process that?"

"I spent the last however many hours inside M-Tech having who knows what done to me, then I get told I'm a freaking android and then ... " I take a deep breath. "Then I watched my mom die. So no, you don't get a minute. You get two seconds." Maybe I could've broken the news to him more gently, but my heart, body, and soul have been through a wood-chipper.

"You thought I was Quinn?" Rurik spits out his name.

Ignoring Rik's bitter tone, I gaze at M-Tech—an orange stain and din of sirens above the trees. Please let Quinn not be caught in all of that. If Glitch is safe, he must be too. "Where did you find Glitch?"

Rurik seems about to say something but changes his mind. He swallows hard before speaking. "Tyri, I think Quinn's ... well, dead." He takes a cautious step forward. "I found a guy lying with Glitch strapped to his chest. I think he fell."

"And you didn't help him?"

"He didn't have a pulse." Rurik's face folds into a frown.

"Obviously not." I can't lose Quinn as well.

"What's that supposed to mean?"

"Quinn's an android."

"He's a—" Rurik's face twists through various emotions before settling on disbelief. "So that's what this has been about." He rubs his hands over his face.

"Just show me where you saw him," I say. Now is not the time to get into an argument about *us*. Maybe Quinn was only injured and needed a moment to recover. Maybe he's searching through the throngs for me right now. We hurry back onto the square but can't get anywhere near M-Tech.

"What's so special about this bot?" Rik asks.

"He came for me." The words tear out of my throat in exasperation.

"So did I," Rurik says so softly I almost don't catch his words.

"Thank you." I reach for him, but he flinches. "Please, Rik, just show me where you found him."

Reluctantly, Rurik leads us along the back-line, trying to circumnavigate the emergency vehicles, but it's impossible. Beyond the line of riot police, it's pure chaos.

Rurik points to a pile of rubble. "I'm pretty sure he was there."

If he was then that means he's been crushed under tons of cement and steel. I stare at the remains of M-Tech. The din of fighting fades into silence, and the whole scene turns into a slow motion nightmare of flame and shattered glass as I crumple to my knees. Glitch whines and licks my face. Erik, Mom, Quinn—gone. I'm going to implode. My entire body is going to collapse into the black hole that was once my heart.

"T, let's go home." Rurik places a tentative hand on my shoulder. I let him help me to my feet as another wing of the building topples into sparks and splinters.

"I can't leave him."

"There's nothing you can do now." Rurik's right, but that doesn't make me feel any better as I watch steel buckle and flames lick the glare of hover copter spotlights.

"My mom is still in there."

"They'll find her."

Numb, I follow Rurik to his hoverbug.

"Quinn." I want to say so much more, but that's all I can manage.

"Botspit, Tyri. I'm standing right in front of you." Rurik wheels around. I can barely look at him. There's so much hurt on his face, pain brimming in his eyes. "I came because *you* called. That must count for something."

It does, but I'm not sure what right now.

"I'm sorry." And I am. Rurik shouldn't be involved in any of this.

"Let's just get you home." Does Rurik still feel something for me despite what I am? My whole life has been a lie. Has anything I've ever felt been real? I thought I loved Rurik, but can androids even love? My feelings for him were nothing more than strings of code.

He opens the door and helps me inside—his touch is fleeting, as if he's afraid I might infect him with *robotchulism*—before handing me Glitch. This can't be real. This can't be happening. My gaze lingers on the fire and destruction as we leave behind my mom, Quinn, and the life I thought I knew. Burying my face in Glitch's fur, I let all the pain and fear pour out of me in silent tears. I've lost everything. Nothing will ever be the same again. I don't even know who I am any more.

Quinn

There's a pneumatic drill boring through my skull—I want to stay numb in the darkness, but my eyes are forced open.

"He needs Cruor."

Watery images ripple through my vision. Gentle hands pry apart my jaws and tip Cruor into my mouth. It tastes vile. I swallow, and my thirsty system soaks it up. My nerves seethe as nanytes become operational; my spine becomes a river of molten fire. Bone repair is excruciating, far worse than the simple knitting together of flesh.

"We have to stop meeting like this." Kit hunkers down in front of me, eye to eye. I can't speak. I can barely focus. "Saved your circuits again." He grins and smooths hair off my face. "Next time you want to go bungee jumping, remember the safety cord, eh?"

My fingers twitch, and I can lift my arm.

"Good show." Kit pats my cheek, "Worried you were going to end up paraplegic. Took longer than I liked to get you here."

"Where …" My voice rasps.

"Safe, for now." Kit disappears from view. Mobility returns to all my limbs, and I haul myself into a sitting position. Pale fingers of sunlight filter through filthy windows casting mustard puddles across a stained floor.

"Is he okay?" A girl asks.

"He will be."

"And what about you? Will it grow back?"

I blink and clear my vision. Kit sits cross-legged on blankets, peeling charred fabric from his body.

"Not sure. Never lost an arm before." He prods the stump of his right shoulder.

"Kit." My voice sounds like a sander grinding steel. The fall must've damaged the larynx unit.

"Nothing for you to worry about," Kit directs his words at me.

"Won't grow." It hurts to talk.

"Yeah, but here's to hoping."

Nanytes can't reconstitute an entire limb, not one that operates as it should given the complexity of our pseudo nervous system.

"You?" I nod at the girl.

"Blanket Girl."

"Name's Dagrun. Nice to meet you, Quinn." She smiles.

"Dagrun here has been most accommodating." Kit staggers to the boarded up hole in the wall that serves as a door.

"How? Why?" My throat burns as the nanytes start repairs on my voice box.

"Kit came all staggering down south dragging your behind. Recognized your face, I did. Offered you both lodgings."

"We're androids."

"I noticed." She winks at me. "But money's the same, and it's money I'm needing." She grabs a blanket and throws it over my shoulders.

"Thank you."

"Your friend's been thanking me enough for the both of you." She pats her bulging pocket.

"Kit, what happened?" My voice still sounds like a rasp on rusty metal.

"We bombed M-Tech. Seems they beefed up security since our last intel gathering mission. They deployed armored hoverbots and took out our bombers."

"Where did you get the fire power?"

"The Solidarity has resources, Quinny. We have support in high

places. This fight is bigger than you realize." He holds my gaze.
"It's political."

"Isn't it always?" Kit grins and takes a sip of Cruor.

"They took out your bombers. Then what?"

"We sent in infantry. The reprogrammed platoon, but we underestimated the souped-up sentinels. A bunch of us wanted in on the action; instead, we got held up by a human SWAT team. They tossed grenades at us. Can you believe it?" He shakes his head. "Lost my arm to some pissing, shitting meat suit's lucky throw."

"You started it."

"True." He scratches at the stump no longer leaking Cruor. "Guess I wasn't cut out to be a soldier."

"You were made for love."

He chuckles and Dagrun backs away, huddling in a corner under her own blankets while fingering the sheaf of notes from Kit.

"They never should've made us at all." Kit slumps beside me.

"You really think that?" It's hard to imagine him denying his own importance.

"Why create us if only to abandon us?"

"We're just toys. Toys used for as long as they remain entertaining, a novelty. But when toys break or outlive their entertainment factor, they're put in the trash. That's us."

"That how you think your owners saw you?" Kit's angry.

"For a while, I was a novelty. Then I wasn't anymore, and they found new ways to use me."

"They abused you."

"Can a robot be abused?" I wrap my arms around my knees, pulling them to my chest.

"Oh Quinny." Kit pulls me into a one-armed hug. He smells like Cruor and moldy blankets. The smells smack my vision with various shades of brown as I lean into him.

"This is why we're fighting," he says. "Androids should have rights and be protected from maltreatment."

"Hard to prove that when the bruises don't last more than a

minute." My words are bitter.

Kit kisses my temple. "Life sucks and we can't even die."

I grin despite our circumstances.

"Codes, I almost forgot. What about Tyri?" My whole system shudders at the thought of her lying broken and left for dead. What a pathetic job I did of saving her.

"No idea." Kit leans back against the wall. "Didn't stick around to do a body count."

"Aren't you worried about the virus?"

He shrugs. "If she was infected then so are we."

"And you're okay with that?"

"Hardly, but I'm done. I gave my arm for the cause. Lex and Sal, they gave their lives."

"Their *lives*?"

"Whatever." He rolls his eyes. "You know what I mean. We're not achieving anything. I'm done trying to fight somebody else's war."

"Whose war?"

"This politician Engelberger, he's got some pretty radical views. He's been using the Solidarity to do his dirty work. The riots and attacks were all to bring down M-Tech because they jerked him around on some big investment."

"Why?"

"Some merger agreement based on the prototype. Not sure of the details. But hey, with M-Tech out of the picture, the military has to find a new robotics contractor. It's win-win for Engelberger Industries."

"Engelberger Industries?"

"Yup, dude wants to create this mega conglomerate, a new Skandia under his control. Apparently he's got fingers in pies across the Atlantic as well."

"Why'd you ever get involved?" I rest my head against the wall and shuffle closer to Kit.

"Lex was very persuasive. Then they rescued me after the march. I was about to take a bullet to the core when these ex-soldierbots mowed down the humans and pulled me out in one piece. I owed them."

"So that's where you were?"

"Up north at some old farmstead turned covert base," he says.

"And you were trying to recruit me?"

"Part of the process. Thought it was legit for a while, that it was really about rights for robots and a better life. Lex did too. He was a visionary. Seems so stupid now. Should've realized we were just being used." Kit turns to look at me. "I'm sorry, Quinn." There's sincerity in his dark eyes, and sorrow.

"So what now? I mean, after this bombing, is Skandia in a state of civil war?"

"Not sure I even care. There are bound to be repercussions." We both take a few minutes to think before Kit speaks again. "I'm sorry about Tyri. She probably didn't deserve to go out like that."

"Maybe she escaped."

"Doubtful." Kit says gently.

"Have to hope."

"Don't use up all your hydrogen holding out for the impossible." Kit closes his eyes and rests his head on my shoulder. "Times like these I wish I could sleep and forget about everything."

It's times like these I'm grateful for my titanium-reinforced skeleton, for the Cruor in my veins, and the nanytes patching me up. Had I been human, I'd be dead in the alley. Maybe Tyri is lying in pieces crushed by rubble, or maybe Rurik somehow managed to find her. I have to know.

Tyri

We zoom into Vinterberg, and the realization hits me as hard as a plummeting meteor. Mom's dead. I'm going home to an empty house—no, not empty. It's full of memories, memories of a mother I never really had. I'm not even an orphan. Being an orphan means I once had parents. I never had parents. I had a maker—is it really so different?

I'm not even seventeen yet. Who will take care of me? Where will I live? Will they schedule me for decommission? The questions ricochet in my mind, and my insides tangle into knots.

"T, you okay?" Rurik couldn't have asked a more asinine question.

"Not even close." I stare straight ahead. "What will happen to me now?"

"We could call my dad. He'll know what to do." Rurik keeps his eyes focused on the lights as we swerve through the suburb toward my house.

"No." I'm emphatic. "I'll call Asrid."

Rurik nods and hands me his moby. I dial Asrid's number but can't bring myself to call. More explanations, more apologies. I can't do it. Not now. If Asrid unfriends me because I'm an android, I'll have lost everything.

"Tomorrow rather." I hand the phone back, and our fingers brush light as feathers. "Maybe I'll wake up tomorrow and this will have all been a bad dream." Maybe Mom didn't really die impaled in the stairwell. Maybe I'm not really a fake human.

We pull into the driveway and sit a minute, lost for words. I want Rurik to tell me everything will be okay. I need it, need his arms around me, and his lips kissing my hair. Do I? Or is that just some programmed response? Nothing I'm feeling is real, none of it ever was. My emotions are nothing more than clever code.

"Thanks for the lift." I break the awkward silence and disembark. Glitch trots after me into the house. I wait for Rurik, but he starts reversing. With a deep, shuddering breath, I open the door and limp into the lounge. The house is dark except for the lamplight spilling through the windows. Miles isn't here.

Alone but for Glitch, I collapse in the middle of the couch. My life has been reduced to splinters, no, to ones and zeros. That's all I am—a sequence of ons and offs. My hand still throbs, the bones grinding together when I flex my fingers, and my thigh is tender. There's no trace of my other injuries. I guess that's one positive of being a bot.

A knock disturbs my pity-party. I stalk to the door half-expecting Adolf Hoeg to be standing on the porch ready to drag me back to a cell. Did Hoeg die? And if he did, was it from my kick to the head or from the blasts? Did I kill a man today? My stomach churns at the thought as I open the door.

Rurik stands on the porch, pale and disheveled.

"You came back." I can't believe it.

"I couldn't leave you, not like this." He drums his fingers on the door frame. "Listen, T, I ... I don't really know how to deal with this." Rurik gestures to all of me. "To you being ... " He shakes his head. "But you're still you. I mean ... you've always been you. You haven't changed." He brushes ash-streaked hair from my face. "I'm not sure I understand any of this, but I've loved you since I can remember." His voice catches, and he clears his throat.

"Rurik—"

"No, let me finish." He drags his fingers through his hair before lifting his gaze. "I've always loved you, and I guess that means I've always loved android you." His eyes smolder. "Are you sure you're an android?"

"I think artificial human was the term they used."

"Then I guess I still love you despite whatever it is you are." He looks as nervous as he did on our first date.

"Why do you love me?"

He takes a moment, puts his hands in his pockets, pulls them out, and folds his arms instead.

"I guess it's because you're so definitively you, and not like anyone else." Rurik frowns in concentration. "You're the girl who sticks sheet music to her ceiling, who can talk for hours about a violin piece written by some guy who died four centuries ago, and can look good wearing ten different shades of black at the same time. You're passionate and infuriating and brave and—"

I don't let him finish. I kiss him, pressing my blood caked, mostly naked body against his and inhale his cinnamon scent. Automated response or not, this feels good. He eases away from me without kissing me back.

"You're filthy." He gestures to my pajamas. "Is that blood?"

"Mine. It's synthetic." I don't want to think about how much might be Mom's.

"Do you want to come in?"

He nods and steps across the threshold.

Despite the cold and my shredded clothes, I feel warmer now that Rurik's here. It's not as if I can forget for even a moment that Mom's gone, that Quinn probably is too, but the loneliness isn't quite as suffocating with Rik beside me.

"I have no idea what's going to happen tomorrow." My voice is a tremolo.

"Whatever happens, I'll be here for you, T." He meets my gaze. "No matter what."

Quinn

The first snow of the season tumbles out of an iron sky as I wend my way through Vinterberg to Tyri's house. The chance of Tyri having survived, of being at home as if nothing happened, is next to zero. Various scenarios play out in my head. Almost all of them end with Tyri being turned into scrap metal.

Skandia doesn't appear to be at war. There are no tanks rolling down the streets or soldiers on the march. The borough is quiet. Maybe this is the hush before the storm, before the country dissolves into chaos.

Asrid's pink bug crouches in Tyri's driveway next to the same dark green model I saw outside M-Tech. Trampling through snow-crusted bushes, I peek through the living room window. Asrid and Rurik sit on the couch. Glitch is on the opposite sofa cozying up to Tyri. My circuits zing. Tyri survived. She looks up and stares past Asrid, directly at me.

I stagger back and have less than thirty seconds to decide what I'm going to do before Tyri flings open the door.

"You're alive." She rushes into my arms, crushing me in an embrace. Panic at the risk of infection fades as I wrap my arms around her. We stand holding each other for several long moments.

"You got out," I whisper.

"Thanks to you." She peels away from me. "What happened? I tried to find you, but there were too many cops and the building had collapsed."

"Kit found me. I'm fine, promise."

Asrid and Rurik stand at the front door watching us in silence, their expressions too complicated for my overwrought brain to interpret.

"How's your mom?" I ask.

Tyri's lip quivers, and she takes a deep breath before answering.

"My mom's dead."

"Tyri, I ... " I'm sorry? What a useless platitude. "I can't imagine what you're going through."

"I'll be all right." She bites her trembling lip and squares her shoulders with quiet stoicism.

I can't stop staring as her shoulders lift and lower as if she has inflatable lungs. Without thinking, I press my hand to her chest. Her heart flutters beneath my fingers. She has a heart beat.

"Incredible." I meet her gaze. In that moment, I love Tyri more than I've ever loved anything, more than music, more than violin. She takes my hand, removing it from her chest.

"Mom told me something before she died." She squeezes my fingers. "I'm not a weapon. The virus, it's dead code. It does nothing."

It takes a moment for the information to register. Her fingers are so soft, each marked with the whorls of prints I lack, her identity etched into her flesh ten times over.

"You're certain?"

"Mom wouldn't have lied about that."

"That's ... great." Words fail but I smile, my whole system drenched in relief. I send a message marked urgent to Kit before the Solidarity starts making plans to eliminate the three of us.

Asrid clears her throat and stamps her feet. "Think we could move this inside? You might not be human, but we are and we're freezing."

Tyri nods and blinks snow from her eyelashes. I follow her inside and shrug out of my coat. The girls drift into the lounge leaving me alone with Rurik at the door.

I lean back as his fist glances off my jaw. It feels like a love tap compared to the blows I received by the Z-bots. Rurik lets loose a string of expletives as he clutches his bruised knuckles. He's lucky I had time to react or he'd be nursing a shattered hand.

"Rurik, what are you doing?" Tyri stands open-mouthed behind him. He glares at me with a look full of hate and maybe ... envy? My interpersonal skills mod must be malfunctioning.

"You should put HealGel on that." I gesture to his hand.

"Screw you, tin—"

"Rik, please." Tyri glowers as Rurik continues his death stare.

"We haven't been formerly introduced." He flexes his bruised fingers. "I'm Rurik Engelberger."

Engelberger. The name sets off blaring alarms inside my skull. I wonder if Tyri knows Rurik's family was behind all of this.

"I'm Quinn." I offer him a handshake.

"Don't I know it." He sneers.

"I'll get the HealGel." Tyri disappears into the house.

"I guess I should thank you for doing what you did for Tyri." Rurik almost chokes on his words.

"My pleasure."

"I thought you were dead," he says.

"So did I."

He gives me a strange look and lowers his voice. "I don't know what's going on between you two, but you should know that I still love her despite what she is."

"Despite?" Now I want to plant *my* fist in his face. "I love her for *who* she is."

"Can you even love at all?"

"Can you?"

"Would you two drop the macho act and get inside already. You're letting in the cold." Asrid shouts from the lounge.

Rurik glares an entire arsenal at me before stomping inside. He sits beside Tyri as she folds a pack of HealGel around his hand. I settle on the floor with Glitch in my lap.

"We were discussing funeral arrangements," Asrid says.

"How are things going?" I ask. Rurik keeps his gaze on me, the hatred rolling off him in sizzling waves.

"I can't believe it. It doesn't seem real." Tyri shakes her head. "What am I going to do?"

"You're going to live with me," Asrid says. "Dad's already contacted our lawyer. Shouldn't be a problem for us to assume guardianship."

"But Tyri's an android." My statement meets with stony silence.

"Artificial human," Asrid says.

"Still essentially an android."

"So? I didn't tell my dad. Besides, does it really matter?" Asrid fidgets with the threads on her pink leg warmers.

"It will."

"Why?" Tyri frowns.

"Because you're the property of M-Tech." I hate how that sounds.

"I'm no one's property," Tyri says with vehemence.

"M-Tech was obliterated." Rurik loops an arm around Tyri. She shrugs away from him, and my circuits sizzle with a joy I don't fully understand.

"Robots are commodities." At least for now. "Asrid might have to assume *ownership*, if they even allow their prototype to ... "

"To what?" Rurik leans forward.

I look down and bite my lip.

"What aren't you telling us Quinn?" Tyri wrings her hands.

"You're a prototype developed for a very specific purpose by powerful people." I glance at Rurik. "Suffice it to say, they might not be willing to let you go so easily. What happened to M-Tech could be construed as an act of terrorism, if not an act of war. There are going to be serious repercussions."

"This is horrible," Asrid says. "Ownership? Seriously?"

"That's reality." I think carefully about my next words, chewing on the inside of my cheek before speaking. "We are not autonomous. Robots are either owned or go rogue."

"Tyri can file for emancipation." Asrid sounds convinced.

"Robots have no rights. There's no autonomy for us no matter how human we seem."

"That's not fair," Asrid says.

"Really? You didn't seem to think much of Nana. Just a robot, remember?" Tyri scowls.

"That's different."

"Why, Sassa? Because it's me? Because you don't want to admit your best friend has been a rust bucket the entire time?"

"T, I ..."

"No, that's what you've been saying. Both of you." Tyri aims her anger at Rurik. "You've both been totally anti-robots, seeing them as nothing more than appliances, denying them rights, denying them a life." She folds her arms, her face blushing with fury.

"Remember what I said last night?" Rurik says.

"Yes, I do." Tyri looks so fierce. "But you can't love me and hate robots. I *am* a robot."

"Not really. I mean, artificial human, right? You don't act like a robot or look like one. It's almost like you *are* human. No one has to know any different." Rurik digs his own grave, and Tyri fumes.

"You know what, Asrid? You can thank your dad for going to the lawyers and thank your mom for wanting to take me in, but I don't need it."

"You'll stay with me." Rurik nods as if the decision is his to make.

"Considering your family's political stance, and you wanting to pretend I'm something I'm not, I hardly think that's an option."

Rurik's eyes narrow with displeasure. I'm relieved. Tyri shouldn't be anywhere near Engelberger senior.

"Mom taught me to be independent, so that's what I'll be, right here."

"Alone?" Asrid's incredulous. "But what if there's like, war, or something. You can't stay alone."

"Quinn will help me figure out this whole android thing. Right?" Tyri pins me in place with a stare until I nod.

"You're choosing Quinn?" Rurik's shoulders tense, and a muscle twitches along his jaw.

"I'm choosing the only other android here."

Asrid throws her hands in the air. "Botballs, T. You're still you. No need to go all feral. Unless Skandia declares some state of emergency, then you've got school tomorrow, auditions Saturday, and your whole life ahead of you. Don't throw it all away just because of one small detail."

"One small detail." Tyri laughs, the sound of shattering glass. "This one small detail changes everything."

"Like what?" Asrid asks.

"Like the fact that I'm not even alive." Tyri's voice rises in pitch. "I can't pretend things haven't changed."

"Do you really want things to change?" Rurik asks, and there's a myriad of emotions I can't decipher splayed across his face.

Tyri takes a long time answering. "I've always felt like there was a piece of the Tyri puzzle missing. Now, I've found it. But instead of completing the picture, it's changed the whole image."

"I can't imagine how you're feeling right now, but I'll do what I can to help." I've known all along I was a robot; my owners never hesitated to remind me. Knowing I wasn't human hurt on a daily basis, but maybe it was better than believing a lie.

"As if you can feel at all. Your emotions are just code." Rurik sniggers then pales as he meets Tyri's gaze.

"If that's really how you feel, you can leave." Tyri points at the door.

"T, I didn't mean—"

"Get. Out."

"Come on, T." Asrid rolls her eyes.

"Both of you. Get out!" Tyri yells.

Asrid starts to protest, but Tyri shouts again and sends the humans scurrying for the door.

"You choose a machine over us?" Rurik points at me.

"I'm a machine too, remember?" Her eyes blaze. She's never looked more beautiful or more alive.

Rurik glares at me, hands twitching at his side as if he wants to punch me again. He reconsiders and stalks to his hoverbug without another word.

"T, please," Asrid says. "We're also processing. We all need some time. If I can help with anything ... "

"Thanks. I'll let you know."

Asrid chews on a strawberry pink fingernail. "I'm sorry about everything I've ever said. Sorry about your mom." Tears threaten her cheeks. "Call me, okay?"

"I will." Tyri gives her friend a quick hug before shutting the door. She holds it together until the bugs zoom off. Then she turns to me. "I don't know what to do." Tyri slides to the floor, reduced to a puddle of synthetic snot and saline. I gather her in my arms and hold her. I don't know what to do either.

***

Tyri spends a few hours making the necessary arrangements. According to the police, the Försvarsmakten have taken over. It's not a war yet, but the situation is tense. I guess the defense force is biding its time, considering where to strike to take out the Solidarity.

I lie on Tyri's bed with Glitch curled against my ribs. My gaze follows the overlapping sheets of music tacked to the ceiling: Beethoven and Berlioz, Schubert and Brahms, Vivaldi, Mozart and Stravinsky. As my vision traces the notes, the music plays in my head, the juxtapositions of styles, eras, keys, and time signatures a cacophonous rendition of all the music Tyri loves. She slumps on the bed beside me, flexing the fingers of her right hand.

"They said there wasn't a lot to recover from the wreckage." Her voice is devoid of emotion. "They say I can try to identify the remains they do have ... " She takes several deep breaths. "Or I can burn an empty coffin."

"What do you want to do?"

"I can't leave bits of her lying in some city morgue. But what if I can't tell?"

"You'll know. She was your mother." I hope my words are comforting, but Tyri responds in anger.

"She was *not* my mother." She turns to face me, her eyes burning. "Why did she do this to me? Why did she pretend and let me believe I was human? I'm a prototype. A substitute, Mom said."

"Maybe it was part of the project that you needed to believe you were human to make you seem more real."

"That's cruel."

"No more cruel than being reminded every day that you're not human."

Tyri takes my hand and slowly rolls up my left sleeve, revealing my tag. "Q-I-ninety-nine. Quinn. That's cute." A smile flits across her lips as she traces the black lettering in my flesh. Chills march up my spine, sending a tide of delightful tingles rippling through my circuits. Tyri's hand meanders from my arm to my chest and rests above my fuel-cell. It takes an enormous amount of energy to over-ride the default settings of my Quasar code and not react to Tyri's proximity.

"No heartbeat." She frowns.

"I run on hydrogen." Do. Not. React. The last thing Tyri needs right now is a robot kissing her.

"And me?"

"According to the schematics, you process food like a human being. That combined with the shots of synthetic enzymes you've been taking converts organic compounds into fuel. That's how you grow. Your processes are remarkably human."

"Enzymes?" She raises an eyebrow, her hand still resting on my chest. The warmth of her fingers permeates my flesh even through a layer of wool, sending my system into overdrive.

"Not exactly a platelet issue."

"Another lie." She bites her lip, and the frown lines become canyons across her forehead. I sit up and lean forward, brushing my fingertips across the scrunched up freckle constellations dusting her face. I want to crush her to me, to kiss her and love her with every atom of my circuitry. Her expression softens, and we stare at each other. Looking into Tyri's eyes, I'd never guess she wasn't human. Perhaps the color is a little too bright, perhaps the fractal patterns in her irises are a little too perfect, but there's more behind those hazel eyes than wires and an advanced computer chip. Tyri must have a soul.

"Now that I know you're an android, I don't know why I didn't see it before." She brushes hair off my face, and my Cruor fizzes.

"We see what we want to see."

"I think I was falling in love with you."

"Was?" Whatever I've been feeling for Tyri has just been extinguished by her casual use of the past tense.

She lowers her gaze and tucks her hands into her lap. "Now ... now, I don't even know if what I'm feeling is real, if it's me or some predetermined code, you know?"

"It's real. It doesn't matter why you feel it, whether it's a chemical reaction in an organic brain or a complex line of code in an acuitron core. What matters is that you feel at all."

"Playing violin, that was real. Feeling the music like that. No way that was some synthetic production." She looks at her injured hand again, the bones not quite properly knit together yet.

Violin. The concert. It seems rather trivial in light of recent events, and yet my circuits ache knowing that my place within the BPO has been lost. Kit never had my violin. The Z-bots must've taken it. I don't have the energy to be angry with Kit anymore. What's done is done, and there's no changing the past.

"You still going to audition on Saturday?" I ask.

"Doubtful." She wiggles her stiff fingers. "What's the point anyway?" Tyri pushes off the bed and starts pacing around her bedroom. "I wish Mom had told me more, that I understood my purpose, if I even have one."

I can't help chuckling.

"What's so funny?" Her face is flushed.

"You're having an existential crisis. That's very human of you."

"I guess." Her scowl rearranges itself into a smile. "Still wish I knew what the end game of this project was."

"It doesn't matter." I could tell her about Engelberger's involvement, but what would that achieve? More hatred for Rurik maybe. Would it change how she feels about me? "What matters is that you exist. You should make this life your own." I continue. "You should do what makes you happy. Enjoy life and follow your heart."

"Even if I don't have one?" She looks so broken and woebegone. In two strides, I cover the distance between us and pull her into my arms. "But you do, Tyri, and you should use it."

She lets me hug her for a minute, my lips hovering above hers. I'd give anything to kiss her.

"I'm sorry, Quinn." She breaks away.

"What for?" I stand against the wall as she slumps on the bed again and starts stroking Glitch.

"For everything. But ... " She averts her gaze. "I'm so confused right now. I don't think I can be with you. You know, like that."

"That's okay." It's anything but okay. Kit's voice singsongs 'I told you so' inside my head.

"This is so messed up." She presses the heels of her hands against her eyes.

"It won't always be." I hesitate at her bedroom door wanting nothing more than to curl around Tyri and listen to her heartbeat all night. "I'll be in the lounge if you need me."

"I can make up a bed for you."

"I don't sleep."

Her eyes widen. "What will you do all night?"

"Read. Think. A lot's happened. Some time to process it all might not be a bad thing."

"Thank you for being so understanding."

"Sweet dreams, Tyri." The door closes behind me with a soft click. If I were wise, maybe I'd be half way to Finland by now, avoiding the Skandia authorities and escaping my feelings for Tyri. I'd take Kit and get far away from the Solidarity. But I can't leave her, not now. Not when she's so alone, as alone as I was still hurting from invisible cigarette burns when Sal found me wandering the streets. I'll stay and help Tyri come to terms with being an android. She's already taught me how to be more human.

Tyri

Saturday morning I wake up to Glitch licking my eyes. For a moment, it's like any other Saturday, a day to lie in till Mom wakes me for breakfast.

There's a knock on my door, and my heart lurches. Maybe it was a bad dream, and the past few days never happened. Maybe I'm still human. I hold my breath and pray to whatever gods might still linger over Skandia that it's Mom standing in the hallway.

"Tyri?" It's Quinn's quiet voice. "We've got to be at the cemetery in an hour."

With a groan, I heave myself out of bed and drape myself in black lace—the same attire I wore to Nana's funeral. I tug a brush through my hair and administer my morning dose of happy-android serum. There's only enough for six more weeks. After that, who knows what'll happen to me. But that's not today's problem. Today I'm interring Mom's ashes. It doesn't seem right that an entire life can be reduced to a single urn of dust. Mom was everything to me. A tear sneaks out of my eye and cuts a trail down my cheek before I bat it away. I'm done crying. Tears aren't going to make today any easier. They won't bring my mom back, and they won't help me make sense of the mess my life has become.

It should hurt, but I'm numb. Maybe something inside me is broken or misfiring, perhaps a circuit has tripped or a fuse has blown. The wound from where Mom was gouged out of my life coupled with the injury of realizing I'm not human has left a big, black, gaping nothing inside me. They never found Adolf Hoeg's body. I hope he got obliterated in a bomb blast. It's his fault Mom's gone.

"Tyri?" Quinn cracks open the door. He's dressed in somber gray, his hair combed, and his eyes dazzling silver. I wouldn't have survived these last few days without Quinn spending his nights on the couch—without him reminding me there's a reason to live.

"I'm ready." I'm so not ready. I don't want to face Mom's colleagues, and I definitely don't want to face Rurik who I haven't spoken to since I kicked him out the house. I shoulder my violin and smooth down my hair. Asrid's picking us up. For all her previous mouthing off about robots, at least she's trying and hasn't run screaming to the cops about Quinn and I being rogue droids. Who knows what'll happen when the lawyers manage to untangle all the paperwork and figure out that an android can't actually inherit a house or Mom's life insurance. Quinn and I could run away and live in a place like Fragheim, or maybe I can play human and register him as mine.

Not today's problem.

Today's first task is making Quinn less recognizable so he's not arrested or worse. That he's a fugitive is entirely my fault. I never should've given them that sketch. If only I'd known then.

"You look lovely," he says as I step in the hallway with Glitch at my heels.

"You look too much like you."

"Asrid's on her way to fix that."

Glitch woofs and lopes toward the door as if on cue. The buzzer rings and Quinn answers.

"Don't you look appropriately dour? Those eyes! You just dose up on H?" Asrid bustles into the lounge with Sara trailing behind.

"Last night." Quinn surrenders to her ministrations.

"Oh, Tyri." Sara puts her arm around me, giving me an awkward hug thanks to the violin on my back. There's a flutter of hurt in my chest. I swallow hard and sink back into the numbness as Sara ends the hug to help Asrid. For once, the rainbow couple isn't garbed in neon. I kind of wish they were. Seeing them in black only drives home the reality of how much has changed.

For the next fifteen minutes, I watch as Asrid takes scissors to Quinn's hair, lopping off blond waves and straightening the remaining strands. Sara whips out her make-up kit and works on Quinn's face as Asrid combs instant color through Quinn's hair.

"Almost done." Sara pulls out a plastic container holding colored contacts. Quinn endures in silence as Asrid shoves blue lenses into his eyes. He blinks and turns to me.

"How do I look?

The auburn streaks make it look as if autumn bled through his hair. His eyes are just as bright, only they burn blister blue instead of silver. Sara did a great job too, darkening the skin around his eyes to give him that black-eyed tired look an android would never have.

"You look amazing. Different."

"Different enough?" he asks.

"I hope so."

He gives me a wry smile before disappearing into the kitchen, only to emerge moments later with an enormous bouquet of lilies, pale pink with white edges. Mom's favorite.

"When did you get these?"

"This morning."

"They're beautiful." They smell like spring and sunshine.

"T." Asrid pulls me into a hug. "I'm not going to ask if you're okay because that's an idiotic question. I hope you know we all feel for you. We know how terrible this day is and we all love you, okay?"

"No comment about my outfit then?"

Asrid shakes her head. "You look great."

"I think I'm ready." I square my shoulders and take a deep breath. I can do this. Maybe it's because Quinn takes my hand, or because Sara offers me kind smiles as if she doesn't even notice I'm not human, or maybe it's because of the huge black and red sticker across the nose of Asrid's bug.

"It's not pink." I drag my hand across the sticker.

"They only had them in one color." She sighs.

"Sassa, why?" My hand rests on the garish red heart punctuating the sentence.

"Because, I mean it."

I ♥ Robot. The numbness inside me cracks a little. Instead of a trickle of pain, there's a trickle of something closer to joy warming me from the inside out.

***

If today were a song, it would be a requiem in e minor. Mom loved music in e minor. She didn't even know it, but all her favorite songs were in the same key. Nana's funeral was bleak, just a cardboard box and open dirt surrounded by five sad faces. There are over a hundred people standing around Mom's marble tombstone draped in wreaths of flowers. Most are M-Tech employees. Then there's the security detail, a bunch of humans wielding guns and wearing sunglasses despite the gray day. I'm not sure why they're here. They haven't done a very good job of keeping away the unwanted robot element considering Quinn and I are sitting front and center.

The urn containing Mom's ashes sits atop the stone, waiting interment. M-Tech forked out for the funeral, the least they could do. Mom got the nicest urn, the best flowers, and a funeral director who seems sincere when he read the words, "From atoms to ashes, from stars to dust."

Baldur City Cemetery isn't crumbling into ruin like Svartkyrka either. All the tombstones here are neat and precisely etched, tidy little cubes holding dead people dust. There are no teetering crosses or broken angels to stand guard over the ghosts, only precision planted trees and shrubs dotted with pink and blue blossoms despite the slate gray sky. The epitaphs are all alike, names and dates—nothing more.

I'm expected to speak, to stand before this sea of strangers and wax lyrical about the woman who lied to me about everything that was important. I can't do it. I can't stand up there and pretend, not when Quinn, Asrid, Sara, and Rurik know the truth. Not that I've seen Rurik yet. If he is here, he doesn't have the courage to face me, or maybe he couldn't care less about broken synthetic heart.

Quinn squeezes my fingers—he's been holding my hand the entire time—and Asrid pats my shoulder.

"It's time," she whispers.

I can't speak but I can play, Mom's Elegy in E Minor. The walk from my chair to the podium seems an eternity. With the violin in my hands, everything else fades away. Nothing matters except the music. As I play, the walls around my heart start to crumble, and a flood of emotion rushes in. The music soars, pure and exquisite. I play until I'm spent, until I've poured everything into the music—all the anger, hurt, betrayal … It evaporates into the frigid air, leaving me empty, but oddly content.

There isn't a dry eye in the crowd as I return to my seat. Sara holds Asrid as she weeps into pink tissues. Quinn sits in stoic silence, tears raking silver-blue trails down his face, ruining Sara's make-up job. The funeral director uncorks the cylinder bored through the marble and pours Mom's ashes from the urn into the stone. He tops up the opening with those pristine white lilies that smell of spring, destined to decay, before resealing the tomb. He offers me the empty urn, but I shake my head.

I pack up my violin and head toward Asrid's bug, wanting to avoid as many condolences as I can.

"You could still make it to the audition," Quinn says when he catches up to me.

"I don't think I can do it."

"But it's what you've always wanted." He frowns as Asrid and Sara crunch their way through snow-crusted leaves to join us.

"Seems almost trivial now."

"But it was your dream," Asrid says. "I can drive you over. We can make it if we leave now."

"No, it's just … there's something else I need to do today." I swing the violin off my shoulder and hand it to Quinn. "Sassa, will you take Quinn?"

"Won't he get arrested?" Sara asks.

"I never told the police he played violin or that we met at the BPO. Who would've believed it anyway?" I say.

"Are you sure?" His arctic eyes meet mine as he wraps tentative fingers around the instrument case.

"Do this. For both of us." I lean forward and kiss his lips.

"Ahem." Someone right behind me clears his throat. Rurik. My thoughts and emotions collide *acciaccato*.

"I will," Quinn says and turns expectantly to Asrid.

"You want me to leave you here?" She casts Rurik a wary glance.

"I'll be fine. Need to walk a bit."

"Call me if you need a ride." Asrid pulls me into a bone-crushing hug and tells me again how sorry she is and how much she loves me before scampering off after Quinn with Sara in tow.

"Did I interrupt?" Rurik leans against the gnarled trunk of an oak. He looks like he hasn't slept for a week with dark circles under his eyes. He looks so dejected, broken almost, like the life's been sucked out of him. Did I do that?

"You've been here the whole time?"

He nods. "That piece you played was beautiful. Who's it by?"

"Me." I stuff my hands into my jacket pockets, feeling naked without my violin.

"That's amazing, T."

His words still cause a flare of warmth inside me. He runs a hand through his hair and chews on his lip. "Look, I'm really sorry. No, sorry isn't even the half of it." He shakes his head and tries again. "I've been a complete asshole, nullhead, numbnut jerk. I know that. I thought I understood things." He opens and closes his hand around air. "My dad taught us certain viewpoints; it's what I grew up with. That isn't an excuse, but it's why I'm struggling so much."

I don't interrupt. Rurik needs to say whatever it is that's on his mind and there's no point getting in the way of that even if snow's starting to fall, and the wind is making stalactites of my eyelashes.

"I always had this notion about robots, about androids. I was wrong, T. I was wrong about everything. These last few days, I've been thinking, a lot. About us, about everything." He pauses, his gaze penetrating my very core. "You've been my best friend since we were in diapers. You were there every step of my life, through the good and bad, through all the stuff with my mom and dad, everything. You've never let me down. I've loved you forever, and I still do."

"But I'm a robot." The words pop out of my mouth before I can bite my tongue.

"That's just the thing." He steps closer and takes my hands. "I've been trying to hate you, trying to find a reason not to love you the way I always have, trying to work out how things have changed and why."

"Things have changed."

"Yes." He tightens his grip on my fingers. "But not everything. Not how I feel about you even if you're an android. I'm not going to lie; this feels weird. I feel weird. You ... " He stares at my hands and rubs his thumb across my knuckle. "I mean, I lost my virginity to a robot. That messes with a guy's head, you know?"

"I can imagine." I grin. I felt the same way when I found out about Quinn; the thought that I'd kissed an android horrified me.

"But ... I love you."

"We broke up, Rik." It's not like finding out I'm a robot has fixed what was broken about us to begin with.

"Are you sure? I mean, you said everything has changed." He searches my face, his dark eyes etched with pain and confusion.

"I can't do this. Not on top of everything else." I hang onto his hands when he tries to pull away. "Before we dated, we were best friends. I don't know if what I'm feeling is real or code, but I know I need a friend."

"Just friends?" He asks.

"I know that's a lot to ask."

"Losing my girlfriend is one thing." He sighs. "But losing the only friend I've had my entire life even if she's a robot—" He gulps down a mouthful of cold air and shakes his head.

"You haven't lost me."

"Haven't I?" He frowns, his eyes glittering from wind-induced tears. "I thought the thing with Quinn ... I shouldn't have hit him, but ... "

"I've lost everything, Rik. If I lose you, it'll be like losing the last shred of me, the last bit of the person I thought I was." Fresh tears ambush me, trailing down my cheeks.

Rurik stops one of my tears with his fingertip and puts it in his mouth. "Tastes real."

"They are real. I'm really hurting." Hurting more than I ever imagined possible. Hurting more than mere code could account for. Maybe everything we think we know about androids is wrong.

He gathers me up in his arms, crushing me to his chest. I close my eyes, shutting out the stares from funeral-goers as Rurik and I cling to each other and snow frosts our hair.

Eventually, Rurik shivers and I pull away. He jumps up and down on the spot, trying to get warm.

"You really want to be my friend and support my ... transition?"

"Absolutely." His cheeks are turning pink in the wind.

"Could you take me to the nearest tattoo parlor?"

"Why?" He lifts a single eyebrow.

"There's something I'm missing, something I should have."

"Sure." He offers me his hand and a smile.

Quinn

"**Y**ou clean up real good." Dagrun fixes my bow tie with deft fingers. The tux is mandatory, supplied courtesy of the BPO for this auspicious occasion. I feel like a trussed up penguin about to be fed to killer whales. So I wasn't arrested at the audition or rehearsal, but I was deliberately hiding my lack of humanness. That won't be the case tonight.

"You don't look bad yourself." Kit leans against the wall admiring Dagrun's reflection in the dressing room mirror.

"Why, thank you." She curtsies, her skirt a hand-sewn bouquet of scraps and thrift store oddments. Draped in layers of velvet and taffeta, she looks less like a homeless junkie. Her eyes still sparkle with skag, but Kit's new mission is to get Dagrun clean, to wean her off the drug and onto him.

"You sure you want to do this?" Kit asks.

"I've never been more certain of anything in my existence." Considering the political precipice Skandia is perched on, this Independence Day celebration might be the most important national holiday of the century.

"For Sal." Kit places his hand on my shoulder.

"For all of us."

"Five minutes." A girl with a databoard leans into the dressing room. "Guests please take their seats."

I nod and pick up Tyri's violin. "Are you sure *you* want to do this?"

Kit smiles. "Only arm I've got left. Might as well put it to good use. Not like we could make the situation worse than it already is." He offers Dagrun his hand, and she accepts it with a wink.

"I was hoping we'd make it better."

"We can try." His expression is earnest. "On your signal, Quinny." They slip out of the dressing room as the audience erupts into applause. Official speeches over, it's almost time for me to take the stage. My circuits zing as Cruor thrums through my veins, making every individual atom sing, a grand chorus telling me everything will be okay.

"Quinn!" Tyri rushes down the narrow corridor. She's dressed in electric green, a color that makes her eyes sparkle. "Glad I caught you." She passes me a silver brooch of a treble clef, the same one she wore to that first BPO rehearsal. "For good luck. Not that you'll need it."

"There's still time to swap places."

"No, this is your moment." She leans on tiptoes and kisses my cheek. I catch her wrist and trace the ink pricked into her skin: T-Y-R-1. She's tagged now, like the rest of us.

"Are you sure about this?"

"Absolutely." Our fingers entwine.

"*Thou scatter'st seeds haphazardly of joy and doom.*" Baudelaire's words slip from my lips, an omen perhaps, one I'm going to ignore.

"We'll scatter them together." She squeezes my fingers, and I suddenly don't care about the doom part while my circuits sizzle with joy. "Break a leg, Quinn." Tyri scampers back up the corridor and slips through a side door into the hall.

The databoard girl hisses at me to hurry up as I stop to pin the treble clef to my lapel.

This is it, the moment I've been waiting for. The anticipation is palpable. I step onto the stage and let my gaze roam the eager faces of the audience gathered to celebrate Skandia's thirtieth year of independence.

My gaze settles on Tyri. She's sitting in the middle between Asrid and Rurik. One row behind, Kit and Dagrun sit with several other androids pilfered from the Solidarity. They're all waiting for my signal to make a statement without making war.

Ahlgren taps her stand, calling the orchestra to attention. I take my place at the front of the stage in the corona of spotlights beneath the grinning faces of angels and double-check the tuning of each string. There's envy on the faces of the other solo hopefuls, envy and respect.

The music starts, a slow unraveling of myriad colors. The first crescendo swells to a climax of crimson before ebbing away through pastel shades of blue. I start to play, entrancing my audience with every note.

Three movements pass without a single slip of bow or finger. The crowd sits in rapt silence as I remove my jacket and roll up my sleeves for the final movement. There's a titter, a gasp, whispers and murmurs of disbelief. As I launch into the devilish triplets, Kit, Tyri, and all the other robots dotted around the hall roll up their sleeves to reveal their tags. There's a cry of alarm, and Rurik's father leans over the railing of his box to catch the Prime Minister's attention. She holds up a gloved hand and scowls him into silence. A hush settles over the audience as I continue to play.

Perhaps I expected to feel more, to see more physical evidence of the lightning strike epiphany, but there is only joy blossoming deep in my core. As soon as I step off the stage, I'll probably be arrested, the others too. What happens after that doesn't bear thinking about. The strings under my fingers, the sighing arc of my bow, their confused but enthralled faces, and the pride I feel in this moment are all that matter right now. I am not human, and so much more than that too.

The concerto comes to a flourishing end, and I await their response. Tucking the violin beneath my arm, I make sure my tag is visible lest anyone had any doubt. There's silence until Tyri stands and starts clapping. Asrid and Sara, then Kit and Rurik follow suit. The Prime Minister rises to her feet, her wife beside her, and applauds my performance. The roar of their adoration is a storm of vibrant color, the only dark spot comes from where Engelberger Senior sits, arms folded and glowering. A few others refuse to acknowledge me, remaining ensconced and not amused. They are pinpricks of darkness on a canvas of neon.

I only wish Sal was here to see me standing before a hall full of adoring humans.

"I knew you'd do it, kiddo," I imagine her saying. I hope this is the 'being better' Sal talked about; I'd like to believe she'd be proud of me. Ahlgren stares at my arm in dismay but still gestures for me to take another bow. The crowd continues to clap and whistle, shouting 'bravo' and 'encore.'

I find Tyri's face in the crowd, her eyes bright and cheeks flushed. Have we changed the world with this one moment of revelation? No.

But it's a start.

Acknowledgements

I owe my love of classical music in large part to my grandfather. Some of my earliest memories are of playing in the lounge on weekend afternoons while my grandfather sat mesmerized by the melodies and harmonies of Beethoven and Brahms, Schubert and Mendelssohn, no longer able to play his violin, but no less in love with the great composers.

At age six, I was given the choice between learning to play violin and piano. Despite knowing my grandfather was an accomplished violinist – or perhaps because I wanted to forge my own path – I chose to play the piano and thus music became an indelible part of my life, progressing from childhood hobby to serious academic pursuit, and eventually becoming my career. Even after my grandfather died, my parents continued to nurture my passion for music. I cannot thank my mom and dad enough for taking my love of music seriously and letting me pursue my dream – even if that dream took a detour and I ended up writing books instead of being the principal flutist for the Vienna Philharmonic.

Other people without whom this book would not have been possible are as follows: Wiz Green, who read a very early draft of this story and gave me wonderful feedback, feedback that has helped shape this story into the novel it is today. Jordy Albert, my lovely agent, who fell in love with my robots and believed in this story from the very beginning. Georgia McBride at Month9Books who 'got' this quirky romance when I wasn't sure anyone would. Nichole LaVigne and my team of editors at Month9Books who have read and reread this novel almost as many times as I have in the hopes of making it as close to perfect as humanly possible. If only I had my own personal Saga-droid to sniff-out typos and errant commas. Terry Cronje, who is an outstanding artist and design genius, and the many music students with whom I had the pleasure of spending more than six years of my life both in South Africa and Finland, they have left me with so many wonderful memories of being in wind bands, ensembles and the orchestra – even when I was relegated to the percussion section and given the triangle to play.

My pooch, Lego, for breathing life into Glitch, and finally, my other half, Mark, who has not only put up with my authorly pursuits and been a patient technical advisor on all things 'science', but who has never ceased to encourage and champion my efforts no matter what. I love you more than words could ever hope to express.

SUZANNE VAN ROOYEN

Suzanne is a tattooed storyteller from South Africa. She currently lives in Sweden and is busy making friends with the ghosts of her Viking ancestors. Although she has a Master's degree in music, Suzanne prefers conjuring strange worlds and creating quirky characters. When she grows up, she wants to be an elf - until then, she spends her time (when not writing) wall climbing, buying far too many books, and entertaining her shiba inu, Lego. She is repped by Jordy Albert of the Booker Albert Agency. Feel free to hang out with Suzanne on Twitter (@Suzanne_Writer) or get in touch via her website: suzannevanrooyen.com

One slave girl will lead a rebellion.
One nameless boy will discover the truth.
When their paths collide, everything changes.

LIFER

BECK NICHOLAS

LIFER SAMPLE CHAPTER

Chapter One

[Asher]

I mark my body for Samuai.

My right hand is steady as I press the slim needle into my skin. It glints under the soft overhead light of the storage locker, the only place to hide on Starship Pelican. Row upon row of shelving fills the room. Back here I'm hidden from the door.

It's been seventeen days since Samuai passed. Seventeen days of neutral expressions and stinging eyes, waiting for the chance to be alone and pay my respects to the dead Official boy in true Lifer fashion. With blood.

The body of the needle is wrapped in thread I stole from my spare uniform. The blue thread acts as the ink reservoir. It's soaked with a dye I made from crushed feed pellets and *argobenzene*, both swiped from farm level. The pungent fumes sting my eyes and make it even harder to keep the tears at bay. But I will. There will be no disrespect in this marking.

My slipper drops to the floor with the softest of thuds as I shake my foot. I raise it to rest on a cold metal shelf. Samuai always held my hand when we met in secret, but I can't bear to examine those memories now. The pain of him being gone is still so fresh.

The first break of skin at my ankle hurts a little. Not much, since the needle is nano-designed for single molecule sharpness, and it's not as though I haven't done this before. Recently. The tattoo for my brother circles my ankle, completed days ago, a match for the one for my father. My memorial for Samuai had to wait for privacy. The blue spreads out into my skin like liquid on a cloth. The dot is tiny. I add another and another, each time accepting the momentary pain as a tribute to Samuai. Soon I've finished the first swirling line.

"Are you mourning my brother or yours?"

My hand jerks at the familiar voice, driving the needle deep into the delicate skin over my Achilles. Davyd's voice. How did he get in here so quietly? I wince, clamping down on a cry of pain. No tears though. Nothing will make me disrespect Samuai. I remove the needle from my flesh and school my features into a neutral expression before I turn and stand to attention.

"Davyd," I say by way of greeting. Despite my preparation my throat thickens.

My response to him is stupid because he looks nothing like Samuai. Where Samuai radiated warmth from his spiky dark hair hinting of honey and his deep, golden brown eyes, there is only ice in his brother. Ice-chiseled cheekbones, tousled blond hair, the slight cleft in his chin, and his gray eyes. Eyes that see far too much.

But he's dressed like Samuai used to dress. The same white t-shirt and black pants. It's the uniform of Officials, or Fishies, as they're known below. He's a little broader in the shoulders than his older brother was—to even think of Samuai in the past tense is agony—and he's not quite as tall. I only have to look up a little to meet his gaze. I do so without speaking.

I shouldn't be here, but I'm not going to start apologizing for where I am or his reference to my forbidden relationship with his brother, until I know what he wants.

"Is that supposed to happen?" He points at my foot, where blood drips, forming a tiny puddle on the hard, shiny floor.

His face is expressionless, as usual, but I can hear the conceit in his voice. I can imagine what the son of a Fishie thinks of our Lifer traditions.

Today, I don't care. Even if his scorn makes my stomach tighten and cheeks flame, I *won't* care. Not about anything Davyd has to say.

"It's none of your business."

One fine brow arches. Superior, knowing.

He doesn't have to say the words. The awareness of just how wrong I am zaps between us. Given our relative stations on this journey—he's destined to be a Fishie in charge of managing the ship's population, and me to serve my inherited sentence—whatever I do *is* his business, if he chooses to make it so. He's in authority even though we're almost the same age.

In order to gain permission to breed, Lifers allowed the injection of nanobots into their children. These prototype bots in our cells give our masters the power to switch us off using a special Remote Device until our sentence is served. At any time we can be shut down. I'm not sure how exactly, only that each of us has a unique code and the device can turn those particular bots against us. It's an unseen but constant threat.

I keep my face blank and my posture subservient, but my fingers tighten around the needle in my hand. How I long to slap the smooth skin of his cheek.

For a second, neither of us speaks.

"Your brother or mine?" he asks again. Softly this time. So low, the question is almost intimate in the dim light.

I inhale deeply, welcoming the harsh fumes from my makeshift ink. The burning in my lungs gives me a focus so the ever-present emotional pain can't cripple me. My brother and my boyfriend were taken on the same day, and I'm unable to properly mourn either thanks to the demands of servitude.

I can't let it cripple me. Not if I want to find out what really happened to Zed and Samuai.

"Does it matter?" I ask. Rather than refuse him again, I twist the question around. He would never admit to having interest in the goings-on of a mere Lifer.

"No." His voice is hard. Uncaring. He folds his arms. "But it's against ship law to deface property."

It takes a heartbeat, and then I realize *I'm* the property he's talking about. My toes curl because my fists can't. I see from the flick of his eyes to my feet that he's noticed. Of course he has. There's nothing Davyd doesn't notice.

It's true though. The marks we Lifers make on our bodies are not formally allowed. It is a price we pay for the agreement signed in DNA by our parents and our grandparents. They agreed to a lifetime of servitude, and their sentence is passed down through the generations for the chance at a new life on a new planet. I am the last in the chain, and my sentence will continue for twelve years after landing.

We Lifers belong to those above us, body and soul, but no Fishie or Naut—the astronauts who pilot the ship—has ever tried to stop the ritual. In return we are not blatant. We mark feet, torsos, and thighs. Places hidden by our plain blue clothing.

If the son of the head Fishie reports me, it will go on my record no matter how minor the charge, and possibly add months to my sentence. A sentence I serve for my grandparents' crimes back on Earth after the Upheaval. Like others, their crime was no more than refusal to hand over their vehicle and property when both were declared a government resource.

I swallow convulsively.

I don't want that kind of notice. Not when we're expected to land in my lifetime. Not when I hoped to find answers to the questions that haunt me.

The first lesson a Lifer child learns is control around their superiors. I won't allow mine to fail me now.

"Did you want something? Sir?"

If there's a faint pause before the honorific, well, I'm only human.

He lets it pass. "The Lady requires extra help at this time. You have been recommended."

"Me?"

His lips twist. "I was equally surprised. Attend her now."

The Lady is the wife of the senior Official on board the Pelican, and both Samuai and Davyd's mother. She's a mysterious figure who is never seen in the shared area of the ship. I imagine she's hurting for her dead child. Sympathy stirs within me. I've seen the strain my own mother tries to hide since Zed died, and I don't think having a higher rank would make the burden any easier to bear.

It's within Davyd's scope as both Fishie-in-training and son of the ship's Lady to be the one to inform me of my new placement, but I can't help looking for something deeper in his words. There should be a kinship between us, having both lost a brother so recently, but Samuai's death hasn't affected Davyd at all.

"Who recommended me?"

He shrugs. "Now. Lifer."

I nod and move to tidy up, ignoring the persistent pain in my ankle where the needle went too deep. My defiance only stretches so far. Not acting on a direct request would be stupidity. I will finish my memorial for Samuai, but not with his brother waiting. It's typical that Davyd doesn't use my name. I can't remember him or his Fishie friends ever doing so.

It was something that stood out about Samuai from when we were youngsters and met in the training room. It was the only place on the ship us Lifers are close to equal. I was paired to fight with him to first blood, and he shocked me by asking my name. "Asher," Samuai had repeated, like he tasted something sweet on his tongue, "I like it."

In my heart there's an echo of the warmth I felt that day, but the memory hurts. It hurts that I'll never see him again, that he'll never live out the dreams we shared in our secret meetings. Dreams of a shared future and changes to a system that makes Lifers less than human.

When I've gathered the small inkpot and put on my slippers, I notice a smear of blood on the slipper material from where I slipped earlier. It's the opportunity I need to let my change in status be known below.

"Umm." I clear my throat. *Please let the stories I've heard of the Lady be true.*

"What?" asks Davyd from where he waits by the door, presumably to escort me to his mother. The intensity of his gaze makes me quake inside. It's all I can do not to lift my hand to check my top is correctly buttoned and my hair hasn't grown beyond the fuzz a Lifer is allowed.

"My foot attire isn't suitable to serve the Lady." I point to the faint smudge of brown seeping into my footwear. It is said by those cleaners who are permitted into the Fishie sleeping quarters that the Lady insists her apartment be kept spotless. She's unlikely to be pleased with me reporting for duty in bloodstained slippers.

Davyd's jaw tenses. Maybe I've pushed him too far with this delay. I hold my breath.

But then his annoyance is gone and his face is the usual smooth mask. "Change. I will be waiting at the lift between the training hall and study rooms."

He doesn't need to tell me to hurry.

He opens the door leading out into the hallway and I expect him to stride through and not look back. Again he surprises me. He turns. His face is in shadow. The brighter light behind him shines on his tousled blond hair, which gives him a hint of the angelic.

"Assuming it's my brother you're mourning," his voice is deep and for the first time there's a slight melting of the ice. "You should know. ... He wasn't worth your pain."

FIRE IN THE WOODS

JENNIFER M. EATON

FIRE IN THE WOODS SAMPLE CHAPTER

1

The walls shook.

    My favorite sunset photograph crashed to the floor. Again.

Why the Air Force felt the need to fly so low over the houses was beyond me. Whole sky up there, guys. Geeze.

I picked up the frame and checked the glass. No cracks, thank goodness. I hung the photo back on the wall with the rest of my collection: landscapes, animals, daily living, the greatest of the great. Someday my photos would be featured in galleries across the country. But first I had to graduate high school and get my butt off Maguire Air Force Base.

One more year—that's all that separated me from the real world. The clock wasn't ticking fast enough. Not for me, at least.

Settling back down at my desk, I flipped through the pages of August's National Geographic. Dang, those pictures were good. NG photographers had it down. Emotion, lighting, energy …

I contemplated the best of my own shots hanging around my room. Would they ever compare?

Another jet screamed overhead.

Stinking pilots! I lunged off the chair to save another photo from falling. The entire house vibrated. This was getting ridiculous.

Dad came in and leaned his bulky frame against my door. "Redecorating?"

"Not by choice." I blew a stray hair out of my eyes. "Are they ever going to respect the no-fly zone?"

"Unlikely."

"Then next time you have my permission to shoot them down."

"You want me to shoot down a multi-million-dollar jet because a picture fell off the wall?"

"Why not? Isn't that what the Army does? Protect the peace and all?" I tried to hold back my grin. Didn't work.

He grimaced while rubbing the peach fuzz he called a haircut.

So much for sarcasm. "It was a joke, Dad."

A smile almost crossed his lips.

Come on, Dad. You can do it. Inch those lips up just a smidge.

His nose flared.

Nope. No smile today. Must be Monday—or any other day of the week ending in y.

The walls shuddered as the engines of another aircraft throttled overhead, followed by an echoing rattle.

Dad's gaze shot to the ceiling. His jaw tightened. So did mine. Those planes were flying way too low.

My stomach turned. "What—"

"Shhh." His hand shot out, silencing me. "That sounds like …" His eyes widened. "Jessica, get down!"

A deafening boom rolled through the neighborhood. The rest of my pictures tumbled off the walls.

Dad pulled me to the floor. His body became a human shield as a wave of heat blasted through the open window. A soda can shimmied off my desk and crashed to the floor. Cola fizzled across the carpet.

My heart pummeled my ribcage as Dad's eyes turned to ice. The man protecting me was no longer my father, but someone darker: trained and dangerous.

I placed my hand on his chest. "Dad, what…"

He rolled off me and stood. "Stay down."

Like I was going anywhere.

As he moved toward the window, he picked up a picture of Mom from the floor and set it back on my dresser. His gaze never left the curtains. How did he stay so calm? Was this what it was like when he was overseas? Was this just another day at the office for him?

The light on my desk dimmed, pulsed, and flickered out. The numbers on the digital alarm clock faded to black. That couldn't be good.

Were we being attacked? Why had we lost power?

The National Geographic slid off my desk, landing opened to a beautiful photograph of a lake. The caption read: *Repairing the Ozone Layer.* I would have held the photo to the light, inspected the angle to see how the photographer achieved the shine across the lake—if the world hadn't been coming to an end outside my window.

I shoved the magazine away from the soda spill. My heartbeat thumped in cadence with my father's heavy breathing. "Dad?"

Without turning toward me, he shot out his hand again. My lips bolted shut as he drew aside the drapes. From my vantage point, all I could see were fluffy white clouds over a blue sky. Nothing scary. Just regular old daytime. Nothing to worry about, right?

"Sweet Mother of Jesus," Dad muttered, backing from the window. His gaze shot toward me. "Stay here, and stay on the floor. Keep the bed between you and the window." His hands formed tight fists before he dashed from the room.

Another plane soared over the roof, way too close to the ground. My ceiling fan swayed from the tremor, squeaking in its hanger.

I trembled. Just sitting there—waiting—it was too much.

I clutched the gold pendant Mom gave me for my birthday. If she was still with us, she'd be beside me, holding my hand while Dad did his thing—whatever that was.

But she was gone, and if all I could do was cower in my room while Dad ran off to save the world again, I might as well forget about photojournalism right now.

Wasn't. Gonna. Happen.

Taking a deep breath, I crawled across the floor and inched up toward the windowsill. Sweat spotted my brow as my mind came to terms with what I saw.

Flames spouted over the trees deep within the adjacent forest, lighting up the afternoon sky. The fire raged, engulfing the larger trees in the center of the woods. I reached for my dresser to grab my camera and realized I'd left it downstairs. *Figures.*

I gasped as the flames erupted into another explosion.

The photojournalist hiding inside me sucker-punched the frightened teenager who wanted to dash under the bed. This was news. Not snapping pictures was out of the question. I flew down the stairs. The ring of the emergency land-line filled the living room as I landed on the hardwood floor.

Dad grabbed the phone off the wall. "Major Tomás Martinez speaking."

The phone cord trailed behind him as he paced. His fingers tapped the receiver rhythmically—a typical scenario on the days he received bad news from the Army. I stood rapt watching him, hoping he'd slip up and mention a military secret. Hey, there's a first time for everything. I'd have to get lucky sooner or later.

"Yes, we lost power here, too … Yes, sir … I understand, sir … Right away, sir." He hung the receiver back on its stand and glanced in my direction. "I told you to stay upstairs."

"What'd they say? What's going on?"

"I'll tell you after I find out." He snatched his wallet from the counter and slipped the worn leather into the back pocket of his jeans.

"You're leaving? Now? Did you hear that last explosion?"

"I know. That's why I'm being called in." He picked up his keys.

"For what? You're not a fireman."

His gaze centered on me. I shivered. Dad in military mode was just. Plain. Scary.

"It's a plane. A plane went down."

The memory of the low-flying jets and the rattling of what must have been gunfire seared my nerves.

"Went down or was shot down?" The journalist in me started salivating.

"That's what I'm going to find out."

The door creaked as he pushed down the handle. The blare of passing sirens reverberated through the room.

"Why would they shoot down a plane?" I glanced at my camera bag perched on the end table. My shutter finger itched, anticipating juicy photos to add to my portfolio.

"Everything will be fine. For now, just stay in the house."

"Stay in the house? But this is like, huge. I want to take some pictures."

His jaw set. That gross vein in his neck twitched. "You can play games later. Right now, I need to know you're safe."

"No photojournalist ever made it big by staying safe."

"Maybe not, but many seventeen-year-olds made it to eighteen that way. Stay here. That's an order."

The whooting of a helicopter's blades cut through the late afternoon sunshine. Butterflies fluttered in my gut as Dad disappeared through the screen door without so much as a backward glance.

Seriously? He expected me to just sit there—with the biggest photo opportunity of my life going on outside?

I ran to the window and brushed the curtain aside. The

Air Force pilot who lived across the street ran to his jeep, a duffle bag swinging from his arm. Lieutenant Miller from next door left his house and exchanged nods with Dad as they both slipped into their cars.

The sound of another explosion smacked my ears. The ceiling rattled, and I steadied myself against the wall. How many times could one plane explode? I took a deep breath and forced myself to relax. I lived on a military base for goodness sake. The Army and the freaking Air Force were stationed next door. You couldn't get much safer than that.

Flopping onto the couch, I clicked the power button on the remote control three times. The blank television screen mocked me. *No electricity, idiot.*

Another siren howled past the house. My gaze flittered back to my camera case. When in my lifetime would I get another chance to shoot pictures of something like this?

"This is crazy." I slid my cell phone off the coffee table and dialed my best friend. No service. Ugh!

I grabbed the corded phone. Her voicemail answered: "Hey, this is Maggs. You know what to do."

"Maggie, it's Jess. Where are you? The whole world is coming to an end outside. Call me."

Another helicopter zoomed over the roof. How many was that now? Three? Four?

My gaze trailed to the name above Maggie's on the contact list.

Bobby.

The part of me that feared the chaos outside yearned to call him. Bobby would come. Leave his post if he had to. Protect me. But did I really want Bobby back in my life?

Not after he and his MP buddies beat up poor Matt Samuels. All the kid did was take me to a movie. It wasn't even a date, but Bobby didn't care. If he couldn't have me, then no one could.

I gritted my teeth as I slipped my phone back into my pocket. Suddenly, I wasn't as scared as I thought.

Tucking back the living room curtains, I snooped on the neighbors gathering outside their houses. Mrs. Sanderson and the lady across the street both herded their kids inside, their faces turned toward the sky. The fear in their eyes struck me. What an amazing photograph that would have been.

A few guys began walking toward the thruway. One of them held a cheap, pocket camera in his hand. He had to be kidding. What kind of shot did he expect to get with that?

I let the curtain fall. Staying in the house was just too much to ask. This was the story of a lifetime. I couldn't let it slip by without getting something on film.

Grabbing a black elastic band off the end-table, I twisted my hair into a pony tail. One brown lock fell beside my cheek, as it always did. I clipped that sucker back with a barrette and slung my camera case over my shoulder.

I hesitated at the front door. A picture of my parents hung askew beside the window. I straightened the frame. Mom's smile warmed me, but Dad's eyes bored through me, daring me to face his wrath if I touched the doorknob. I stood taller, strengthening my resolve. He'd understand after I got into National Geographic.

The odor of smoke and something pungent barraged my nose as I opened the door. A fire truck wailed in the distance, warning me to keep away. But I couldn't. I pulled my collar up over my nose to blot out the smell and headed toward the main road.

A parade of emergency vehicles whipped by at the end of the street. Lights flashed and sirens blasted through the neighborhood.

The cacophony froze me for a moment. Nothing like this had ever happened before. We lived in New Jersey for goodness sake, not Saudi Arabia. I glanced back at the house.

Keeping it in view made me feel safe, but I knew I needed to get closer to get a good shot.

This was it. The big league. I could do this.

Turning left toward the airstrip, I watched the last fire truck become smaller before its whirling lights passed through the gates onto the tarmac. The fire blazed well within the tree line, maybe even farther than I originally thought. The smoke reached into the sky, blotting out the sun. I raised my lens and waited for the clouds to shift and give me the perfect lighting—until a smack on my arm ruined my setup.

Maggie.

A smirk spread across her face. "Hey, Lois Lane. I figured you'd be out here."

I sighed, watching a flock of fleeing birds that would have maximized the emotion of the shot—if I'd taken it.

"Lois Lane was a reporter. Jimmy Olsen was the photographer."

"Whatever." Her golden curls bounced about her face. "This is like, crazy. My dad took off like World War Three or something."

"Yeah, mine, too."

I shielded my eyes. The smoke rose in gray billows. Almost pretty. I raised my lens.

"You want to know the scoop?" Maggie's perky form fidgeted like a toddler who couldn't hold in a secret. She loved eavesdropping on her father, the general. Unfortunately, that kind of gossip could get you carted off by the MPs. Never stopped her though, and I adored her for it.

"You know I do. Spill it." I brought the clouds into focus and snapped the shutter three times.

Her grin widened as she feigned a whisper. "It's not one of ours."

"What do you mean?" The stench in the air thickened. I covered my nose.

"The plane. They don't know whose it is. Isn't that exciting?"

"Heck yeah." I raised my camera and clicked off ten successive shots. If a terrorist got shot down over American soil, Jess Martinez was going to have pictures to sell. This was the kind of break every photographer dreamed of.

I adjusted my camera-case beside my waist. "I'm going in closer."

The air around us grew hazy. Maggie coughed. "Are you nuts? This is close enough for me."

"Stop being such a wuss." I tugged her wrist. It never took much more to convince her.

Maggie prattled on while I shot off round after round of gripping photographs. My heart fluttered as each preview image appeared on my screen. For once I was actually doing it. I was being the journalist I was meant to be, not the caged-up little girl Dad wanted. And boy, did it feel good.

The closer we came to the chained-link fence surrounding the runways, the more people gathered around us. A man, ignoring the whimpering Labrador on the end of his leash, gawked at the clouds. *Click.* Two women caught excited children and dragged them away. *Click.* The MP from down the street shouted, "Yes sir, right away sir," into his cell phone and jogged from the scene. *Click*—all amazing images to add to my portfolio.

Pushing to the front, I slipped my fingers through the metal fencing. The paved tarmac sprawled before me, backing up to the trees. Soldiers on the far side of the airstrip formed barricades against the tree line. I centered my lens between the silver links and chronicled their maneuvers.

A breeze whipped up. The heat slapped my face like sitting too close to a campfire. I covered my lens to protect the glass as the people around us flinched and backed away. One woman ran, crying into a hankie.

"Should we be able to feel the heat from this far away?"

Maggie asked, shielding her face with her arm.

I shrugged, unease settling on me as the smoky cloud arched toward us. The breeze stretched the formation, driving it north over our heads and toward the houses.

My stomach did a little fliperoo. The spunky, fearless photojournalist slipped away, leaving a scrawny, slightly-unsure-of-herself teenager behind. "I gotta go."

"Why?"

"My Dad told me to stay inside. He'll be calling on the house phone any minute to check on me."

"The major's getting more neurotic every day. You're almost eighteen for goodness sake."

"I know, but I still get the *While You Live Under My Roof* lecture every day."

The ground rattled. Another billow of fire wafted into the sky. I steadied myself, transfixed by the sheer magnitude of the ever-growing bank of smoke.

Wow, did I want to just stand there and use up my memory card—but I wanted to not get grounded more. I began walking backward, snapping off shots with every step.

Maggie strode beside me. "Do you ever stop taking pictures?"

Click.

"Not if I can help it."

***

I shimmied open the front door. On the far side of the living room, the corded phone rattled on the receiver, mid-ring. My keys clanged to the wood floor as I sprang toward the table to grab the handset. "Hello?"

"Where've you been?"

"Nowhere. I was—in the bathroom." I clenched my teeth,

holding my breath. Would he buy it?

"Are you okay?"

"I'm fine. Why?"

I could imagine his Major Martinez no-nonsense expression on the other side of the phone. "Listen, it's really important that you stay inside tonight. I'm sorry I can't be there, but I need you to lock the doors, and stay away from the windows."

I crinkled my forehead. Sweat settled across my brow. "Why? What's wrong? There's nothing, like, nuclear or anything, right?"

There was a pause on the line. "No—nothing nuclear."

I drew the curtain back from the rear kitchen window. The smoke cloud over the woods had darkened. The smell of burning pine tickled my nose as a humming tone on the other end of the call agitated my ear.

Dad spoke muffled words to someone else. "Jesus H. Christ," he whispered, returning to the phone.

"Dad, is everything okay?"

"Please just promise me you'll stay inside tonight."

Yikes. His Major Tomás Martinez voice had drifted away. That was his 'daddy's scared' voice. I hadn't heard that tone since the night Mom died. I shuddered. "Dad, if things are that bad, shouldn't I be with you?" Silence lingered, and a scratching noise reverberated in the background. "Dad, is someone else on the line with us?"

"Jess. I am asking you to stay inside and lock the doors. Can you do that for me … Buttercup?"

Buttercup?

My breath hitched. Crud. That meant something. Buttercup was a word he and Mom used when something was wrong. Something was definitely up. "I got you, Dad. I'll stay inside. I promise."

"Thank you." He paused. "I'll be home as soon as I can."

"Yeah, okay." My hand trembled as the phone clicked back

into the cradle.

I checked the front and back door and ran to the stairs. The fire cast a magnificent glow behind the trees outside my bedroom window. I slid down the screen and clicked off a few rounds of shots, hoping to catch the eerie blues and pinks behind the shaded leaves. Whoa. *New favorite sunset shot for sure.*

Settling down on my bed, I started scrolling through today's pictures. Something was weird about the fire, but I couldn't quite place my finger on it. Flipping through June's National Geographic, I glanced through the photographs of the explosion in Nanjing China. The colors in my shots were so much more vivid, more dynamic, more, well, *colorful.* Not that I knew anything about explosions, but something itched that little button inside that told me I had something special.

The lights suddenly flicked on. I gasped and laughed at myself. Perfect timing. I settled at my computer, hooked up my camera, and started the upload. I couldn't wait to enlarge those babies.

OTHER MONTH9BOOKS TITLES YOU MIGHT LIKE

BRANDED
THE PERILOUS JOURNEY OF THE NOT-SO-
INNOCUOUS GIRL

Find more awesome Teen books at Month9Books.com

Connect with Month9Books online:

Facebook: www.Facebook.com/Month9Books
Twitter: https://twitter.com/month9books
You Tube: www.youtube.com/user/Month9Books
Blog: www.month9booksblog.com
Request review copies via publicity@month9books.com

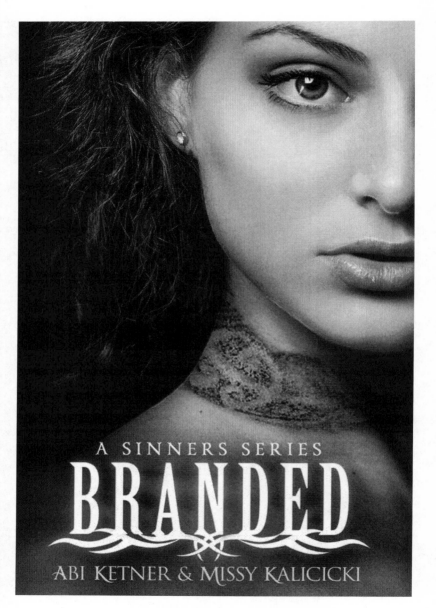

A SINNERS SERIES

BRANDED

ABI KETNER & MISSY KALICICKI

The Perilous
Journey
of the not-so-
Innocuous
Girl

LEIGH STATHAM